to Michael
+ Kate
Happy reading!
Carlota Findsay
Xmas 2006

Searching
for the
Jaguar

Searching for the Jaguar

ᨀ ᨀ ᨀ ᨀ ᨀ ᨀ

Carlota Lindsay

10617-LIND

This book was printed in the United States of America.

To order additional copies of this book, contact:
Xlibris Corporation
1-888-7-XLIBRIS
www.Xlibris.com
Orders@Xlibris.com

To my husband
And to the reader's imagination
and sense of humor

Contents

I
Brazil, Rio de Janeiro:
Deb

THE HUGE BIRD is soaring, its wings stretched taught, high above an endless, undulating surface of green. Responsive to the slightest change of direction or wind current, it tips to the left as it begins to circle. Will it start a slow descent, or will it glide upward farther into the cloudless cold blue sky? From this elevation, only the sharp eyes of a bird of prey can distinguish life beneath the thick tangle of vegetation. What can those eyes see in the dense cover of shrubbery? As the bird begins to float in a slow descending spiral its vision pierces from every angle to perceive an irregular movement. It can single out a small rodent scurrying from one shaded area to another, unwilling to risk its life in the light, or a monkey, or a native child learning to walk in the jungle, unaware of the menace circling in the sky above. There are other dangers, too, lurking unseen: a silent form crouching at the side of a path, large open jaws filled with gleaming teeth under the river's surface, disease, famine, white man, extinction.

Through the oval window, Hank watches the mass of green extending below, his mind still half in the trance brought on by the constant shrill hum of the large jet. He turns toward the woman sitting next to him and tries to focus his mind. She looks up from the book she is reading and smiles at him. He has just enough time—before he falls back into his daydream—to remind himself that the woman is Deb, that she is his wife, and that they have been married for three weeks.

This time it is Deb, whose image like photographs in a well-kept album, inhabits his wandering thoughts. What do I know about Deb, really? Not in my feelings, which are so intense that I can't sort them out, least of all at this moment on an international flight when there is so much to think about in preparation for the coming months.

Let's see. One thing is clear: she has accepted a job in Brazil; that's why we are flying to Rio on this enormous winged beast gorged with three hundred people. American tourists, for the most part, dressed in their short pants and loud sport shirts. Many must be business people; they are reading the *Wall Street Journal*, like the fellow sitting in front of me, with a front page article exclaiming about the "economic miracle" in Brazil and how the business climate is steadily improving under the new government.

She will start work in one or two weeks as part of a team whose purpose is, among other things, to immunize poor Brazilian adults and children against a whole array of diseases, many of them endemic to tropical areas, and others brought in from foreign countries and spreading rapidly because the bacteria or parasites have no natural enemies in the region. Also, she will provide health care to other Brazilians who are suffering from infections or chronic conditions. Who knows? She might get to treat lepers or people with elephantiasis who need to be transported on wheelbarrows to support a monstrous leg or testicle. And that's not all. When time permits she will work in the planning and educating branch of her organization. That Deb is looking forward to this work is obvious in her expression and vivaciousness. I am happy to be tagging along, without any particular duties of my own or even much of an idea of how I will spend my time during her two-year assignment in Brazil.

I first saw her at an ice-skating rink in Los Angeles. She was in school after having returned from two years in the Peace Corps in Costa Rica. Dressed in a kind of knitted suit that looked like tights with a cape, she skimmed effortlessly around the rink. As she approached I could see the animated smile of someone absorbed in the sensation of her body in motion; as she passed by I became equally absorbed in the outline of her right thigh, which moved in a steady rhythm. When she had disappeared from sight, the fluttering of the cape made me wonder if I would ever see this apparition again.

A month or so later I saw her on a college campus where I was auditing some courses. I followed her to the pharmacology lab she was headed for and succeeded in obtaining her attention when I cut a corner short and bumped into a large glass contraption, smashing test tubes and retorts that were perched precariously close to the edge of one of those large experiment tables. I told her later that I had seen her at the rink, recognized her on the lawn outside, and that at the moment I felt like an absolute ass.

The rest went fast. We had coffee together. She told me she would be happy to teach me how to ice-skate and to walk safely around tables in laboratories. I have no idea of what I told her, but soon we were going out together. Then we slept together. Then we lived together. After five months, when she learned she was accepted for the job in Brazil, we decided to get married so that I could go along as a dependent. The ceremony was small and took place in a chapel I had helped build in Arkansas.

"Funny," Hank said out loud. "Every time I think about you I end up thinking about myself at the same time."

"That's not surprising. We have hardly been apart since we met."

"Every time I look at you it seems to me that you are the more beautiful when you are lost in a deep thought."

"What was it you were thinking about me?"

"It's hard to say, exactly. I was taking an inventory of everything I know about you, you see, just the facts. But I found that I knew hardly any facts, which makes me feel that you exist only when we are together, and that's scary."

"Don't worry. I won't disappear when you look the other way.

But I like your idea. It's my turn now. Can I think about you out loud?"

"Please do. I'd love to hear you think."

"Okay. But don't expect anything like a case history. I like geography a lot, so I'll start there. You're from a small community in Arkansas. You grew up in a depressed area, I saw it when we were married, and I can imagine that when you were a child it was worse than it is today. Your parents are truly humble. You had a brother, younger by a couple of years, to whom you were deeply attached. From what you tell me the two of you were inseparable. Then when you went off to a state college about a hundred miles away from home, he became lonely, hung out with the wrong crowd, and ended up dead on a street corner in one of those senseless drug related crimes no one understands even now. I wonder what you did to get over that."

She paused and squeezed his hand in hers before continuing.

"In any event, by holding down part-time jobs, getting scholarships, and studying like hell you graduated with a degree in anthropology. And here is where the story becomes confusing. Instead of going on for a higher degree, or getting a job with some security, or starting a family, you began to wander. Across the country a couple of times by Greyhound, sleeping who knows where. Then you found it was cheaper to travel in empty freight cars, where you made a whole new set of friends, mostly peaceful bums. I admire that, especially since I couldn't do it myself. That's how you went through the Middle West and New England. Then you discovered the joys of hiking, and with a friend you went up the Pacific Crest Trail all the way from the Mexican to the Canadian border. I forget how long that took you. Then with another friend you bicycled to the Yucatán Peninsula and found work there for a year or two guiding American travelers through deserted areas you barely knew yourself."

Hank looked out his window and saw a straight tan line cutting through the dark green vegetation.

"After bicycling back to Arkansas, you decided to return to

school, rode your bike from Arkansas to California and enrolled in the Linguistics department at that college where we met."

"Bravo! You got just about everything right. I also wonder what made me do some of those things, and I still can't find an answer."

"But that's why it omits everything important. To begin with, you seem to have an easy time with other people. They like you right away, for your openness and lack of obvious defenses. You have many friends, but you don't seem to need them; I think you are happiest when you are alone . . ."

". . . with you."

"Thank you, my love."

By this time, the passengers could feel in their ears that the jet was beginning an approach to land in Rio. Below them now they saw large empty spaces on the earth's tender skin, like streaks of scar tissue. Looking out the window, Deb and Hank caught a glimpse of blue ocean embracing an undulating coastline. They stretched and smiled at each other. Hank leaned over and kissed her on the lips. Voices came over the loudspeaker giving instructions in several languages about fastening seat belts, putting up trays, not smoking, feeling at home in the beautiful city of Rio de Janeiro, preparing for customs inspection and passport check. Through their window Deb and Hank watched the intense blue waters of the Atlantic penetrating the innumerable inlets of a coastline constantly rewriting itself along sensuously shaped hills covered with vegetation. In the clear morning light, it was a view of incredible beauty. Right before landing, the jet turned above the city, and the passengers were able to observe an amazing array of tall modern skyscrapers mushrooming in the flat areas. As they came closer they could make out the shacks and huts covering the hillsides.

Sharing the excitement of the other passengers, Deb and Hank sensed that coming to this city would change their lives but without knowing in what way.

After checking through customs, they walked out into the open air. The palm trees were swaying in the sultry tropical breeze and everywhere they could hear the sweet sounds of spoken Portuguese amidst the noise of cars honking as they dashed by.

It is hardly necessary to describe the harrowing ride they experienced in the cab that drove them from the airport to downtown Rio, or the four hours it took them to come upon an inexpensive yet decent hotel where they could find their bearings and gather their wits. Nor is it important to relate how they were virtually held captive in their hotel room for two days by a conspiracy of jet lag, fear of being mugged, and a painful diarrhea that struck them both as soon as they had shut the door of their room.

"It must be a rite of passage," Hank said to Deb as they passed each other in the narrow door that separated the bath from their room.

"We make lousy tourists," she told him. "Let's get busy. Maybe we'll feel better."

They took a bus tour of the beaches, remaining as much as possible in the air-conditioned bus. When they returned they found they were hungry, and after fruit juice and a snack near the hotel they made their way to the American Express to collect mail, cash traveler's checks, and meet other Americans. Deb noticed a bulletin board with cards pinned to it bearing messages, ads, and announcements of available rentals. One of them appealed to her. After several failed attempts and coins lost in the entrails of a public phone, she succeeded in establishing contact.

". . . Follow the highway for about five kilometers, then take a left on the Rua Visconde de Nácar, and after two streets, right before the sign that points to the top of the hill, turn right and go straight for a kilometer and a half. Then take the second right after a small store and follow a narrow curving road until it ends. That is Rua dos Ventos, you can't miss it," said a man's voice on the phone, in English. The voice belonged to Erik Nielsen, an

American who had listed a cottage for rent and who would be "delighted" to show it to Deb and Hank in the morning.

They got out of their rented car at the end of the road and started to look for Rua dos Ventos, but they found no sign with that name. They stopped at a small open park surrounded by an iron fence from where they could see the nearby hills covered with mist. A morning shower had filled the air with a humid, fruity smell, and as they walked they felt water squish under their shoes. Seeing some children playing in front of a house, they asked for directions to the street they were seeking. The children answered all at the same time, pointing in different directions, which confused Hank and Deb even more. Finally a dark-skinned boy of about ten took Deb's hand and, after leading the way down a curving road, stopped in front of a house and called out: "*Dona Maria, tem duas pessoas aquí procurando pela senhora!*"

In a door surrounded by overgrown vines appeared a short woman with brown hair and hazel eyes. "You must be the American couple who called about the apartment." She led them into a small room, and after they were seated in wicker chairs she served iced tea and fresh tropical fruits, chatting cheerfully in Portuguese. Deb and Hank eventually understood that Erik Nielsen was out and was expected to return shortly.

When Erik walked through the door soon afterward, he impressed his guests with his height and an athletic stride unusual for a man in his sixties who had just come in out of the midday heat. He leaned over to kiss his wife.

"Come! I will show you the apartment." He led the way down tiled steps, across a neatly kept vegetable garden, passing an orchard with fine old trees, which, he explained, "bear a large variety of tropical fruits: guavas, mangos, papayas, avocados. That is the cottage," he added, pointing with his head toward a brick construction surrounded by fruit trees. "It was originally the outer kitchen building. Maria and I lived there years ago when we were first married."

Deb and Hank went in, and, looking around, found the apartment of their dreams. The interior had been remodeled, and, although sparsely furnished, everything was clean and freshly painted. On the walls hung watercolors and pastels of stylized tropical landscapes, done years ago by his wife, Erik explained. Deb felt her heart beat fast as she asked what the rent and utilities would come to, knowing full well that they could never afford to live in such an appealing house which seemed to materialize right out of the most unreal fairy tale.

"We'll take it," Hank shouted without consulting Deb when he heard Erik's answer. "What references do you want?"

"Your word and a handshake," Erik replied. "It's interesting, isn't it, that I posted the notice for the cottage yesterday morning, you read it in the afternoon, and now it's rented. Talk about luck! Please excuse me for a moment. I need to speak with Maria. I will be right back."

Deb and Hank embraced energetically when he had left.

"You can't imagine how happy we will be in this place, Hank! But how in heaven's name are we going to pay for it?"

"Beats me! We'll figure out something. I'll find a job somewhere."

"How about lunch with us?" Erik asked when he returned, interrupting their whispering. "Maria and I would like to celebrate your arrival and our future association. You can move in this afternoon, if you like."

The four of them sat around a table on a tiled patio under the cover of flowering vines and drank a pale yellow liquid from tumblers filled with fruit and ice. "This is *batida;* it is made of coconut milk, crushed pineapple, and *cachaça,* a kind of rum," Maria explained as she refilled the glasses.

"I'm originally from Wisconsin," Erik told them. "My father was an engineer, and against his wishes I followed in his footsteps. He had something professional in mind for me, but I wanted to build bridges and roads to bring far places and people closer together. When I graduated they needed engineers to build

Brasília, so I came down here and joined in." He looked at Maria and smiled. "Soon we met and got married; I haven't left Brazil since except once, when my parents died."

Looking at the Portuguese style wall and windows facing her, Deb asked: "How long have you lived here?"

"Our children grew up in this house," Maria answered. "It belonged to my grandparents. Let me show you around." She took Deb's arm and led her into the house with its cool, thick brick walls and tiled floors. From the iron-grilled verandah on the second floor Deb could see the nearby hills shimmering in the early afternoon sun.

"At night we can leave the windows open; the shutters offer protection from the light and insects while the air keeps on circulating through the louvers. You can do likewise in the cottage. It is more comfortable that way. It lets you hear insects sing at night, and when the sun rises birds begin their concert. Having many birds around is a way of life for us."

The lunch table was covered with colorful dishes: avocados stuffed with curried shrimp, wedges of watermelon wrapped in prosciutto, black beans and rice, baked papayas with spiced ground meat filling, watercress with slices of red tomatoes and white onion rings. Erik poured a chilled white wine in plain glasses from a clear bottle without a label.

"The fruit and vegetables are from our garden; Erik made the wine," Maria answered when Hank praised the spread.

"I have never heard of wines from Brazil."

"Only certain areas grow grapes fit to make wine from. I have an Italian neighbor who belongs to a large family from Rio Grande do Sul, that's the state farthest to the south, just up from Uruguay. Every year they send him grapes after the harvest, and since he is too old to process them, he gives them to me. They come from a town called Garibaldi, of course!"

"Of course!"

Dessert consisted of fried bananas in a dark syrup and demitasses of thick Brazilian coffee, which Maria called *cafezinhos*. They remained at the table for the rest of the afternoon getting to know each other. The talk inevitably centered on Brazil and Rio, which turned out to be Erik's favorite subject, and he proved to be well informed in his somewhat old-fashioned and ponderous way of saying things. Speaking at length about what he called the "tragic disproportion between wealth and poverty," he went on:

"I don't believe you came here to see the fun-loving face of Rio most tourists expect to find: the beautiful, carefree city, full of luxury hotels, restaurants, nightclubs and discos. It won't be long before you notice the swarms of homeless children roaming the streets. The expression in their eyes gives the other face of Rio its poignancy." He went on to describe the illiteracy, the lack of housing, the spread of disease, the prevalence of crime, prostitution, and drugs.

It was dark when Erik finished talking. Silence followed, taken over by the sound of croaking frogs and nervous cicadas.

Deb and Hank began to move into the cottage on the following day. Seeing Deb busy carrying suitcases and supplies, Erik asked her to join Maria while he helped Hank with the heavy work.

"You will have to carry all sorts of supplies when you start your job," he told her. "I would much rather carry these loads than watch you strain yourself. Anyhow, I'm old fashioned, as you can see, and stubborn. Maria hasn't carried heavy loads since we were married."

Maria winked at Deb, shaking her head imperceptibly, smiling. "Do as he says, Deb. He really wants to help you. I can see he likes you both."

With the help of Erik's strong back and ingenuity, Deb and Hank were installed in one day.

"Usually people have to wait years to have a phone hooked up in this city, if not longer. I'll try to hurry things along." Erik called a number of friends with the result that a new phone was installed in a few days. Deb called the office of the clinic where she was to work.

"Nothing to do until next Monday," she announced. "There will be meetings for a whole week and a large reception for the new recruits next Friday night. It will be something big, I guess, and you are invited, Hank. Until then I'm free. We can get acquainted with the city."

"And with your permission," Erik interposed, "Maria and I will show it to you. It is a difficult city to know since there are so many different sections separated by hills and bays. So do let us have the pleasure of giving you a guided tour. We have a car and plenty of time. And, Deb, it might be wise to ask Maria about what to wear at a reception at that hour. This country is very different from yours."

ERIK DROVE HIS wife and new friends through the main arteries of greater Rio. They visited tourist attractions and locations of great beauty, enjoying the views of the ocean and sampling the beaches. He took them up the cable car to the top of Sugar Loaf, drove them around the Lagoa Rodrigo de Freitas and through the Jardim Botânico, where they walked amid tall palm trees and later had lunch nearby. They followed the *avenidas* south between high rises and beaches, visited the Hotel Naçional, and returned through the Tijuca National Park, where they saw what was left of a tropical jungle, which, Erik told them, once surrounded the city; then they admired the statue of Cristo Redentor and the view from the top of Corcovado. From there they traveled north, skirting the enormous Maracanã Stadium and visiting the Museu Nacional, where Erik led them through the exhibits featuring the different peoples of Brazil. Better than any tour guide, Erik, who had a sense of humor and a flair for telling stories from the history of Rio and Brazil, drew them ever deeper into the past and the mythology of the places they visited.

The next day, they "did" the city's center, going through churches, cathedrals, monasteries, theaters, libraries, the Museu de Arte Moderna, still being renovated after a fire, the Museu Nacional de Belas Artes, the central bank and, next door, the Casa França-Brasil. "The rest we will have to see another day," Erik said as he led them to a dock where they took a ferry across to Niterói and the Ilha da Paquetá. It took another day to visit elegant neighborhoods and some quaint cobble-stoned places that still remained within the city. When they arrived wearily at home, Erik told them he needed their patience one more day, when he proposed to show them the "other side" of Rio.

Deb and Hank had perceived, on the previous days, signs of misery and poverty lurking around corners, prowling near the wounds inflicted by construction sites, and slipping down the edges of hills like lava floes. Now, after warning his guests to leave all valuables at home, Erik drove them through the ugliest and poorest favelas imaginable. "Seeing these neighborhoods is the only way you can get an idea of the way the majority of Brazilians live. This is the result," he said, gesturing with his hand toward a writhing mass of corrugated metal roofs, "of rapid industrialization, mismanagement of rural areas, overzealous anti-communism, military governments, and uncontrolled foreign investment. No one had the time or the interest to concern themselves with a population displaced by progress."

Although Deb had done an internship in the slums of Los Angeles and was used to the sight of suffering and squalor, she was hardly prepared for what she saw. "I suppose I'll see a lot more of this, before long," is all she said.

Erik's car entered one of the many tunnels that pierce the jutting rocks, uniting one part of Rio with another. In the middle they came to a sudden stop behind a line of stalled automobiles, suffocating in the heat and the exhaust.

"*É um assalto!*" Maria said in a nervous voice.

"This won't be pleasant," Erik warned. "We are all being robbed. It will take a little more than an hour. Just give them what they want. Fortunately we don't have much. By now it has become routine."

Twenty minutes later they could see a group of husky youths confronting drivers and passengers in the cars ahead; they were holding handguns and moved quickly between cars, searching trunks, and threatening passengers.

When the muggers came to the car window, Erik had a key to

the trunk ready for them, and enough money to make it look as though it was all he had on him. They gave orders in English: "Money, watches, jewelry, cameras! Quick! You no give right now I shoot!" Deb moved so as to cover her camera with her skirt and arm. One of the men saw her motion and pointed at the camera with his revolver, gesturing her to hand it over. He accepted Hank's wallet, which he threw back in his face when he found it empty. Maria gave them her rings and a bracelet. In the meantime another man opened the trunk and, finding nothing in it, slammed the lid. That was all.

It was another fifteen minutes before the line of cars was able to begin moving again.

"I always wear the cheapest jewelry I can find when we go out. I buy it just for these occasions. Could you tell that I was praying all the time? That is why they didn't hurt us."

"What can you expect?" Erik asked. "There are over twelve million *abandonados* in the streets of Brazil's large cities, children without homes, abandoned by their parents who cannot provide for them. If they are lucky enough to avoid disease and death squads, there isn't much for them to do when they grow up besides what you just saw. The ones who make a living by stealing live in places like this," he added, pointing to the crooked shacks clutching at the stoney hillside to keep from collapsing. "You can be sure there is no running water or sewers around here."

To dispel the gloom engendered by what they had seen and experienced that day, they went out to a restaurant for dinner and an evening of samba and bossa nova. At midnight, on the way home, Deb noticed that Erik ran through all the red traffic lights. Other drivers seemed to be doing the same. She asked why.

"So we don't get robbed again. At night you can't even slow down for a curve; you're only safe if you're going at top speed. That is known as Rio life, as opposed to fairy tales and fantasy."

It was on a Monday morning that Deb reported for a day's orientation program. The Organization for Medical Assistance to the Indigent, an international agency funded mostly by the International Red Cross, the World Health Organization, and various North American groups. In Rio, OMAI was located in the Andaraí district in a large building that had once been a warehouse, then a vocational school, a barracks in the 1970's, and only in the last few years had its interior walls been rearranged to make it more or less suitable for its present clinical use. Deb learned during the first presentation of the day that this was the central administrative office serving seventeen smaller facilities situated along the east coast between São Paulo and Fortaleza and three in the interior. It was also the largest clinic and educational center of OMAI in Brazil.

In the early afternoon Deb and five other new recruits were shown around the facility and introduced to the directors of the various departments. She noticed that the waiting rooms were full, mostly of pregnant women, mothers, children, and old people. The temperature was in the high nineties; there was no air conditioning, and the odor was at best dubious. "Sanitation," one of the recruits observed, "doesn't seem to be of primary concern to the administration."

"The environment is not ideal," a head nurse reminded them. "But we do our best in a difficult situation."

When the official tour was finished in midafternoon, Deb decided to visit the areas she would be working in. She had a dual appointment as nurse and social worker. The clinic was located on the second floor. The waiting room was packed with patients standing or sitting, looking vacantly into space. Many were smoking, and there were no windows to provide circulation. Inside the door of the treatment room a woman behind a large desk directed patients to one of a series of card tables where they sat and pulled up a sleeve to receive a shot. Each table had a sign in Portuguese indicating the illness the immunization was intended to prevent.

Deb met her supervisor, Ms. Converse, a tall, lean, and masculine woman of about fifty.

"You will spend alternately time here and time on the road. This is to avoid burnout, which in this climate and at the pace we work, comes fast. A recycled U.S. school bus takes our staff to rural areas and into the interior, where the work is essentially the same as it is here. They have arranged for you to do your family planning work there as well. It would be easier for me if you worked exclusively with us, but there is no way I or anyone can change the minds of the administration. God's will, I suppose. Over here is our sterilization equipment. We now have clean needles, thank the Lord. For five years we held the needles in a candle flame for a half minute between patients. It saved time, but it didn't quite meet sanitation standards, especially with so much AIDS around."

"Where do you keep the charts?"

"Do you think we have time to work with charts? Get this straight right away. We don't treat individuals here, we treat populations. That's why you won't find any charts in this building. Our records are over there, on the wall. Take a look. Statistics, that's all, and lists of names of the people we treat. Ah! There's the doctor. You should meet him now, before you start work. Dr. Powers! Here is our new recruit . . . what was your name? Oh, yes, Ms. Myers."

"Great! I was hoping you would arrive as soon as possible. Thank you, Clara. So you are Mrs. Myers. What's your first name?"

"Deb."

"Gladtomeecha, Deb. Won't you step in my office? We can chat a little."

He motioned her into a small room with a desk, an easy chair, diplomas and a picture of a woman and another of three children on the wall, an examination table and equipment usually found in physician's offices. He gestured toward the easy chair and sat down behind the desk.

"Do you smoke? No? Mind if I do?" he asked and without waiting for a reply lit a cigarette. "I was interested in your application, really, and I chose you from among a large number of applicants because you had both the skills of a nurse and those of a mental health care provider. My staff wanted a full-time nurse, but I asked for you. Do you speak Portuguese?" he asked. "Why don't you call me Bernie?"

Deb found this doctor amusing, with his incessant chatter and habit of asking personal questions rhetorically. She looked at him. Dressed in jeans and sport shirt, he looked young for a man in his early forties.

Bernie leaned back in his chair as he continued smoking and told Deb about himself and how he managed the unit; in addition to injections, he was also in charge of the diagnosis and treatment of a number of diseases common to the area around Rio.

"You will wear a nurse's uniform, won't you? I insist on that in my department; you see, it reinforces the respect your patients have for you and makes them behave. I don't care what you do when you are out in the mobile unit, but here it's part of the dress code. My colleagues think I'm old-fashioned, and they let their nurses and aides dress any old way, but I figure that's their problem, not mine."

"Will I be working at one of those card tables?"

"Heavens no! The ones giving injections are aides. They learned all they know right here. Few have as much as an elementary school education. You will have an office like this one, although you may have to share it with another nurse or two. Here nurses function like M.D.'s; you have your own case load, for which the entire responsibility is yours—examination, diagnosis, treatment, follow-up, the works! All the doctors are as harried as I am; if I need to consult with one, I have to tackle him as he walks down the hall. Sometimes they run when they see me coming. It's a regular sports arena—all effort and perspiration. We don't smell good at the end of the day. You are probably tired and sweaty yourself, Deb, after today's ordeal. What do you say to having a drink with me? I know some nice places. Then I'll drive you home."

"Thanks, Bernie. I still have to visit the mental health area, and my husband is picking me up at six. Maybe another time?"

Deb took leave of Dr. Powers, said good-bye to Ms. Converse, and hurried over to the psychiatric unit. It was closed for the day. She then dashed up the stairs to the Women's Health unit. The door was locked. It was a few minutes after five. For an hour, Deb wandered around the facility, killing time and avoiding being seen by Dr. Powers. She walked down empty halls, taking note of the location of the different departments and trying to remember the names she saw on cards pinned to the doors. She went into the women's john and, sniffing the air, decided to wait until she got home. Unsure of whether it was safe for her to stand outside the clinic on the sidewalk, she glanced through a window and saw Hank waiting in Erik's car at the curb. She rushed out and gave him a kiss.

"Let's go straight home. I have to go, bad!"

Hank handed Deb a letter from the Consulate, which had arrived during the day. She tore it open and read it out loud while Hank drove.

"What does that mean, exactly, Hank? They don't need me for another two weeks. I wonder why. Maybe they haven't got the space yet."

"It sounds to me like your work starts two weeks from today and from now to then you are supposed to have some fun. Not a bad idea."

When they arrived home, Maria was preparing a light dinner. At the news of the two-week delay in Deb's schedule, Maria burst out:

"Then you have time for a honeymoon! Hank told me you didn't have one when you were married. That was very bad, a very bad thing to do. It will cast a shadow on your marriage. I stayed awake last night worrying about that. *Vocês têm que ter uma lua de mel!* Your marriage is not complete if it hasn't been blessed by the spirits of happiness, the ones who watch over people's honeymoons. But you can still make up for it, and the spirits will be satisfied." Maria thought for a moment. "Erik! Erik! Come here! Where can that man be, just when I need him?"

For a small person, Maria had a large voice. Erik heard it where he was cultivating a garden plot behind the cottage and came running.

"What is it, dear? Hi Deb, how was your day? Tired, right? Now Maria, what sudden disaster has struck? Or is it time to eat?"

"Come on, Erik. Help me now. This is serious. These young people have to go on a honeymoon, right away, before it is too late. Could they go to Juscelina's house on the island? Just for two weeks. What do you think, Erik? Do go and try to call her. It is too late to do it by mail."

"I'll do my best. When can you start? Tomorrow?"

"We will be free after the reception Friday night."

Friday's reception at the Consulate was a once-a-year affair. The Consul General and various members of his staff received on this occasion: Peace Corps participants, Fulbright scholars, Ford Foundation and other grant recipients, U.S. citizens coming to Rio for the year. Some cynics claim that half those invited are connected somehow to the CIA, FBI, GM, or GE, but no one believes them. A number of curious people also get themselves invited: journalists in search of a story, idle men wanting to ogle the new crop of female students, business representatives looking for connections, drunks from the Ambassador Bar looking for champagne they don't have to pay for. The important guests are invited to remain for a late dinner. Deb and Hank were not among them.

The party was already well under way when Deb and Hank arrived and were ushered into the grand reception room. People were standing holding a champagne glass, inquiring about the other to find out who he was and in what section of Rio he lived. Hank as usual was successful in drawing a number of people around him, eager to find out more about this fellow who spoke freely about himself and listened intently to what they told him. Here he was the odd man, the one without a function, here for the ride, so to speak. After Deb was whisked off by Dr. Powers to meet some members of the medical community, Hank kept on talking and listening and finally found himself in the midst of a group of nature and hiking enthusiasts. Someone asked him where he had hiked, which brought him to describe the Pacific Crest Trail and the Yucatán Peninsula. This was quite interesting to a graduate student from Yale who had spent his weekends and summer vacations in the Blue and White Mountains and in the Appalachians. He had also climbed the Jura, the Schwartzwald, and the Italian Alps. Hank's mind began to wander.

A man dressed in a white suit came to his rescue.

"I'm John Webb; I work in the cultural attaché's office. Couldn't help overhearing what you were saying."

Hank introduced himself and explained how he happened to be at the party. They talked about their mutual interest in outdoors activities.

"I happen to be forming a group of Americans interested in going on weekend trips to different parts of Brazil. So far mostly business people have shown interest, but I'm trying to broaden the base. How about you? Oh, there is one of my charter members. Herb! Come over here! I have someone you must meet."

Webb introduced Hank to Herb Kater, telling him everything he had just learned about Hank. Kater hardly looked like an outdoor enthusiast. Dressed smartly in what seemed to Hank the latest fashion, his head was slightly stooped and he was certainly overweight. His eyes focused with intensity, almost accusingly, on the person he looked at; his voice was low, without modulation, and his words came rapidly in long, complex constructions.

Kater asked Hank leading questions about his past and what he wanted to do while in Brazil, so that after fifteen minutes Hank felt he had bared his soul to this unknown person. He finally brought himself around to asking what his new acquaintance did for a living.

"Well, I work for a company that is interested in developing avenues for commercial groups to advance the profitability of their activities in this part of the southern hemisphere. It's called Southern Overseas Development Corp. or SOD for short. We are really consultants who make things happen. We work closely with agencies of the U.S. government and are often under contract to them, and at the same time we have cordial relations with the Brazilian bureaucracy, so we are able to provide considerable assistance to U.S. enterprises, both large and small."

"How long have you been here?"

"Just over three years. I wanted to get away from Washington for a while and ended up here, the true land of opportunity. It's virgin territory, just waiting to be carved and served up."

Listening to Kater, Hank noticed Deb walking across the room in the company of a tall man with glasses.

Kater talked on for the duration of another glass of champagne and then placed his hand on Hank's wrist.

"Here is my card. I'd appreciate it if you would give me a call in a few weeks. You like the woods, and you enjoy a good hike, so I think you might find one of our projects to your liking. You speak Portuguese and Spanish and can easily learn other languages. For that we can pay well, and you could keep busy while your wife is at work. When you phone, just tell the secretary who answers that your call is C-14. You will get right through. Can you remember without writing it down?"

After Kater had disappeared between groups of guests, Hank looked around the room for Deb. Not seeing her, he explored the areas of the Consulate that were accessible, then moved back into the reception hall. There he saw Deb looking for him, with the same tall curly-haired young man in tow.

"Hank! *Je t'ai cherché partout*," she said in French. "I want you to meet Roger Bonot. He's a journalist, from Paris, *n'est-ce pas*, Roger? He's doing some fascinating research on slavery in this century. *Voici mon mari*, Hank."

"Well, I don't know if it is all that fascinating to anybody else, but I find it quite absorbing. Actually I am preparing a thesis on *l'esclavage moderne dans les pays sous-développés*. There is a lot of material to be found in this country."

"I didn't know there were still any slaves in Brazil."

"There are slaves wherever there are people," Roger answered. "It is a question of giving to the term slavery a broader acceptance than it usually connotes. But the essence remains the same. The only element that has changed is the structure: the coercion is no longer by punishment, it is economic in origin."

Hank looked at Roger and felt glad that Deb had found a friend, someone they could talk with. The acquaintances he had made that evening were hardly exciting, he thought, although he may have succeeded in landing a job.

"I noticed earlier you were talking with a man dressed in a tan suit. I have seen him around Rio at functions like this one. Can you tell me who he is?" Roger asked as they walked out to the street.

Deb and Hank took a cab to Erik and Maria's house. There on a table in the cottage they found a note from Maria: "*Vocês vão para Angra dos Reis*! You can leave tomorrow. Sleep well."

"ANGRA IS THE most beautiful place in the world," Maria declared the next morning. "My cousin Juscelina has a villa there on one of the islands, and she has invited you to be her guests while she is doing business in Pôrto Alegre. Everything will be ready for you this afternoon. Erik has arranged for a rental car. It will be delivered soon."

"But Maria . . ."

"Please don't worry about anything. Juscelina is very rich, so you mustn't offer to pay her. You won't see her, anyway. Just leave a few gifts for the servants. That is all you will have to do, other than enjoy your honeymoon. While you are on the island you won't need your car; Juscelina owns a garage in Parati right across from the dock. You can park it there before taking the schooner to Jipóia. When you arrive on the island, all you have to do is say 'Juscelina,' and someone will take you to her villa."

"Can you believe what we are doing? I can't!" Deb exclaimed as they headed west along the coast road.

"I don't even know where we are going," Hank answered, swerving to miss an oncoming car in his lane. "Tell me again."

"I have a map here. We are on our way to a place called Costa Verde, which most people call Angra. It's a little bay with quaint villages and islands where rich Brazilians and foreigners live in their elegant villas to escape the hustle-bustle of the cities and enjoy a bucolic life with fishermen and humble villagers. I feel ambivalent about this sort of place; it sounds to me like Big

Sur or something on Cape Cod or Long Island Sound. But if we keep our fingers crossed behind our backs, we may be able to enjoy ourselves for a while. I am a little strung out, I must admit."

"Me too! It has been a strain; traveling always is. But I am beginning to agree with Maria: we need a honeymoon, or let's just call it a vacation. A time during which all we have to do is get up in the morning, eat, love each other, walk, eat and love some more, and sleep. We have never done that."

"Notice how we are going up and up? I suspect we will be driving along a narrow road on the edge of a cliff. Wow! Did you see that? He passed us on that curve with no visibility at all. This may not be the most restful of drives. Look at those little shrines! All along the road: crosses with flowers. Do you think they are offerings to Yemanjá?"

"They are more likely for people who were killed there. It's not surprising, really, when you see how fast they take the curves."

The route was spectacularly beautiful. When they were able to take their eyes away from the road, they saw fantastic vistas of mountains, forests, and the ocean, all bathed in the afternoon light that follows a gentle rain. A few hours later, as their anticipation began to heighten, they suddenly found themselves driving along a devastated coastline and through industrialized wastelands; they could see supertankers crowding the docks, and the acrid smell of a nearby oil refinery made them shut the car windows. In the distance they could sense the ominous presence of a nuclear power plant.

Continuing their journey around the edge of the Baía da Ilha Grande, they came to Parati, a town of white colonial Portuguese buldings with colorfully painted doors and windows. The white façades of the houses and churches reflected the late afternoon sunlight, and the hulls of yachts and sailboats floated calmly at their moorings. Hank found a café on a path leading to a small marina, where he invited Deb to have tea and ice cream. It was almost night. They stayed at a small, comfortably furnished hotel where they were practically the only guests in the dining room.

After dinner they were able to walk without fear in the roads made of irregular rock. Before turning in they watched the southern constellations from the end of a pier and listened to the lapping of the water against the moored boats.

A cool breeze from the ocean accompanied them the next morning as a schooner they had boarded skimmed by a peninsula and several small islands. Once they were beyond the islands, the sea had an unmistakable swell, even though they were within the bay. Jipóia, their destination, was the first of two slightly larger islands; another, the Ilha Grande lay beyond. A horse carriage took them and their baggage from the fishing village, where they had disembarked, down a winding path under the shade of large trees to what looked at first like a small stucco house set in an elaborate garden with paths and beds full of colorful blossoms.

A handsome black woman of about thirty, wearing a starched dress, flowered apron, and a little lace cap, met them at the main entrance, smiled broadly, and politely declined to let them carry their belongings any farther. This was Martita. She served them a lunch of fresh seafood on a patio overlooking the bay.

From that moment on Deb and Hank discovered what it was like to live the life of the rich. They spent their days sitting in the sun or shade, depending on the time of day, swimming in a small inlet located at the end of a path leading from the house—it was so secluded they gave up wearing swimsuits after the second day—or hiking in the hills and discovering new beaches. At night they drank tea or cool wine sitting on the patio listening to Juscelina's vast collection of LP's and CD's. There was also a well stacked library of Portuguese, French, and English classics in red leather bindings. On other evenings they called for the buggy to take them to the village, where they drank beer and chatted with tourists and well-healed local residents. Since everyone living on the island seemed to know and respect Juscelina, at the drop of her name they were invited to other villas for dinner, entertainment of all sorts, and sailing expeditions.

On one day they took the schooner to Ilha Grande where

they explored as much as they could on horseback. There wasn't enough time for Hank to climb an alluring mountain, Pico do Papagaio, which beckoned to him from every street corner in the village of Abraão.

Another day Deb received a call from a new acquaintance to have an impromptu luncheon at noon in a villa at the other side of the island. Martita was away getting provisions, so Deb left her a note saying they would be gone for lunch, and wouldn't she like to take the afternoon off to be with her family? When they returned at seven, there was Martita looking bewildered, with lunch still on the table. The note was where Deb had left it in the kitchen.

"Maybe she can't read, like half the population of Brazil," Hank suggested.

The following day, in the course of a morning chat, Martita told Deb that her youngest son was ill and that she would have to take him to visit a *mãe de santo*, a candomblé priestess, to bring him back to health. In that case she would send one of her daughters to do her work.

The next morning a tall, big-boned girl of about fifteen came and started doing the chores Martita usually did. When the same girl came again, Deb convinced her to lead them to Martita's home. She and Hank followed their reluctant barefoot guide down paths through scrub-covered areas, over a high ridge, into another part of the island. This side of the island was treeless and the soil was gravel; shacks and hovels without walls were crowding everywhere. Here is where the island poor live, Hank thought as they crossed a rivulet of grey water trickling across the path. Martita's shack was clean yet shabby. She thanked them for coming and said she was sorry for the inconvenience their trip had caused. The neighbors were setting up for a procession; Martita's child had died.

The next day the weather turned sour. After a week of self-indulgence, Deb and Hank found themselves shut-in by the almost constant downpour of a tropical storm hovering off the coast. There was little left to do on the island; most of the acquaintances they had made fled to the mainland when the clouds first showed signs of gathering above them. Hank rolled up in a couch under a heap of novels he had always wanted to read. Deb began to study the photographs on the walls.

When she first arrived she could see, from the number of photographs signed by eminent musicians and dancers, that Juscelina was an avid patron of the arts. Now, to the rhythmic sound of rain against the windows and on the roof, Deb undertook a methodical inventory of the pictures lining the walls of the hallway leading to Juscelina's bedroom. These were mainly of choreographers and dancers signed and dedicated to "my good friend, Juscelina" and even to "my esteemed colleague." Deb felt like an intruder in a Rogue's gallery of ballet personalities: Nureyev, Fonteyn, Cranko, Béjart, Graham. She called Hank. He remembered seeing somewhere a photo album of scenes from classical ballet that featured a single, unnamed dancer.

Seated in a large armchair with that album on her knees, Deb turned the pages slowly. There were shots of a little girl in pigtails going through steps and stretching at a bar. Sometimes she was in a long fluffy white dress, more often in tights. A number of pictures showed a teenager performing in the corps de ballet in the Teatro Colón in Buenos Aires. Finally Deb came to pictures of solos and ensembles. The female dancer was the same young woman with stunning black hair combed into a bun and large dark, dreamy eyes. In the pas de deux she shared the stage with different male dancers.

"I'm convinced this is Juscelina," Deb told Hank. "It's a pity she isn't here so we could ask her about her career. If only we could find some newspaper reviews of her performances!"

"For a professional dancer she is mighty modest," Hank put in. "There don't seem to be any portraits of her anywhere in this house. All the paintings are either landscapes or abstracts. How can one have a career as a dancer and at the same time be self-effacing? The two seem contradictory."

"Maybe her mementos are in her apartment in Pôrto Alegre. But we can surely find more pieces to the puzzle somewhere in these rooms."

From bits of evidence found here and there in the villa, they reconstructed a life dedicated to ballet that came to a sudden stop at the height of her career. What had happened?

"Could it be this?" Hank asked as he brought a framed photograph from a night table. It showed a Juscelina of about twenty-five, radiant and relaxed, with her head leaning on the shoulder of a man about ten years older.

The next day when a neighbor stopped by to ask about Juscelina, Deb invited her for lunch. It was to this neighbor that Deb owed the remaining pieces of Juscelina's career and marriage.

During a tour Juscelina performed at the São Paulo Opera, she caught the eye of a young member of a rich family, Otelo Borja de Pessoa, who fell in love with her from his box seat. The Pessoa family had made a fortune in shipping between Brazil and Portugal, maybe even doing some slave trade when that was still legal. Before long they were established and respected, and two family members had been elected to the provincial government as deputies from the moderate left. Otelo himself was a n'er-do-well: rich, spoiled, without ambition. He showed no interest in the professions, let alone the priesthood or military. He had travelled a number of times to Paris and Lisbon, spent most of his time there in libraries, cafés, and the opera and returned to Brazil with a decided taste for mezzo-sopranos. This preoccupation lasted until he was well over thirty and caught a glimpse of Juscelina doing *Beauty and the Beast* at the Teatro Municipal in São Paulo. He immediately saw himself as the Beast and began to court his Beauty with more energy than he had been able to muster for any other enterprise. He took her to the Museu de Arte de São Paulo where, among the Impressionists, he pleaded his case. She pretended to be shy at first, then let him understand that if he asked her to marry him she would take his proposal seriously. After a long, old-fashioned engagement, during which he got himself appointed to the board of directors of theaters and museums, the opulent society of São Paulo was invited to their wedding. From then on Otelo channeled his energy into raising money for the arts and promoting, even financing, large scale performances throughout the city. Eventually he became manager of operatic and dance productions at the Teatro Municipal, a position naturally accompanied by a good deal of power and prestige. He let himself be influenced by his wife's taste and, occasionally, personal ambitions. He was careful, however, to support real talent wherever he found it, with the result that he became admired and respected by the cultural elite and even some of the politicians. The next step for him was to have himself elected to the city council, but before he had a chance to wage his campaign, the political climate of the country had shifted: the new, more repressive government of General Médici took office, death squads multiplied, the U.S. Ambassador was kidnapped by guerillas, and the economic miracle happened. Otelo had made the mistake of producing a program of Cuban dancers and performances by the Hungarian Opera. Furthermore he had not hidden his contempt for the successive military governments or ceased demanding explanations for episodes of police brutality and torture. He himself was arrested in 1970, just after a cousin of his had been expelled from the State of São Paulo legislature. Juscelina was never able to learn why her husband had been arrested or where he was held. He simply did not return. Only after the 1982 elections did she find out that Otelo had died in prison 10 years earlier. All documents referring to his case had been destroyed. She wondered if his death had occurred at the hands of torturers imperfectly trained in the techniques of interrogation, the ones who miscalculate how much torture a prisoner can tolerate and still be able to make a confession.

Juscelina grieved for years; to this day she avoids contact

with people she doesn't know well, preferring to spend the rest of her life with close friends and ghosts from the past.

It was late in the evening when Deb and Hank returned to Rio. On the next day Deb started work. She also received in the mail an invitation to attend, with her spouse, a fund-raising celebration for the Indian tribes of the Amazon basin. Sponsored by FUNAI, the government agency in charge of Indian affairs, the "Grande Baile dos Indios" was to be a major cultural and social event of the season. A large convention center in a downtown hotel was transformed into a veritable tropical jungle paradise, with rock and samba bands imitating primitive music, and an entire native village, huts and all, was transported all the way from the Xingu National Park and set up in the middle of the main ballroom. Cages with live jaguars, enormous snakes, caimans, and aquariums filled with flesh-eating fish were securely placed amid trees and vines provided by the Jardim Botánico. FUNAI had arranged for exhibitions of native artifacts and public lectures by well known anthropologists. But best of all, the culmination of the whole affair, was to be the ball, a grand costume party for the elite of Rio and Brasília society and the local international set.

"What in heaven's name can we wear?" Deb asked of all who were within hearing. "I'm used to ghost and goblin costumes for trick or treat, but this will be on a more ambitious level. It may be like the Carnival we've heard so much about, where everybody prances around in sexy outfits, dancing for days and nights on end."

"For a high school costume dance in Arkansas, I searched my grandfather's trunk in the attic for clothes. Let's ask our friends if they have such a trunk."

"It depends," Erik said when he understood their predicament, "whether you want to see or be seen. Maria is looking through her closets to see if we have anything appropriate."

Soon Maria came bustling in, her arms full of seemingly shapeless pieces of cloth. "If you don't mind wearing tights and a tutu, these might do. Juscelina left part of her professional wardrobe here. Let's try this. You'll look real cute!"

It was a praying mantis costume meant for a ballet, now forgotten, set to a piece by Villa-Lobos.

"I absolutely refuse to let you go in that!" Hank exclaimed. "The prognosis is not good for your mate. Furthermore, any suggestion of cannibalism might be considered in bad taste if Carib Indians are present. What else do you have?"

"I couldn't wear it in any event," Deb said sadly, holding the costume to her waist and looking in the mirror. "Juscelina must have been anorexic in order to squeeze into this!"

"Here is *Afternoon of a Faun*. It is for the modern version that Juscelina did at the end of her career. She was heavier then, so it might fit without too much adjustment."

Deb tried it on. "It's too sexy, with all that gauze over see-through tights. What else is there?"

"A pity. I'd make a great faun. Look at these legs; they would be the envy of all the old goats at the ball."

"Here are costumes from *Prince Igor*. You can choose between the Captive Princess or the Polovetsian Girl, Deb. Hank will have to be the Chief Warrior. Look at the colors! Aren't they beautiful?"

"At least my legs will be covered," Deb said, modeling the Polovetsian Girl's gown, which fit perfectly. "What do you think, Hank? Do I look beautiful? Could I wear this and the Princess's crown, Maria? The girl's cap is a bit drab."

Now it was Hank's turn to look like a Tartar or Mongolian warrior. "I like the costume with all the Turkish rug designs. But the face isn't right. Too damn western!"

"That's where a skillful makeup artist comes in. Maria will be able to fix that."

It took an afternoon of sewing, adjusting, and applying makeup to prepare Deb and Hank for the ball. "*Vocês parecem muito bem!*" Maria exclaimed while Erik loaded his camera to catch them as they entered their taxi.

It was indeed a fabulous affair. There must have been a

thousand people crowded into the ballroom, talking, drinking, dancing, laughing, and looking at each other more than at the exhibits. Already the smoke was so thick that it was difficult to breath.

A few Tupi Indians fluent in Portuguese were crouching outside huts, busy making arrows and grinding manioc as they explained what they were doing and why. Their faces, arms, and legs were decorated with colorful designs; they wore native attire made of grass and feathers. The women, however, had their breasts covered.

The guests were by far the most naked to be seen. White women were dressed as if for Carnival with tinsel blossoms held in place by an invisible net to cover their nipples. Deb and Hank noticed that a small triangle shape made of white fur with a dark line in the middle was almost enough to conceal a woman's sex; it was held in place by a studded velvet belt that worked its way upward to encircle the hips and, in back, descended again to disappear between the buttocks.

Going native was the rage. Women and men had hired the most talented and expensive artists to paint wild designs on as much of their body surface as was exposed, which in some cases was most of it. Swirling geometric streaks in garish colors converged at crucial points of anatomy to accentuate natural peaks and valleys, often giving the impression of lava or glacier floes. Bodies were decorated with painted scenes done in minute detail. A man's chest and stomach represented a map of Amazonia, with the great river flowing into the sea at his left nipple. Another's back narrated the disappearance of the British explorer Fawcett in the last century. There was every possible variety of skirts made from grass. On some women they were short, on others they extended to below the knees; in either case the strands of grass were attached in such a way as to separate often, revealing long legs and elegant high heeled sandals. The men wore grass skirts as well, even portly businessmen. Native masks, purchased at chic boutiques, were worn by both sexes.

Hank was relieved to think that this was probably the most elegant and ambitious social affair he could ever expect to be invited to, and he marveled at how spontaneously the overweight and underdressed guests were able to amuse themselves in public. Deb let herself enjoy every minute, holding on to Hank's arm and feeling anonymous yet well enough dressed to be noticed.

DEB BEGAN HER work. She spent the mornings doing physicals and prescribing injections and medications. Four nurses worked with her, all under the supervision of Clara Converse, who had the ability to be everywhere at all times and to talk without taking a breath. Dr. Powers whisked in and out, greeting everyone but talking little. In the afternoon Deb worked upstairs in the Woman's Health Unit, where it turned out she was the only person qualified to work with mental health cases. In a cubicle just large enough to fit two small chairs, she met with pregnant, sterile, or grieving women, trying to help them cope with insolvable problems in constructive ways. She had fifteen minutes for each patient, less the time it took to scribble notes. Her day included a lunch break, not long enough for her to go home so she stayed in her office catching up on files and studying the rules and regulations in force at the clinic. In three weeks she was scheduled to leave in the school bus for the area around Belo Horizonte, where she would continue doing physicals in a tent and giving lectures and demonstrations on birth control in empty lots, village squares, or sports fields, since the Church refused to lend its facilities for this purpose. She was puzzled by the instruction she found in her English language policy booklet, underlined and in italics: "The staff is not authorized to mention abortion, either explicitly or implicitly; infringement of this policy may result in dismissal of personnel responsible and curtailment of program." Where did this order come from, she wondered. Was it still in effect?

Hank felt something like abandonment as he realized that Deb would be away every day from 7 a.m. to 7 p.m. when in residence in Rio. Whenever she was away in the field, he would have to shift for himself. In her free time she would have to squeeze in sleeping, eating, doing laundry, shopping, social events, being alone by herself, and doing the work she wasn't able to finish at her office. This schedule hardly seemed exciting to him.

The day after making these calculations, Hank called Herb Kater and using the code C-14 was able to recognize Kater's voice without delay.

"I'm glad you called. After that reception—when was it? Oh, yes! three weeks or so ago—I saw John Webb again. He liked the idea of our getting together in a business kind of arrangement. I also asked some questions for security reasons. We will have to ask for an official security check, but since that will be a formality we won't have to wait on that."

"Can you tell me what you have in mind? I don't have a real impression about what I will be doing except that it seems to involve some walking and looking around. That sounds like fun to me, but it would help if I knew what I will be looking around for."

"Look, Hank. Why don't you come in tomorrow at one, and we can go over the whole project together. I'll introduce you to some people who can brief you in on the details. We'll also discuss the financial aspect. It will be over four digits, for sure, and there won't be any applicable taxes. Plus a couple of benefits and perks. How does your wife like her job? We have heard good things about her."

"She just started. I haven't heard much about it, so I am amazed anyone else has. I'll be there tomorrow. How do I get there?"

After giving addresses and directions, Kater asked:

"By the way. That fellow you talked to after we separated at the reception, what was his name? I can't remember exactly, oh, yes! Bonot. Do you see much of him?"

"I had just met him that evening. I haven't seen him since."

"Just as well maybe. He's one of those reporters who ask stupid questions at news conferences and don't know when to stop. Sort of a smart ass. Well, see you tomorrow."

Hank reached the headquarters of SOD early enough to look around. It was housed in an old mansion on a shaded street without traffic, and there was no sign to identify it. No cars were parked at the sidewalk in front although the rest of the street was crammed. As Hank walked up the concrete steps toward the front door, a man in a uniform like the one you see outside elegant apartment buildings came to meet him. Upon learning what brought Hank, the concierge smiled and invited him into a reception area, where he was asked to fill out a security form and given a plastic badge for identification. Then the guard accompanied Hank to an antique elevator from the inside of which he manipulated three ropes to make the car rise silently and slowly to the top floor where the cage came to a smooth stop.

Hank waited in what looked like a rich bachelor's apartment. The walls were covered with intricately carved panelling portraying erotic scenes, one consisting of shepherds, shepherdesses, sheep, and unicorns. Another showed a man and a woman, both naked, riding through a forest on horseback without saddles. The furniture consisted of overstuffed chairs upholstered in needlepoint and highly polished tables with elaborate candelabras. A young woman in a smock, seemingly unaware of Hank's presence, was dusting the furniture with a rag that smelled strongly of disinfectant. After a few minutes she went on her hands and knees and began silently polishing the floor around the edge of the room between the molding and the Oriental rugs. She did not look up when Hank was summoned into another room.

He was met by Herb Kater, three men, and a woman. They invited him to join them at a conference table where they held an informal meeting that lasted almost three hours. The room had once been a dining room. It was panelled with dark carved wood; on top there was a shelf which still supported light blue Chinese plates standing on edge and leaning against the wall. As the afternoon wore on, Hank was able to observe a mural that covered the walls above the panelling. With the sun illuminating one end, he could see a medieval knight taking leave of his mother; an hour later as the light moved he saw the knight entering a king's festive court; later, on another wall, he was visiting an invalid in bed. The last panel was situated above the windows behind Hank's chair, so he was unable to find out how the story ended.

"Don't mind those murals!" Kater told him. "Weird, aren't they? We haven't gotten around to repainting this place. It used to belong to some eccentric. It's warm here, too. Would anyone like a Coke?"

Hank talked easily in answer to a request to introduce himself. His audience seemed more attentive than he had expected, especially when they asked for clarifications about certain periods of his life. Their questions were specific but neither pointed nor intrusive. Then Kater asked the man next to him to outline what they had in mind for Hank to do.

"We are here at the behest of our government, you might say under contract, to monitor the passage of drugs, in particular cocaine, through Brazil. In other terms our effort is to uncover the new pipeline created by drug traffickers to use Brazil as a transit country for Colombian cocaine destined for the United States and Europe. You can appreciate how important our findings will be for the War on Drugs effort. SOD covers Brazil; different organizations have been chosen to do the same in various Latin American countries. So far we have been able to send agents, people like you, to track the drug routes through most of northern Brazil—along the border of the Guyanas, through the Amazon network, around Brasília and the coast north of here. This has involved many informants and cross-checking of sources. But our personnel is limited, as is the time allotted to us to gather the information. That is why we are interested in your participation in this effort. Do the rest of you concur with this presentation?"

"Absolutely," the oldest man present put in. "You might add that we are working in close connection with agencies of our government and of the government of Brazil, who are kept in full knowledge of our operations. We keep in contact with Brazil's military, security, and police divisions, to whom we supply technical assistance. We enjoy a fully cooperative relationship with them. It's a pity General Soarez was unable to attend this meeting. He is such a fine gentleman."

"It sounds to me as though you have been able to cover a lot of territory. What happens after you have finished gathering your information?"

"We don't have any real input into the follow-up, but my understanding is that once a drug route is observed and verified, Washington alerts the local authorities who, with the assistance of U.S. agents and equipment, seal off the access and choke the pipeline."

"What areas do you still want to cover? How can I be of help?"

"You may have noticed that I mentioned the area north of Brasília. We are doing such thorough work that the traffickers are heading south. We assume that they are currently entering Brazil from southern Bolivia or northern Paraguay, somehow making their way across the great Pantanal swamp into the state of Mato Grosso do Sul and eventually getting to São Paulo and Santos or to Curitiba. What we have in mind is for you to travel west from São Paulo, by whatever means you choose—by jeep, foot, or canoe if necessary. The idea, if you haven't already gathered, is to discover what route these transporters of lethal drugs are using to get across southern Brazil. It will be up to you to decide how to proceed; we can't make too many assumptions here, because the terrain is so different from what it is in areas we are familiar with. But there is one thing we are sure of: the ordinary routes followed by travelers, business people, prospectors, and local residents are avoided by the traffickers for fear of being detected. So it will probably be in your interest not to use the Transcontinental Highway or the railway to get to where you are going. From what I understand you have time on your hands, and like to be on your own, hike, meet people along the way. You talk easily, in three or four languages, and people take a liking to you, as we are discovering right now, I am happy to admit. And of course, we will pay handsomely for your services."

"Mr. Jones, here to my right, will help you get started, make suggestions for the equipment you will need and tell you everything we know about the territory you will be covering. Miss Peppercorn will explain the financial arrangements and take care of obtaining the necessary documents from the government of Brazil to permit you to sojourn in the interior of the country. She will also supply you with your initial spending account, some telephone cards and code numbers for quick communication with us and your wife, and, of course, a fake identity card. Briefly, what we had in mind is paying you $6,000 for two month's work in the field, depositing half of it at the end of one month in your bank account and issuing you a check for the rest when you return. It would be in everyone's interest to complete the job within the given time frame, since continued funding is not a certainty."

The meeting continued for another two hours. When Hank arrived at home that night he found Deb in conversation with Maria and Erik and a mixed couple with two children.

"Come in, Hank, and meet our daughter, Maria Sofia, and her family," Erik called out. "They came over from the other side of Rio, where they live. It takes them three hours to drive here, so it is a real treat when they come. This is our son-in-law, Carlos Orós, and our grandchildren, Jorge and Amelia. I'm sure I told you, that Carlos is an architect. Maria Sofia is a painter of murals, which means that she is invited to do her work in the beautiful mansions of Rio and Petrópolis."

"I do that, and I am also asked to paint historical narratives on the walls of new public buildings, but most of that market is all sewed up," Maria Sofia said in perfect English.

"It is just as well she doesn't work much now," Carlos added. "You know how it is. When she is gone I have to take care of the children. But since no one can make a decent living in architecture around here, I have two other jobs to help make ends meet. I didn't tell you, Erik, I am now assistant manager in the newest McDonald's in Rio. You would think it is the best restaurant in the city, since the burgers are made of beef, which is hard to find in the markets, and the Cariocas are starved for beef. You know, the people who live in Rio," he added to be sure Hank would understand. "I don't know where all that beef comes from, but it is ground and safe to eat, believe me!"

"What is your other job?"

"I work at the counter of a copying shop."

"When do you find time to do your architectural work?"

"At night, after the kids are in bed, when the lights are working, that is."

Deb asked Maria Sofia where she had learned English.

"From Dad, of course. You have probably noticed that he has a slight Danish accent he got from his mother. The rest I picked up at Reed College, in Portland. Dad sent me there for an education and to get me out of danger's way when the military were in power in Brazil. He knew that if I stayed in Rio I would demonstrate, and that was a sure passport to the other world. As it was, I got arrested a couple times in Oregon, for exercising my freedom of speech. That's where I met Carlos—in jail! But I loved it in the Northwest. You're from Seattle, aren't you, Deb?"

"Yes, until I left for the Peace Corps in '85. Were you in Portland then?"

"We were already back in Brazil."

"Tell us how the two of you met. Carlos is Brazilian, isn't he?"

"His father is a doctor and sent him to Lewis and Clark for the same reason, to keep him out of political trouble, which was no joke at the time."

"But how did the two of you happen to meet in jail?"

"We both signed petitions and demonstrated in front of the hotel where a Brazilian government official was visiting. He was part of a commission traveling around the country to get support from business people and loans from bankers for the military government. We cornered him in a hotel corridor and bugged him by asking about the fate of fifteen people we knew who had been detained, tortured, and listed as *desaparecidos*. I remember shouting at him while he dodged our questions. He stalled just long enough for the police to come and whisk us off before the reporters arrived. We were together wisecracking in Portuguese while they searched and interrogated us. They put Carlos in a cell next to mine, so we were able to whisper all night, and almost touch! After that they wanted to deport us both. Somehow the colleges intervened and got us permission to stay until we graduated. After that there was no way Carlos could avoid me any longer."

Maria invited the group to the courtyard, where they sat at a round table under the cover of trees and shrubs.

"New brew!" Erik announced, bringing in a tray of clear glass mugs filled with a dark liquid and overflowing with foam. "This batch has aged long enough to taste fairly good. I haven't shown you my brewing area and equipment, Hank. You have already tasted my wine; tonight we celebrate this ale, which is the only kind of brewed beverage Maria and I can tolerate these days. Even Carlos is beginning to enjoy its dark flavor."

Deb was curious to know about Hank's job interview in the afternoon. He explained as much as he had understood, which wasn't much, about what he was to do and who his employer would be.

"I don't know what to think," Erik commented. "Things have changed so much in this country, one really doesn't understand what is happening outside one's home and neighborhood. I find it hard to imagine what all those busy people in the fancy buildings are up to. If you ask them, they answer with a bunch of initials, like your employer, Hank. I even wonder if they know what they are doing. It made more sense in Brasília, where thousands of people were working on one enormous project, to build a new city. But now it's all fragmented and dispersed; we're running in opposite directions, and we would never dream of asking someone where he is going."

"That's no problem for me," Carlos said. "If someone wants a new building, I design it, and I don't ask what it is for except to get the right number of rooms and provide space where they need it. As long as it looks right and I get paid, I'm satisfied. If I started worrying about what it might be used for ten years down the pike, I couldn't even finish a first draft."

"As an architect," Deb asked, "can you explain how the shacks in the favelas can remain standing on those steep slopes? It looks as if they will all come tumbling down with the first strong wind or a heavy rain."

"Good question. Poor people must be born with an instinct to build in impossible places. And it's amazing how fast they work; they are like ants. When the rich construct fine apartment complexes in Barra, for example, the next day they are already surrounded by tin-roofed hovels; so they move farther out, set up razor-wire barriers, and hire thugs to guard their neighborhoods from the *favelados*. And don't believe it's romantic to live in a favela the way movies show it. Up on top you can't see the ocean any more or feel the warmth of the sun because of the high-rises. Of course if you like the smell of sewage in the gutters . . ."

Carlos continued, turning to Hank. "Your project sounds fine to me. Personally I can't stand mosquitoes and mud, so I have stayed as far as possible from the interior, especially the swamps and jungles. But if you like that sort of thing you'll probably enjoy it. In the beginning Brazil consisted of a narrow strip along the coast where people lived. My theory is that they should have remained there. The interior was meant for Indians and runaway slaves, and they should have been left alone to live in peace. Nobody thinks about the Indians except when they get in the way of progress and shoot it out with prospectors who want claims on their land. People like Rondon and the Villas Boas brothers are piously praised for what they did to help the Indians, but nobody really cares, do they?"

The children were becoming restless in the midst of all the talk. Maria distracted them as well as she could with games and stories.

"I just have to say one more thing. Erik, keep this beautiful house and garden just as they are now. Nobody is building anything like it in Brazil today, no matter how much money they sink into their mansions and town houses. The idea of a garden is out of date."

Hank spent the next few days preparing for his departure. It was difficult to know what supplies and equipment he would need in an area he knew next to nothing about. Erik put him in touch with a friend who had traveled in the Mato Grosso do Sul and who advised Hank to lay in most of his supplies at the last outposts in order to be able to travel light through the more populated areas. There were some items, however, that he should buy in specialized stores in São Paulo, because quality can make the difference between life and death when one ventures so far from civilized areas. Hank received the necessary shots at Deb's dispensary. Miss Peppercorn drove him to the offices of the Bureau of the Interior and to FUNAI, where she whisked him to the front of long lines of people waiting at windows, making it possible for him to apply and receive the necessary permits for his trip into the backlands in one afternoon.

His plan was to drive in the jeep, supplied by SOD, to Santos where his lodging was already arranged. After making inquiries there, he would decide what route to take into the interior. Kater had already mapped out what he thought to be the most fruitful route for over half the way to the Bolivian border, as far as Campo Grande, but he wanted Hank to be free to follow his instinct in discovering the most frequently used routes. From Santos Hank would go to São Paulo and stay long enough to make further inquiries and purchase supplies. Then he would weave his way across the country, sometimes moving diagonally north and south, like a sailboat tacking against the wind. Where he went and how far depended on what he was to discover. He was aware that he would be moving westward more or less along the Tropic of Capricorn.

His jeep was to be delivered to his house at noon. In the morning he and Deb drank their coffee in the gazebo outside their cottage.

"I am happy for you, and I'll miss you, of course. I can't really see you sitting here while I'm giving injections and lecturing people about health. On the weekends I have Erik and Maria for company, and then there are also my friends at work. But I do hope you will take care of yourself. I can't help worrying a little. How long will we be in contact, at least by phone?"

"I'll try to phone every third day or so, in the evening. After a month that will become more difficult because there won't be many phones, so I'll call whenever I find one. You can expect several calls one week, then none the next week. If you get used to the idea now it won't be a problem when it happens. When it gets hard to communicate with you, I'll start writing in that diary you gave me, so that you can keep in touch with me day by day, at least in retrospect."

"You said 'spying activities.' The word is a little awesome, really, for me in this moment. Is that what it will be?"

"The more I think of it, the more that sounds like what I'll be doing. They said the worst that could happen is that I could be arrested by the local militia and put behind bars overnight on suspicion of trying to buy cocaine for myself. I have full instructions as to what to do under those circumstances. And don't forget, this operation is overseen jointly by the U.S. and

Brazilian governments and their private enterprise subsidiaries. So it looks pretty safe to me. You have the names and numbers of the people in charge; you can phone them if you become anxious. They said they sort of expect it."

"I'd like to think it is some sort of research project, like if you were to go and gather information about Indian languages. The word 'spying' gives me the creeps."

"Let's not use it anymore, then. Let's pretend I am going out to the wilderness to measure the skulls of the headhunters, in centimeters, of course. That would be safe enough."

"That would be dreadful. The first hunter whose head you tried to measure would grab his bow and arrow and start hunting yours."

"No, no! That's not what I meant. I would ask his permission to measure the skulls in his possession. They must keep a collection somewhere. There is nothing safer than that."

They both laughed and then looked at each other in silence.

"The jeep is coming in an hour and a half. Let's use this time well. Come, Deb," Hank said as he took her hand and led her into the cottage and into the bedroom, where he shut the door quietly. The time passed quickly for them, for it was meant to encapsulate two months of joyous play, to be a down payment to carry them through the next sixty nights. They were even able to sleep a few moments, embracing each other tightly so that their naked bodies and skin could learn the imprint by heart and recite it whenever solitude threatened.

They awoke to the sound of the jeep's powerful engine. Hank was ready to leave in ten minutes. Maria had made a picnic lunch to see him safely to Santos, and after he drove off, she invited Deb to spend the afternoon with Erik and her.

ON A MONDAY morning after Hank's departure, Deb went to her clinic at five in the morning to meet a peculiar vehicle called Nova, which was to transport her and two other nurses, three aides, and a volunteer medical student from New Mexico. Also on board were the driver, someone's friend who was going to visit relatives, a patient of the clinic going home to Belo Horizonte for a vacation, and another person Deb couldn't identify. There were also a few exotic birds in cages and some suitcases and cartons that didn't seem to belong to any of the medical members of the group.

Nova was once a school bus that had seen service in a rural area of Louisiana where it carried junior high school children to and from school, dances, football games, band concerts; it had also taken the school spelling bee team across the Mississippi into Alabama for a match, which they lost. On the return trip there was trouble with the brakes so the school board decided to sell the bus, putting it up for bids. No one wanted it until some hippies saw it rusting away in a school yard and offered to take it away for fifty dollars. They fixed the brakes, painted the body with psychedelic designs, and headed south across the border. It was those same hippies who, a year later, donated it to the American government by abandoning it on the sidewalk in front of the Consulate in Rio. The then director of the clinic learned the bus was up for grabs and, hoping it could be transformed into an ambulance, asked that it be placed on his equipment inventory. It broke down on its first emergency mission, obliging an accident victim to take a cab the rest of the way to the hospital. That is how the ancient bus, baptized Nova (pronounced *não-vai*, meaning: it doesn't go) and always driven by the same loquacious driver, found its true vocation: delivering medical personnel and supplies.

The driver, a chubby, unshaven Brazilian smelling of perspiration, talked without interruption about the weather, the lousy condition of the roads, and what his horoscope had to say about the day's soccer match while birds, passengers, and baggage were being loaded. As he backed out of the clinic entrance, forcing drivers on the street to come to a screeching halt, he began to sing. His song, which had no identifiable melody or words, continued until after lunch break when he turned on the radio for the afternoon match. This lasted until the passengers arrived in Belo Horizonte, eight hours after they had set out, their ears ringing, their bodies exhausted from the heat, and their heads dizzy from the sharp curves along the mountainous route and the frequent jolting stops.

Trapped between hills, Brazil's third largest city suffers from a chronic onslaught of smog, and Deb found it singularly lacking in charm, despite its promising name. She was housed along with her female colleagues in a low-lying building situated in the outskirts. To avoid the guilty feeling that comes from not doing enough sight-seeing in a foreign country, she planned to spend her weekends on bus tours of the historical towns of the state of Minas Gerais—Ouro Prêto, Cogonhas, Tiradentes, Sabará. This provided the only real pleasure Deb had outside her work. Walking the narrow streets of these towns, she found herself in a world of cobblestones, ancient churches, mansions, water fountains with sculpted faces, and tiny white houses, until at noon when they were overrun by foreign tourists, and the spell was broken.

Her workday consisted of riding Nova to a different town or village each day. There a large tent was set up in the town center, and people quickly gathered in a line waiting in the sun for their turn. Deb's working hours were spent diagnosing and prescribing treatment. Once she had begun work, she found that her colleagues and sponsors had little or no enthusiasm for the educational functions she had intended to assume, and anyway, there wasn't enough time for her to talk to women about the advantages and methods of birth control when the line of sick people waiting outside her cubicle was endless.

One after another, she interviewed patients and listened to their belabored breathing. Why, they asked, was it so hard to get enough air? They were mostly miners, but some simply lived in smog-ridden Belo Horizonte, and others had smoked for as long as they could remember. Emergency patients were rushed in suffering from heat exhaustion after working long hours in the sun. There were the chronically malnourished women and children; Deb learned that usually there was little for them to eat at home, even when they lived in one. Men came, their faces, necks, arms, and chests covered with cancers. Seeing their pleading eyes, Deb knew they believed she had magical powers to heal them, and she wondered what she could do for these people with her little black suitcase. What about the women with ten or more children? Give them *preservativos*, the unreliable local condoms? What could she tell people with eye disease and tooth infections when there were no ophthalmologists and dentists to refer them to? During her first week she saw and diagnosed parasite infestation, mercury poisoning (from gold mines?), syphilis, malaria, calcium deficiency, tuberculosis, running sores, hookworm, and a case of scleroderma.

On Friday afternoon, when she was nearly exhausted, Deb took out a few minutes to shut her eyes and rest before calling in the next person in her line; she imagined herself in the cottage in Rio with Hank, enjoying a drink with him before going out to dinner together.

"Well Deb! You look mighty busy there! How about a break?"

She opened her eyes to focus on the smiling face of Bernie

Powers; he was standing in front of her, dressed casually for the heat and held a suitcase at his side.

"Bernie! What are you doing here? I thought you were so busy at the clinic in Rio."

"Aw jeez! I needed to get away. The tension got so bad it was giving me chills, and when you get chills in Rio you know you're sick."

"What about your unit? And your patients?"

"All that can wait. It's better to have a relaxed doctor tomorrow than one who is going bananas today and can screw everything up."

"What are you going to do while you are here, Bernie?"

He took out a cigarette and began lighting it.

"Please, not here, Bernie! I'm trying to get the patients to refrain, at least in the tent."

He stuffed it out in the palm of his left hand. "Well, I had some business here, some people to see, and I decided to see how you were doing. I have to be back Tuesday. What about that break—you look all strung out, ready to hang on the clothesline to dry. I think you should have an iced tea with me and quit for the day."

"That would be for the weekend; today is Friday. Look! I have at least ten people waiting. Who knows how far they came from, how long they have been standing there. It'll be two hours before I can break. I appreciate your thought, Bernie, but really, I can't."

"Okay! Let me take half of them, you the other half. You'll see who wins. Want to learn how to do a fast diagnosis? Just watch; when I want to finish in a hurry I'm a streak of lightning. Next! Come in and stand there!" he shouted in a gruff and thickly accented Portuguese.

Maybe he's right, Deb thought as she finished her third and last diagnosis. Bernie was already outside having his smoke after dispatching eight of her patients. Yet she somehow felt cheated, as if he had stolen them from her, preventing her from knowing and helping those eight souls in the way they deserved as fearful, suffering human beings.

She packed up her things and said good-bye to her aide and the other nurses, who were still hard at it. Bernie was standing next to a red Alfa Romeo parked in the sun.

"I told the bus driver you wouldn't be waiting for him. Hop in! We'll be back in Belo Horizonte in a half an hour. I know a great place for a cool drink. Then we can have dinner at the only place with a view and a good show. It's in Savassí, a suburb."

He started off with a screech, slowing to under 110 km. only on the most acute hairpin turns. The wind whistled in Deb's ears and her hair was blowing in all directions. She was unable to answer until they came to an abrupt stop in front of her dormitory.

"Take your time getting ready. I'll be back in forty-five minutes."

"Wait, Bernie! You aren't taking me to dinner; I won't have it, it's not right."

"Deb, don't be a fussy little girl! We're all grown-ups, professionals, and we have a right to get to know each other and have a little fun. I'm married, too, so don't worry. Indeed, I'm a dutiful husband, you can't believe how dutiful I am. Aren't you enough of a feminist to know that going out to dinner with a male colleague isn't a sin? It's a sign of your independence, that you are intelligent and can control your own behavior, to know how to say no . . . or yes, as you choose. I suppose you didn't know I am a confirmed feminist. Well I am! Equal rights, equal opportunities, equal obligations. My vision of a good world is to be able to work with female doctors who don't go running home to their little husbands after work but feel free and secure enough to go out and have a couple of beers, play some pool, and chitchat about work. That's how doctors get educated, by communicating with each other. As a matter of fact, Deb, I'm not taking you out to dinner. The clinic is picking up the tab. It's a new policy that went into effect a few months ago. They want us to keep in touch with all the medical personnel. Maybe you haven't heard about it yet. See you in forty-five minutes, then. Ciao!" Bernie sped off thunderously.

Deb showered, changed, feeling fresh and quite determined not to let things get out of hand. When he returned, Bernie looked resplendent in a white suit that almost gave the impression that he was handsome.

"First I'll drive you around a little so you can become acquainted with this town, which isn't as awful as it looks. The night life is okay if you don't ask for perfection. How do you like the sound of Bang Bang Burger? The waiters all look like cowboys. Naw? After a drink we'll go the newest natural food place; you'll like it."

Bernie ordered a *caipirinha,* giving instructions on the exact proportions of *cachaça,* lime, sugar, and crushed ice for it to be, as he said, "a work of art." Deb had a *chopp,* a pale cold beer.

"Tell me, how are things going for you here in the back country? Are you happy? Do you get enough rest? What are the working conditions like?"

There wasn't much to say except to describe the heat, the frustration, and the long-term tedium that was settling in.

"I try to picture my patients at home when they return to begin their treatment, whatever it is. But I can't get a clear image because I am not acquainted with their surroundings. We should do home visits, Bernie. It would be much more effective."

"Just try to convince the Board of that! Can you imagine the cost? You would kill yourself going from one hut to another hovel."

He went on to describe how the majority of Brazilians live, day after day in shacks without plumbing, sleeping in bug-infested beds. "If you can call a pile of rags a bed, that is. What we can do for these people is a relative thing. If you can make them feel a little better about themselves, about their lives, you have accomplished a lot, even more perhaps than if you cured them of whatever they have, if that was possible. I work fast with them, act like someone who knows everything and can do everything. Since they come in with the hope that I can relieve their suffering,

I encourage that hope, because it doesn't cost anybody anything, and it does them a world of good. Their life will never get any better, we all know that. I give them a vague suggestion that they'll feel better in three quarters of an hour; most of the time it works. They go out with a dream that will nourish them better than a sack of free groceries. I give an illusion that I know will be satisfying, at least for a while. And there are no side effects."

"Do you knowingly deceive them? That would be dreadful."

"Oh, come off it, Deb! You know damn well that the scientific part of our functions accounts for a lot fewer than half of the cures we achieve so heroically, patting ourselves on the back as we deposit our fees. People cure themselves! All we do is make that possible with smiles or snarls, an occasional shot in the ass, and a pill or two."

"You have much more experience than I have, Bernie. But I would have to quit if I subscribed to that kind of thinking. And I certainly would end up smoking and drinking as much as you. How many have you had?"

"Four. You're right that it helps. At the end of each day I dope myself up so that I can face the next with something like equanimity. At least I know it's an illusion, that tomorrow when I wake up sober I'll see the world for what it is. You're living in a dream day and night, just like your patients. Only they go out feeling better, and you, well, you will age fast, get wrinkles, start to stoop, unless you learn how to get away from that line of patients waiting for you. Our mission, and all that shit! Relax, baby; you've had it if you don't. What are you doing over the weekend? I'll drive you to Ouro Prêto tomorrow; we'll leave good and early and be there before the rest of the tourists arrive to spoil it for us. Spend the night in a nice inn and come back late Sunday. What do you say?"

"I'm sorry Bernie. I'm going there with a friend on the bus. I couldn't let her down."

"Shall we have dinner? I'm ready. Since it's not far, let's walk."

Bernie held her arm somewhat unsteadily as they made their

way in silence across a square and down a wide street to the restaurant. There Deb let Bernie order for her, feeling the fatigue accumulated during the week rise up inside her, and paying little attention to what she ate or what he said. She did find enough energy to ask a question.

"Tell me about your wife and family, Bernie. Do they live in Rio?"

"I was afraid you'd ask that, but I knew you would sooner or later. You see, we don't get along all that well, that is, my wife and I. So she spends more and more time back in Illinois with her parents. She says it's better for the kids to go to school there where they can get a decent education in the public schools; in Rio they would have to attend a private school while we got up to our armpits in debt. She's right, of course. But I really think it's because she can't stand the sight of me for more than three months a year, which is what it comes to."

"How many children do you have? What are their names?"

"Do you really want to know all that Deb? Haven't we better things to talk about? We have three kids: Mary, Donald, and Alex, ages eleven, eight, and seven. Now, don't you want to know about my wife and me? What our problem is?"

"I know you are dying to tell me. Go ahead if you feel like it; but if you want to keep it to yourself, that's alright as far as I'm concerned."

"Purely and simply put, our problem is sex. That's all, there isn't any other. Doris is a model wife. You couldn't ask for a more courageous, hardworking, conscientious, economical, steady, faithful, thoughtful, unassuming person to be married to. Name a strength of character, she's got it. And she's good-looking and a safe driver to boot."

"What else could you want, really?"

"To be as far away from her as I can get, for the longest time possible. Of course, I miss the kids."

"I can imagine."

"She was a nurse, like you. We met during my residency. We used to make the rounds together. She would prepare the patient and take notes while I did the examinations; we totally agreed on procedure, which made us a good team. I forgot to mention that since I was in the hospital as a kid for some childhood disease, I have been haunted by visions of nurses and nurses' uniforms. That's why I went into medicine—one reason's as good as another, as long as you are any good at it. Anyhow, one evening when we were on rounds, there was this patient who could hardly move, and he was facing the wall, so Doris had to lean over him to remove a bandage for me to check out his suture. It was a time when nurses were wearing short skirts, so watching from behind I had a good view of her thighs, which were admirable. Then I . . ."

"Are you sure you want to tell me all this, Bernie? You could certainly find a more sympathetic audience somewhere. This isn't my favorite kind of story."

"Oh, shut up and listen, Deb! This is what life is all about; you'll realize that when you've had more experience. Well, I went and caressed those thighs with my hand. Then I explored some more. It was hot in Springfield that summer, and the hospital didn't have air conditioning. Consequently she was wearing loose panties, and my hand could go just about everywhere it wanted. By this time I was hyperventilating, and my heart was pounding like a sledge hammer. Then Doris disengaged herself and announced calmly that I could proceed with the examination. When we were out of the room, she picked up one of those iron rods they use to jack up mattresses and clobbered me over the head, I mean, with all her strength. That is how our love/hate relationship started. I was hospitalized for a week with a concussion; she was fired. She came to apologize, and we were married a month later. For a while things were great; she gave up nursing but always put on her nursing uniform when we had sex. Then after the third child was born she threw out the uniform, and in my frustration I decided to go off to Brazil . . ."

An hour or so later Bernie drove Deb back to her dorm.

"Are you sure you can't cancel the trip with your friend and let me take you to Ouro Prêto?"

"No way. She has been looking forward to this as much as I have. Thanks for the ride and the meal." Deb walked quickly to her door.

Deb fully enjoyed being alone on the bus the next morning and anticipated with pleasure two days of sight-seeing. The trip took long enough for her to begin feeling relaxed again, at one with the hilly landscape she watched pass by. When she got out of the bus and turned around after picking up her suitcase, she found herself face to face with Bernie Powers.

"Why did you lie to me, Deb? You don't need to be afraid of me, you know."

"I didn't lie."

"Where is your friend, then?"

"Right here," she answered, gesturing to herself. "It meant I wanted to be alone, and that is the truth."

Bernie had driven to Ouro Prêto the previous night, after seeing Deb to her room.

"I had business here, but what I really wanted was to show you around. Anyway I never did believe in that friend of yours."

Bernie turned out to be an excellent guide. He showed her the quaint little town inch by inch, explaining its history, architecture, and customs with enthusiasm and considerable humor. He took her through all eleven churches and then led her to little chapels and private oratories and a whole series of *Passos* or Stations of the Cross, impressing Deb with his intuitive grasp of Brazil's bizarre Catholicism. Along the way they visited the municipal buildings, the mining college, and the museum, where he was able to explain the episode of the *Inconfidência* uprising and describe in lugubrious detail the leprosy of Aleijadinho, Ouro Prêto's great architect and sculptor. Along the way they took in most of the fountains and bridges, reserving a visit to Mariana for the next day. Deb let herself gradually become caught up in Bernie's enthusiasm, and by the end of the day she was enjoying herself in the freewheeling and irreverent way he

skipped from one monument to the next. She couldn't find any
obstacle to having dinner with him that evening.

"You know that so-called medical problem, the one everybody
is talking about and governments are constantly wrestling with,
and pharmaceutical and insurance companies are spending
fortunes to maintain their influence over, all that can be easily
solved," he told Deb between courses at dinner, after a few drinks,
which that night made him confuse his syntax more than usual.
"All they have to do is make doctors happy; that is absolutely all
it would take. If they earn enough money to satisfy their desires,
whatever those might be, they will willingly cure their patients in
the most efficient and painless way and do their utmost to prevent
the spread of disease and injury. It doesn't matter so much who
pays their fees—governments, insurance moguls, or the patients'
meager savings, so long as they are paid enough."

"Isn't it slightly more complicated than that? I don't think
anybody other than doctors would be satisfied with your utopian
solution. Nurses wouldn't."

"Look at it this way. Humanity is hierarchical by nature. Take
physicians, for instance. What do they want, basically? They
want to enjoy their own life by whatever means. Some like to
travel, others like to sail; then there are all those who spend their
time in libraries doing research, those who collect stamps and
ride horses, and the ones who play the violin. These are all
worthwhile activities, there's no denying it. But they cost money,
and the happy doctor is the one who can pursue his enjoyment.
Mine is sex, no question about that. Just one more story, Deb.
Hear me out!"

By now, Deb was resigned.

"A few months ago, at the clinic, I came in after lunch and
caught sight of the most delicious morsel you have ever seen
waiting in line for treatment or advice of some sort. Don't ask me
her name. She was a very light-skinned mulatto, about sixteen,
maybe younger. Her dark hair curled just above her shoulders,
she was wearing shorts and a long loose T-shirt. I could tell her

breasts were small but developed, her waist was thin, and her bottom seemed compact although you couldn't really tell because of the shirt. Dark eyes darting all around at everything, and a pleasant expression. I fussed around with X-rays on my desk until she got close to the head of the line. Then I started receiving patients myself so that when her turn came I would be the next examiner ready. It worked. She came in to my office and asked for something to treat itching and skin inflammation. Lifting up her T-shirt and moving the elastic band of her shorts down an inch or so she uncovered her abdomen where I right away recognized the signs of an allergic reaction. I didn't need to prolong the examination at all, but you can see the length we go to in order to satisfy our need for enjoyment. I asked where else the rash was. She lifted her shirt and let me examine her breasts, which I did close up, with extreme care. Anywhere else? She lowered her shorts, uncovering her bottom and thighs. She was wearing one of those crazy bikini swimsuits so popular here, the ones they call 'dental floss' because the back is nothing but a string, so I could examine her rash with great concentration. I prescribed some pills and a lotion to prevent itching and told her to come back just before lunch in three days, although there wasn't the least necessity for a follow-up. I know that was stupid without your telling me with that pained look on your face. But that's not the issue. This isn't a lecture about medical ethics, it's a parable about how making one physician happy can benefit others. She returned as scheduled and showed me how the rash had disappeared. When I saw that she was wearing the same swimsuit under her skirt, I laid her right there on the floor of my office. Sounds awful, doesn't it? But wait. For the next three months she came two or three times a week just before lunch break, and each time she took with her stuff she could use at home: syringes, pills (no hard stuff, just pain killers and vitamins), one day a flashlight, the next day a stethoscope, tongue depressors, pencils and paper, even food other patients had brought to me as offerings. I never asked what she did with her

loot, whether she sold it or gave it to family members or a
boyfriend, but in any event it made her content to go out hiding
some of the wonders of modern medical technology in her
shopping bag. But the miracle is what it did for me: it blew away
the depression over my absent wife and kids, I worked with
incredible energy, seeing twice as many patients each day as I
had previously, and for a while I even entertained the idea of
doing some research and writing it up for medical journals. Then
after a month or so she didn't come one day when I expected her,
and there has been no sign of her since. I'm still running on the
momentum of that experience, but I can feel it begin to wear off.
One of these days I'll relapse and sink into a slump again. But at
least I have learned what it takes to keep me going and alive.
Deb! Are you awake?"

"Of course. I was just thinking of something. I'm afraid I
missed a lot of what you were saying because I suddenly
remembered a patient who came in early yesterday with
emphysema. He said he was from the North. What's the
connection, Bernie?"

"That's where the mines are, and when you say mines you're
talking about unbelievable wealth for owners and managers; for
everyone else nothing but skin cancers, heat exhaustion, chemical
poisoning, and the inevitable closing down of their lungs because
of the conditions they work in. Of course, they smoke, too, which
accelerates the process," he said, flicking the ashes from the tip
of his cigarette. "We join the chorus of social workers and rich
old ladies to scream about the bad health of the miners in Brazil,
but nobody listens, everybody ignores the laws and regulations
about employment. Whenever someone tries to enforce them he
is either fired or arrested. You are going to see a lot more of that,
Deb. They come down here because they believe the air is better
and will cure them. What can you expect? The social problems
here are so immense you get diseases like my ulcers just thinking
about them."

"I remember the gargoyles and the sad faced bas-reliefs of

diseased and starving people we saw today in that one old church. Do you think the sculptor had sin and damnation in mind, or did he foresee what was going to happen to the majority of Brazilians?"

Bernie stuffed out his cigarette and, looking directly into Deb's eyes, paused before answering.

"The greatest art is prescient, if you want to know what I think. When I see a painting that tells even obliquely what's going to happen to innocent people, tears come to my eyes. The best of us can't do much more than alleviate the suffering of just a few people, if we're lucky. Not even the dedicated scientists in their billion-dollar labs can figure out how to get food to undernourished Brazilians. There are forty million of them, believe me, almost a third of the total population. Not to mention the sixty million who don't have sanitation, drinkable water, or decent places to live. Don't be surprised by what you see dragging into your consultation room; do the best you can for each one, and try not to expect lasting results from your efforts. I'm beginning to admire you, Deb. I don't want to see you hurt."

After a night in separate hotel rooms, they continued sightseeing the following day.

One of the patients Deb saw the following week had her puzzled. It was an older man who refused to talk about his injuries other than to show where he felt pain. He complained about discomfort in the area of his kidneys. Deb noticed that he had no nails on his fingers or on his toes and could see scar tissue from burns on his hands, feet, and thighs. When she asked about it he was silent.

"You'll get used to seeing just about everything, Honey," an older Canadian nurse told her later when she described the patient. "Torture victims of the military government still come in, even though the *abertura*, the political easing-up, has been here for a decade."

W HEN DEB RETURNED to Rio, her work picked up where it had left off, only her case load increased by fifty percent.

"In Brazil, everything submits to the laws of inflation, and it isn't just a question of currency," Bernie told her when she complained. "Your only choice is between efficiency—in the way you treat your patients—or burnout. Please pick the first. There are no funds for me to replace you with."

A month later Rio was busy preparing for the Earth Summit, which was scheduled to begin in June and bring to the city thousands of delegates, journalists, lobbyists, and curious people from around the world to jam its streets and facilities. It was to be the feather in the cap of this country, which had long been among the most egregious of polluters and spoilers of natural resources, to host the elite of ecologists, to play the gracious facilitator to foreign governments wanting to show concern for the future of the planet. This was at any rate the way Deb viewed the events that were about to take place in Rio, and it explains why she had paid relatively little attention to what was to become an important date in history.

"Anyway," she told Erik and Maria at dinner several days after her return, "everything is already decided. They have hammered out all the provisions of Agenda 21, making so many compromises that nobody is really satisfied. Now it is a question of arguing about relative pronouns and conjunctions and then ratifying a document that doesn't bind anybody. So, is President

Bush going to appear? The party won't be complete if our President doesn't show."

"It was announced today that he has decided not to come. Everyone was on pins and needles, you can be sure, because, as you say, without him the meeting will be a flop."

"Do you really see much difference? By the way, did you hear from Hank today?" Deb asked.

"No, not since the last time he called. Remember that he said he was having trouble making phone contact? Maybe none of the phones work out there."

Soon Deb could no longer avoid taking interest in the Earth Summit conference, for the radio and television programs were full of interviews of eminent scientists and commentaries about what the different countries expected to gain, politically and economically, from the deliberations. Every newspaper and magazine cover loudly proclaimed the world-shaking character of the events, and President Collor de Mello gave unctuous speeches about Brazil's leading role in the affair. Special concerts and exhibits were scheduled; posters and graffiti were everywhere. The Dalai Lama was expected, and thousands of extra tourists would soon pour in.

"*Bom!* Good! It is just like the Olympics," Maria said. "Everybody measures and compares the strength and the beauty of the national teams or lineups, and the inaugural ceremonies will be spectacular! But in the long run the games will get boring, and we will fall asleep in front of our TV sets and wake up just long enough to hear the scores: US.—9.8, Russia—9.4, Brazil—8.3, and so on. The performance of each country won't be judged according to its ecological record but to the points it makes during the conference by promoting or effectively preventing action."

"Don't forget how important it is that the delegates look sexy on television," Erik added. "But Denmark will score much better than it ever has in sporting events. I wanted to tell you, Deb, that a cousin of mine is a member of the Danish delegation, and he will be staying with us. He is an expert on food production and population shifts. I hope that it won't inconvenience you to have another person here."

It didn't inconvenience her at all; she found the presence of Aage Bording a healthy distraction from wondering where Hank might be. The Dane came to the summit meeting with mixed feelings. "We are starting at the wrong end of the problem," he told Maria, Erik, and Deb at dinner. "To do anything for the environment, we must first deal with poverty and control population growth. Remember, Erik, how they used to explain to us that there is no wealth without poverty? That was a clever way of telling us not to shed tears about the poor. But still the saying is true, although the opposite is not. Just watch: one day there will be plenty of poverty, and no wealth."

It took Deb a while to understand what Aage meant. She went on to ask him about the tropical rain forest and if it could be saved.

"The world is watching Brazil," he answered, "because the rain forest is quickly disappearing. The real culprit isn't just the poor farmer who cuts trees to eke out a living for a year or two until the soil goes bad. It is the developer and the international corporations that send in dollars and equipment to hurry up the process of destruction. There is no legal way of stopping them."

"I'm hoping the meetings will inaugurate some new kind of consciousness," Erik, said, always optimistic. "Once people become aware of how complicated the problems of the environment are they won't be able to forget. This is the beginning of a process; first it needs to mature, then it will bear fruit . . ."

Aage interrupted him. "There's preserving the planet on the one side, and on the other is the economic system with industry, banks, labor, votes, government, and so forth, that thrive on pollution and deforestation. There is no money in ecology, in spite of what the romantics say."

And then, to lighten the conversation, Aage explained how in his country one can offer a toast to anyone else at the table, preferably a beautiful woman, and can expect reciprocation.

Thereupon he nodded and winked at Maria and Deb, said: "Skaal!" and raised his wine glass to his lips.

A few days later an incident at work made Deb aware of the underside of the Global Summit. In the afternoon a woman came to her in anguish. Deb had given her counseling a month earlier. The woman had born ten children, four of which died at birth, and she didn't want any more; with Deb's advice she decided on a tubal ligation. Suddenly, during a roundup of homeless children in Rio, part of an effort by the government and the police to clean the streets for the conferees and tourists and create a break in everyday crime, her three youngest had disappeared.

"Bom, você sabe que they weren't homeless; they were just roaming the streets. Then a squad of uniformed men came and loaded them in a truck full of *abandonados,* and we haven't been able to find out anything about them. Was it a death squad, the off-duty police who are hired by businesses to kill kids to make neighborhoods safe? Or were these children temporarily 'removed' by the government? In that case they will be returned, won't they?"

Deb couldn't answer these questions. But she sensed behind the woman's tears and panic the fear of not being able to replace her children with others, and Deb felt largely responsible.

The next day, she found out that she was assigned by the clinic to help run a first aid station at the convention. It was there that she was recognized by Roger Bonot, who was covering the meetings for his news agency.

"Salut, Deb. Ça va? Est-ce que Hank est déjà parti pour l'intérieur?"

"Yes. He left over a month and a half ago, and now he must be miles east of São Paulo. I expect soon to learn where he is."

"Let me know how he likes it. I have always wanted to go there myself."

The Earth Summit meetings did not start until after lunch each day, which gave Deb time to relax in the morning before work.

She enjoyed being alone in the cottage, picking up, sitting in the morning sun drinking fruit juice, and writing long letters to her mother in Seattle giving a faithful account of her daily activities.

She also wrote letters to Hank. "I am missing you more and more. Maybe the anxiety is building up. Maria always says that no news is good news, that if anything has happened I would hear. I let that console me for a few days, but then I don't believe it any more. Thank goodness I am so busy with these meetings! Without them I would start worrying for real. I prayed for you last night, for your health and safety, and for you to return soon to Rio. Little did I know as an adolescent that one day I would pray again. It came quite naturally. But I have no idea to whom I prayed. Maybe it was one of the spirits people talk so much about in Rio. Given the choice again, I would urge you not to go on your trip.

"I saw Roger Bonot at the conference yesterday. He asked about you. He is an interesting guy and has quite advanced ideas, especially about the conditions here. We are planning to have coffee together during one of the breaks at the conference. Erik and Maria's guest, the Danish delegate, is very much the gentleman, quite amusing to be with. But how depressing it is to listen to him. He said last night that the title of the Earth Summit, UNCED, stands for United Nations Conference on Environment and Development, and then he went on to say that in his view environment and development are antithetical, they form an oxymoron that no amount of talk or good will can bridge. 'It's like,' he said, 'making fire and water, oil and vinegar, cats and dogs, estranged couples, the north and the south, the developed and underdeveloped countries, live together in peace.'

"Oh, Hank! Come back soon and cheer me up."

She carefully placed her letter in an envelope dropped it in a drawer on top of several others, all of them stamped, lacking only an address.

Someone knocked at her door. It was Maria, dressed in black, holding a small bouquet. The shock of seeing her in mourning took Deb's breath away.

"Maria, why are you in black? Has something happened?"

"Nothing has happened, Deb. If you come with me you will understand."

Deb dressed quickly and followed Maria who was already on the street. They walked in silence in the direction of the mountains, away from the city. After several turns in the road they arrived at a tiny graveyard hidden behind a stone wall. With a large key Maria opened a cast-iron gate with sharp points on top and led Deb slowly up an incline between two rows of graves.

"This is a place without pretensions, without large stones or mausoleums," Maria told her. "It is where people who were neither rich nor poor repose. You can see they are well tended to. Many of them were people from foreign lands, Protestants and others, who wished to remain almost anonymous in eternity. That explains the simplicity of the stones."

As they walked up the hill Deb was able to see inscriptions carved in many languages, although for the most part the slabs— they could hardly be called monuments—bore only names and dates. Some were in Hebrew, Arabic, and Greek script. Maria stopped and kneeled before a modest stone set slightly back and to the side. "Julia Nielsen. Age 13." Here Maria set her bouquet, carefully making the earth even with her hands. She then took out a handkerchief, knelt, and began to weep silently; Deb knelt next to her, placing her arm around Maria's shoulders and feeling tears come to her own eyes.

They returned slowly the same way they had come. The silence was interrupted only when Maria said: "Leukemia." A few steps further she went on: "We wanted Julia close to our home. At first I used to come every day. Now only once a week. It becomes more difficult for me as time goes by. It takes more out of me, out of my heart, and I almost wonder if I can keep on coming here at all, knowing of course that I will, up to my last day. If I ask Erik to come with me he always does, but I know he wants to have his own private time with Julia. He goes on his own, and although he never tells me when he has gone I always know, for he looks more at peace. The one thing in our lives we haven't been able to share is our grief. I think it is because we sense each other's suffering too deeply."

"Thank you, Maria."

That afternoon Deb accepted Roger's invitation for coffee in the cafeteria at the convention center. She told him about her experience of the cemetery and what she knew about Maria and Erik.

"They sound like interesting people," he said in his usual French accent. "I'd like to meet them. As an American who has lived down here for many years he could undoubtedly tell me things about Brazil that would take me forever to dig up on my own."

"How can you do research for your thesis and at the same time write articles for newspapers, with deadlines and assignments?"

"*Oh! C'est facile!* During the day I check out leads and write articles. Then at night I translate them into complicated thesis language, and after several articles I'll have five hundred pages of thesis, enough for a doctorate. My life is pretty simple. I live alone, without a TV or much in the way of entertainment. I eat sparingly, at little restaurants, just as I would at home. There is not much in the social life of Rio that interests me, even among journalists and in the French community; so I have plenty of time to put my nose in all the corners and observe, and then I write at night."

"Would you mind telling me what you are finding out with your nose? I imagine your sense of smell is pretty good."

"Actually I was going to ask you about what you are doing at your clinic, but you asked first, so here goes."

He sat back, took off his glasses and wiped them clean.

"By the way. How much time have we got? This isn't the sort

of thing one tosses off in ten minutes. Right now the representative from Moldova is speaking, and I know what he is saying without listening. He is asking for money to help clean up the environmental mess in his country. And he's saying that it is the competition of the great Cold War powers that created the mess; all his people did was stand by, watch the Russians build factories, and now they breath the acid air. Will you be needed soon?"

"I'll go check." Deb scurried over to the temporary sanitation and health area, found a doctor snoozing on a chair in front of a fan, and asked the nurse at the desk to let her know at the cafeteria whenever she was needed.

"All is quiet, at least for now," she said, returning to the table where Roger was paging through a newspaper. "We treated a minor heart attack yesterday, and that tired us out. I need a refreshment to cool myself to your subject. You too?"

"What a good idea!" Roger signaled to a *moço*. Then he spoke at some length about how he justified his research in present-day slavery at a time when most educated people believe that slavery had disappeared in the last century. He had documented how in Brazil and the U.S. the vestiges of slavery continued decades after it was officially eliminated, differing in each country according to "the structure of human domination," as he put it.

"In Brazil," he continued, "the economy never really recovered from the shock of slave liberation, at least not until the military dictators came along and created a new form of oppression that had the look of an economic boom. Right now I am working on the dialectics of this new slavery that comes with freedom and is called poverty. This form of slavery happens everywhere, but it is most flagrant right here in Rio, in São Paulo, and in the northeastern part of the country. If you want to see misery, that's where you should go. Up in the Northeast they don't look at you or at cameras; they just go about living on nothing, without a future, without a glance, and then they disappear into the cities to die of starvation, HIV, cholera, or gunshot. Slaves used to be forced to work for nothing; now they have to live for nothing. I don't know how much sense this makes in the way I'm telling it, trying to stuff the entire evolution of sardines into a small tin."

"It makes sense so far. Go on."

"What is hard for people to accept is that slavery has always existed, and just about everywhere. Look at any advanced civilization and you will find slavery behind the great accomplishments, the pyramids, the temples, the cathedrals and castles, the great Inca and Aztec cities, modern factories and skyscrapers."

"But, Roger, it's different now, surely. Slaves must have been whipped mercilessly as they tugged the rocks up the incline of a pyramid. The same with the galley slaves; I remember an illustration in one of the pirate books I read as a child, and it made a lasting impression on me. The slaves, many of them white, were chained to their oars, and a big oaf was standing at the stern with a long whip curled up under his tattooed arm. They couldn't just up and quit; it was work or walk the plank. But today nothing keeps a factory worker from saying 'shit!' and walking out the gate to find another job."

"It was nice to have those old book illustrations, wasn't it, Deb? It made you feel so far from those awful, brutal times, cozy here in the twentieth century where there aren't any pirates anymore, and people are civilized, safer, protected by our police . . ."

"Okay, Roger. I get your point: I'm seeing the world through rose tinted glasses. The worker can't quit if there isn't another factory down the road ready to hire him. But he can in theory, at least."

"I'm not even sure of that."

"How about you, how about me? Where do we fit in that scheme?"

"Just a few minutes ago, Deb, when you rushed over to your emergency medical unit, you looked like the perfect, obedient slave ready to forego everything when they call you to come and put cold compresses on some overheated delegate's brow. As for me, I'm marginal, innocuous, outside history; I'll never make a difference one way or another."

"Come on, Roger. Won't your thesis on slavery help people be aware of their state, give them pause to think, maybe even rebel?"

"But first I have to finish it, which isn't a sure thing at all. Then I'll have to pass a public examination on it's content and ideology. Then there is the little matter of publishing the book so that people can read it. I'll have to borrow the money to pay for the printing, or beg for a grant. I forget what it was you asked, Deb?"

"I have forgotten, too, and also I'm depressed just listening to you. But I understand how you can feel marginal, since what you do for people is intangible. I may be a good, obedient slave, as you say, but my satisfaction is real. When I give an injection and feel the tremor in a child's frame from pain or apprehension, I know in my bones that I am helping heal that child, or preventing a sickness from entering his body."

"I like what you say, Deb. But to give you a sense of what I mean when I say that slavery is still with us, I will take you one day to see Serra Pelada—it's a gold-mining region about three hundred miles south of the mouth of the Amazon. It wasn't mined before 1980, but already the whole area looks like an inverted anthill with thousands of little cubicles and squared sections where the ants crawl all over, up and down, carrying heavy loads on their backs. If you look closer, and it is hard to do so because the area is enormous, you see that the ants are men, over sixty thousand of them, mostly black, covered with grime and sweat, digging in the hard, dry earth with their hands, spitting out brown dust, and carrying heavy bags of dirt up two hundred feet of improvised ladders. You can imagine what you would see if you took a look inside their lungs! The land there has already been destroyed by clearing, digging, and mercury. After the ants deliver the sacks of earth for thirty or forty cents a day, the prospectors wash it, and they in turn are cheated by the officials who weigh the gold dust. You have probably seen photographs of those mines. Everybody knows about it, yet nobody does anything. It makes you wonder if the concept of freedom makes any sense in our world."

"I remember seeing horrible cases of emphysema in men who had worked in the mines, so I know what you are saying. But tell me one more thing, Roger. What brought you to write about slavery in the first place?"

"That's another story, and it's a personal one. My family comes from the Atlantic coast of France, near the mouth of the Loire, and we are fairly well off, comfortable, you would say. Here is how we got that way: after the upheaval of the Revolution and the wars Napoleon got us into, my ancestor Hyacinthe Bonot hired on as a sailor on a ship out of Nantes. It turned out to be a *négrier*, used to transport blacks from Africa to anywhere in the Americas. You have probably heard how they were stuffed into the hold with little air, water, or food and kept in chains for the whole trip. One night the captain and first mate were murdered by crew members, and Hyacinthe, the only remaining one with brains, found himself in charge, in the middle of the Atlantic. Clever enough to dodge the British navy, he got rich carrying slaves one way and returning with a hull full of sugar, hides, or fine hardwood. This arrangement worked perfectly until the British caught up with him and shot off one of his legs, providing him with a reason to retire from the slave trade. He headed home, married, started a business, became mayor of his city, and ended up with a full-length portrait hanging among other *notables* in the Musée de Nantes. I suppose it was a bourgeois form of guilt that struck while I was reading through the family papers as an adolescent and found an article by Hyacinthe describing how the number of slaves in a ship could be increased by fifty percent if they were placed on their sides, alternately, one facing aft, the other facing fore, instead of all in one direction. In his old-fashioned prose you wouldn't suspect that he was talking about human, or even living beings. It was as if he were describing the most efficient way of stacking cordwood in piles. I've been atoning for what Hyacinthe did ever since."

Roger continued talking for a while. Deb felt somehow uncomfortable. She wondered if it was that she was expecting to be called back at any time for an emergency or if Roger made her uneasy. She recognized the importance of what he was saying, yet at that moment, to her, it didn't seem relevant any more. Roger stopped and looked at her seriously.

"Deb, when is the last time you heard from Hank? How long has it been?"

"Around a month ago. He phoned and said there would be a while between communications until he got back to a more populated area. I wish he would call soon."

"That seems like a long time to me, especially around here, where anything can happen. What have you done to find out where he is?"

"Nothing, really. I've been so busy, and anyway he always manages to pull through the scrapes he gets in. Where would I start?"

"I would start now, if I were you. A call to his employer certainly wouldn't hurt. Go over to the Consulate and pester those people. Then decide from there where to look next."

"Roger, do you think he's in trouble, or hurt? If he were I'd feel it, I'm sure."

"Don't trust your intuition too much in these things. It is definitely biased in favor of thinking all is well. I just think that is a long time for a man to be out of contact with such a beautiful wife—I'm not being facetious, either. Every man's young wife is beautiful, especially after he's known her only for as short a time as you and he have been together. You say he likes to be alone. Possible, but only for so long."

"I have seen so many suffering people, I couldn't bear to think of him sick or depressed."

"I would be more concerned about something else. You can't assume that people are safe in this country because it is supposed to have a modern, democratic government, whatever that may be. You have heard about the way children are murdered on the streets in Rio by respectable business and law enforcement agents. You have also heard about the political disappearances in Argentina, Uruguay, Chile, anywhere in this hemisphere, Brazil included. Out in the rural states and in the tropical areas, there really isn't much incentive for law and order, especially among the tough guys who can make more money through brutality than honest work."

"Now you are really making me anxious. What do you think has happened to him?"

"All I know is what could happen to him. Anyone who takes off into the savanna and is inquisitive about other people is at risk."

"This conference is supposed to be over the day after tomorrow. I'll start then. My landlord will help, too, I'm sure. He will drive me around, and he is good on the phone. Can you give me any hint as to where to begin?"

"Let me think about it for a while and make some inquiries. We journalists have connections that aren't available to everyone, and I'd be happy to put them to work."

"Roger, I don't know how to thank you. I think you have brought me to my senses."

"I'll get back to you in a couple of days. What is your phone number?"

Deb is in the tent in Belo Horizonte or another town away from Rio. It is hot, and she has been talking to people suffering from all sorts of conditions, only half of which she can diagnose with any certainty. Increasingly the symptoms just don't add up in a meaningful way. She takes a glance at the line of patients waiting to see her; it is too long for her to count. It will be late into the night before she can rest.

A woman is standing in front of her, holding an infant. Deb has difficulty taking its pulse, which is weak and fading. Yet the baby is squirming and full of energy. Perhaps the mother is tubercular, with that dry cough. She may be pregnant, too.

Deb dismisses them. She studies the chart of the next patient, but it is too wrinkled for her to read. She looks up. It is Hank. He looks frail and tired; he hasn't shaved for days. The hat he is wearing is shapeless. He is covered with dust or ashes and has a blank look in his eyes.

"Why did you come here? We could be together in Rio."

"It was hard to find you. I was told you would be here, because of your work."

He begins to slump toward the floor. To prevent him from falling, she leads him to the chair; when he is seated she holds his head in her arms. She can't find his pulse.

When Deb awakes, she describes her dream in a letter to her mother.

DEB ANNOUNCED AT breakfast that she intended to start the wheels turning in an all-out attempt to locate Hank. Erik and Maria nodded in approval. They had felt uneasy about him for some time, but had hesitated to mention their concerns. Conferring at the breakfast table they held a strategy conference. It was agreed that Deb would ask for time off from her work. In the meantime, Erik would find out what he could on the telephone, and once Deb was free they would both take to the road in Erik's car, going first to all official addresses in Rio they could think of and later, if necessary, into the bush to follow Hank's tracks.

That night Deb informed them that Bernie would grant her two days off to look for her husband. "He will see to it personally that my patients receive competent attention while I'm gone. What were you able to find out, Erik?"

"The names and phone numbers you gave me this morning were helpful," he told her. "At the consulate they wouldn't tell me anything because I am not related to Hank. And they won't tell you anything either, Deb, unless you go there in person. When I asked to speak to someone with more authority I was put on hold, and after twenty minutes we were disconnected. I remembered the person's name, a certain Mr. Goetz, so I phoned and asked to speak to him. He was in a meeting. I finally caught him just before he went to lunch, and he was most obliging. He told me you would have to come to him personally and fill out the necessary forms for a missing-person search. How long would it take? Up to a month for the paperwork; the actual search would be another matter, and for that he hesitated to make predictions."

"By that time who knows where Hank will be. Did he say where else we could inquire?"

"Yes, he did, and I'll tell you what I came up with. First there is that office Hank works for, the Southern Overseas Development. I talked to seven different people at their office, and none of them could, or wanted to, tell me much. There was no record of his working for them; he wasn't on their current list of agents. He did say, though, that it would help if you came to their office personally and talked to him. His name is Remick."

"What about Kater? Did you talk to him?"

"He is out of the country for a month or so for surgery, and his secretary has no access to his files during his absence. And that Miss Peppercorn and Mr. Jones you told me about, the ones who interviewed Hank have all been transferred to other offices."

"So what do we do now?" Deb asked, already feeling desperate.

"*Vamos comer primeiro.* We sit down and eat a good dinner," Maria said. "You can't accomplish much on an empty stomach. But Erik, you went somewhere this afternoon. Where was that? You were gone a long time."

"I was at the Ministry office where Hank got his permit to visit the interior. I had to wait in three lines. The first one turned out to be the wrong one when I got to the window; the second closed when only two people were ahead of me. At the window of the third line an old gentleman in thick glasses went to the bound files that line the wall, got up on a ladder, came down, moved the ladder, climbed up again, and each time at the top he read the spines of the volumes from up close, about two inches, his eyes were so bad. I thought he was going to topple over as he leaned to the left and to the right to decipher the inscription on one more volume. When he finally found the correct file, he brought it to the window and paged through it, wetting his finger with saliva every fifth page, and squinting mightily to make sense out of the document he was reading. It turned out to be Hank's original application, which was stamped and countersigned several times. Then he looked up, squinted at me and told me that according to this document Hank was somewhere in Mato Grosso do Sul and that if he had gone into another state since filling the form the office wouldn't know about it. Then he noticed that part of the form wasn't filled out completely and went to consult with a colleague. When he came back he told me that Hank might be arrested when he returns because of irregularities in this form. But of course, he added, 'if the gentleman in question does not return he will not be arrested.' Encouraging, isn't it?"

"What do we do next, Erik? I'm almost ready to give up. It's weird to feel so helpless. Hank must be in some kind of trouble, somewhere out there. How could I have let it go for so long without even thinking of doing anything?"

"That kind of thinking won't get us far. I'll keep inquiring. Then when you get your days off, we will go to the Consulate and make a stink."

Deb worked the next day. In the evening she had a call from Roger.

"I'm on to something, but I don't quite know where it will lead. It is sort of complicated. Can we get together for a while? I'll try to explain what I know. You'll have to give me your address."

An hour later Roger drove up to Erik's house in a battered Citroën. Deb was waiting for him at the door. They went to a nearby luncheonette which was filled with smoke and the sound of a music box turned on as loud as possible.

"What is it you found, Roger? Tell me right away."

"My information is that Hank got as far as the Grande Pantanal, that enormous swamp, near the border between Brazil and the southern part of Bolivia. He did it on foot at least part of the way, which is quite an accomplishment. Just think! He walked at least a hundred kilometers through rough . . ."

"Get to the point, please, Roger! I need to know how and where he is, not how he got there."

"Okay. *J'arrive!* I'm getting there. It seems he was about to take off time to explore the swamp and then come back to Rio. My source doesn't know if he entered the swamp or not. He was seen in Corumbá, which is on the border, but doesn't appear to have stayed there long. That's the last trace that I have been able to dig up."

"How long ago was that?"

"I'm sort of vague on the chronology, because my informants don't seem to keep diaries or look at their watches, if they have any."

Deb feared she was about to cry. Roger went on.

"Apparently he made friends along the way. One in particular, a drug trafficker from Bolivia was with him for a week or so just before the time we are talking about. That fellow must have helped him get across some pretty difficult terrain."

"I wish I could see exactly where he was. Do you have a map?"

Roger took out a pen and drew a sketch of southern Brazil on a paper napkin; he placed dots to represent Rio and São Paulo, made a long skinny triangle between them and Corumbá, drew in the Rio Paraná, and made blotches to indicate Paraguay, Bolivia, and the Grande Pantanal.

"Is he alive, Roger? Is there anything you are not telling me? If there is, that would be cruel."

"I'm telling you absolutely everything I know. The rest is only hypothesis. Personally, I think he is alive somewhere. My guess is that he went with his friend to Bolivia. If he is a mountain climber as you say, that is where he would want to go."

"But he would have sent word! That is what I can't understand."

"Most of us would keep in touch, I know. But it sounds like Hank is an original kind of guy. He makes new friends, is completely absorbed in them and in what he is doing. He learns about the wonderful rock and mountain climbing in the Bolivian Andes and simply goes there. He is more focused than the rest of us. Then after a month or two he is surprised to come home and find that you are worried to death about him. 'I wrote you a postcard from La Paz,' he will say, and then find it in his backpack when he is looking for a souvenir to show you."

"What you say describes him very well, and I want to believe it. What other hypothesis can you cook up?"

"That he figured he was done with his work and decided to come home going a different direction. So he took a boat or a canoe or a raft down the Paraná and will phone you one of these days from Buenos Aires or Montevideo. It would take just as long that way."

"You do make him sound like an irresponsible teenager, but I can accept that scenario, too. Thank you, Roger. Can you keep looking?

"I'll do what I can. If I don't come across something definite pretty soon we could go to that part of Brazil and look for ourselves. It would be a nice trip."

The two days of free time promised Deb by Dr. Powers became a reality by the end of the month. Erik had made an eleven o'clock appointment for her to see Mr. Goetz and drove her along the wide boulevards toward the Consulate.

"I would feel much more secure if you would come with me, Erik. Together we can think of all the questions we should ask."

"I would be happy to. You do the talking. I'll join in when I think of something that needs to be clarified."

He parked his car in the shade under some large trees. They entered the main entrance, asked directions, and took an elevator. Crowded in with them were a well-dressed, elderly woman, a small boy holding on to her hand, a dark skinned female clerk with an armful of files, and a man with a round face, large mustache, dressed in a suit. The adults concentrated on the numbers shining above the elevator door; the child looked at Erik, perhaps because he had never before seen anybody so tall.

The light behind number ten went off and number eleven

started to shine. As the elevator came to a halt all the lights went out, and the passengers found themselves in total darkness.

"*Ah, outra vez faltou luz? Não!* No, not again!" a female voice broke out in Portuguese. "This happened last week, during a bomb scare. People were stuck in the elevators until late in the afternoon, almost quitting time. I had to use the stairs all that time." She lit a cigarette.

"Please do not smoke," an older female voice requested in English. "There is not enough air in here, and the boy shouldn't have to breath the smoke."

"Will it really take that long?" A male voice asked in Portuguese. "I have to catch a plane in three hours, and I can't afford to miss it. *Merda!*"

"You see, Manuel," the older voice continued. "This kind of accident happens in a world where everything is mechanized and there is no janitor around to fix things. All we can do is pray for deliverance from this captivity. I did so hope Manuel could receive his visa today. Now we will have to come back another day. Can't anybody do anything?"

"Not in this light, ma'am," Erik said, "I can't see a thing."

They waited what seemed to be a long time in silence. Suddenly Deb remembered the flashlight she carried in her purse. She took it out and felt for Erik's hand.

"Now we are making progress," he said, turning on the flashlight. "What else is there in that purse?"

The clerk put her files on the floor and sat down next to them. The round-faced man stared straight ahead. Erik turned the flashlight on the control panel at the side of the door and pushed the alarm button, which produced a long wailing sound somewhere far below them.

"Now what I need is a screwdriver." He tried his fingernail to no avail, Deb handed him a tongue depressor.

"Too fat. It won't fit."

"Would this be helpful, Sir?" the old woman asked, holding out a metal fingernail file.

"Excellent! Excellent! Deb, would you hold the depressor and this knife; be careful: it's sharp. Now, young man," he told the boy, "you will hold the light and make it possible for me to work." He lifted the boy up, placing him securely on his shoulders. "Try to aim the light right where my hands are so I can see what I'm doing. Keep it steady; don't move it. There!"

In a matter of minutes he had removed the panel and pulled out a knotted tangle of colored wires. "That won't help; there's no electricity, anyway. Manuel, point the light up, where my hand is, on the right. Good job! Now follow my hand upward. Okay. Keep it there."

He moved the inside gate, the one that runs along a track and has an ingenious construction of slats loosely connected to each other, to the left. At the edge of the outside door, located at this moment just below the roof of the elevator, he started turning screws. When four or five of them had fallen on the floor, he bent a metal molding and inserted his hand and wrist into the opening. Deb could not see what he was doing inside the wall, but he was clearly exerting some kind of pressure, and his breathing was difficult.

Finally he took out his hand and asked the round-faced man in Portuguese to help him pull the solid door to the left. This required a good deal of moving around in the small space available. The clerk had to stand up, but as she did she slipped on the files that were on the floor. The grandmother moved to where the man had been standing, and Deb took her place. The door opened an inch, but it was uneven on its track, so it had to be shut half an inch. Then with great effort they worked the door open, half inch by half inch, far enough so that the boy could scramble out on the eleventh floor. With Erik's support from behind the grandmother followed, expressing great embarrassment for her awkward position and complaining about her knees and stockings. Deb followed, and then she understood the old woman's complaints. The opening, about two feet by a foot and a half, was six feet from the floor of the elevator; she had to slide her head and shoulders through while Erik held a foot in one hand and pushed her bottom with the other, and once through she had to roll over in order to sit up and then try to stand, feeling dizzy. The clerk came next, leaving her files scattered over the elevator floor. Then came the man, who had trouble making it through the opening, and finally Erik, who had to twist his torso for his shoulders to squeeze diagonally through the mouth of the hatch. When they were all standing, somewhat unsteadily, they found themselves face to face with an armed Marine guard who informed them that they should have waited patiently in the elevator until they had been released. An aide came up and told Deb that the Consulate was closed for lunch and that Mr. Goetz had left for the day. He then showed them to the stairway exit and locked the door behind them.

"Let's go, Deb," Erik said softly. "We'll call for another appointment."

When Deb and Erik were ushered into Mr. Goetz's large office, they found him sitting behind an old-fashioned dark red hardwood desk. Impressive looking dossiers lay in neat piles to his left and right; the windows were covered with heavy drapes, and on the walls native artifacts hung in profusion. Diplomas from Yale were in evidence. The man behind the desk, impeccably dressed in a dark suit, was smoking a Sherlock Holmes pipe; his graying hair and steel-rimmed glasses barely concealed a benign, easygoing expression.

"You will excuse me if I continue smoking. I am just breaking this pipe in and would like to be finished soon; my mouth has tasted like the bottom of a bird's cage for three days now. Now let's see," he said looking through his dossiers, pulling one, quite thin compared to the others, and opening it.

"Yes. Henry Myers. You must be Deborah, and this is Mr. Nielsen, who called? I'm glad to meet you both and hope I can be of assistance. Tell me, Deborah, may I call you Deb? Thank you. Do you smoke, either of you? They are made locally and are really quite delicious," he went on, handing them a box of thin, long cigars. "No? Probably just as well. You will live longer. Where was I? Oh, yes. Tell me, Deb, everything you know about your husband, let me see, ah! his name is, is Henry. Tell me everything that happened since you and Henry arrived in Brazil."

Deb filled him in on what she felt were the important events, stressing Hank's character and activities and giving exact names and addresses wherever she was able. Erik interrupted now and then to add a comment or to clarify whenever Deb's geography of Rio was vague. Mr. Goetz took notes in longhand, scratching the surface of several sheets of legal paper with a large fountain pen. At one moment he sat back and watched Deb as she talked, took out a handkerchief to clean his glasses, and then began taking notes again. Her story took three quarters of an hour to tell, and when it was over she added, looking down at the knotty patterns in the surface of the desk:

"Even though Hank is quite capable of taking care of himself, you will agree that I have reason to be worried. It has been more than two months since he has contacted me. His American employers don't even have record of his existence. One of the things I would like to know is what the status of the Southern Overseas Development Corporation is. I mean, is it a legitimate company doing business in Rio?"

"You are asking me a number of questions all at once. Let me begin with the last one. That company is certainly legitimate, but we don't have much contact with the people there because they are doing business under the aegis of other branches of our government. Consequently, I can't even tell you what kind of work they are engaged in. But they are fully funded by . . . I think it is the Department of the Interior, or is it the Department of Justice? At any rate they are fully registered with the U.S. and Brazilian authorities, and they are on the U.S. payroll. Those people are well established. All you have to do is call for an appointment with their manager or chief officer and go to see him. Tell him the same story you told me, and he will certainly do all he can to help another American. What I will do is write him a note that you can take along, to serve as a kind of introduction."

He took out a sheet of stationary, wrote down part of a long sentence, reread it, then tore it up, saying:

"Better yet, I'll phone him and get back to you. In that way he will be prepared for your visit." Mr. Goetz scribbled himself a short note.

"What did we learn from Mr. Goetz, Erik?" Deb asked as they went out the main entrance.

"That he is a very nice man."

The next dream Deb remembered had her baffled. She described it in a letter to her mother:

"The beginning was vague. At one point I saw you briefly, in front of the house. Later I was with Hank in our Los Angeles apartment. Then Erik and I were searching for Hank, in a car, driving through a *favela*, noticing something dripping down rotted wooden steps. Was it sewage? rainwater? blood? We entered a shack where there were a number of people seated in silence. We went up to the boy, Manuel, and his grandmother, who told us to sit, wait patiently, and pray. We were all in the elevator then; the boy was holding my hand, telling me something I couldn't hear or understand. The man with the mustache was eyeing us suspiciously. When the lights went out and the elevator stopped, I took Erik's arm and felt comforted. He asked me for a flashlight; I fumbled through the objects in my purse, dropping pencils and bits of paper on the floor. Finally I found the flashlight, and, trying to turn it on, discovered that it was an erect penis. It still would not turn on so I gave it to Erik, who said: 'Excellent! Excellent! Now we are making progress,' and began to open a metal panel to the side of the elevator door. When the panel was loose, he pulled a tangled mass of wires out and turned toward me, and I saw there were tears in his eyes. 'She's dead,' he said quietly."

"What do you make of that, Mom?" she wrote.

Deb went back to work. One day during her lunch break she saw Roger at a luncheonette.

"My connection on the Bolivian border might be able to contact Hank's friend in La Paz. If he can stay sober long enough, that is."

Erik continued his search, spending whole mornings at newspaper offices and police archives reading the record of deaths and disappearances in Southwestern Brazil. He found nothing.

Mr. Goetz's secretary phoned while Deb was at work. Mr. Goetz, she told Maria, would be attending important functions in Brasília and Petrópolis. He intended to call again when he returned to the Consulate.

Then it was time for Deb to ride the school bus to work at another temporary clinic. When she returned to Rio three weeks later, Maria was all smiles.

"Now we are going to find him, Deb. We will use the right connections, the dependable ones. Spirits! We go to a séance tomorrow night at eleven. That is the best time to contact them. It's my friend Praia who will take us there. She will explain everything and tell you what you have to do."

"T HEY CALL HER Praia because as a teenager she spent all day at the beach. She was always wearing skimpy swimsuits, the kind my other friends and I would never dream of appearing in. She just loved to have fun, that's all she lived for. *Dirija com cuidado!* Please drive carefully, Erik. You know how many curves there are on these suburban streets. Then when she completed her studies, got married, and had children, she became serious. You'll see what she is like. I wonder if her husband is coming."

"Maria, you should explain that Praia is married to a well-known plastic surgeon and that they are very wealthy. It's not unusual, Deb, for professional people to belong to these spiritist groups, and often they constitute the majority of the members. Most of them are good Catholics, too. They don't see any contradiction."

They drove quickly along tree-lined boulevards. Deb could sense the presence of large houses on each side behind tall iron or stone fences.

"I haven't had any experience with séances or mediums except in the movies," Deb said in a quiet voice.

"It's different here from anything I had known back in Wisconsin. There someone's great-aunt would invite old friends over to her parlor at night, and they sat around the table holding hands in front of a candle. The great-aunt then delivered a message from someone's departed husband; they would all cry and feel better. Or they might use a ouija board to receive the message. Supposedly a skilled medium can make the little pointer dance around the letters on the board and spell out a coherent message in a jiffy. It was all pretty hush-hush back when I was young, and none of the adepts would admit during the day what they did at night for fear of the Lutheran pastor getting wind of it and scolding them for aiding the devil in his work. Here it is quite open; the spiritists are organized into societies that hold conventions and sponsor charities. It isn't my favorite kind of activity: I like it about as much as going to church or to funerals, so I will leave you both here."

Erik drove through a gate and up a driveway leading to Praia's mansion, which was surrounded by an English style park with lawns and tall trees. A butler opened the car door and led them up several marble steps to an imposing entrance covered by a portico. A thin woman somewhat older than Maria met them inside the door. She was elegantly dressed in a black silk gown that matched her short died black hair, *corte Chanel* style. She spoke with the hoarse voice of someone who has smoked all her life.

"The chauffeur is just now coming with a car. *Muito prazer.* I am so happy to meet you, Deb, and I grieve to think of the worries you must have. Maria is a good person to bring you with us."

Deb immediately took to this person with a penetrating look of concern and sympathy in her eyes. Even her accent and stilted way of speaking made her seem more caring.

The three women sat in the back seat of a limousine driven by a black chauffeur wearing a gray suit with shirt and tie. Praia placed her gloved hand on Deb's arm and continued:

"We are taking you to one of our usual *sessões*, how do you say it, Maria?"

"Sessions, Praia."

"That is it, sessions. We will sit around a table. Sooner or later a spirit will descend and enter into our medium and through her deliver an urgent message to one of those attending. If someone comes needing to be healed from an illness, we will lay hands on that person or a spirit will send vibrations to cure. Or we may also give spiritual advice to an attendant who is in need."

"Who will be our medium tonight, Praia?"

"We are fortunate to have Fürelisa, one of the best. You know her, I am sure, Maria. That is not her real name, but it is what we call her because by day she is a piano teacher and gives lessons to children in the best homes and makes them all play that same piece by Beethoven. She is a spinster and dedicates her entire life to music and the spirits."

"How might I benefit from the meeting?" Deb asked.

"You will be given a turn to tell your story for all to hear, my dear. Then, if your husband is dead, his spirit will take advantage of this occasion to contact you, to comfort you, or give you advice. Or maybe another spirit will know about him and wish to communicate to you. All of the spirits we receive are evolved; we do not have contact with the low spirits, like the ones who visit the Umbanda mediums."

Praia was quiet for a few minutes. Then she added:

"Tonight we will be seeking to unite the visible and invisible worlds. We are spirits, but in the material envelope of life we are unable to perceive the eternal spirit-world of God, until we are liberated from it by death."

Fürelisa lived in an apartment with thick drapes covering the windows, heavy furniture and rugs, a grand piano, and paintings of ethereal figures. A large oak table stood in the center of her living room with some twenty chairs around it, many of them already occupied. A short middle-aged woman with flashing eyes smiled briefly at the newcomers and pointed to the empty chairs; then she sat down at the other end of the table in front of a small dark velvet table mat, a glass of water, a large pad of writing paper and a pencil. Two chairs, one on either side of her, were empty. A young man got up, sat in one of them, and started talking to her in a low, monotone voice that Deb couldn't hear well enough to understand. When he was done Fürelisa explained to the people present that the young man's pain was the result of suffering, ignorant, spirits who had not found their way after death.

"The spirits are perturbing him because he does not have enough moral strength to send them away. In the meantime, the most secure beings present will lay hands on him to assuage his pain." She then pointed to five people seated at the table, pausing between each one—Praia was one of them. They crowded around the chair occupied by the young man while the medium pronounced some words in a singsong voice. They approached him and placed their hands about an inch away from his chest and shoulders, while the medium continued chanting. Then she got up and placed her hands on the man's head and moved them in a circular motion concentrating mostly on his eyes and temples. The man, whose eyes were shut all this time, began to jerk his head to each side and shrug his shoulders, wringing his hands and letting out guttural sounds. Then he subsided, slumped back in his chair, and heaved a long sigh. Fürelisa returned to her chair and addressed the audience.

"We have completed a battery healing. The combined spiritual power of us all has entered into this man to buttress his soul via the perispirit which, in its semimaterial form, unites his body to his soul. This took place during the time his body was in movement, which reflected the reception of our healing vibrations." Meanwhile the young man, absorbed by whatever was happening inside him, remained oblivious to everything around him. Those who had placed their hands near him returned to their seats, and after a moment's hesitation, he followed suit.

The medium then asked who else wished to contact the world of spirits. Praia spoke up and gestured toward Maria, who introduced Deb as an American woman whose dear husband had disappeared and who wanted to know if he was alive or dead and, if the latter, to learn if his spirit was in peace. Fürelisa invited Deb to sit next to her, took one of her hands, gazed at length into her eyes, and then asked her husband's name.

"Hank."

"*Muito bem.* We will try to make contact."

Fürelisa and Deb sat facing each other, staring into each other's eyes. The medium then released Deb's hand and placed both her hands on the velvet mat in front of her. Deb could see her eyes start to look upward, the pupils disappearing underneath her upper eyelids. There was complete silence in the room, broken by the medium when she said that she was making contact but that she could not say the words. Deb felt her heart beating wildly within her chest and saw that her hands were trembling.

"Spirit! Can you speak through me in Portuguese? *Muito bem.* Give what you want to say in letters."

Without looking Fürelisa took the pencil and made ready to write. She paused a long time, as if listening. Then she wrote four letters: M-E-U-D. She repeated the letters as a question, wrote them again. She then crossed out the E and over it wrote an A.

Deb felt relieved; obviously this had nothing to do with Hank. Yet at the same time she was drawn into this experience of the other world in a way she had not expected; she was believing everything she saw, giving it some kind of meaning she could not fathom.

The medium's eyes returned to normal focus.

"I am making stronger contact now. I am hearing Portuguese."

She sat back, letting her eyes turn upward again, closing them. Her breathing increased in tempo, her face lost some of its color, and behind her eyelids, Deb could sense a movement back and forth.

After ten minutes of intensifying silence, Fürelisa began to speak, but with a different voice; her words were clipped, rapid, with an unusually brittle accent for Portuguese.

"I am seeking, looking for . . . Please tell me where to find . . . Ever since I died I want to return to mood [*sic*]. How will I explain to her that now I am neither man nor woman? Can I cross the ocean?"

"Yes, of course. Spirits can go anywhere on earth."

"I am lost. Why are you interested in speaking to me? I don't know anyone here."

"Are you Hank?

"No."

"What is your name?"

"I have no name."

"We are seeking Hank."

"I don't know Hank. But he is alive."

Deb started to tremble throughout her body; she was sweating and felt cold at the same time.

"Where is he?"

The voice said a word Deb did not understand. Then it seemed to sign off: "I am going across the ocean. She will be there."

Fürelisa's eyes stopped moving, and her face regained its color. She opened her eyes, looking around as if surprised to find herself in the presence of the people around the table.

"I hope you learned what you seek to know. I cannot answer your questions, if you have any, because I was not present. You may return to your seat now."

The séance went on for another two hours. Afterward Deb could not remember anything. Her mind had gone blank.

"That shows you that he is still alive!" Maria told Deb as Praia's chauffeur drove them home. "The spirit who possessed her was that of another person, obviously."

When they arrived, Deb and Maria sat at the kitchen table, trying to write down everything the medium and the spirit had said.

"Maria, where did the spirit say Hank was? I couldn't understand, and now I can't remember the name or what it sounded like."

"Must have been in some foreign language. I didn't get it either. *Que pena!*"

"I am completely at a loss to know what to think about it. It makes sense, and yet it doesn't make any sense at all." Deb had just finished recounting her experience at the spiritist session.

She was sitting with Roger in the luncheonette that had become familiar to them.

"*Ça, évidemment, c'est curieux. Moi, je . . . je pense que . . .*"

"But wait! It's even more curious than you think. Let me explain that the spirit said that it was neither male nor female. It—I can't say 'he' or 'she,' can I?—at any rate it also said it didn't know Hank but that Hank was alive. How can that be? Does it make any sense to you?"

"A spiritist will tell you that spirits have no gender since they are all ethereal and have no genitals, no more than they have bodies. Reincarnation can be in the form of either sex. I remember studying this stuff back in France, but I can assure you that I don't believe any of it. I guess it illustrates one's capability of telling oneself stories and believing them. It's a strategy that helps one get through hard times."

"What about the other part, not knowing Hank but saying he's alive?"

"It's the same thing again. Spirits are said to have much greater knowledge than we mortals can summon up, because they aren't limited by their bodies or the everyday concerns of living. That spirit did not have the slightest notion who Hank is, but its knowledge included the certitude that Hank is alive. That can be considered to make some kind of sense and to be good news."

"But if you don't believe it, how can it be good news? Now you're not making sense, Roger."

"*Parce que* something tells me that he is alive, and the spirit, if you can give it any credence at all, would seem to confirm it. At least it isn't bad news! And anyway, just because I don't accept a system of beliefs doesn't mean that it is pure garbage. There are some two or three million Kardecist spiritists in Brazil, and they are getting something positive out of it. Like folk medicine, which may have been fully discredited by modern medical theory, but that doesn't prevent it from healing thousands of people each day all over the world."

"I have seen that. One of my patients was dying of diffuse peritonitis. I gave him antibiotics and ordered rest and plenty of water, but he was impatient with the treatment and went to a witch doctor out in the bush. He returned a few days later to tell me he was cured and healthy."

"Many Brazilians believe in the intervention of the spirits, even people from the higher classes, as you saw last night. Professionals, wealthy businessmen, people at all ranks of government, even military officers. This high class spiritism is called Kardecism, after Allan Kardec, a French schoolmaster who in the middle of the last century wrote down what the spirits told him through a medium. He is pretty well forgotten in France today, but a traveler smuggled his books into Brazil and his ideas spread like wildfire, especially in Rio and the urban centers. Most of the Kardecists are well educated; someone even wrote that being a spiritist is one way of being an intellectual. Can you understand why I can't dismiss it all as nonsense? I'm giving it the benefit of the doubt, since I want you to have Hank back and the spirits seem to be saying to you that he is alive somewhere."

"I so hope I can believe you! The spiritists and you make strange bedfellows, but together you keep me from giving up hope. Thank you." Deb took one of Roger's hands in hers over the table.

"It's good you have your work, Deb, to occupy your mind during the day. If I can help your morale in the evening, so much the better. Tell me. Do you want me to go to the interior and look for Hank? For you I'll do it."

"Have you ever been there?"

"No."

"How much have you done in the way of climbing the Alps or crossing the Sahara Desert?"

"Nothing. One might say that I have spent most of my life in bookstores, libraries, cafés and riding the subway. As a teenager I wanted to become a sailor, but it turned out I was afraid of the water."

"Then stay here, Roger. You are much more useful to me in Rio. If you were to go after Hank, I'd lose you in just a couple of days, I'm sure. You are no match for crocodiles or cannibals, let alone muggers or the fire ants people talk about. I have lost enough already."

"Then all I can do is keep you busy. Let us plan to go together to observe some of the African religious cults here in Rio, to see how they function and understand some of their beliefs. I have been fascinated by them since I came here, and I can introduce you to some strange and exotic practices. What do you say?"

"I would like that. I have heard about Umbanda and Candomblé, but I have no idea what they are really about. If I get my mind off Hank he will return sooner."

During the next weeks Deb and Roger went out in the evening together visiting countless neighborhoods of Rio in his old automobile, which, miraculously, did not break down on the steep hills it was expected to climb. On one occasion his *bagnole* lost its muffler, which clattered down the potholed incline of a narrow street in a hillside favela.

"If only it doesn't strike and hurt somebody! No sense in going after it. Someone will use it in one of these shacks for a sink or a flower pot."

At work, Bernie proved to be more understanding than Deb had anticipated, and he made it easier for her to take time off to continue her search, sometimes giving her whole days free. On most of those occasions she spent the day with Roger visiting curious sights in out-of-the-way parts of Rio and its environs. She did not feel it necessary to inform Erik and Maria of what she was doing.

"Deb, dear! Would you be kind enough to help me tonight? *Eu estou péssima hoje.* I don't feel particularly well and I need to get things ready."

"Sure thing, Maria! What is the occasion?"

"Some old, old friends of Erik's are coming over in an hour to play cards. It has been a tradition ever since he was working in Brasília. Here: we'll need to wash, peel, and cut this fruit and then cover it and put it in the refrigerator. How much cold beer is there? That's the most important ingredient. Four people times two bottles, adding two more for good measure, and some for you, that makes . . ."

"Twelve; how about you?"

"I don't know if I want any, but put fifteen to be safe. There, those dark brown bottles in different sizes. They prefer to play here because there is always plenty of the beer Erik brews. They won't start to drink until they have played for a couple of hours. This is very serious business. I'll fix the cheese; will you reach that bread and cut some slices?"

"Do you play with them?"

"Not usually, unless one of the players suddenly can't come. Women can play, but it is a man's game. I don't enjoy it because it makes me think too hard."

"What do they play? Poker? Or something like bridge?"

"Neither one; it's more intellectual. You probably haven't heard of it; it's called skat, and it is sacred institution for these men. When everything is just right, they are lost to the world, completely involved in their effort and mental calculations. They only relax when it's all over and beer is served. We can join in then. I always try to sit with them afterward, because they are interesting people with good stories to tell."

Erik came into the kitchen, looking preoccupied, a little nervous.

"Will everything be ready, Maria? They are coming at nine. You are welcome to join us when the game is over, Deb. They are my good friends, although I hardly see them except when we play."

"Who is coming, Erik? Otto?"

"He has never missed a game, has he? He is a former engineer like me, but instead of retiring and living the quiet life after Brasília was finished, he got involved in other projects. Then there is

Beto, you know him, and Joachim, someone who played with us last month at Otto's place."

"So one of you will have to sit out during each game. That is something I don't understand, Deb, how they always have four people to play a game for three players. Can you think of anything more boring than watching other people play cards for long stretches at a time?"

"Maria, sometime you will learn the virtue of patience, the enjoyment of doing nothing while your friends do something," Erik said pretentiously. "It is a lesson in humility, and that's what a good card game teaches. I'm sure our souls are better for it, just as our minds learn to make quick calculations and our memories learn how to retain the probable location of other people's cards that are hidden from sight."

"Yes, yes, Erik. I'm sure you are right. But now let us eat so that we are ready when the guests arrive."

Otto came first. Deb would have taken him for a sea captain with his faded mariner's cap, pipe, and bushy short beard behind which a good-natured smile and stained teeth flashed as he talked. Joachim came with him, a tall, clean-shaven man with his head and shoulders slightly bent forward, whose pallid features and hollow expression made Deb run through in her mind the symptoms of jaundice and cirrhosis she had memorized. Beto arrived soon afterward, giving Maria an ostentatious hug and a kiss on both cheeks. He winked at Deb and immediately told her that he regretted he was not young enough to invite her to go dancing.

Within five minutes the four men were seated at a card table, concentrating, almost silent. As Deb and Maria sat in the kitchen reading and talking quietly, they overheard an occasional: "18!" "20!" "30!" The cards were shuffled, dealt, taken up. Sometimes a player hit his knuckle on the table as he snapped his cards down, as if to emphasize their value. There was some discussion, presumably after each game. After an hour or so Erik called to Maria to bring them each a glass of beer. The game continued, but from the sounds Deb could hear, it was less serious. Then when all the players began to talk at one time, Maria invited them to the yard where she and Deb had set a table with food and beer.

"Now tonight, no talk of politics, right?" Otto said emphatically, in a heavily accented Portuguese. "It spoils the aftereffects of a good game. As tonight's winner, I proclaim this new rule of the game: no talking about fraud, corruption, or economics. Only soccer, maybe. You will support that, Maria, won't you?"

Deb poured Erik's dark brew into tall glass steins, taking care to leave just enough foam.

"Yes, Otto. But before that rule goes into effect, you have to hear this. It's priceless!" Beto took a long draft and wiped his mustache. "The newspapers were questioning the governor of Sergipe about his sudden wealth. They had noticed that he was taking vacations in Paris, returning with a shipload of clothes for his wife, a Mercedes Bentz, and a few Volvos. It's simple, he explained; he had been lucky in the lottery, that's all. But how lucky? Well, he had won on 24,000 lottery tickets in his province. Can you imagine? All in a matter of weeks! I'll bet no one else in his province won a single *cruzeiro*."

"If anything, that will help his chances for reelection," Erik brought in. "If your governor gets rich, that means the economy is healthy and therefore you vote for him, even though you can't afford to feed your cat."

Otto asked Deb what brought her to Rio. She explained that she was a nurse.

"That's interesting! Joachim here was a doctor once, weren't you, Joachim?"

"Yes, until about twenty years ago."

Deb wanted to ask why he had changed professions but couldn't find the Portuguese words she wanted.

Erik pursued his thought about luck and the economy, despite Otto's objections. "When the economy is expanding and the soccer team has a winning streak, we in Brazil are happy; nothing else counts."

"Don't forget stability, Erik," Beto was talking now. Otto looked glum and resigned. "You can put all that into a catchy tune and we will forget the repression of the military government and the *escuadrão da morte* and vote again for someone like General Médici. The poor cheer the soccer team and the rich get richer, and the paranoids sleep better because communism is held in check by the security squads. And we all sing along with the TV ad thanking our government and the continued support from the USA."

Deb listened, wondering if all this was true; then she remembered Juscelina's story. While the men continued joking about politics, Maria explained to her in English how Brazilians had suffered through a succession of repressive military governments after the *coup d'état* in 1964. "Your President Johnson sent a wire congratulating our generals on the afternoon of the coup. It was a period of intense suffering, and these gentlemen can't talk about anything else when they get together after a game of skat."

"We are like World War II veterans," Erik interrupted her. "When the trauma is bad enough, you can't forget it. Torture was widespread."

"To think someone would want to make others suffer! At the clinic I see suffering every day; but at least the cause is impersonal, nobody wants it to happen, nobody inflicts it. Nobody in his right mind, at least."

"That's what was remarkable about our courageous military leaders," Erik was speaking again. "They were of sound mind and body, likable, modest, polite, even cultured. They didn't do the torturing themselves, they delegated it to others, who were simply obeying orders, so no one is to blame. Tell Deb about General Leitão, Beto. That will help her understand."

"It's hardly a pleasant story, but here goes. General Belmiro Jayme Leitão was my wife's uncle, and he used to entertain us a

few times each year in his villa. He was Commander of the Fifth
Army in the Province of Paraná. Mild-mannered, a devoted family
man and devout, practicing catholic, his favorite sport was flying
gliders in the mountains around Curitiba. I understand that he
was not active in politics, although he voted with the other officers
when they decided to get rid of President Goulart and he favored
increased military control of civilian affairs in the years that
followed. Like the others he was anxious about subversion and
feared that the labor unrest and student protests of 1968 would
spread. But he was opposed to military participation in groups
like OBAN and DOI-CODI. The Army wasn't trained to be garbage
collectors, I once heard him tell his guests."

"Those were internal security units," Erik explained to Deb,
"that were supported by prominent São Paulo business interests;
they were made up of civilian police and military security officers
trained in the detention and interrogation of political suspects.
And that's a sore spot for me because one of the main supporters
of OBAN was a Dane who had become a citizen of Brazil and had
grown rich in the liquid gas business. He collected funds for
those thugs from multinational firms and big executives."

"The military cadres," Beto resumed, "got increasingly
involved in interrogation, torture, and censorship, when some
guerrilla groups started kidnapping foreign ambassadors to
embarrass the government and demand release of prisoners and
other concessions. General Leitão was fairly neutral until his oldest
son was arrested in a student demonstration. Up to then the
families of the political, military and business elite were not
bothered by the police. Mainly it was workers and students without
connections who were interrogated. The general's son, who was
studying geology in São Paulo and probably went to meetings to
protest the dismissal of a few professors, was detained and held
in one of the interrogation centers. The High Command called
the General in and gave him an ultimatum: if you resign your
command, you will receive a pension and your son will be
released. Otherwise we can't guarantee his safety. He stuck to

his guns, literally, and returned to his job. When one of his aides informed him that his son had been tortured—the electrical shock treatment—and was in bad shape, the general phoned his wife, told her that he would not be home to dinner, and took a military flight to Iguaçu, where he went up in a glider, floated over the Falls, and after shooting himself, crashed somewhere on the Argentinean side."

"What about his son?" Deb asked.

"I never heard. The subject wasn't discussed much in my wife's family, and even my wife won't talk about it. You can be sure they made inquiries, especially after the elections. My guess is that nobody knows."

"Actually I can tell something about him," Joachim broke in. Everyone looked up, since he hadn't spoken for several minutes. "That is, if you really want to know."

"Maria and Deb shouldn't hear this. Let's wait until they retire." Erik looked at them both.

"I have heard many a torture story, like all mothers who have lived in Brazil, or anywhere else in South America. How about you, Deb?"

"I have a particular reason for wanting to know what happens to people who disappear. Tell the story, and I'll explain afterward."

Joachim seemed reluctant to talk at first. "I seldom mention my experiences in the 1970's because in a sense they weren't any different from what happened to the rest of us. But still I can't forget them. At the time I was fresh out of medical school and an intern at the Santa Cecília Hospital, in São Paulo. My mistress had just given birth to a little girl, and I needed to earn some money to keep them both alive. So I went to the Avenida Angelica Armory, where according to rumor, anyone with medical training could earn some extra cash. It was worse than I had expected. Inside the bowels of that great brick building there were a number of training and exercise rooms which were used at the time to house workers, students, and intellectuals suspected of subversion. It was upstairs, in one of the towers that pain was inflicted and bones were fractured. My function was to visit the suspects and give them immediate medical attention like preventing death by bleeding for those whose ears or genitals had been hacked off. Then on the report I was required to write there was a final query pertaining to how much longer each prisoner could be expected to tolerate 'sustained questioning.' I asked one of the military physicians what that meant. 'Oh! simple,' he said. 'That means before he croaks.' It was confirmed when one prisoner whispered to me while I was examining the burns on his neck and face to bring some cyanide the next time I came. The torturers usually wore hoods, but there were also others around, out of curiosity, even businessmen in their suits."

"If you will excuse me, I will retire for the evening," Maria said. "Thank you all for coming. *Boa noite.*"

"You want to know about Gaetano Leitão, the General's son? When I saw him he told me that he had been arrested in front of the Butantã Institute where the students made jokes about some prominent political and military figures belonging inside rather than outside the famous *serpentário*, the great collection of poisonous snakes. Once inside the Armory he was subjected to electrical shocks of increasing voltage in an effort to make him identify his friends and acquaintances. I asked him what I should write about him on my report. 'It hardly matters,' he told me. 'If you write that I can bear one more day of shocks, that's what will happen. If you say I can't, then it's the firing squad. Anyway, someone told me my father is dead, so I don't really care.' By the time I left at three in the morning I had decided to quit that work and to give up medicine. When I reached home I found my flat had been ransacked and my mistress and daughter were gone. Please do not ask me about them. I took a bus to Uruguay and spent the next ten years in Paris."

"Doing what?"

"Working for Amnesty International, drawing up statistics on torture."

Deb described briefly what she knew about Hank. It was Joachim who answered her.

"That's what makes life so hard to bear. You can't help anybody."

10617-LIND

IN THE WEEKS that followed, Deb grew more and more depressed. Her work exhausted her, especially when she was away from Rio. She felt uneasy when her friends tried to cheer her up with forced humor or insisted on speaking comfortingly about Hank. At work her supervisor, Ms. Converse, was at great pains to relieve Deb of unpleasant chores and to speak to her quietly, as if to a sick person. Bernie decided that it was unseemly, under the circumstances, to flirt with this unfortunate woman, although he continued to arrange his schedule so that he could remain near to where she worked, keeping her, so to speak, under his eye. Being at home with Maria and Erik was particularly tiring because it seemed that their entire conversation, even when it was about trivial or indifferent subjects, resonated with a constant undertone of despair. Whatever was said had as an implied footnote questions such as "Where is Hank? Is he still alive?" Erik spent hours each day going through archives, telephoning agencies, or driving around Rio to check out a tip, and at the end of each day he had to tell Deb that it had all been in vain. He was elated to be able to arrange an interview with the U.S. Ambassador on the occasion of his passing through Rio to attend meetings with visiting business executives. The three met at the Consulate; the Ambassador listened sympathetically and suggested that Deb remain in touch with the U.S. agencies in Rio; he for his part would alert all of the consulates of Hank's disappearance and ask to be personally informed of any new developments. Driving home with Erik afterward, Deb tried without success to think of something to say.

She had to admit to herself that she was changing. It seemed that the subtle and slow corrosion brought on by the lack of hope was taking its toll. At night her sleep was shallow, intermittent, and troubled by short, pointless dreams. Her appetite faded as the days went by, and nothing Maria could do in the way of preparing varied and enticing meals was capable of unblocking Deb's jaws and throat. "If only Hank were dead and I knew it," she thought, "I would be able to breath again, and eat, and sleep." The most difficult for her was waiting endlessly for an answer, which by now she was convinced would be devastating when it came.

She bought a camera to replace the one that had been stolen in the tunnel, and hoping to distract herself, she took snapshots of scenes in Rio whenever she could. But the distraction was only temporary. She found herself looking for Hank among the faces she saw through the sight of her new camera.

It took Deb some time to escape a feeling of guilt and admit that she thoroughly enjoyed her outings with Roger Bonot. It was a break in her waiting; she felt the answer she so feared could never come while she was walking with Roger up the slopes of some favela or sitting with him in a café listening to a group of musicians. No news could reach her then, for Deb was careful to keep this part of her life to herself. How could she explain to Erik that she was enjoying the company of this man precisely because it prevented her from thinking about her husband? What made her realize how much she needed this diversion was that when Roger took her to a restaurant, and he knew them all, she was able to eat, making up for the meals she had missed on previous days. Roger smiled as she ate hungrily, telling her the names of the food and describing the very tastes she sensed in her mouth. She even wondered, on one occasion, if she wouldn't sleep more soundly in Roger's company, but she quickly dismissed the thought, wondering where it had come from.

Each time they came together, usually in the evening when Erik and Maria had retired, Deb would walk a few blocks to a designated meeting place where Roger was waiting in his car. He always began by asking if there were any news, and then the subject would not come up again. The purpose of their wanderings, or *randonnées* as he called them, was to show her the hidden corners of the city where the real Rio was waiting to be discovered.

"This is where the city vibrates to the rhythm of new music, to the breathing of thousands of Cariocas living only for the sensation of the moment. Look at that fellow dancing down the alley! He must live in a hovel around the corner, if he has anywhere at all to call home. But that doesn't matter. He lives in his flesh and bones, in the movement of his arms and legs. He has no future to think about beyond what he is going to do in the next few minutes. You can't imagine, Deb, how much I would like to be that guy, to be that rhythm for just an hour, to climb out of my rationality and leave it here in the street like the skin a snake has discarded."

December came. Deb dreaded the idea of Christmas in this hot country. There was no joy in her world, only momentary suspension of loneliness. Her life, though full of scheduled events, felt like the hallways of an empty building, exchanging echoes in the late afternoon. Only once had she spent Christmas with Hank, a year ago in Los Angeles, and she felt herself losing even that memory among the spreading shadows.

Erik and Maria did their best to cheer her up, and sometimes they even came close to succeeding. One day Maria told Deb her life story. She was an only child and had lost her parents in a train accident before she was ten. Her grandparents brought her up in the same house she was living in now.

"Sometimes I wonder how I kept my sense of humor in the company of those austere people. They were kind and loving, and they cared for me like their own child, but they never laughed.

I remember coming out here into the garden to find relief from the seriousness of life. One day I watched a caterpillar climbing up a branch, and when he almost fell off the leaf he was eating, I laughed and felt young. You could hear the Cariocas singing and dancing in the street outside the gate, but my grandparents said that one of the consequences of wealth and position was that you couldn't sing or dance because only the lower classes did that. The best part of my childhood was when they sent me to stay for extended periods with my aunt and uncle in Belém; they had many children who sang and danced as much as they wanted. My grandfather would frown when I returned home and described everything my cousins and I had done together."

"How did you and Erik meet," Deb asked.

"Actually it was right here in the garden where we are sitting. After my grandparents' own children had married and gone their various ways, they began to rent out the cottage, mostly to foreigners. One of them was a tall, serious engineer who had come down from Brasília where he was constructing roads and fancy government buildings. Before then I had hardly seen a man other than my cousins from up close. He was seven years older than I was and took absolutely no notice of me; as a result I fell hopelessly in love with him, especially after he returned to Brasília. I became depressed and morose, which must have favorably impressed my grandfather. Then one day he solemnly told me Erik had written to him proposing to marry me, and he wanted to know what I thought. Of course I said it was out of the question and fainted right away. After the wedding Erik and I lived in the cottage, just like you and Hank, until my grandparents died leaving me the property."

One of Deb's friends at work, a young black woman with the impressive name of Claudia Maria das Graças Mato de Sousa, invited Deb to an Umbanda ceremony. A few years earlier she had been a *sambista* or samba dancer and had passed out from exhaustion during Carnaval, but unlike the many others who suffered the same fate and recovered, she began wasting away, without energy or the will to live.

"A relative took me to an Umbanda center, and during the ceremony the *pai*, the leader, placed his hand on me, and I started to tremble. After that I swooned and fell to the ground, and while I lay there the spirit of a saint came into me and cured me. Now I am healthy and can dance two days and nights in a row without being tired in the least. See this?" She took her necklace in her hand and showed Deb the ivory amulet in the shape of a clenched fist with the thumb protruding between the first and second fingers. "It's a *figa*, and it protects me from evil spirits. I never take it off."

"What sense does it make for you to work every day at this clinic and then at night go deal with the spirits?"

"That way I am twice as healthy. It's like going to mass in the morning and to Umbanda at night. I have all the saints on my side."

Roger drove Claudia and Deb to the Umbanda center, a two-story building in a lower middle-class neighborhood. People were coming and going, the rooms were strewn with altars and what looked like bits of sacrificed animals. A row of drummers made a constant rhythmic din, and the rooms were filled with the smell of tobacco smoke and incense. In the main hall, where the ceremony was already under way, a number of middle-aged women in long white skirts were kneeling with their arms and heads on the floor, writhing in the grip of the spirits that possessed them. Others were standing or leaning from the waist with their elbows against their thighs, waiting for a trance to come to them. An older woman, dressed in an immaculate white blouse and long skirt, was smoking a large cigar, her hair disheveled and her face covered with sweat. She wore about fifteen necklaces of different color beads, crystals, and shells; at the end of some of them were metal crosses or icons printed on coins; in her hand she held a white rose. In another room the *pai de santo* presided, greeting the *orixás*, or spirits, with formal salutations; the drums moderated their rhythms with the arrival of each new *orixá*. When mediums and celebrants fell into spirit possession they received white shawls or scarves on their shoulders thrown by attendants who offered their hands in assistance. Claudia joined a group in the center of the hall. Her eyes began to roll; she cried out, arched her back, and her face was contorted into an unrecognizable grimace. When she began to stagger someone helped her to a stool next to a respectable looking businessman walking on hands and knees and whinnying furiously. Then the music ceased, the people consulted with the *orixás*, who were now present through the mediums. Finally lighted candles were passed around, and the session ended with prayers and hymns. The celebrants sat with eyes shut, then left quietly.

Claudia was silent as Roger drove her home. Afterward he took Deb to a little bar where he explained as much as he could about the doctrine and the practices of the Umbandas. Deb was so tired she was unable to absorb much of what he told her. In front of Erik's house, Roger took off his glasses and kissed Deb on the lips before opening the car door for her.

During Deb's lunch break the next day, Roger phoned. "There is this new spot in Vigário Geral I want you to see. I haven't been there, but a friend who went last night told me it is terrific. First-rate musicians, they call themselves 'Mágica Realista,' and an outstanding vocalist with a far-out political message, all of it stuck in the most abject poverty you can imagine. Is tomorrow night okay?"

"Where is that? Can I meet you there?"

"Vigário Geral is a rough favela, not the kind of place one wanders into alone, especially after dark. Right now the Red Command is in control there, and that's not an urban guerrilla group out to promote socialist revolution, either. It is an armed gang that specializes in cocaine trafficking and kidnapping; they walk around openly displaying automatic weapons. I've seen them.

Everyone grows quiet when they walk by; it's weird. Shall I pick you up at your place?"

"I'd rather you call for me at work."

"I'll be at the curb near the main entrance. We should dress casually. It'll be hot and stuffy. By the way: I still haven't met your landlords the Nielsens. They sound like neat people, and I'm hoping you will introduce us soon."

"Roger, not for a while. Let me find out about Hank first. Then, maybe."

Deb did not ask herself what she meant by those last two words. But the idea of introducing Roger to Erik and Maria seemed intolerable to her. Just the thought of being in the same room with the three of them made her uneasy.

After work the next night, Deb waited twenty minutes for Roger, then she took the bus home. Just as well, she thought, as she stood on the crowded bus, supported on all sides by the warm, sweating bodies of commuters. Even though I enjoy his company immensely, I need a vacation from him, too. I may have to learn how to be alone again.

"Is that you, Deb?" Erik's voice called out as she closed the front door. "Come in! There's someone here we want you to meet."

Erik and Maria were sitting in the garden with a heavyset black man, dressed in sports shirt, slacks, and tennis shoes. His jovial face was deeply lined, his curly hair trimmed short, and his mouth overflowing with shining white teeth.

"Come meet our cousin Nonato. This is the American woman we were just talking about."

Husband of Maria's cousin, Florina, Nonato was on his way to São Paulo on a business trip from Belém, where he ran a hardware store. Maria's family had objected to the marriage before it took place twenty years ago, but Florina insisted despite the lectures, punishments, and deprivations that were inflicted on her.

"There are no colors in Brazil," Nonato explained. "As long as you are rich, educated, and from a good family, that is. I was none of these. But I had good connections in the form of an important spirit who took a liking to me and instructed Florina through a medium that she should marry me. At the time I didn't even know her, I had only seen her at the *batuque* where I was playing the drums for the ceremonies to make a little money. It was the voice of the *encantado* Acatai, who is an important saint, believe me, who told Florina in no uncertain terms that I was the only man she could marry and if she married someone else a disaster was sure to follow. That suited me fine. I was an orphan and had lived most of my life in the woods outside Belém or in the streets near the harbor, working in the Ver-o-Peso market, not getting into too much trouble, just a little, now and then."

"That's why my uncle was so upset," Maria interposed. "I remember it well, since I was visiting in Belém at the time. Every year my grandfather sent me to spend vacations with my aunt, uncle, and my cousin, Florina, who was two years older than I was. Her father worshipped her. He kept saying that Nonato was a worthless thief that would bring dishonor and cause all the customers of his business to abandon him; furthermore he himself would die of shame if such a marriage took place. Then Acatai spoke again, this time through the most experienced medium of the *terreiro* where my aunt and my cousin went regularly. This time he declared loudly that if my uncle wanted to stay in business he would have to agree to the marriage within a week. Then Florina got an infection, which my aunt blamed on her husband's stubbornness. Finally, only two days to go before Acatai's ultimatum fell due, my aunt told him: 'If there is no marriage for Florina, there will be no more you know what for you, ever!' That was too much for the poor man to contend with, so he gave in. And guess what? The day after five new customers came to him, which he interpreted as a reward and finally joined the *batuque* himself."

"You see," Nonato turned to Deb. "I can't complain. Florina is *mãe de santo*, a leader at our center, and my business is flourishing, which means I am less in debt than ten years ago.

When we were married, she was so skinny I could hardly find her in our bed. Now she weighs over a hundred kilos, so everyone thinks we are very prosperous."

"And do you go into trance, too?" Deb asked.

"Only when I play the drum, which I still do at *batuque* ceremonies. Sometimes a child spirit comes into me and makes me cry while I do the beat. But I am respected for that. Only at the *terreiro* does that happen. When I beat the *carimbó* at night clubs the child never comes."

"That's because you are too busy ogling the naked dancers," Maria said, laughing.

Someone rang at the door. Erik went to see who it was. Deb's heart missed a beat.

"Here is a friend of yours, Deb," Erik said, returning with Roger. "At least that is what he tells me."

"I'm so sorry, Deb. I had to cover today's race at the Jóquei Clube; my boss suddenly decided to go to a beach party, so I was stuck there. I'm Roger Bonot, and I'm happy to meet you all."

Nervously, Deb made the introductions. When Maria heard Roger's name she looked at him. "I like the sound of your name. Roger rhymes with blue jay, and I love birds so."

"Who won tonight at the races?" Nonato asked eagerly. "Was it Little Finn? Or was it Tea for Two?"

"Neither. It was an unknown horse, and I don't even remember his name. We don't cover the races for sports journals but for the celebrity magazines. They want to know who is there, what she is wearing, who is flirting with whom, and who is probably sleeping with someone else. Innuendo is our most important device."

"Do you enjoy that kind of journalism?" Erik asked.

"I hate it, but it is part of the job, and the French read as much crap as anyone else, maybe more. Luckily I get to write on more interesting matters from time to time."

"Don't disparage junk journalism, Erik! Now, listen to me, your cousin Nonato, who can tell you that you can learn more about a country from its fashion tabloids than from the official journal. Tell us, Sr. Bonot, who was the most beautiful woman at the race."

"Well, I'm not a good judge in those matters, but Sra. Silva e Milanesa and her daughter had the biggest crowd of admirers around them. They could hardly get to their seats."

"Bravo! Now, tell me where did the Milanesas get their money? That is what you journalists should be telling us, rather than how much her outfit costs or who she is sleeping with. Do you know that?"

"Personalities don't interest me."

"But it isn't personalities that count, it's economics, it's business, and there's crime hiding in there somewhere behind the scenes, you can be sure of that. Do you want to know what Nonato thinks? Newspapers should have only one section: business. Everything else, society, the arts, local and international politics, that's all business, nothing else. Take any article you write; read it again and you'll see that it is about someone making or losing money. Who knows how they got rich, that Milanesa family?"

"Stocks?" Erik suggested. "Buying and selling money?"

"Not at all, Erik," Maria interrupted. "I read about them sometimes in the tabloids. They are import/export people from Curitiba. They got rich during the miracle years after the coup in the sixties."

"You see, Maria, you would make a wonderful journalist, because you take interest in important things, in matters that have to do with the heart and the pocketbook, not numbers and trends. And you see, too, my other friends, how crucial that is, how much it tells us about Brazil. Let me explain. I am obliged to sell imported building materials: they are no better than the ones we make in Brazil, and they cost twice as much. But if I refuse to sell them, my supplier cuts me off and I'm out of business. It's that simple. I swallow my pride, and it gives me ulcers. Every time I drink coffee in the morning I think about all those people in other countries who drink the coffee from Brazil marked 'For Export Only,' while we, the slobs who produce the stuff, can buy only shit beans in our markets. Everybody else drinks the best coffee in the world and believes that those Brazilian bastards are the luckiest people ever, since they live in a tropical paradise where the beautiful red beans grow. Meanwhile the Milanesa family invests its money and goes to the races where they can be seen and envied."

"But won't the inequalities level out under free market conditions?" Deb put in, remembering what she had learned in an economics course. "It did for us in the States. And when free trade between nations becomes real, then every country will benefit, and that will trickle down to the people."

Nonato looked at her thoughtfully. "The trouble with Americans, and I don't mean you necessarily, Deb, is that you think freedom equals free market. Do you know who profits from the change? You guessed it: black marketers and the mafiosos, and don't forget the foreign investors."

"What about Brazil? Won't it benefit from being able to trade freely?"

"In Brazil free trade means that the poor, around eighty percent of the population, get poorer, and the landowners and CEO's consolidate their fortunes, enjoy their privileges, keep the laborers and tenant farmers off their land, while they cooperate with American and foreign investors. What does Brazil get from cooperating? Millions in loans to buy foreign supplies, and now we can't even afford the interest on those loans."

"But certainly you oversimplify." Roger had been wanting to talk for some time and went on to frame the matter in dialectical terms.

When Roger had finished, Nonato sighed. "That theoretical talk reminds me that I have to get a good sleep before going to São Paulo tomorrow morning. I like better what Rufino, one of my workers told me. The other day he said, in his Northeastern accent, 'Brazil was raped by the Portuguese, who then kept her pure by fending off the Spanish, the French, the Dutch, and the English. What happened next? Well, Panama, who in a pinch always helps the U.S., did Big Neighbor a favor one night by bending and letting it slip down and sodomize Brazil up the Amazon, using Florida as its prick.' Just look at a map. You all know how people say Belém lies at the mouth of the Amazon, don't you? Well, Rufino says 'they got their directions wrong; it's more like a sore hemorrhoid, and that's why we are the first to get shafted.'"

Maria took Nonato to his room. Erik and Roger went on talking, and Deb noted with relief how much they enjoyed each other's company.

Christmas came. Erik and Maria invited Roger for dinner, along with their own children and grandchildren.

On New Year's Eve Roger took Deb to the beach to witness the celebration in honor of Yemanjá, goddess of the sea. At sunset, as the last of the sunbathers retreated to the cover of bars and restaurants, the beaches filled with worshippers dressed in long white dresses and scarves, carrying candles and offerings to the goddess, chanting hymns to the rhythm of drums. Bonfires were lighted, candles were set in the sand amid flowers, bottles of wine and beer, and plates of food. Someone drew magical symbols in the sand. As the festival gathered momentum, some of the worshippers began to dance to the sound of painted drums. Others consulted with cigar smoking Umbanda mediums for spiritual advice. Increasingly the devout who were dancing appeared to suffer seizures, gyrating and writhing on the sand, and then collapsed as the spirits released them.

"In a few minutes, Deb, at midnight, you will see these people go into the water and offer gifts to Yemanjá for her protection, hoping that their wishes for the next year will come true. They have to choose carefully, for she doesn't accept all gifts."

"What sort of thing does she prefer?"

"Whatever you see now on the beach. She also likes mirrors, jewelry, even sacrificed animals."

Then the crowd suddenly surged toward the water with a cry. Deb stood up and followed them. When the water reached her thighs, she took off her watch and threw it between two waves. She returned to the sand; Roger placed the light jacket he was carrying over her shoulders, and they sat next to an abandoned bonfire.

"I know what you requested. I hope it will be granted."

"Thank you, Roger."

He found some wood to throw on the fire, which burst into flame again. Deb leaned her head on his shoulder. After a silence she said:

"Tell me, Roger, were you ever married?"

"No."

"Do you know what it is like to lose someone you love?"

"All too well. It was always my fault, too."

"Do you recover?"

"Depends . . . on how deep in you are. A couple of times I was in so deep I didn't resurface for over a year, and I'm still trying to piece together what happened. I guess that's how you must feel, except that you aren't to blame for anything."

"I would like to think that, but if I'm honest with myself I can't. One day I may have to admit how much I am to blame. I've avoided that so far."

"You are lucky that you can keep things separate, Deb: your work, Hank, anything else you choose to do. I can't do that."

"Would getting married have solved your problem, Roger? I mean, if you had married her might you have avoided the pain?"

"I gave up any thought of marriage when I was still a child. My parents weren't the best example, and I used to wonder why they bothered to stay together. I knew myself well enough to realize that with my work and my character I would have to keep moving. I would make such a rotten husband I can't bear to inflict myself on anyone. So whenever I get involved I make it clear from the beginning that it can't be permanent, that both of us have important things to do beyond the relationship, and finally that I couldn't imagine adding to overpopulation, even in a small way."

The beach was quiet now. Other groups of people huddled around fires and candles; some were asleep. Roger put another piece of wood on the fire before him and took off his glasses. He held Deb tight with one arm around her shoulders and kissed her gently on the temple and forehead.

"I just told you what I have wanted to tell you for a long time, Deb. You understand, don't you? *Et tu sais que je t'aime, n'est-ce pas?* It's stronger than it's ever been."

"Yes, Roger. I do understand but . . ."

"Here's something else I need to tell you. In a couple of weeks I am going to Paris for a little over a month. There are people I have to see, and I need a break. Come with me, Deb! It's what we both need. You should get away from Rio, from your work, from thinking about Hank, because all of that is taking its toll on you, I can sense it more every day. I need to be with you, to love you, to make love with you. Whenever I get homesick, I conjure up Paris in my mind's eye, and now you are there, too, with me."

"Oh, Roger, I don't know. Let me think."

"I don't need to know right away. I can get you a ticket in a day's notice through our agency."

"Can I have a week to decide? I want to, Roger. But there are so many reasons why it is impossible."

"I know what some of them are. If you want I could help you think them through."

"For now, let's go home. I'm absolutely exhausted."

"Can we talk again tomorrow or the next day? *Mince alors!* I wonder where I put my glasses."

The fire, almost out, gave little light. After checking his pockets, Roger sifted through the sand with his hands. Deb joined in the search. After twenty minutes, Roger arrived at a conclusion:

"*Merde! Je les trouve pas.* I can't drive without them."

"I have never driven in Rio, but I can probably get us to your place if you can see enough to direct me."

As Deb crawled slowly along the Avenida Atlántica, Roger suddenly cried out: "Now I know what happened! The glasses were my gift to Yemanjá, which she accepted since we couldn't find them. That means you will accept, too, Deb."

After arriving at Roger's place, Deb took a taxi home.

The next evening Roger and Deb went to their customary bar.

"*Mon amour*, do you know that last night was the most beautiful I have ever spent with a woman?"

As she lay in bed an hour later, Deb wondered what he had meant. Unable to find any hidden meaning in those words, she took them for what they were and fell asleep. Her dreams were senseless and confusing.

Just before lunch the next day, Erik called Deb at work.

"Deb, we have news. Good news! Can I come to pick you up? Then we'll drive to the airport."

II
Brazil, The Interior:
Hank

Hank's Diary. Mato Grosso do Sul, Brazil

I HAVE BEEN gone from Rio three or four weeks. Now that communication with Deb has become difficult, not to say impossible, this scribbling in my diary will have to serve as my only means of keeping alive the illusion that we are still in contact with each other.

In these three weeks, I have made important discoveries, but it seems impossible to tell them to anyone. The telephone system is a wonderland full of mysteries and dark secrets that never get told. The phones work, it seems, and after some delay I am able to get to Rio on the long distance line with the help of the code number Mr. Kater gave me. But once I'm there, the connection turns sour. Deb's number brings a series of earshattering shrieks which occasionally a recorded voice interrupts to tell me that the system is encountering difficulties, and won't I try again. The same happens when I call Erik and Maria. At Kater's office it is a recorded message that tells me over and over that as soon as a receptionist is available, my call will be answered. All this time I am standing in the hot sun cursing to myself. As I work my way toward the west there are no telephones to be found anywhere near the route I am taking, and this makes me feel far, far away from everyone.

I miss Deb dreadfully. I guess this diary is mainly for her, to give her an idea not so much of the hardships I am encountering but of the solitude this trip to the interior thrusts on me during the heat of the day and again at night, when I lie under the mosquito netting and breathe the moldy smell of dank walls in cheap hotels. The hardships are real, but most of them I have encountered before, and I know that they will be over in a month or so. But the loneliness is new to me; it is something I had never experienced before knowing Deb. She is so far away; or is it I who am far away? The feeling that I will see her soon brings no solace, just an enlargement of the surrounding emptiness. I am in such bad shape that I can't even bring myself to say "you," although the diary is all for you, Deb.

The next reason is a little harder to explain, but here goes. I have no idea where I am. According to my best calculations, I should be 100 km. west of Campo Grande, on the western slope of the Serra de Maracaju, heading for the Miranda River, somewhere between the road to Aquidauana and the one, further south, that leads to Nioaque. I can't be any more precise. My compass is shot after passing the strip mines on the way here. It seems that the maps don't correspond to the terrain in this region. I came across a town yesterday and spent the night there. The only way to get to it is on the path I am following, yet neither the town nor the path show up on any map I have seen. The people look puzzled when I ask them where we are. To them it is very simple: "We are here." But they can't locate "here" on the map I show them. Even the names of the larger towns in the area bring only bewildered looks on their faces. Why would anybody want to know where "here" is?

I said I have been gone three weeks, but I'm not even sure of that. I haven't seen a newspaper in days, and my watch fell in the Paraná River, together with the content of my unhappy stomach. I travel days on end without talking to anybody. Along the rivers where my path takes me, the forest obscures the stars, and often I can't make out where the sun is rising or setting. If only I had thought to date my entries as I wrote them in this diary!

It seems, furthermore, that I am becoming distrustful, like so many of the people I meet on this trek. It is true that trying to find about what overland route the drug transporters are taking is delicate work, and in my innocence, I underrated how dangerous it would be. So here I am writing this diary in the most complicated code I could invent in the interest of security. I am using symbols of the International Phonetic Alphabet to transcribe my thoughts in constantly changing languages. For the moment I am avoiding English and Portuguese, which might make the document too easy to decipher. Then the whole thing is done in mirror image, like Da Vinci's journal, so that it looks backward or upside down to people who might be curious about this strange looking text— this rigmarole doesn't give me much chance to use imagery or stylistic flourishes; all I can do is try to be articulate. When I am back, I'll translate it for you, Deb.

I seem also to have lost track, at least for now, of the people I am following. It is true, of course, that I am tracking them backwards: instead of following my prey, keeping my eye on them from behind, I am walking into them, going against the current. If anything, I feel like an ant crawling toward the source of a whole string of ants coming upon me, bumping my head against theirs. Up to Campo Grande I encountered no difficulty in recognizing my transporters. They dressed like peasants, traveled by foot or using an astonishing variety of vehicles: bicycles, wheelbarrows, bus, motorcycle, tractor, burro, llama, even an old limousine. One was on a stretcher. They don't seem to be carrying much, just a few necessary belongings as they travel "in search of work." There is no outward sign of their cargo, which they have stashed away in their clothing—in an inside pocket, strapped behind a knee, sewn into various hems—or in one or more of the orifices of their bodies. I heard of one who was able to insert a plastic bag of cocaine powder into his sinus cavities. They stop in village squares, sleeping next to statues or outhouses. They avoid the larger communities, where there might be police or civil guards, and pitch a tent beyond the outskirts.

They do not look at anyone, seemingly content to go their own way and mind their business. They haven't shaved for a couple of weeks, and their shoes are badly worn and their clothes ill-fitting. I have yet to discover where and what they eat. Occasionally I find one in a bar, after dusk, staring at a candle that burns feebly on a table in front of him.

I should start at the beginning so as to give this narrative at least the semblance of order and sequence.

In Santos, I was so innocent that I couldn't see any evidence of drug running at all; after three days I got wise and suspected every passerby of carrying pounds of cocaine in his pockets. I had to keep on telling myself that I was a perfect novice at this work, even though when at first I was requested to do it, I felt like an old hand, someone who was meant to go after vicious characters, discover their secrets, and capture them if necessary, modestly but heroically. A short while on the waterfront in Santos showed how naïve my assumptions were. I walked around, peeked into corners, and asked questions like: "Do they load ships anywhere outside of the central harbor, you know, where you can't see them that easily?" People must have thought I was raving. All the kids (homeless for the most part) could tell right away that I was foreign to the area, and they hung around me for company between attempts to beg or steal. At least my waterfront Portuguese has improved, and if I needed to find a street corner or a particular dock, about fifty children of all sizes would lead me there, singing, running, and begging on the way. From them I learned that the drug carriers enter the dock area after midnight and that every two or three weeks the police raid the waterfront and either confiscate the cocaine or extort it and sell it themselves. When that happens, the whole exchange system is transformed into one that nobody can predict, since the new system is established rather capriciously, according to arcane, unwritten, and shifting gang laws. I also learned from those children that anyone who wants to be shot needs only to go there before dawn and look interested in what is going on. One boy of about twelve took a special liking for me, it seemed, and after a while offered me his sister. If I didn't want her, he had several others; each of them, according to him, had different color eyes and hair, and all of them were virgins. He seemed sincerely disappointed when I refused, as gently as I could. Then he smiled and added that he had brothers, too.

I drove to São Paulo where I looked up a professor of linguistics with whom I had studied in Los Angeles. I was shocked at how unhealthy he looked. His cheeks were pasty, and his breathing was markedly labored, but I was happy to be able to converse easily in Portuguese with him and his wife, a beautiful, tall woman with long dark-tan hair that gave her face a light chestnut effect. They invited me to dinner on the terrace of a restaurant in a park on the edge of an artificial lake. The food was plentiful and exotic, the drink, copious. I was interested in what he had to say about the newest theories of pragmatics, but had to admit to myself that those matters seemed less significant to me than they once had. When we got around to what I was doing in Brazil, I told him about my mission, thinking that he would applaud my efforts and propose ways to make my work easier.

"If I were you," he said after hearing my explanation, "I would get out of that business. The 'company' you are working for is either a front for some intelligence agency, owned lock stock and barrel by them, or a front for the drug lords. Whichever it is, you will be dead before two months."

His wife looked at him with a soft, serious gaze as he smoked and spoke. She was, I think, more concerned for his health than for my safety.

"But surely they are legitimate," I objected. "I met them at the Consulate, and it was a secretary of the Consul who introduced us."

"That doesn't mean anything, or if it does, you've got the meaning wrong. The best way to describe what you are getting into is to call it 'Operation Strange Bedfellows.' Travelers in the eighteenth century never knew whose bed they would have to share in the roadside inns. They could be strangled or seduced before morning, I am not sure which was preferable. I suppose you have never seen a cop sleeping with a drug peddler. I have, figuratively speaking, and it's enlightening to watch how they threaten each other and come away, both richer than they were before. Do you get what I mean?"

"I understand what you are saying, but I'll stick with my mission for a while, at least until I get to see the interior."

"My love, come, it is well past midnight, and you are tired. Let us take you to your hotel, Hank, and forgive us for retiring so early."

"But Hank, at least stay alert and keep an escape hatch open at all times. And don't forget to bring your wife to São Paulo sometime soon. I don't travel much these days, and we both want to meet her."

His advice was a bit unsettling, I'll admit, but since I had enjoyed myself immensely with those good people and felt invigorated by the *cafezinhos* and liqueurs, I felt I was up to the task I had taken on; I was at ease with what I was doing, I felt invincible.

My travels westward were uneventful and quite enjoyable. The carriers were becoming more easy for me to spot, so that I was able to avoid suspicion. The lake area was gorgeous, situated as it was between mountains and in deep valleys. I traveled through hilly coffee plantations and ranch land. Slowly the terrain shifted, and before long I realized I was working my way through jungle. Eventually I came to the Paraná River, and it was there that I made my first discovery.

Back in Rio, during my briefing at company headquarters, Herb Kater and his associates had made it clear that the carriers were coming downstream: after crossing the swamps from eastern Bolivia, they made their way through the northern Mato Grosso plateau, going over mountains and embarking somehow on the Paranaíba River south of Brasília and then turning downstream on the Tietê, and from its source, to Santos. They all knew what they were saying; any hypothesis other than theirs would be absurd. My job at this point was to discover the exact routes the carriers took, where they embarked, and where they crossed the Paraná. But everything I saw and heard convinced me that their scenario was mistaken. The carriers did indeed arrive on small boats, but they did not drift downstream as Kater had claimed. Instead, they rowed or paddled against the current from another river to the south. Nobody I talked to along the river knew where they were coming from, and most denied that there was any river traffic at all coming from the other bank.

As there was no phone available in the river villages, and I couldn't receive further instructions from Rio, I decided to cross the river at this point to the location on the other side where the carriers were coming from. I ditched the jeep along the bank and hired one of the small boats I saw unload what I suspected was a carrier. I asked the boat pilot to take me to the place he had come from on the opposite shore, believing that he would transport me to the spot where he would take on another carrier. Instead, he chugged a third of the way across and then drifted downstream. The river was swift and rough, and for the first time in my life I was seasick and could only object feebly to his maneuver.

"I get you across, don't worry. We are going to . . ." he said giving a place name I didn't recognize. "Only place you can stay. Hotel there."

My frantic pointing upstream was of no avail. The crossing lasted for what seemed hours of misery. When we arrived at an inlet, the boatman deposited me on a half-submerged pier. After walking to the first building, I turned and saw the boat disappear in the distance.

None of the people in this town were in a mood to talk, so after a night in a house shared by people, cattle, and several cats, I found a gravel road leading north along the river and hitchhiked. Late that afternoon a beaten-up truck stopped and a pipe smoking peasant called out in Spanish *suba*, and I jumped aboard. Judging from the smell in the cab, the truck was loaded with some kind of domestic animals I couldn't see through the slats. The driver was talkative, telling me that life wasn't the same in the area since it had been overrun by "foreigners" who were doing "what they shouldn't be doing."

"Where are the 'foreigners' coming from?"

"From hell, that's where."

"How do they get here, then?"

"They come down the Pardo River, like water spiders skating on the surface without getting wet. They don't sink because they are still hot from hell, and they smell of sulfur. They also come on rafts, pushing themselves along with long poles. Others are disguised apes. They swing from vines in the foliage and put on human clothes when they come to the Paraná. My mother-in-law saw one of them when he landed; he quickly donned a shirt and tie, pants, and a hat, which he tipped in her direction as he passed, smiling with great civility. My mother-in-law hit him on the head with her walking stick saying: 'Get away with you, Satan!' in her Indian language. He laughed and moved on. Others are fish; they swim downstream and crawl out like reptiles on the muddy bank, and within seconds they look like men, but they still smell like fish, and you can see the scales on their cheeks if you look close enough."

"How do they get from hell to the Pardo River? It is pretty far, isn't it?"

"From a hole in the earth in the north of Paraguay. They come out with the lava all red and happy. Half of them remain in Paraguay, where they become politicians. The other half stuff their pockets with powdered coca and head for the ocean. They want to corrupt the world. When I deliver these animals, I'll take you back down to the Pardo and I'll show them to you. You can't mistake the glow in their eyes. We'll stop at the church first to get some holy water. Soak your handkerchief with it, and it will last for hours."

"Are we going north right now?"

"¿*Qué importa?* Don't you pay any attention to that. If we are headed north we will be going south in five minutes. *Al que pregunta demasiado el diablo le contesta.* Don't ask too many questions or the devil will answer and send you downward. If you know where you want to go you will arrive there. You are lost aren't you? Pray to St. Anthony for forgiveness and to show you the way."

It was now totally dark. Either my driver didn't believe in turning headlights on, or his truck had none, but he seemed to be able to drive along this twisting gravel road set among tall trees without slowing down on even the most sudden curves. I wondered if I would be seasick again. Then I fell asleep, exhausted.

At dawn we stopped in a village where the driver delivered the animals he had been carrying. Later he took on a load of what looked like refrigerators and washing machines in cartons on which the names G.E., Westinghouse, and Gibson had been scratched out but were still visible. We had breakfast and headed downstream again. At the end of the day we crossed a highway, and soon after that we came the banks of the Pardo River, stopping in a small town called Tronco. My driver friend unloaded again, telling me it was all "black market." He continued on his route while I remained there for three days at a tiny run-down hotel, resting, trying unsuccessfully to hire a small boat and observing whatever I could.

To my surprise, I overheard at least six men speaking English in the dirt streets and others speaking Portuguese with a distinct American accent. Their beards were unkempt, and their jeans and short-sleeved shirts had accumulated several days of sweat and grime. They seemed familiar with the town and were as relaxed as they would be anywhere in Texas. What could they be doing in a town like this lost in the jungle? Thinking I might find out, I went into the bar. A muscular fellow with a serious expression came up to me and said flat out:

"I don't know who you are, but it doesn't matter. This is not a safe place to hang around. If you got no business here, take my advice and beat it. There's nothing here for tourists to look at. It's safer you stay in Rio, go shopping, or watch the chicks at the beach."

"What could happen?"

"Anything. Nothing good. You could get sick. The diseases here kill you in a couple of hours. The miners shoot when they get drunk. Lots of people don't get to go back home because they are too fucking curious for their own good."

I was about to ask him what he was doing in Tronco but thought better of it. Another man came up to us.

"Who's your friend, Bill? Not often we see a stranger in these parts."

"I was just telling this bozo it's time for him to move on. Not everyone is full of booze like you are to keep the bugs and crocodiles away."

"That is perfectly correct, what he is telling you. If you wanna keep alive, just drink this," he said, holding out an unmarked bottle filled with a clear liquid. "All of it, fer a starter."

This is one kind of social situation I am never really prepared to extricate myself from, but my first acquaintance saved me.

"What you trying to do, Jeff? Kill him before he gets shot?" Turning to me he explained: "Jeff's private reserve burns a hole in your stomach before it even gets to rot your brain, like it did his. But even that won't make it safe for likes of you around here."

I decided to act honest. "I'm here to test my endurance, to see if I can hike alone all the way to the Andes Mountains, and then, if I have any strength left, cross them and take a swim in the Pacific. What you say bothers me a little; I would hate to have to turn back here."

"I'll see you get two days to rest. After that don't count on me to keep you alive. In the meantime, don't look so hard at people, they don't like it."

We drank together for a half hour, but their talk didn't reveal anything further. I slept deeply after the long truck ride and the local brew.

The next day I set out to buy supplies to last me for another week, and as I walked to the single general store, I noticed I was being followed. When I finally managed to let my "guide" catch up to me, I saw that he was a *mestiço*. I asked him in Portuguese to show me around town, promising him a handsome tip. He was nervous at first; when I insisted, he grudgingly agreed in an Indian language I was acquainted with. Hearing me say a few words in his own tongue gave him some degree of confidence, and while we sat together on the bank of the river where we could see that we weren't being observed, he explained, as well as he could, that the Americans who hired him to track me had been in Tronco for a long time to "help with coca."

"Was it Bill? or Jeff? or someone else?"

"Bill. And someone else, too. Mike. You won't tell, no?"

"No, I won't. You can say I bought supplies and left."

I was unable to unearth a more coherent story from him but decided that I had found out what I needed to know. I gave him twice the amount I had promised and left town that afternoon, well ahead of my deadline.

That I was glad to leave Tronco behind goes without saying. It was clear that I needed a guide to help me complete the rest of my trip and to keep me out of the way of unforeseen trouble. I would hire one in Campo Grande. As I was walking along a path on the eastern shore of the Pardo River, I noticed the shadows lengthening, and I wondered where I could spend the night. I remember that I was looking at nearby trees to hang my hammock when I felt myself picked up forcefully by powerful arms and carried away, my head covered in some kind of burlap bag and my hands tied behind me. At first I struggled to get loose but was unable to break free. I could hear heavy breathing and the sound of a machete cutting through foliage. After some time I was laid on the ground and shortly I heard the sound of burning wood.

I COULD ALREADY feel the warmth of an open fire on my arms and legs when the bag was removed from my head. It was dark except for the light coming from the fire. I was lying on my side in a clearing; I was thirsty, and my wrists were stinging from the cord tied tightly around them. A short stocky figure was moving nearby, tending to the fire, and setting up some kind of equipment at the fire's edge. He seemed unaware of my presence as I watched him in silence. When his face finally became visible in the light, I could see the features of an Andean native with dark eyes, a bushy mustache, and several days' stubble on his cheeks and chin. He was dressed in a colorful poncho and a wide-brimmed sun hat. Finally he turned toward me, came closer, kneeled, and looked me in the face. His eyes showed neither hatred nor fear.

"*Me llamo* Juan José María Jesús Valdés," he said in Spanish. "*En un rato*, when you are calmed down, I will release your hands and feet. Do not try to escape from me. You would perish during the night. *¿Entendido?* I mean you no harm; I want only to talk to you. Then you will be free to go, or to come with me, if you wish. We will eat soon."

I answered in my broken Spanish that I felt calm and that I would not try to escape. I added that if he released me I would be glad to listen to him.

Without saying a word, he cut the rope from my wrists, then from my feet. He took two handfuls of some kind of mash from a pouch and heated it in a pan over the fire. I turned around, faced the fire, and watched his preparations. Silently he put small strips of dried meat into the pan on top of what was already there and added some liquid from a bottle. This mixture was finally served on tin plates along with a tin cup. We ate with our hands.

Juan spat his first mouthful on the ground; then he smiled and broke the silence, saying: "For Pachamama; all this comes from her." We fell back into silence as we ate. I was hungry and devoured my portion despite the taste. The liquor was fairly strong and sweet. He sat, absorbed in his thinking. I leaned against a clump of vegetation and, feeling relaxed after several stressful hours, fell asleep, facing the fire.

My companion woke me after an hour or so. It was still dark and the weird noises of the jungle at night sounded louder than I had expected. He stirred the fire, which made me aware of how cold I had become from sleeping on the ground without a cover.

"This will make you feel better," he said handing me a leaf and taking another for himself, carefully placing it between his teeth and beginning to chew.

"Before you judge me, you should realize that I am married and have two children. They are my whole life, and my aim is it to feed them and bring them up decently. Whatever sins I have committed are for them, and those are sins I do not regret."

"What are their names?"

"My wife is called Soledad; she is a good woman, and she bore me a daughter, Concepción, and a son, Circuncisión. They are waiting for my return after three months travel, praying that I come home safely from what they know is a dangerous job. Do you have children?"

"I have a wife but no children. We have only been married for a few months."

"Are you taking something back to her, that you should be walking through the jungle in the same way I am?"

"Yes, many things, but the only one I can think of now is money."

"You see! We are the same, we risk our lives so that our families will not starve, *es nuestro destino*."

"Can you tell me now why you captured me? Was that destiny, also?"

"No, that was chance. I have been tailing you for some time. I saw you watching poor people like me who carry their livelihood through the jungle. You stop somewhere, in a village, and then you pursue your way through the thicket, watching, watching, as if you wanted to divine our secret. I captured you so that I could tell you our secret, and then you would no longer need to spy on us and risk your own life doing so. I do not know what your purpose is; perhaps you will consent to tell me before long. I hope it is not to betray us; that would be a grievous crime against helpless people. You are a gringo, ¿*no*? Everything about you says you are. My friends who do the same job I do have seen you, and they wonder what it is that you want. I told them I would find out."

He paused to catch his breath. Then he added almost as an afterthought: "I should also say that ever since you left Tronco you were being followed . . . by a person who is known to me. For a price he causes people to disappear in the jungle."

Juan chewed in silence for several minutes.

"Now I must tell you my secret."

I thanked him for leveling with me, adding that I was interested in learning his secret.

"I am a *mestizo*," he began. "You cannot know what it means to have two races under one's skin. I come like the salamander out of the crack between two cultures. When you look at me, I am not sure which one you see, the Spanish or the Indian. My Spanish blood gave me energy and ruthlessness. My Indian blood gave me my love for Pachamama and the acceptance of whatever fate is in store for me. From that blood comes also the realization that our lives are only threads of a cosmic fabric. Like this poncho the threads of our lives make the pattern, and when one pattern is finished a new one is started. From up close we can only see single threads, not the pattern."

He paused again, this time as if searching for the loose strands of his thought. I was just beginning to wonder if he would find them when he resumed. "The gringos in the North need our coca paste so badly that they make it a crime to have it or carry it, as I do. When you return to your country you will teach them that coca is the gift of Pachamama to the Indians. She taught us to use it sparingly for survival and for health. Tell the gringos to let us use our coca the way we always have, the way Pachamama taught us. Tell them also to bring us different seeds so we will be able to give the world food instead of coca. Now you know my secret. What else do you want to know?"

"Tell me now about the path you took to arrive at where you are."

"My story is the story of my people, and it goes back generations. It really starts when Columbus and the conquistadors came, because that is when it became a sad destiny, when my ancestors had to learn to be slaves. My grandparents came from the Huallaga Valley in central Perú where they worked the land for a big landowner. During the rubber boom they moved to Iquitos, a jungle town on the Amazon River. There was plenty of work, and everybody prospered. Then someone smuggled rubber tree seeds from Brazil and planted them across the Pacific Ocean on an island. Our prosperity followed the seeds, leaving our area destitute. My people had to move again to find work.

"With seven children my grandparents crossed the border into Colombia to work on coffee plantations. After years of toiling from dawn to dark, they were able to own a small coffee farm. My father married, I was born, and four more children came. I helped in the fields, but I also went to school and decided to become a teacher. Then coffee prices fell, we lost the farm, and the whole family moved back to Iquitos. There I learned a new trade: trapping tropical fish and birds for illegal export as pets to rich nations. It brought in money and despair, because I knew all along that I was harming Pachamama and that in the end she would harm me. By then I had been married two years and had two children. I became a guide for a company catering to tourists who wanted to enter the jungle and see naked Indians in their villages. I took them down the Amazon by boat. Since the pay was rotten, I had to supplement it by going down the Huallaga River to buy cocaine, which I sold to my American tourists.

"The need for cocaine kept rising, and in no time the fertility of the Huallaga Valley was devoted to that single crop. I became a full time trafficker, because that job pays the best. I carried coca paste into Colombia, where it was refined into a powder for smuggling overseas. After each trip my young family could eat and be clothed. But a few years later armed conflicts started involving the local police, the militias, the army, the rich drug people, and the guerrillas. Trafficking to Colombia became too dangerous, so I moved to Bolivia with my family and settled in La Paz. Soledad does not have to work in the fields, the children can go to school, and we have a house in the outskirts of the city. You will come to visit us, and you will like it." He paused. "After I pick up my coca in Perú I deliver it in Santos. I go by truck, train, river, helicopter; sometimes I walk. When I make enough money I fly back to La Paz. A month ago my son became sick, and I am walking as a way of doing penance for the bad way I earn a living. I pray to Santa Rosa de Lima for divine forgiveness. And walking back I saw you. Now you can tell me who you are and where you are going."

I hesitated a long time before answering. This could be a trick to see if I would betray my employer. Juan may also be dangerous, a member of an outlawed drug mafia or a terrorist. Even if his story is true and his motives are what he says they are, should I tell him anything? Aren't I after all a spy, a secret agent, the bearer of important secrets that one doesn't reveal, even under torture?

"When did you first see me, Juan?"

"You were walking along a path where the forest begins. You

moved slowly, watching the carriers as they came toward you. It was the slowness of your pace that made me notice you. Everybody walks fast, they can't wait to get back and start another trip east, the only trip they get paid for. You seemed to be wandering aimlessly. Why does this gringo want to make a contact with dangerous people, I wondered. Then the thought came to me that you might be an agent looking for particular carriers, maybe ready to shoot them on sight. I lost you at the Rio Paraná. I saw you again as you left Tronco. That is when I started to follow you."

"Before I answer, can you tell me what the Americans are up to in Tronco? I hadn't expected to find so many in a Brazilian village far from anywhere."

"Is it possible that you do not know? Didn't you drink with them a few nights ago? All gringos around here know each other."

"They are completely unknown to me. Someone named Bill told me to get out of Tronco for my own safety. Then there was a drunk called Jeff. And they talked about another man, named Mike."

"I don't know them either, but I heard that they are engineers who came here to find oil for some American company, and they expect to find lots of it several miles up the Pardo River. Mike is their leader, and he is fearful that someone else will discover the oil before he does. I have heard of Bill; his job seems to be keeping journalists and competitors away from the area. A friend of mine told me that Bill once bought his entire load of cocaine. That saved him the trip to Santos. He thinks Bill is an agent sent along to make things easier for the oil prospectors."

"Thank you for telling me this, Juan. It helps me to learn what is going on here. I thought my mission was simply to find what route the carriers take when they bring their goods across the southern part of Brazil."

"But they know it already! You have wasted your time and effort. Everybody knows precisely where the carriers enter Brazil, what route they take, and how and where they dispose of their loads! Not just in Mato Grosso do Sul, either; the Northern routes are even better known. Here! Give me your map; I'll draw our route in red ink. You can take that to your employers and retire. You will live a longer life. Do you miss your wife?"

"Immensely."

"Go back to her soon. Then bring her with you when you visit me in La Paz. Now we will go together to Campo Grande, and from there you can tell your employer that you have completed your mission and get paid."

We slept near the fire. Juan was up at dawn, preparing a breakfast made of berries and leaves for both of us. At his suggestion, we returned to Tronco; there he found a river boat which took us the eighty odd miles upstream to Ribas do Rio Pardo. A bus took us the rest of the way to Campo Grande.

"I have asked to postpone completing my penance so that we could travel together. Here I will leave you, friend. Be careful." We embraced and parted after I agreed to visit him in La Paz.

Campo Grande was a disappointment, but I needed to stay long enough to contact my employers and settle affairs with them before heading for Corumbá, on the Bolivian border, where I expected to be able to explore the Pantanal, an enormous swamp with all the wildlife imaginable. I couldn't phone Mr. Kater until late that afternoon. By then he had left. The person who answered—whose name I didn't catch—said that he had enough authority to take my message. I explained what I had accomplished and that I would send the information to them the next day. I went on to tell him that it was my impression that the route of the carriers was well known to everyone, especially to the Americans, and that most of those I had talked to, including the oil prospectors in Tronco, were somehow involved in the drug trade. Upon hearing I was headed for Corumbá, he gave me precise instructions. He told me to seal my report and take it to a certain Mr. Dourada at the Lux Hotel there.

It was the next day that my phone connections were all but lost. I tried to ring up Deb several times, then Erik and Maria. Later Mr. Kater and the Consulate in Rio, unable to get through to any of them. So I spent my time in Campo Grande in my hotel room, with a mirror in my left hand and writing this diary with my right, acquiring in the process the worst headache I have ever experienced. But that was preferable to letting the feeling of isolation overtake me. I have been gone so long, looking forward to sharing some of these adventures with my loved one, only to have myself shut away again, now farther than ever from her familiar voice.

Once I was on the bus I resolved to phone Deb from Corumbá without using the credit card that Kater gave me. It was the bus ride that lifted me out of my feeling of forlornness. As we approached the Pantanal the bird life grew more varied than I had ever seen it, and a few Indians with painted faces, holding their bows and arrows, waived to us as we passed by. When not watching the scenery, I was fascinated by the other passengers: Bolivians, Paraguayans, some of them doubtless carriers returning for another load of cocaine. There were heavy women with three or four crying children, nursing the youngest ones, middle-aged men staring absently in front of them, young men, cages with chickens, some pigs and goats. We stopped briefly in every hamlet or town: Jango, Aquidauana, Miranda, where the bus broke down, stranding us for hours.

Corumbá is fascinating. I am sitting writing on a bench overlooking the Río Paraguay. To my right are elegant nineteenth-century buildings crumbling as their ornate windows gaze at the river, still wide enough to accommodate freighters, which no longer come this far from the ocean, hence the depressed look of the town. When I checked in at my hotel I was warned not to venture forth at night for fear of being robbed or beaten, so I am enjoying the shade during the afternoon heat while waiting to call you, Deb, when you come home from work. As I look at this magnificent river, I realize that to the south it cuts across Paraguay and after following the Argentinian border flows into the Río Paraná. Tonight, when I phone you, Deb, I'll tell you my new idea for a return route: find a boat that will take me down this river as far as Buenos Aires and then fly back to you in Rio. In the meanwhile, I will pay my respects to Sr. Dourada.

At this point there is an interruption in Hank's diary. The following pages are written not in a notebook but on legal-size lined paper. They are folded and inserted in the diary.

DEB, YOU WON'T believe what I have just gone through. I have only the vaguest notion of what has happened during the last few days, and I don't have the faintest idea of the date, the day of the week, where I am, or what I am doing here, wherever that is. Furthermore, who knows how long I have been zoned out, either drugged or unconscious.

I woke up in this sparsely furnished room; the heavy wooden door is locked from the outside. There are three hardwood chairs and a small table, on which I found this pad of paper and a ballpoint pen. There is a high window protected by metal bars. The walls are bare. I have on the clothes I was wearing that afternoon by the Rio Paraguay, but none of my other belongings. There is a bulge in my left pocket: something wrapped in paper and tied with a string. Oh, yes! The last thing Juan Valdés did was to give me this package, saying that I might need it. Let's see: a little statue. It looks like the *ekeko* he always carried around his neck. He told me it is an Indian image and assures him material success. I could use a lot of that at this moment and maybe some old fashioned luck for good measure. It is small, rather squarish, and has the smiling face of so many Inca artifacts; I'll keep it with me. Now what are these? Leaves of some sort, like small bay leaves, coca maybe. He chewed them often and offered some to me saying they were good for high altitudes and hunger. I don't know at what elevation I might be, but I do know I am starved, so here goes. One leaf is enough for now.

How did I get here? I remember being told by the hotel clerk in Corumbá that I would find Sr. Dourada at a certain address, to which a bellhop was to take me. Apparently I was hit on the head from behind on the street as I was with him. I came to in a small propeller plane that night, feeling sick. I threw up and passed out again. The rest is confused, but when the plane landed, after what seemed ages of rough flying, I was blindfolded and bound, shoved into some kind of vehicle for another jolting ride. When I was finally unloaded and put into this room, I passed out again. I awoke a little while ago, my hands free and the blindfolds gone.

The building is quiet. The only noise comes from a distance where there may be a highway with trucks or other heavy vehicles. I can smell tropical trees and flowers. The room is spotless; the walls bear no sign of mold or scuff marks, the floor is highly polished.

Oh! Hang on. Someone's at the door.

Here I am again. It must be something like three hours later.

A smart looking young man with an expressionless face opened the door of this room with a large key and told me in Portuguese, rather politely, to make myself ready for an interview with a Sr. Braulio. He brought me a bowl of water, a towel, a comb, and a tray of food, telling me he would return in half an hour. It felt good to freshen up.

We walked down several corridors richly decorated with wall hangings and painted portraits of ancestors. From the windows I could see that the building is in the middle of a large lawn surrounded everywhere by great trees, something like the English idea of a tropical estate. At a corner a soldier stood at attention wearing an ornamental uniform with sword in scabbard. The cap, wig, buttons and lace reminded me of the lackeys one sees in old

movies. As we advanced the wall coverings became more elaborate
and the guards more numerous, each one saluting us with gravity.

Finally we arrived in a large salon where another uniformed
man was seated at a desk, but his wig was longer and his pale
face covered with lines and pock marks. I thought this might be
my man, but as I sat down in front of him after being invited to do
so, he told me in a serious tone:

"You have been granted a private interview with Sr. Braulio.
This is a rare opportunity only a few fortunate ones have enjoyed.
I advise you to pay attention to every word he says and to be on
your best behavior. Your future depends in considerable measure
on the success of this meeting. Think carefully about what you
say and always remember that what Sr. Braulio says is the truth,
that what he ordains will occur. Do you have any questions?"

I felt like asking if I had entered the gates of heaven and was
about to meet God, but I thought better of it when I saw little
room for humor in the man's expression. He added:

"Sr. Braulio is currently writing a letter. You are to sit patiently
until he addresses you."

A new lackey ushered me into an inner office where somebody
was writing at a wide desk. The lackey held a chair for me to sit
in and remained standing behind me. I sat there for what seemed
like an hour while the person behind the desk, presumably Sr.
Braulio, wrote a word or two, then paused, crossed something
out, paused, wrote something again, took out another page and
went on writing, moving his lips as he wrote. I had plenty of time
to observe. He was using a fancy fountain pen and took obvious
care in his penmanship. The desk had intricate carvings on the
corners and legs; on top of the highly polished hardwood surface
were two ornate phones, a fancy table lamp, and a photograph of
a boy in a silver frame. Behind the seated man was a larger-than-
life portrait of someone who resembled him. On either side were
open French doors, and vertically lined pale blue and white
wallpaper extended to the corners of the room.

He looked up, told the lackey to leave, and smiled at me.

"I have been writing a letter about you, my friend," he said in carefully articulated English, placing the sheets in a neat pile and making an effort to smile. "How I finish the letter depends largely on you."

He paused and looked at me.

"I must beg you to forgive my pilot the rough air passage you received. Unfortunately the sky conditions are not always ideal, especially when one is obliged to fly at a low elevation to avoid detection. It is not always easy to steer an aircraft, even a small one like ours, just above the tips of the forest trees at night with no lights. I know, for I have often done so myself under similar conditions. But I see that you have arrived safely and alive; that is most important. Will you take tea with me?"

"Yes, thank you."

He pressed a button, which produced the same lackey with a tray of tea and cakes. While the latter were being distributed, he went on.

"Your name is Henry David Myers, also known by your friends and relatives as Hank. You are from Arkansas, California, and other places in the United States, currently in Brazil engaged in an ill-fated enterprise about which the less said the better. So you see, I know a good deal about you. Now to make our relationship less uneven, let me tell you something about myself."

He stood up and placed his right hand on his breast. "I am Braulio Silvio Caetano Souza e Rego d'Ouro." As he stood and pronounced these names with solemnity, I could see that he was about six feet tall, broad shouldered, dressed smartly in a uniform that sprouted several colorful badges and decorations along with a good deal of gold thread and many buttons. His black hair was curly and well trimmed, as was his mustache. His dark eyes landed on me occasionally, but most of the time his gaze wandered around the room, apparently at random, while he talked. These eyes were neither sharp nor penetrating, and they were placed, I thought, rather close together for such a broad face.

He sat down and continued. "You can see from these

surroundings and the portraits on the walls that I descend from a line of aristocrats and people accustomed to ruling and being obeyed. Let us say that I belong to a lower branch of the Brazilian royal family tree that ruled Brazil for a century until the nobility became corrupted and brought our monarchy to its unfortunate downfall. But you might say also that I am out on a limb, so to speak, since my lineage is of no use to me now except for procuring invitations to uninteresting social functions and being appointed to chair committees to raise funds for aiding the worthless. There's no money in being of royal blood; we can't even pay our servants or taxes these days. You may talk, if you wish to ask questions or comment."

What can one say after a prologue like this? As I searched for some moderately intelligent and uncompromising answer to all this, I was rescued.

"Ah! What have we here? These are my friends," Braulio said watching the entrance of two large Dobermans, one with a crazy looking monkey sprawled on his back. "Let me introduce you. This is Thunder, who frightens the neighborhood with his barking, and this is Lightning, my fast protector and avenger, giving a ride to Anjinho, my little angel and right-hand monkey, the only servant in this whole establishment I can fully trust; he is my valet, food taster, and confidant when life becomes difficult. Now can you fellows amuse yourselves quietly while I talk to Hank?" The two dogs and monkey looked at me with what seemed like curiosity, with eyes neither more nor less human than Braulio's. Instead of coming to smell me or be petted, the dogs curled up on an Oriental rug, and the monkey sat down in front of a TV monitor on the floor nearby and started pressing the buttons of a remote control. Soon he became quietly absorbed in what he was watching.

"Let me explain our situation clearly, Hank. There is nothing so refreshing as placing one's cards on the table. Since you have no cards at all, I will proceed to show mine. As I mentioned, I am currently a bit short of funds, and for one who is forced by the historical process to use democratic means to become powerful, that is most unfortunate. My goal is to regain control of this great country. Ah! You Americans talk about your country in those terms, but you hardly know what greatness is. To control a country these days requires one to be an elite member of the military or popular enough with the masses to be elected. Since a minor physical defect prevented me from being enrolled in the military academy, I cannot count on a coup engineered by my colleagues to put me at the head of a junta. So the only route open to me is through the hearts of the people. We are all aware, of course, that the only way to travel that route is to be extremely rich. The same is true in your country, where one has to be rich enough to buy into a political party and own the media. One also needs enough patience to wait for the inevitable downfall of the democratic forces at work in our society, here and in other countries as well. This, my friend, is my theory: with the rapid increase in population, societies will be unable to pay the price of a decent life for an ever increasing number of unruly people. All governments—socialist or capitalist—are doomed to failure; only the regime authoritarian enough to force its people to live peacefully in poverty can succeed. What do you think?"

Now there was something to talk about, and since I seldom become upset with ideas I don't share, I could think of a few comments and questions, which he answered readily, apparently interested in initiating a dialogue. We chatted for a while before he continued.

"How do you make a lot of money without strengthening the economy of a regime you despise? Simple. You go into drugs. Now don't mistake me. I do not touch the stuff myself. Nor does my son. Nor do my servants if they want to continue in my employ. It is strictly a matter of convenience, a way of making the money I need to be elected. If there were another way, I might try it, but with the end of the cold war, there aren't many choices left: James Bond and his enemies have all been obliged to retire. Here in Brazil we can't compare with Colombia and Perú in ability to cultivate the coca plant, although we do grow some in the north, along with marijuana. So my fortune has to come from somewhere else. Since the thirst for narcotics is so unquenchable in your country and your drug agents have been busy sealing off the most convenient routes for drugs to arrive on the streets of America, cocaine has taken a detour across Brazil. It is my business to oversee its passage, with the help, of course, of people with influence in this country and in yours; I can also count on the cooperation of local police units and of the crocodiles who eat my recalcitrant carriers. In this way I am able to carve out a decent living and make considerable contributions to my election fund. It is interesting work and safe, as long as I stay out of circulation. That is why I reside peacefully in this modest abode— with its sixty rooms and several gardens, swimming pools, tennis courts, you will see them all—going out seldom and thus avoiding the stray bullets of rivals, disgruntled drug lords' hit men, and leftist guerrillas. I am not discriminating against leftists, by the way; but those to the right have been more cooperative. They are very busy people and have little time for looking into my activities.

"Now where do you fit, Hank, in all this? You are here precisely because you have become an embarrassment, both to me and to your employers. I happen to have many friends in the Free Trade Consortium, the so-called independent environmental and commercial development corporation that oversees the people who hired you. When I complained about your activities along the Paraná and the Pardo Rivers, my friends were already unhappy with the outcome of an experiment cooked up by your boss . . . Mr. Kraper, I don't quite remember his name; but that hardly matters since I doubt that he will last long anyway. My friends in Rio were at their wit's end wondering what to do with you, saying that you knew too much already, and so forth. Sr. Dourada, an accomplished double agent, sent you to me, and I, in my usual magnanimous fashion, volunteered to help out and to entertain you while they come to a decision one way or another."

What bothered me the most was the "and so forth" and "one

way or another." What Braulio didn't say seemed more ominous than what he did.

"What about my wife?"

"Oh, you don't have to worry at all about her. The embassy has probably informed her that you have been temporarily detained by a local constable or leftist terrorist, whatever is more plausible, and they are entertaining her with harebrained plans of using political pressure or sending the Marines to free you. They can keep her busy for months. That you have a wife, who is most likely anxious, hysterical, phoning every other minute to some office or other and making a great nuisance of herself, that is all for the good, for it assures me of your cooperation."

He called Anjinho and presented him with three cookies, telling him in Portuguese to share them with his companions. Then he turned to me:

"Now Hank, there is no reason for you to be uncomfortable during your stay as my guest. You will have everything you need: food, drink, women, material comfort, a library with the latest newspapers and magazines from around the world, the magnificent views from the balconies. You will lack only the convenience of freedom and of communicating with the outside. When I have receptions or parties, you will not be invited, but you can watch the festivities, which can be quite diverting, and I assure you that you will eat as well as the other guests. In addition, you will have two boon companions. One is the future King, God willing, of Brazil, my son João, whom we all respectfully call Ivan. I can't urge you enough to befriend him and to entertain him with your wit and experience, for he finds it rather tedious living in this mansion with few distractions and no friends. The other will be your roommate, Boris Keiner, of whom we will talk later. All you need to know now is that he is my guest, like you, and he is a very clever fellow, only he may perhaps be a bit too clever for his own good. Let us again hope for the best."

Braulio stood up, giving a clear signal that the interview was over. Then: "Oh! I need to tell you one thing. There are no guards here, in the usual sense. The servants you see in the corridors are peaceful souls; they carry no other weapon than swords they hardly know how to use. But we have taken security measures to insure that you accept my hospitality with good will. Anjinho will explain them to you while I retire for a short siesta. We will continue this conversation at your leisure. Of that you will have a plentiful supply."

He whispered something to the monkey on his way to a large paneled door. One of the Dobermans followed him. When he was gone, the monkey signaled me to come sit on the floor next to him; then he manipulated his remote control to start a video tape. On the screen I could see images of a spacious mansion and beautifully kept lawns and shrubs. As the camera followed a path leading through groves of trees and flower beds, it came abruptly to a stop before an eight-foot hurricane fence. On the other side was a no-man's-land without vegetation other than short weeds, and about forty feet farther there was another similar fence. A person walked up to the first fence, smiled at the camera, and threw a large chunk of fresh meat into the cleared area. He then opened the fence and let a large dog run after the meat. After running about ten feet the dog was blown to bits by a large and fiery explosion underneath him. At that Anjinho burst out laughing, holding his sides, and rolling on the floor. Then smiling at me and nodding he rewound the video tape and started to run it again.

I had seen enough and stood up. The door immediately opened and the same lackey beckoned me to follow him. We walked down a hall with high ceilings and portraits on both sides. Then at one point he pressed a button in the wall, and a hidden door slid open. Inside we followed a narrow unadorned corridor with pink stucco walls back to the room I had left earlier. My guide told me in broken English that he would be back in a half an hour to move me to my new quarters, and would I please gather my things. Indeed, there on one of the chairs were the rest of my belongings: backpack, wallet, jacket, boots, even my diary.

Only later did I discover that my fake ID, the plastic phone card with Deb's number stuck to the back, and Juan Valdés's map had been removed.

Oh, Deb! In what words can I tell how I feel right now? I am terrified by all this, for you and for me, and I guess for the human race. But I can't help laughing at a good deal of what went on. Who is this buffoon Braulio? After all he told me, I still don't know if he is real. Or whether I am really here, or if I'm dead after all and this is some kind of parody of an afterlife. Having written down all this helps me see the humorous side of what I am going through, and for that I am thankful. But the writing does nothing to dispel my longing for you. I can bear the nightmarishness of it all but not the emptied-out feeling I have inside. It wasn't so bad when I was in the forest and the dangers were real, natural. But in this world of threats, traps, deceptions, and man-made inhumanity there is no place I can locate you. How can I imagine you walking into this room right now? It would be like in those old paintings of the Annunciation where the angel is illuminated with an unearthly light and belongs obviously to another dimension. I try to feel you here, and it doesn't work. I try to imagine us in bed together, to sense your caresses and the warmth of your limbs against mine, but all I get is this empty room and a feeling of deep desolation inside.

Come Deb! I need you so badly!

RIGHT NOW I am more optimistic about what is in store for me. It makes me feel better to know one sane person who is at ease in a situation very much like mine. He, too, is a prisoner in this house, but he doesn't find his captivity at all painful; in fact he is prepared to enjoy it to the hilt. Let me describe him to you, Deb; you may find his portrait as amusing as I do.

Boris Keiner, as Braulio explained to me yesterday, is my roommate; but that needs some qualification. We actually share a suite of rooms: each of us has his own bedroom, bath, and study; there is a common living area which comprises two sitting rooms and a balcony that has a view of the gardens and of a swimming pool, which is at our disposal. The furnishings are a little old-fashioned, but they are comfortable and attractively arranged. If anything, this place looks like a Hollywood set from the 1950's. Books line the walls of one of the sitting rooms; there is also an upright piano, badly in need of tuning.

When I entered, followed by two lackeys carrying my things, Boris was sitting at the piano trying to pick out some old rock tunes, singing at the top of his voice and making wild gestures. As he saw me come in, he stopped, took on a solemn expression, and struck up a funeral march, getting most of the notes right.

"Now that you have died to the world, welcome to your new life here in Braulio's paradise. Sing on, angels, sing your praises of our heavenly host and of this newly disembodied soul." As he said this his expression shifted from the mock tragic to a good-natured smile, and he jumped up and hugged me.

"I am so glad to see you! God! Am I glad," he exclaimed in English. "Come on in, Hank. I know your name already, and I'm enjoying the thought of having someone to talk to. These," he said, motioning to the lackeys who were standing lost in some kind of contemplation, "are no company at all. They speak only Portuguese and even in that language they have nothing to say. They must be afraid of Jove's thunderbolt clobbering them if they express an opinion." Turning to them, he said in Portuguese: "Bring us a couple of beers, would you?" In English he added: "Then we won't need you for another five years."

In fifteen minutes we were sitting down in front of a lunch of delicately prepared fruits and cold fish along with several bottles of Belgian beer. We talked for hours, drinking, smoking, feeling more and more at home with each other. With my limited capacity for alcohol, I began feeling tipsy quite soon but kept on drinking nevertheless. I was able to follow his story and tell him a little about myself, and, of course, about you.

Boris looks like no one I have ever seen. He has a stocky build, and his wavy black hair is held in check by a spotted neckerchief; he is wearing a purple designer sport shirt unbuttoned half way down his chest, which is well endowed with curly hair. His Mediterranean look is belied by an obvious German accent. He apparently speaks several languages but none of them correctly; he learned them all in the street and admits that he can't write in any of them. From what I gather, he dropped out of school when he was thirteen, which explains why even his German is haphazard.

His story runs something like this. He was born in East Germany to a woman who had been abandoned by her Russian soldier/lover when he learned she was pregnant. He grew up in and around Halle with his mother and grandmother, who had joined some fundamentalist Christian church and spent their days in pious activities while talking about God's will, and a grandfather who kept a collection of Nazi memorabilia hidden in a closet which he would show the young Boris on special occasions. Boris survived all this by dreaming about his father and the day he would be reunited with him.

Fed up with poverty, piety, and his grandfather's stories, he ran away on his thirteenth birthday and hitchhiked to Moscow, somehow getting across Poland and through border inspections. I gather that he is adept at urinating somewhere out of sight when the passport official comes by and at walking across borders at dusk during blizzards. From Moscow he walked thirty miles west to a state-run farm where he had learned his father worked and presented himself at the door. Once he had explained who he was, his father took him outside, threw him into a snowdrift, and warned that the next time he would shoot. Boris made his way back to Moscow, and after spending what little money he had stolen from his mother, he found the Soviet equivalent of slums and rummaged around long enough to become attached to some black market operators. When these were arrested and sent to Siberia, he took over their clientele. Soon he shifted his attention to drugs—whatever was available there at the time. He found he could always bribe the police and secret agents with the LSD that he had learned how to manufacture in the basement of an abandoned building. Eventually he was able to amass a small fortune in rubles but was unable to deposit them anywhere or even spend them without raising suspicion. So he bought a motorcycle on the black market, sewed his rubles into his coat, and headed for the Czech border, where he was nearly captured but saved himself by leaving most of his rubles with the border patrol. With the few he had left he made his way to Western Germany.

After having grown up on a steady diet of anti-American propaganda, his aim was to become an American. When he arrived in Wiesbaden, Boris called himself Jack Keiner and, becoming a taxi driver, quickly made himself indispensable to servicemen stationed there by delivering them to bars and whorehouses and supplying them with heroin and other drugs he had learned how to market effectively without getting caught. Soon his clients included officers and civilian businessmen to whose abodes he would deliver prostitutes and drugs until one day he was knifed in the thigh and robbed by the sponsor of his most sought-after whore. Unable to obtain medical help without proper identification and disowned by his influential clients, he crawled to a sanatorium in the hills of Hessen, where he fell in love with a complacent nurse and lived with her for a year while he healed his wounds and resumed his business activities.

After exhausting his nurse's modest savings, he packed all he had in two suitcases and, leaving no address, took a train to Paris. There he hung around a Left Bank café with some German expatriates and eventually shacked up with Ondine, a young Frenchwoman with good connections. Boris convinced her to move with him to Málaga, where, with money she had borrowed from her parents, he started painting—while stoned—acrylics based on the science fiction novels he was always reading and opened a gallery which specialized in his own works. In the meantime, Ondine had a daughter, whom they adoringly called Clone and tried to bring up naturally, along with several cats, dogs, and ducks, on a farm in the outskirts, which he had purchased with money borrowed from a local business connection. He avoided the necessity of repaying that loan by getting himself arrested and deported by the new Spanish Monarchy's anti-drug squad. He hadn't even enough time to kiss Clone or Ondine good-bye. They neither saw nor heard from him again.

By now my head was swimming in all the beer I had consumed, not to mention a few glasses of brandy, and I have little recall of the rest of Boris's story. Apparently he had traveled around a bit and eventually showed up in Rio, where he took up the same life style. I guess you could say he is good-looking, and he is certainly appealing to women. The important thing is that he offers me friendship, and I am sorely in need of it.

When I awoke the following morning, Boris had already

ordered a sumptuous breakfast that included, among other things, transparent tropical fish served raw in a pungent white wine sauce. They were resting inert on brilliant white plates that reflected light eerily through their eyes, bones, and intestines. I wasn't quite sure at first if my stomach, still recovering from last night's drinking, could accept this new challenge, but Boris reassured me.

"These tiny creatures are the best cure for a hangover known to man. You have to be careful when you go fishing for them, for although they generally restrict themselves to a diet of minuscule plant life, they quickly become carnivorous when they get the scent of meat. Fishermen have been known to lose the flesh of a hand just pulling out a net full of them. How are you by the way, after our bout last night? *Gehts gut? Ça va mieux?*"

After a few bites, I felt miserable and told him so. His expression suddenly softened. "Then don't eat any more, don't eat anything all day; you will feel better for fasting. You can drink this iced fruit juice until you have recovered. Relax. Later we will go out and explore the grounds."

I slept a few hours and woke up refreshed. After lunch Boris led me down a series of corridors and passageways through a heavy wooden door to an expanse of lawn and paths separating well kept beds of tropical plants, the whole covered by the foliage of wide-spreading shade trees. Everything looked as if it had been recently manicured.

"It's beastly hard to grow any kind of lawn in this climate, but old Braulio is not to be discouraged by nature. If he wants a lawn, he gets it despite all odds. And he's just as capable of destroying it as he is of creating it. I'm afraid he deals with people in the same way. He's sort of a pragmatist, really. Let's sit in the shade here, and you can tell me something about yourself. Soon Ivan will arrive from lessons with his tutor, and we will feel obliged to entertain him. So what brings you here to Petrópolis, as if I didn't already know?"

"So that's where I am! I've heard about the summer home of

the royal family, still elegant today, as it seems from these grounds."

"It is a nice place, although I prefer towns where there is something happening, where they don't roll up the sidewalks at night. But if you have to be locked up like we are, this is as decent a place as any. Can you imagine rotting in some hole north of the Amazon delta, in a cell, with brutal guards, insects all over you, and nowhere to take a shit except under your mat? Let's face it, Hank. We've got it good, so good! You been locked up before, I suppose; who hasn't?"

"Well, actually, no; somehow I've avoided that."

"You mean you have never been in the clink? Man! Where've you been? Where I'm from, practically everybody's been sent up at least five times. The laws and the authorities change so fast you take it for granted you'll be arrested twice a year on an average. You don't even know about a law until you've been caught breaking it. Brazil's different, though; here there aren't any laws; everybody does what he wants and generally gets away with it. Rob, rape, pollute, destroy, no problem. But just try getting in the way of someone with power, pow! you're done for, like you and me, sitting around waiting for the outside world to remember us. I don't know about you, but I'm totally forgotten. What are you in for, anyway?"

"Frankly, I haven't the vaguest idea. Braulio said I had become an embarrassment to him. Do you know what that means?"

"Sure. That means you were spoiling his little game just by being somewhere at the wrong time. Where were you?"

"In Corumbá, on the Bolivian border."

"Bad place to be. That's one of the locations where Braulio extracts a fee from coca traffickers. If they don't pay him, he turns them over to the police; if they do pay, he gives a percentage to the same police. Everybody has a good deal. What the fuck were you doing there? Don't worry. Braulio respects our confidences. The joint isn't even bugged; I checked the walls, fans, and electric outlets when I first got here."

At this point I wasn't ready to confide in anyone, so I mumbled something about hiking, physical fitness, and exploring the swamp.

"Bullshit! If that's true, you would have accidentally fallen into the jaws of one of Braulio's crocodiles. You may be an embarrassment to Braulio, but you are also useful to him, and that's why you are here; don't forget that if he threatens you. It will help."

Boris lit a cigarette and went on. "I'll try to find out what they've got on you. Maybe Ivan can help us figure out what Braulio has in mind. He's a weird kid, but he's smart. Here's how I got trapped in this paradise. It so happens that when I arrived in Rio, I checked out the bars and found where the American expatriates and tourists went for drugs and what the prices and obstacles were. Then I started my usual taxi-driving, show-the-tourists-around routine but ran afoul of a taxi drivers' gang. In the end I found trafficking more lucrative and a lot safer. After a while I became a cog in the local distribution systems, arranging deliveries to hotels, consulates, bars, and bordellos. I supplied bellhops, doormen at luxury apartments, guards at consulates, and madams. It worked. Someone else made delivery; I collected the money. That was fine with me because I don't use crack, just pot and hash, ever since the time when I was so deep into LSD that my balls nearly shriveled up, and I quit experimenting. Anyhow, Braulio got wind that I was making a lot of money and managing it well, so he offered me a job in his organization, saying that in the end I might even help him politically, how, I don't really know. I told him to go screw himself, that I was content with a small-size operation. So the next day two of his thugs picked me up on a street corner, right in broad daylight; I fought like hell, and there was a squad car ten feet away from where they clubbed me, and the cops just sat there writing reports in their notebooks! That was about fifteen weeks ago. I'm biding my time, waiting for him to improve his offer."

As Boris was talking, the sound of a helicopter began to throb in the distance and grew progressively louder.

"There he comes," Boris said, pointing to the sky. "Special delivery by air. It is Braulio's preferred type of transportation, for himself and his son, and, as you know, for his captives." By now I could hardly hear over the roar of the approaching aircraft, which touched ground in the middle of an open area near where we were sitting, causing the trees and grass to blow violently. We ran over to it just as the propeller came to rest and the noise subsided; the pilot and a small figure descended. When he caught sight of Boris the boy ran in our direction, jumping into Boris's arms and hugging him vigorously.

"Get off, you hooligan; you're going to wreck me," Boris switched to Portuguese. "Here, meet our new friend, Hank."

I don't know how to start to describe Ivan. He eyed me with suspicion in his dark brown, almost black, eyes hidden below bushy eyebrows. I was struck by a birthmark, about one inch wide and two inches long, starting half way down his neck and extending to below his collarbone. It consisted of a patch of darker skin with short black hairs growing all in one direction. When we shook hands he smiled at me and his expression became accepting. I would have guessed him to be fourteen years old, but he turned out to be sixteen. His hair was cut neatly short, with a triangular mound on top to one side. His clothes looked American: flowered sports shirt, slacks, belt, brown leather shoes. A slight odor of shaving lotion drifted about him.

"Tennis, and a swim?" Boris proposed. "Do you have shorts, Hank? I guess not. We'll ask for a pair, tennis shoes, and a racquet, too."

Soon a young man came (I learned later that he was the son of the majordomo who had lectured me outside of Braulio's office) carrying my duds and a pair of swimming trunks; he joined us for doubles. He was the most skillful player of all, but he measured out his ability carefully, keeping the score close and managing to let Ivan and Boris win in the end. He did not come with us to the pool. After sunning and horsing around in the water for a couple of hours, I felt like a kid again, healthy and optimistic. Before going out, we held on to the edge of the pool, chatting.

"What courses did you have today?" Boris asked Ivan.

"The same old crap. Geography, history, and literature of Brazil. Today we did the rivers, you know, how long the Amazon is, how many sources it has, how many thousand cubic tons of water it carries per minute, et cetera, et cetera. I don't remember a thing except that Manaus must have been a neat place with all those gunfights back in the days of the rubber barons. The rest was a drag."

"What do you know about the Rio Pardo?" I asked.

"Rio what?"

"Rio Pardo; it flows into the Rio Paraná in the Mato Grosso do Sul."

"It's not on my list."

"Put it on your list to visit some day. Just recently I happened to be in that area and got to know the river, sort of intimately. It is a beautiful river, and it speaks its own language, at least to me. It is an untamed language, unlike that of any other river I have known, and you have to be there to learn it."

"How did you travel? By ferry?"

"On foot, hitchhiking, rowboat, and once on a man's back, blindfolded."

Ivan looked at me. He seemed to take interest, for the first time since we met.

"Neat! Hey, tonight before dinner I'll show you around the house. You will be able to pick out the best ring-side seats for observing Dad's big party. I wish I could watch it with you. But I'll have to be with the guests stuffing myself with all that food and then going out and puke so I can stuff in more. Have you met Severina?"

"No. Who is that?"

"That's the castle cook," Boris answered. "She's a real character. By the way, Ivan. I could use some amusement tonight. Could you arrange something? I'm sure Hank has needs as well."

"See what I can do."

I had no idea what they were referring to.

B ORIS AND I rested in our quarters. He turned on the radio to listen to the latest pop tunes from Rio. While he dialed from station to station in search of music he wanted to hear, I fell into a deep sleep and had a series of strange dreams. I found myself walking in an unknown landscape, half forest, half grassland; it turned into a row of strip mines and then into a large unknown city. The sound of the music made its way into my dream on the rhythm of tennis balls bouncing repeatedly and voices calling the score: my opponent's was astronomically high and mine was always love. I was happy to float away from the game on a raft in the middle of a river with foliage covering the banks on both sides. Strange sounds of human utterances came over the brown water toward me, and try as I might I was unable to identify them or take note of them in phonetic script. As I attempted to write, the symbols I was using came to resemble more and more the clumsy handwriting of my childhood. I awoke to the sound of the shots that killed my brother.

It took me a while to come out of that dream and realize that I was alive in the real world of solid objects and people. Ivan had come in, and he was talking to Boris. We were to eat at nine. In the meantime we could explore the building.

"It is a two-layered world," Ivan explained, "like something out of that old Greek guy, you know, Pluto, Plato, or maybe someone else. In one realm the blessed spirits play, free of cares or obligations. In the other, the less fortunate roam, wondering where they are going, cut off from the light of the sun. That's where you two belong; in the other my esteemed father dwells. I cross from one to the other as I wish. Today you can freely traverse from your area to the more exalted set of hallways. Tomorrow, after six o'clock, the doors will lock in preparation for Sr. Braulio's great dinner party. But I'll tell you about that later. Come."

He took my hand and led us out of our quarters, down a corridor, through a sliding door into a large hall adorned with drapes, Turkish rugs, and portraits in gilt frames. For a while we walked along a carpeted hallway looking through wide doors into large rooms with half-closed shutters, full of heavy furniture and decorated with hunting scenes and portraits of horses between cases full of neatly arranged leather-bound books. Next we arrived at the entrance of a large ballroom. There three old men, all of them bald, were walking back and forth in felt slippers pushing fluffy mops across the parquet. The adjacent room was as long but less wide, and it was occupied by a table with enough chairs to seat two hundred people.

"This is where the feast will take place. Soon those three old brothers will mount the table with cloth knee pads and polish it so bright that you will be able to make out the color of your neighbor's eyes reflected on the wood in the candlelight. Then they will set the silver, the plates, and the wine glasses—three or four for each guest—and finally they will come with a measuring tape to see that everything is set within the correct millimeter of the edge of the table. After they are done, if I can, I'll sneak in and move one fork or spoon a little out of line and tell the head butler that these fellows have fucked up again. You will be able to hear the altercation all over the house, the bald brothers will resign in unison, and they won't come back until the head butler goes and apologizes and reminds them that if they don't return and prepare the hors d'oeuvres immediately my good papa will have them thrown in jail, or maybe worse."

Ivan took us through a hidden door up a narrow staircase that led to a kind of balcony enclosed in pane glass, from where we would be able to watch the festivities in the dining hall below. There were already binoculars set next to the chairs. We walked back to our quarters and waited for dinner playing pinochle and drinking vermouth.

Then a lackey came and announced that some people were requesting Ivan at a back entrance to the building. He said he would meet us at dinner.

"Fine company, isn't he?" Boris said, stretching and yawning. "He is so awfully lonesome and bored that he will do anything to liven things up. It will make the days bearable for us while we are here.

Dinner was served that night in a small dining room. As Boris and I entered, Ivan was in conversation with two young women, one of them black, the other Asian, both dressed as if to go to the theater. We were joined by Roberto, who had been my tennis partner earlier in the day.

Ivan introduced us by first name, without further explanation, and we took our seats at a table, which was carefully set with fine silver and glassware. A waiter poured a white wine while another brought in a soup made from what looked like fish heads and innards; I could clearly distinguish a floating eye staring blankly at me. For a while the conversation consisted mainly of Roberto's comments on the weather. I was occupied in trying to figure out who we all were, especially the women. Were they also Braulio's prisoners? Boris watched them as he devoured his soup, not saying much until the next course, a tasty breaded cod. Then he started teasing and asking questions. Rose, who talked and laughed a lot, explained to us that she came from Bahia and that Yih, who was originally from Singapore, lived with her family in Santos until recently. The women were attractive despite the layers of makeup that hid their faces. I couldn't determine if they spoke Portuguese with a regional accent or if their speech was riddled with slang. Ivan looked pained through most of the meal, as if he wished to be somewhere else.

As a veal course was being served, Roberto announced that

he intended to visit the U.S. sometime during the next few months, and he wondered if there was anything anyone of us would like him to bring back. Rose immediately called out for him to bring some postcards of Disneyland.

"That is my dream, Deesnaylandia. I have always wanted to go there, and I will one day, I assure you. You have been there many times, Senhor?" she asked turning to me. "Please tell me all about it."

"I must admit that I have never actually gone there."

Rose, Yih, and Ivan all chimed in at that point to say something to the effect that I must have been a philistine to have resisted such a beautiful opportunity. The two women right away deferred to Ivan.

"Disneyland is more than a place," he stated somewhat pompously in his as yet unchanged voice. "It is an ideal that has become solid reality, incarnate, as our priest would say. For anyone who hasn't had the good fortune of visiting it in person, it is a dream, the object of a desire," he added, looking at everyone present with intensity. "And I should add that in reality it is better than anything you can imagine; I know, because I have seen it on television and in movies. Everybody knows that all Disney movies are filmed there, so it is more than an amusement park: it is a great studio where images are created to satisfy the emotional needs of millions of people."

"And to think that Mickey Mouse lives there!" Rose exclaimed. "What a wonderful actor he is! If I had to name the lover I most dream of, it would be none other than Mickey."

"I don' know about that, really," Yih was ready to hold forth. "But all those castles and scary forests with dragons breathing fire would be a great place to make love. Just think, Rose, doing it in one of those tall towers that looks like, you know what, up there in the window with music everywhere and people all around."

Boris thought that was awfully funny; Roberto looked mortified yet amused, and Ivan seemed not to hear. I have no idea how I looked, but I did try to join in.

"Disneyland is expanding, did you know? There is one in Florida, and another one is being built in France for the Europeans. Maybe one day there will be a Disneyland just outside Rio for you to visit."

"Of course we know all that," Ivan answered abruptly. "But they are all travesties. Fake Disneylands. Not the real thing. In France no one goes there because it lacks the spirit of the original, it has been corrupted by the loose morals of the French people. There can never be any Disneyland but the original, true, sacred one, built and blessed by Walt Disney himself and his helpers. And here is proof: my father is the only person I know who has been there, and when I ask him about it he answers, gruffly: 'Disneyland doesn't exist!'"

"How is that proof of anything?" Boris wondered.

"Because my father doesn't believe in anything but the sacred mission of Brazil and his own vocation in creating it. So for him to deny something makes it more real."

By now Rose was about to start weeping, obviously drunk. Since the fish course she had eaten nothing but had smiled each time a waiter filled her wine glass. Boris turned to me and said in English:

"What do you think? Which one do you want? Tonight you choose."

How the hell do I get into these situations, Deb, tell me! Or rather, tell me how to get out of this one! I need you to inspire me quickly, before I make an ass of myself. Actually I was beginning to enjoy Boris and Ivan; Roberto, Rose, and Yih were entertaining enough as dinner companions. Oh, shit! Deb! I need you more now than I did in the swamp!

I managed not to say anything at the time, but as we got up from the table I told Boris straight out that I wasn't interested and reminded him that I was married.

"Suit yourself. Tell Ivan; he'll get rid of Rose." Boris disappeared holding Yih's arm.

As soon as we stood up after coffee I drew Ivan aside:

"Look, Ivan. I don't want to appear stuffy, and I do appreciate your thoughtfulness. But I'm not interested in a woman. I'm happily married . . ."

"No problem. Let's go play pool."

From then on Ivan was my boon companion. Whenever he was not studying or off in the helicopter to attend classes he hung around me. He liked to discourse about Brazil and its greatness— great expanse, great soul, great opportunities, and also great problems, which its current corrupt bureaucracy was incapable of dealing with. For the Spanish speaking countries of South and Central America he had nothing but disdain. Spain itself was primitive, he thought; Portugal was only slightly more advanced, if only because of its language. In a more abstract way he admired the U.S. and England, but his dream was to move to a tropical island where he could lie in the sun and ride the surf all day.

For my health Ivan proved to be very useful. He insisted that we spend three or four hours a day doing North American sports. I taught him about baseball and our kind of football from what I remembered from school days. Before long, Braulio ordered the finest baseball outfits and equipment from Rio, and we had to enroll Boris and Roberto in our games, and soon we were joined by other household hands on their time off. I also taught Ivan how to jog and then to run, which he took to immediately. We staked out a track that ran through all the paths of the estate, followed along that fearsome fence, eventually becoming a course about two miles long. We began running it several times a day, which helped me survive my forced inactivity and the three heavy meals I consumed each day.

Some days after the dinner with Rose and Yih, Ivan took me to the kitchens of the mansion. There we witnessed an amazing diversity of activities all in preparation for the great dinner. The kitchen was an enormous room with great stoves cooking and fires burning. People were stirring, rolling, tasting, peeling, scraping, kneading, chopping, pounding, and talking at the top of their voices, so that the whole turmoil made my ears ring for hours. I met Severina, the cook, an ancient black walleyed woman with a voice like a man's and the hair on her head sticking out in every direction.

"I keep the guests in this house healthy by feeding them wholesome foods," she said, her eyes moving around the room. "All of the organs in your body need a different substance . . . all is provided by nature . . . nothing by man. Only woman can make the sauces and stews necessary for long life and many afterlives, keep devils away. You eat my food, you are strong and fruitful, and you make many wives happy and shoot arrows straight. You drink strong wine, you talk with God and his saints, you be virtuous and pious. Here, you know what this is?"

She pronounced an African word I didn't catch and showed us on a table a pile of what looked like fine, transparent leaves with reddish veins, about a half an inch long. From what I could see lying on the floor, I presumed that these were cockroach wings painfully separated by hand from the bodies.

"These go in sauces. Here, smell them! They make you potent and keep fungus from your feet. The rest," she said pointing to the bodies, "they go in marinade with red vinegar and garlic and plenty of herbs to make hot sauce. Oh, I forgot to add bat wings! Boil so long they get sticky and nobody knows what they are. Here meat," she said pointing to about forty skinned monkeys, all seated on a table as if waiting for the next step in their own preparation. "They ready. Now you help, too." She gestured to us to throw the animals into an enormous iron pot simmering over a fire. "They come in yesterday from north, sent by Manao people. Very good ones. Tasty. Now we add flour from goat horn," she said throwing handfuls of an ochre powder. "That good for head, keep you think straight and see sharp." When I looked closely I realized the powder was kept in what looked like a human skull. There were cats walking everywhere on the kitchen floor, eating fallen tidbits. "When stew need body, we throw one or two in," she added, pointing at two cats fighting fiercely over a piece of meat.

After watching and helping for an hour, we learned that the menu was also to include *hormigas culonas*, sent from Colombia along with other items, with a note attached, saying: "*¡Feliz cumpleaños!* Your good friend, Pedro." Boris informed me later that these were "double-assed oversize ants"; they were to be served in a yogurt and mushroom sauce. Also on the menu: suckling pigmy feet (am I translating this right?) flown in by a business associate in Angola and snake steaks rolled into wheels and impaled on long swords for the spit. At one table a burly cook was chopping an assortment of bloody objects: hearts, kidneys, liver, tongue, sweetbreads, brain. Another butcher was pounding at a kind of yellow terry cloth towel to make it thin; this turned out to be boiled stomach lining. Finally, waiting to be sliced were avocado-shaped objects and stiff skins in a bushel basket on the floor ("bull's balls and scrota," according to Boris). The ingredients were to be boiled, fried, steamed, broiled, or baked and turned into "delicious broths, sauces, terrines, and hors d'oeuvres," as Ivan explained.

On a large table nearby quantities of bones and entrails of chicken had been neatly piled at one end; rooster heads with eyes and beaks wide open were in a heap at the other. In between were piles of feet and claws, then dark and white meat, along with the gizzards, livers, intestines, and various other glands and organs. The feathers were stuffed into canvas bags under the table. "Use everything! No waste. When meat too tough to eat, we make broth for soup and sauces. These," she said, pointing to the gizzard and liver, "go in pâté. Those," now pointing to a large bowl of testicles, "make tasty salad, with nuts and fruit." The next table bore a similar display of vital parts taken from tropical birds, except that here the large colorful feathers, beaks, and claws had been laid out and groomed with care for table decoration.

At the fish table three cooks were in the process of removing the skin and bones of large fish with ugly eyes and fierce looking teeth, but somehow leaving the heads intact and connected to the filets. Other species of saltwater beasts were waiting their turn: rays, squid, eels, lobsters and crabs (flown in from Bahia), and others I hadn't seen before. Behind them all sat a grim-looking octopus, staring blankly at the activity, his eight arms lying limply at his side.

"The more seafood you eat, the faster you go to heaven. It's all part of the Savior, and brings blessings from the spirits of the sea, and special protection from Yemanjá against devils," she said, crossing herself. Then, lighting a large cigar, she smiled at us. "When this party all over, you come to my room; we make offerings and you can talk to your ancestors. My old mother a good medium."

Before leaving the kitchen we passed a table filled with small furry creatures. Ivan explained that the dessert was the masterpiece of the dinner: *rato açucarado,* or sugared albino mice with feet and ears dipped in gold.

Outside the kitchen, I felt sweaty and somewhat nauseated; I needed a good fast run.

"What is the occasion for this gala event?" I asked Ivan.

"Papa's fiftieth birthday, and the glorious future of Braulio's Brazil!" It wasn't clear if he was joking or serious.

"Let me show you something else," Ivan said mysteriously as he led me down a number of darkly lit stairs. Down below the air was dank and chilled; I suspected we were headed for the wine cellars. Whatever was beyond a big door was certainly well guarded, for two brutes greeted us with automatic weapons and kept us covered until they recognized Ivan, then they apologized profusely while still eyeing me with suspicion. We entered, followed by a guard, into an eerily lighted room where bins of all sizes were on the floor. In each one there was an assortment of stones. From the labels on the bins I could see that they were diamonds, opals, rubies, emeralds, crystals, and the like. Each stone had a label taped to it giving some kind of description.

"These are our family jewels," Ivan explained. "They are useful in an election . . . or a revolution. Maybe these are even more useful," he added pointing to wooden cases of rifles, machine guns, and ammunition at the other end of the room. He then led me into a larger room which was permeated by a sickeningly rich smell. "The real wealth is here;" he pointed to packages wrapped in butcher paper, piled carefully about three feet high on flats. He took one in his hands, opened the wrapping, and showed me a white powder pressed into a kind of brick. "With what you see here you could buy Rio, all of it, including the Sugar Loaf. When God created the coca bush I don't know what He was thinking; His omniscience must have been taking a siesta. Sin isn't half as dangerous as this stuff."

In the late afternoon when we returned to my quarters, Boris greeted us dressed in the most elaborate ruffled shirt, bow tie, and tuxedo, holding a martini.

"Quick! Shower and get dressed! We must be ready to vicariously celebrate Braulio's august fiftieth birthday. Ivan! They have been calling for you!"

"This is going to be the greatest ball of the century," Boris told me as we rushed down the hidden corridors and up narrow stairs into a kind of tower from which we could make out the main approaches to the mansion. On the cobblestone driveway large limousines were already coming in, waiting while others ahead of them paused at the stairway and relieved themselves of their contents to the sound of a hoarse loudspeaker, announcing the identities of the new arrivals.

"The Duke and Duchess Alfredo di Gaetano de Maaz-Salém, of Coimbra, skishzzt, skishzzt, skishzztrchzh." The announcer was waving his microphone up and down during and after every arrival, which produced a shriek of static and more than half of the identifying clauses he provided about the guests were lost.

"Look at that one!" Boris exclaimed, pulling my sleeve. "She must be the fattest marquise on earth who can still navigate for herself!" According to our announcer this was Sra. Gertrude d'Amurá, who was "in the company of General Skisschzt de Monoschizzcht . . ."

"Ambassador and Sra. Rodolfo de Nutrias, of Chile, skoechz skoechzt." They were both extremely tall, smiling self-consciously as they greeted a crowd of servants and lackeys who offered to accompany them into the grand hall.

Another limousine approached. "Sr. skrischt skrischt, . . . sul General of Suriname!" An enormously long Cadillac drove up. "Meesteer and Meesees schgothe schgothe, of Meeneeopolees, skjaeld skjaeld." Could these be my compatriots down there, bowing, smiling, and shaking hands? Then, loudly announced, from within the same limousine came the United States consul general and the cultural attaché in Rio with their wives, obviously pleased to have been invited.

"Any way of getting to these people?" I asked Boris. "I could sure use some of their influence to get out of this place."

"Better not try," he answered. "If you want to get sprung, Ivan is your best bet. We'll talk about that later."

"Señor y Señora Rafael Santos Anatula, skdrght skdrgt."

"They are from Argentina; they left when the generals started losing their influence. They are frequent visitors; he advises Braulio on monetary matters, and Señora makes suggestions about interior decoration. I think she sleeps with him, although Ivan vehemently denies this."

From our perch I could see Señor Anatula shaking hands with the Minnesotan, who then introduces him to the cultural attaché. They all chat, amicably. Cocktail party small talk, from the looks of it.

The next guest to issue forth from a long chauffeur-driven limousine was "Senhor Marlan Guava, the rising star of country muskcrgt!" He was wearing a black cowboy hat, which he removed with a flourish to bow to the people cheering his arrival.

When the next limousine drove up, the announcer screamed in excitement; then he clapped his hands still holding on to the wounded microphone which produced a series of thunderclaps that made us hold our ears. The person so-announced made his way through the crowd of guests with the help of husky bodyguards.

"In case you don't recognize him," Boris informed me, "that's Bicho, the hottest soccer player since Pelé. A national hero, or rather, institution. Braulio is playing high stakes tonight."

After that everything was anticlimactic. A bishop, surrounded by young priests. Portly military officers with their chests covered by medals and an endless number of political bigwigs.

There was some commotion behind us. Roberto, Rose, and Yih entered, with another woman. "Tonight my services are not required down there at the party," Roberto said with exultation. "Just as well; I need time to relax before my trip, and I can enjoy your company. Shall we eat?" he added, turning to the third woman, whom he introduces to me as "a good friend," his right hand resting resolutely on her buttocks.

We descended to the room overlooking the main dining hall, where guests were already taking their seats. A table was set for us, and soon waiters brought us a series of soups, terrines, fish and meat courses, salads, desserts, coffees, liqueurs. Roberto's friend, whose name I learned was Lispeth, identified all the different dishes in Portuguese and tried to find English equivalents for me. My appetite gradually returned as she described the shrimp-eating *peixe* from the Amazon that we had before us and told how the sauce was prepared with sweet onion marmalade, mango, papaya, and herbs.

"And the oil that makes it a true Bahia treat," Rose broke in, referring to *tendé* made from palm oil. "This is authentic cuisine; you can tell by looking at Severina: she's so black and old, and she can't read a word, which means that the recipe didn't come from some book. When I taste just a tiny bit of fish meat dipped in sauce on the tip of my tongue, it takes me back ten years to the time when I would dress all in white and take food and trinkets to the beach at night to lay them on the sand for Yemanjá.

Sometimes it brings back the smell of the water on the stone pavement and walls of the church I used to scrub with my grandmother."

"And then you are going to tell us all about the rest of your regional food and the *farinha de mandioca* you always talk about but nobody in his right mind can eat!"

"You don't believe in anything, Boris, and you grow impatient when a woman speaks. But it is women like us who save the world, including you, from the devils who play tricks to destroy it! This year I will go back to Bahia for the fiesta of Our Lord of Bomfin, and I will pray to the blessed Virgin and to Oxalá to preserve you from evil influences. I may even go through the initiation ceremony, dance, sing, beat drums, and receive the blood of the white goat over my shaven and wounded head to become a *filha de santo*. Then I will know the secrets and be able to cook for the saints, and all my prayers for my friends will be heard."

We finished eating and moved to the window where we could observe the ceremonies outside. The guests were standing in front of a raised dais where musicians were gathering. Then Braulio came to the microphone, followed by Ivan and some dignitaries. I missed the beginning of his harangue while I listened to Rose reminisce further about her childhood, happy to have found a sympathetic pair of ears. After a while it became apparent that Braulio was making a serious speech, one with political import.

". . . and you will witness the utter destruction of our homeland, the beautiful and bountiful land of Brazil. Do not neglect to notice that in my speech I do not include the word republic, that blasphemy! For the destruction and the blasphemy are the same. They are the work of the devil, they are the conspiracy of ignorance. My friends! This land continues to suffer the cold winds from the North, bringing with them the brittle realities of a people with no soul. We have lost our natural resources, we have lost our riches, and of that I must speak. We are in deep debt to the North; our governments, both military and civilian, have kneeled and pleaded before the evil god Mammon and borrowed heavily from the North. We have only our soul left, and now is the moment to prevent our government from selling that, our only remaining treasure, to the North." He paused meaningfully before he said "the North" and each time pitched his voice higher, bringing a thundering round of applause.

"There are few truths remaining in this modern world, but these truths will make us strong and bring power back to us. They tell us that God exists and that the Brazilian people, black and white and native, fear God and love each other. And these same people will demand that the North wind cease and that God return to his favorite land of the rivers. And God will return in the form of his heavenly appointed emissary, his earthly emanation, a king to rule in His name.

"It is my mission, my friends, to promote a new regime, namely, the return of the old kingdom of Brazil. My wealth, my radio and TV stations, my son, and my life will all be devoted to the realization of this ideal. I am happy to announce the creation of new radio and television programs to be aired over all Brazil. They will tell the heartfelt story of a poor woman and her large family and their struggle to survive in a republic that is set to destroy them. Another program will follow, an historical narrative of the old, royal Brazil and its glories . . ." Braulio droned on and on.

Yih came behind me and put her hand gently on my arm. "What's wrong with girls in short skirts, Hank? If they are beautiful and healthy and you are healthy, too . . . Don't ask too much." She smiled, and added: "Come to my room tonight. Ivan will tell you how to find it. Then you will feel better."

"Come and look now!" Rose shrieked. The speeches had ended and the orchestra members were taking their places. When all was ready and the crowd had quieted down, they began to perform music that after a while I recognized as Villa-Lobos's Bachianas Brasileiras. I felt like a silent observer, aware only of the movement of the music like waves breaking on the pebbled shore of the Bay of Sepetiba.

The same musicians, after acknowledging the applause, struck up a series of waltzes of Strauss and Waldteufel, and with that the audience began to talk louder and to mill around in the growing darkness. At the same time other musicians, placed strategically in gazebos and dressed in garish costumes, started enthusiastically playing popular music while singers and guitarists dressed like minstrels wandered up and down the paths.

Ivan came up to our room, looking exhausted but happy to have been able to escape the formalities and festivities going on below. Rose and Lispeth smiled radiantly as they started to dance sambas and afoxés to the sound of the closest group of musicians. At one point they grew so excited they lifted Ivan bodily onto the table and, kicking the dishes and table settings to the floor, engaged with him in a quick set of complex steps, their high heels and tight short skirts making the whole display appear somewhat crazy.

"Don't miss this, Hank!" Boris whispered, pulling me over to the window where I could see better. "It's quite a sight. Look!"

He pointed toward two rows of young girls wearing loose gowns, their hair festooned with white blossoms. They were holding lighted candles and baskets of flower petals which they scattered around the lawn and on the paths all the while dancing in rhythm to the music played by one of the bands. When they arrived at the edge of the large swimming pool, which was decorated with what looked like Christmas lights, they sang a series of verses as they swayed and threw the rest of the petals onto the surface of the water. Then they slipped off their gowns and dived into the water, where they proceeded to perform a kind of water ballet to the sound of a slow, melodious song played by three accordions standing by the edge of the pool. When they finished, they came slowly out of the pool, put their flimsy gowns back on their wet, naked bodies, and mixed with the crowd to shake hands and receive recognition for their artistry.

"Isn't that great?" Boris asked. "They belong to the pre-professional swim team from Rio de Janeiro. They are only thirteen or fourteen years old, and you will probably see them at the Olympic games in a couple of years; only then they will be wearing swimsuits. Braulio is one of their sponsors. Now watch this. It is a *capoeira* display. They are about ready to start. You can't figure out if they are dancing or just about to kill each other." Two men, dressed in slacks and barefooted, came out on the raised platform, and after a long series of ritual preparations and songs sung by the bystanders to the beat of percussion instruments, started to shout and kick each other with such ferocity that I expected the platform to cave in. Yet during the bout, the performers showed no anger; they even seemed to smile with civility to one another.

Soon Boris, Roberto, and I were dragged into the dancing fray. Lispeth was by now bare-breasted and her skirt was split so high that she could accomplish the most acrobatic steps without any impediment. I was sweating so profusely that I removed my shirt soon after Boris and Roberto had; we were barefoot and made a great racket slamming our feet on the floor to the ever returning beat from the band outside. We often paused to have a sweet iced-fruit drink whose alcoholic content seemed to me to increase with each swallow. I don't know how long it was before I passed out, from sheer exhaustion or alcohol. The last thing I remember was when Rose reached down to remove her underwear to be able, she claimed, to move more freely. I had intended to watch the results, but there my recollections end.

After some time I felt Ivan pouring cold water over my face and telling me to wake up. It was early morning and servants were clearing the room; the festivities were continuing outside, but they were much more subdued.

"Come! Wake up! Everybody is gone, they are in bed. Yih sent me to show you how to go to her room. Do you really want to go?"

"Ivan! Tell her I died. Help me to my own room instead. Take her a flower if you can find one."

IT TOOK ME a day to come back to life. Then after that a routine of running, swimming, getting enough sleep, and eating sensibly, as health experts like to say, set me on the road to feeling better physically and more optimistic. After all, I may be a prisoner, but I am enjoying the privileges of the well-off, and I can't say that I am suffering any real inconvenience or pain. I am certainly safer here than I had been in the middle of nowhere a month ago. I am enjoying friendship, too. Roberto spends hours in the evening questioning me about everyday life in the States, and his way of viewing issues and problems often catch me up short. He has a way of remembering what I said earlier and bringing it up again when something I say later is in contradiction to it. He does it not to be nasty but rather to understand a culture that doesn't always make sense to an outsider. It makes me reconsider many assumptions I have accepted for years without scrutiny.

Rose, Yih, and Lispeth often join us for dinner and then spend the evening with us. I never found out where they live or how they make it safely into and out of Braulio's castle. But they bring news from the outside world and can be depended on to express a considered opinion about popular actors and singers or the latest fashion in swimwear. They also know a lot about sports, especially current soccer games and the private lives of the best players. Boris is always entertaining and informative. He constantly dreams up schemes for me to escape, only to give up on each one because it is too dangerous or has little chance of succeeding. But it is Ivan who is the most dedicated to making my sojourn in this place tolerable. Whenever he is free he makes his way to our quarters to propose a run, a swim, or a game of some sort. Sometimes he hangs around reading magazines or listening to Boris's radio. On occasion when Ivan and I sit around the edge of the pool after a swim, he starts to talk about his life.

"You know, Hank, I don't know who my mother was," he told me one day. "There are a number of portraits of women in the great hall, and I used to spend hours looking at them, wondering which of those handsome women provided the thighs I came through to see the light of day. They all stand so straight and have such rigid expressions on their faces, you wonder how any of them could have taken the time to squat down and spread their legs for a little runt to come out. Then I found out that they all died about fifty years ago and that my mother wasn't among those portraits. So I kept looking. My father frowns so fiercely whenever I talk about her that I have given up asking. I do know that one of his wives went mad. She was in her twenties when he locked her up in one of those towers, that one over there to the right. Severina's sister Costa was supposed to tend to her and calm her whenever she started shouting. She was the only servant in the house who could go into the tower; if any other person got close the madwoman would scream bloody murder and try to jump through the bars that cover the windows—you can see they are still there. Nobody saw her until she died, and after that, according to Costa, she started to wander through the building dressed in a flimsy nightgown and visit all the rooms, looking for my father. Many guests saw her walking barefoot down the corridors, several inches above the floor and singing a song about little animals who are helpless and die for lack of love. Do you think she was my mother, Hank? Will I go mad like that one day? My father finally had a *mãe de santo* come from Bahia to exorcise her spirit, and she hasn't been seen around here since. Sometimes I get up and sneak around the halls at night hoping to catch a glimpse of her and ask her if she gave birth to me. Costa says the mad woman died long before I was born and that my real mother was a mulatta from Pernambuco, someone from a family of rich farmers. That one was lucky; she got out somehow, leaving her dowry, her belongings, and her son behind, if you can believe Costa. She couldn't go back to her family in disgrace, so she went to São Paulo and became an exotic dancer."

"I wonder how she escaped."

"Father didn't have the elaborate security system in those days. One could actually walk away into the surrounding woods or streets. Did I show you the dungeons down below? You remember where we saw the guns and the diamonds? Well on the floor below that one there are some dingy cells where years ago the unfortunate enemies of the family languished in chains while rats gnawed at their feet. I used to play down there when I was a kid, pretending to be some kind of political prisoner, musketeer, or prince in a dragon's castle."

"Were there any real prisoners there? I suppose those cells could still serve some purpose. I'm glad your father has a more civilized way of treating his prisoners," I said, feeling uneasy.

"No one has been locked up there for as long as I have been around. But back to the question of who my mother is. Here is another idea. Tell me what you think, Hank. My father has what you would call a handicap, but the kind no one notices. I know, because I used to peek through the key hole while he was bathing. He has a bent penis. No kidding! I looked it up in the medical dictionary, and it's called Peyronie's disease. Father's penis is fairly long, but somewhere on its way to the end it takes a 90° detour to the right, that is, to the left for him. You can imagine the inconvenience. I guess that is why women don't remain long in his company. All of his wives seem to have left soon after their wedding, and he doesn't have a mistress. And to think that, with all his pompous talk of Brazil's mission in the world, he can't even get a good screw! Just an erection brings him the most excruciating pain. He had all the witch doctors in Brazil come in order to straighten him out, but nothing helped. Except that one, who was also a witch veterinarian, told him that if he wanted a decent sex life he should buy a mare from the region of Rio Branco. Their intestine takes a left turn just the right distance in. A young mare could gratify him for years, according to this expert. Hank! Could my mother have been a mare from the region of Rio Branco? Look at me! That would explain why I'm so weird. It's for sure I'm not a mulatto but a *mulo!*"

"Oh! Ivan. Shut up and let's swim."

I was astounded the next morning to see Braulio at the door of my quarters asking for me. He suggested we get together for breakfast in a half hour in the large gazebo next to the pool.

Since our first interview I had only seen him from a distance, usually from a window as he walked in a garden lane below. Once I caught a glimpse of him making his way down a corridor with a covey of attendants or guests following and listening to his words. Of course I had heard plenty about him from Boris, Ivan, and even Roberto. But now I was going to talk with him personally. Right away I felt nervous, knowing that it would be an opportunity to confront him about my status, which was not visibly progressing in any particular direction. Perhaps he had news for me. Could he be ready to release me? I had no idea what was to happen between us, but I somehow sensed that it was my turn to act.

He was already sitting at a white cast-iron table in front of all sorts of delicacies: fruits and juices of various colors and kinds, breads, cakes, a complicated coffee maker, and several bouquets of flowers attracting fierce bumble bees that buzzed incessantly in our vicinity. Roberto's father was seated at his side, content, it would seem, to be outside with the morning sun shining on the pale skin of his aged face. The monkey and dogs were at Braulio's side, begging for food.

"Come, Hank! Let us enjoy a bit of time together. You, who have nothing to do, and I, overcome with concerns and responsibilities, have this in common: time hangs heavily on our shoulders. But we shall not let that separate us, nor will we permit our destinies to draw us too far apart before we enjoy the opportunity of knowing each other. My friend Rigoberto and I were just talking about you, hoping you would come soon to help us devour this fine guava jelly, sent to us recently by a business associate who is traveling in Haiti. Tell me, Hank, how are you enjoying your stay?"

Spreading this famous jelly on some dark bread and waiting for my coffee to be poured gave me a few moments to find an answer to a question loaded with dynamite. I opted for honesty.

"I can't think of a more pleasant way of being held captive."

"I am relieved that you have no illusions about your situation."

"Actually, I can't remember ever benefiting from such generous hospitality. Friends and relatives have put me up for extended periods of time; they have fed and entertained me, but never have I encountered luxury to this extent." I can't believe I actually talked this way; his pomposity was downright contagious.

"But time is moving slowly, and you are anxious to return to your wife and to the exciting life in Rio de Janeiro. I would feel the same way if I were in your shoes. And you can believe that I am doing my very best to expedite the long and complicated process involved in releasing you."

"What is there to prevent you from letting me go right now? I still do not understand why I am here."

"Rigoberto. Please explain to this impatient young man the reasons for which he is taking this extended vacation. You understand these matters better than I do, your mind is more attuned to the legal complexities involved."

Sr. Rigoberto is apparently Braulio's second-in-command, at least in so far as the daily operation of the residence is concerned. What his role is in the overall political negotiations and financial deals for Braulio's campaign for the return of the monarchy is anybody's guess. He is a kind of chief of staff, a glorified secretary and right-hand henchman. At the moment I was glad to be counted among his son's friends.

"Sr. Hank should realize," he began, "that his presence among us, although quite pleasurable to all who have had occasion to know him, is not necessarily what we would have chosen, everything being equal."

Christ! I thought. This clown uses even longer sentences than Braulio. I can see that this breakfast will last forever without my being the more enlightened.

"You are here," he continued, "at the request of various governments, including your own and that of Brazil, and at the request of numerous auxiliary units connected to one or the other government but not quite subservient to either one, thus they operate independently and jealously protect their autonomy. My office is in charge of informing each of these interested entities of your presence here and of obtaining their confirmation. We have just about completed this task and expect to hear from the Office of Roads and Paths of the Mato Grosso do Sul any day now. I believe their agents are searching the route you took to be sure you are not in debt to any transportation agent or wanted by a local police officer anywhere for a minor infraction. We cannot be impatient, as this requires time. All correspondence is done by hand, and the mail is most undependable. Sometimes we have to write four or five times before we receive an answer. We are also waiting for confirmation from one of the units of your government, I forget its name, but it has something to do with intelligence. I first thought that meant part of your educational system, but apparently I was mistaken on that count. Ha-ha! But it is true that they are very smart and know everything there is to know; they have all sorts of magical means of storing and collecting information, so we have little to worry about and can expect to hear from them in the immediate future. The next step will be to obtain permission from all these agencies for your release. I believe that since we have established channels of communication, this will happen much more rapidly."

"What can I do to help?"

"At this point, unfortunately nothing. If they were to hear

directly from you, a virtual prisoner, they would become confused and demand all sorts of clarifications from us that we probably could not supply."

"I really don't understand why you, Sr. Braulio, who are in opposition to the present government of this country and not particularly fond of the United States and its influence in Brazil, why you do not simply open your gates, permit me to leave, and let those offices and agencies deal with the matter themselves."

"But, my dear young man, you have no understanding of the intricacies of diplomacy in the modern world. Before the revolutions which changed everything, I would either have released you or had you hanged. But now I must negotiate with my enemies. There is one aspect of this situation that is definitely to your advantage, and I will tell you about it so that you value it properly. What speaks in your favor is your friendship with my son. Ivan tells me of your kindness and many virtues, and this more than anything else makes me well disposed toward you and wish for your ultimate release into freedom."

"Yes, I enjoy Ivan's company and see no reason why our friendship can't continue after I am set free. I will certainly invite him one day to be my guest in the States and help him realize his ambition of going to Disneyland."

"Speaking of visiting the United States," Braulio went on, "let me tell you some of my adventures when I was a student in California."

If it helps me get me out of here, I'm willing to listen as long as he wants to talk, I thought.

"You should know that all my life I have desired a military career. As I grew up, my games were wars and battles. I stormed this castle many times before I was twelve," he said waving his hand toward his home. "These grounds were the scene of innumerable campaigns as I led my invisible troops to victory along the paths and behind shrubs. I was Alexander the Great, Hannibal, Napoleon, and the great Portuguese generals. All my battles I won in less than half an hour. So it was with great anticipation that I enrolled at the military school in Pôrto Alegre and submitted to the required physical examination. My tragic destiny had it written that I would be turned down, rejected, thrown back to receive the ridicule of my friends, relatives, and enemies."

He fell silent and looked dejectedly at the ground before starting up again.

"At the time many of my cohorts were going abroad to continue their education. Some went to Oxford, others to Cambridge, Paris, Heidelberg. One even went to Harvard and later studied at M.I.T. The less fortunate were accepted at state colleges or normal schools in various locations. Since I had no academic pretensions of any sort, I settled for a public university in Northern California nobody had ever heard of and which was called, if I remember correctly, University of Davis, or something close to that. By proposing to study military 'science' (that sounds demanding academically, but actually it was well within my intellectual ambitions), I received my education without charge and was given book and spending money as well."

He paused again, inviting comments. I felt it incumbent on me to say something.

"I know that area, having been through there a couple of times. Isn't it somewhere near San Francisco?"

"Exactly, but away from the coast, toward the middle of a dry valley where you can smell tomatoes in the night air throughout summer."

"From what I've heard, the school has a good reputation in several areas," I said, thinking to gain his approval.

"Perhaps. But when I was there, before Ivan was born, it was a spot on the map, a farm town broiling in the hot sun. It was a strange place. You couldn't buy a drink or even wine there. When you left the town every road led into an empty field. It was situated on a dammed-up creek, dry most of the year, with an unbelievable name that my throat refuses to pronounce in Portuguese. It was called Putah Creek, and my Spanish-speaking colleagues called

it *Arroyo de las Putas*! There was nothing to do and since my
studies made little or no demand on my time, I tried to obtain a
job teaching in the foreign language department. Can you believe
that they taught no Portuguese at that university? The buffoon
who was in charge of the Spanish section told me in all seriousness
that Portugal and Brazil had such a limited scope of literary
expression and so few literary masterpieces in comparison with
Spain and what he called Hispanic America that it was not in the
best interests of the students or the community to spend their
limited funds to teach a language no one needed. I assure you
that I was strongly tempted to strangle him right there in his
office. Perhaps he saw violence flash in my eyes, or perhaps he
feared my connections with the campus military faction; in any
event, he arranged for me to teach a class in beginning Portuguese
and to be paid for my efforts. What heroic efforts they were! You
are undoubtedly aware of the type of student one encounters in a
North American college. To begin with, they were all girls, with
the exception of one, who may have been anatomically male.
These creatures (how should I call them?) were well scrubbed
and well fed; I had the distinct impression that after being groomed
they were being sent to the market to be chosen and bought by
some football-playing stud. In the meantime they were expected
to become educated, to store knowledge behind their plump
cheeks, blue eyes, and engaging smiles. It was pleasant enough
for me to address this group of beauties, to instruct them how to
form their mouths and make their lips round in order to pronounce
our vowels and consonants properly. But I was well aware that I
couldn't touch any of them or the secret police of *Señor el Jefe* of
the Spanish Department would have me deported or charged
with infamy. But you will have to take my word of honor that I
had not the slightest inclination to touch any one of them. Why?
Because every day of the week I had to listen to these young
mouths produce gruesome imitations of the phonemes of our
beautiful language, like hammers beating a waltz on rusty anvils.
Never have I been so aware of the threat of U.S.A. imperialism

with regard to other cultures as I was when I heard our vowels chewed and spat to the floor by those bubble gum-chewing jaws. You do not realize, Hank, you who, if you do not speak Portuguese perfectly, at least you respect it, you do not realize, I repeat, what an aggressive weapon of war a North American English accent is to sensitive ears. It is also a perfect non-military defense against foreign encroachment."

"That is an interesting linguistic theory," I threw in, "and it may be right."

"Fortunately we have found more efficient ways of attacking the imperialistic giant, of taking revenge for the destruction of third-world economies and the subversion of our cultures. We have discovered the inner appetite for corruption and violence in your cities and we feed it with our secret weapon: cocaine. It is no less dangerous than Coca-Cola or the greedy face of an entrepreneur or the bayonet of a Marine, but it is less ugly, until of course it is unleashed on your streets."

"What other ways might there be to resist the takeover of Brazil that you speak of? You seem to want to avoid war. Why not avoid killing, too? I am acquainted with killing, and I know there is no beauty there."

"You do not understand my emphasis. It is no business of mine if someone far away wants to commit suicide. That is his business, but it is business none the less. I was in the U.S.A. long enough to learn that business is everything, that what counts is the bottom line—in my country such an expression could only be used to make a crude joke. I also learned about market economy, free trade, supply and demand, in short, all the virtues of free enterprise, which used to be called capitalism. I have accepted those values and exercise them with an easy conscience. One does not ask why a population needs Fords, one just supplies the vehicles, and the craving for them increases mysteriously. The United States craves narcotics; I supply them, transport them, and I am paid for providing a necessary commodity. It is all done according to the sacred principles of free trade: no country collects taxes to cause unfair competition, no export or import duties are extracted. If anything, your country encourages our drug trade by raiding and burning its own home-grown product, but that is not my concern. My job is to oversee a well-run operation. A few of my agents are caught and shot: one of the risks of business. Worse things happen to your executives when they lose their jobs, become depressed, and take their own lives.

"I am also a shipping agent. Deciding how to get the drug to your shores and beyond is the most interesting of my activities. The trick is in the disguise. How to make coca paste look like something else to eyes that are not too inquisitive is what Sr. Rigoberto and I spend hours devising. For a while we shipped it with coffee; when that was discovered, we made it look like bananas. You need a crew of well-trained artists in this line. Psychologists, too. They are the ones who use persuasion to create new personnel for us, mainly from among the agents who were sent here to seek us out and destroy us. C.I.A. pilots come in handy, as do D.E.A. career people.

"Hank!" he interrupted himself to exclaim. "What a fine agent you could be for us! Your innocence would be the most marvelous disguise. You could do well in your own country what you did so poorly here in Brazil. At another time I will describe to you the wonderful opportunities you are missing by subscribing to outmoded moral principles."

"Would it help me go free?"

"Yes, but it will take me some time to gain trust in you, as is the case with Boris. At present I feel you are too impatient. But we can discuss this more at another occasion. We do have work to do, Rigoberto and I. Furthermore, I believe a young man is eagerly awaiting you."

"What was that all about?" Ivan asked, joining me from behind a shrub as I walked back to my room.

We spent most of the day together, running, swimming, talking. In the late afternoon, after he had paged through the rest of Boris's magazines, tearing out pictures and articles, and while I was still at work setting down details of the morning's meeting, Ivan looked at me for a long time with a kind of searching, sad gaze.

"You must feel caged-in here, waiting to go back to the world and do your thing. But think how long I have been trapped! As far back as I can remember my life has consisted of wandering among these rooms and corridors, between the walls that you have only known for a couple of months. The only other places I have been were exclusive schools, in Rio and São Paulo, but they were real prisons! The teachers and administrators were like guards and wardens, whose main function was to keep me on leash. The other students had a chance to escape through a window from time to time; they would go to a movie, look at girls, or just feel free walking in the streets, knowing they would only be reprimanded when they returned. I was different; at my father's insistence there was always a tutor or a special companion who kept me in sight, away from the windows. The other students could at least daydream or masturbate when they were alone, but privacy was not among my rights. When I did manage one day to duck out in the rest room of a São Paulo zoo, I was picked up, after a few hours of wandering in the streets, by a secret police agent who returned me here. Those few hours are my most cherished memory; whenever I'm sad I can take that São Paulo walk in my head and relive each street I crossed and each building I saw. I'm also a prisoner here, except when the helicopter takes me to my private lessons. The pilot is a real brute, and my security guard, as he is called, is always with me, during class, at meals, in the bathroom. By now he has learned volumes about the history of Brazil, and he knows exactly how I piss and shit."

I told Ivan how much I was looking forward to being free again, seeing more of Brazil, and returning to the United States. And as he kept on looking at me with his sad eyes, I added what I had told his father, that Deb and I would certainly invite him to visit us when we settled down somewhere. This seemed to cheer him up a little, and at dinner he was the one who got drunk.

Boris and I took him back to our quarters where we set him on the couch to sleep it off. After a long cool drink of *cachaça* in some tropical fruit juice, the two of us turned in.

I was awakened in the middle of the night and found Ivan sitting beside me on my bed with his hand caressing my brow.

"Are you awake? I have to tell you something else, Hank. Can I? Well it's that things have gotten better. When Boris came last year there was something to do. Before that father's prisoners had always been thugs or wrinkled intellectuals, most of them mad. Boris was young and eager to do things, and we hit it off. But still, he always stayed at a distance; he was more interested in what he was doing than anything else. And all he seems to think about is screwing women, as if there weren't anything else worth doing. Then you came, and that changed everything for me. You were willing to do stuff that was fun for us both. It was sort of like when I escaped into the streets of São Paulo, and everything opened up and I felt free. I think visiting you in the States would be super, but I wonder if it will ever happen, if you will ever return there to be able to invite me, if I will ever get to be away from this arsenal. When I remember that nothing ever happens the way I want it to happen, I start to give up hope. Is there a reason to hope, Hank? Say there is!"

All this was beginning to make me feel uneasy. I was moved by this poor kid's story and by his willingness to confide in me. Yet he seemed rather too dependent on me, on my being and remaining in this mansion to be his in-house liberator. And as I set all this down in writing I am aware that I was blind to what he was driving at, to what was about to happen.

"Ivan! I hope a lot and always have. Life can be a bitch, as you have learned over and over. I have found that hoping and working can tame it. Here's what happened to me. See what you think." I told him about my brother's death and how that had nearly destroyed me. Then I went on to explain how I kept busy and interested in what I was doing and how eventually I met Deb, who brought light back into my night. When I had finished he was weeping and exclaimed how beautiful it was that I had loved a young man so deeply. It seemed that he had only heard the first half of my story.

"Look! Hank," he went on. "There is a way we can both get away from this dungeon now, without waiting. If you and I went together somewhere, my father would probably approve, maybe even enthusiastically, as long as it was safe for me. Like we could go to one of the little islands he owns off the Atlantic coast, a real tropical paradise with a few natives living in huts and palm trees swaying in the breeze. We could walk on the beach all afternoon, swim nude in the surf, and then go back to our own little hut. That is something we can hope for, can't we?"

With this he fell on me, still weeping silently, and began to kiss me on the cheeks and mouth. I realized he wanted something from me that was not in me to give. As I felt Ivan's tears and breath on my face, I took him by the shoulders and pushed him gently away.

"Ivan, hold on to your hope to go to a deserted island with someone, but it won't be with me. I have one goal, and that is to leave this house in safety and to return to my wife. I long for her every day and night."

As I said this he backed away, his face without expression, his eyes somehow lifeless. He turned and left my room.

I_N THE MIDDLE of the next morning, Boris was unexpectedly summoned. I had lunch alone, and immediately after I had finished a lackey came to my room and handed me a note. It read:

"The agency of your government has just answered my request for instructions. They say only this, that they 'have no record' of you. That being the case, I have no choices left. Braulio."

Three armed men in military uniform entered, greeted me, told me to gather what personal belongings I wished to take with me and led me away. They took me to the empty room in which I was deposited when I first came here. My original clothes—worn shorts and boots, a shirt, a sun hat, and an empty knapsack, were waiting for me. One of the guards watched while I removed the clothes I had been wearing at Braulio's and put on my old duds.

"What is going to happen now?"

"A ride."

"Where to?"

"In an airplane."

"To Rio?"

"No."

"Where, then?"

"Don't know."

The guard stood there as if waiting for something.

"Please call Ivan. I need to talk to him."

"Gone."

"Roberto, then."

"Gone too. Everybody gone. No more asking."

At that the other two guards came in, carrying what possessions I had brought with me, including this diary and my wallet.

"Put what you want to take along in this," the first guard said, pointing to my knapsack. "Nothing else goes."

The guards saluted and left, locking the door from the outside. Although I felt very tired, I quickly checked my possessions. The diary appeared to be all there, along with some extra underwear. Some food had been added, with a note dictated by Severina, saying in hardly recognizable Portuguese that she trusted Oxalá, God, and the saints would accompany me and save me from evil spirits. In one of the sandwiches was hidden a small, sharp kitchen knife.

Before being able to look through the rest of my belongings, I passed out. When I awoke it was night, and I was lying, bound hand and foot, on the floor of an ancient propeller aircraft, with a splitting headache. A guard was snoring next to me with his hand on an assault rifle leaning between his knees. The compartment had no seats; the floor was made of hardwood slats that had felt the scraping of heavy crates. At one end were a number of empty cartons piled in disorder. I passed out again.

When I reopened my eyes, it was daytime. My guard was in the cockpit, talking with the pilot. The propeller engine made so much noise I couldn't hear what the guard was saying. A few of the pilot's words spoken loudly and in a high-pitched voice were audible. He said something between long and repeated curses about getting rid of the cargo before nightfall and fetching the other cargo after another two days. Something was apparently delaying his normal flight pattern.

When my guard saw that I was awake, he came over, untied my hands, warning me not to sit up, and gave me some dry, tasteless food with a can of warm Coca-Cola. After I had finished, I asked:

"Where are you taking me?"

"Shut up!"

At that point the pilot must have told my guard to take over the controls; he approached me and crouched down, talking rapidly in Portuguese.

"Look. We aren't paid to give information. We have a goddam job to do, and there isn't enough time to do it right. Because of you we have to go out of our way, and we may lose thousands. If you want to know where you're going I'll tell you. You are going to be put down in the rain forest with your stuff," he said, pointing to my knapsack and small blanket roll. "You will be alone, and there is no way you can survive more than two days. These are the orders, to make sure you start out alive. The boss has to keep his hands clean. The rest is a foregone conclusion."

"Which rain forest? How far is it to a settlement."

"Too far to do you any good. What's going to happen is you will be chewed up by soldier ants during the day and by mosquitoes at night. Your legs will be covered by ticks you can't remove. You won't find any water or food, unless you like grubs. That's only if some anaconda or jaguar doesn't get you first. If you want to finish faster, try swimming in a puddle or stream; the piranhas and eels will make quick work of you."

"What will it take for you to deliver me somewhere safe. Give me a couple of days; I can raise the money."

"You don't know what you are saying. I'm not known for kindness. I make an honest living flying and obeying orders."

"I mean a lot of money. You could retire, relax."

"You're wasting my time. There's this one thing I'll do for you. Just sign a release, and I'll blow your brains out before dropping you. That way you will save yourself a lot of suffering, and you'll thank me for being charitable. It'll cost you what money you have on you. What do you say?"

"Don't you understand? I've got a wife and an old mother to

take care of. And don't forget the kids, who are probably starving right now if I don't get back to Rio to feed them. One's a cripple. Do you want him to die, too?"

"Too much talk. You missed your chance. Here, Pedro! Tie him up again and shut his mouth."

In a moment I found myself with my hands firmly tied behind my back and with a large tape covering my mouth. Then I must have been struck on the head, perhaps with the butt of Pedro's rifle, for I passed out and when consciousness returned I could feel what I took to be coagulated blood on my cheek.

The rest of the trip seemed endless. I must have lain there for six or more hours, in considerable pain from the blow to my head and the rope around my wrists. It was difficult to breathe, and the smell of the pilot's cigars kept me feeling constantly nauseated. Eventually I started having hallucinations, which came as a relief.

The next thing I remember was a dreadfully bumpy landing, which added to the pain in my head as it was jerked up and down against the floorboards. I was then carried a short distance toward the sound of a helicopter engine. Eventually the noise became deafening, and I felt the wind from the propeller blasting from above. I was thrown in, on the floor, and after the exchange of loud words by unseen men, the aircraft took off.

An ancient model in bad need of repair, it seems, for the mechanism running the propeller gave a loud and persistent clanging thud. Suddenly I realized that I feared the helicopter might crash and I would be killed. I was able to picture in my mind the fiery explosion that would result when we crashed into the ground. Were it not for the tape on my mouth, I would have laughed out loud at this absurd vision. When we landed an hour or so later, I was more relaxed.

Someone dragged me out and then cut me loose. It was light and the heat already seemed unbearable. A man with a knife pointed to another who was aiming an assault rifle at me. I took this to be a hint not to try anything.

"You're lucky it's morning. You'll be around for eighteen hours, maybe. You have water for a day, and there is your crap."

They walked backward into the helicopter, and as they took off, one of them shot several times in a circle in the dust around me.

When the roar of the helicopter had subsided and I could look around, I found I was in a small clearing with enormous trees on each side spreading vegetation so thick that daylight seemed unable to find its way down between the leaves and vines. I picked up my belongings and walked toward the nearest trees, where the shade began. I rested for a while, trying to figure out what to do. I had no sense of direction or time. From the forested area came muffled sounds and echoes, with occasional shrill cries, while the clearing was filled with the sound of insects in the heat of the sun. I inspected my possessions again, feeling in them an affirmation that I was still alive. Two items were new: a plastic container half-filled with water and an unopened can of Coca-Cola, my transporters' contribution to my well-being. Trying the water, I found it cloudy and foul smelling; I decided to save it for later. Severina's lunch with the kitchen knife was still there, rolled in a light blanket and a hammock. In the knapsack, my document case was empty except for the photograph of Deb, a few receipts, and some matches. My diary was intact; no pages had been torn out or even looked at, as far as I could tell. Some dried meat and cans of fish were still there—but the can-opener was gone. I had always believed in traveling light, I thought as I closed the knapsack.

I sat quietly for a few hours. I don't know if I prayed, and if I did, to whom. My mind went into a kind of semiconsciousness. I thought of nothing in particular, although my thoughts did wander, touching ground here and there, floating most of the time in the past or in imaginary realms. The humid heat must have taken me back to summer afternoons in our backyard in Arkansas, in the sandbox with my brother building roads and bridges. The memory of making love with Deb was extraordinarily clear. Occasions were all mixed up, places, too; but the main event was there, whole, and extremely close. Perhaps it was to her that I prayed.

When I came back to consciousness, I felt relaxed and refreshed. After all, I had survived the trek to the Paraguay River, and there was no reason why I shouldn't be as fortunate again, for by now, I thought, I was an experienced explorer. It was time to move on. With my knapsack mounted and secured to my back and a staff selected from among branches lying nearby in my right hand, I started walking. There must be a stream or a path somewhere in that forest, I thought, as I took the direction that looked the coolest.

The undergrowth was not so thick that it prevented me from advancing in the direction I wanted to go. I could make out where the sun was located in the sky and which way it was moving by looking at the reflections on the leaves above me. Occasionally my way was so completely obstructed, I had to go round the obstacle. At times I thought I had found a path, but it soon disappeared into a thicket. My ears were open to any sound that might indicate the presence of moving water, and I soon became used to the constantly changing orchestration of the jungle. There were cries and yelps from the direction I was approaching, and often they appeared to be quite near, but the area I was crossing was always silent. I was drenched with sweat.

I discovered that my matches were useless, having become soggy in the humidity, and that my water was undrinkable. The dried beef was still edible and I was able to hack open a can of tuna with a stone. Even the warm Coke was welcome. Toward evening it started to rain in torrents; I wondered if the rainy season had suddenly come. I took off my clothes and rinsed them in puddles that formed everywhere. Fresh rainwater collecting in large leaves growing near the ground easily provided enough to fill my plastic bottle. After the rain stopped falling, it was difficult if not impossible to walk any distance in the slippery mud. I set about collecting grubs from the trunks of fallen trees. After knocking off the bark all I had to do was pull the wood apart to uncover whole colonies of wiggling white larva-like creatures. They tasted rather sweet yet sickening because they kept on moving in my mouth while I was chewing. Having eaten a few mouthfuls, I discovered I wasn't awfully hungry anyway, but I was convinced that before long I might be able to subsist on a diet of grubs and rainwater. As it became dark I hung my knapsack on a branch, strung my hammock between two tree trunks, wrapped myself in the blanket, and, with my staff next to me, fell deeply asleep.

I awakened to screeching sounds from the treetops above me and to my own shivering from the cold. There were noises in the underbrush nearby, but it was too dark for me to see anything. Then a deep sound that was half growl, half snore, made me shiver more, this time from fear. It seemed to come from quite near. A jaguar, perhaps. But such an animal would have no reason, I thought, to attack a human unless it was starving. I took my staff handle in my hand and remained still. Everything was quiet, and I dozed off. When I awoke again the heat had already set in.

The ground was firm, but there, directly under my hammock were the unmistakable footprints of a large cat. To judge from the prints, it had paused under my knapsack and turned several times under my body before moving on. Had it sniffed me from below and decided to save me for a meal at some later hour? Or was it simply not interested? In any event, I had to get started. After a breakfast of grubs and rainwater, I collected more water from the leaves in the area, secured my load to my back, and started off in the direction the jaguar had taken. If he had a reason for going there, the same reason might hold good for me.

By noon I was already feeling exhausted. I had no appetite, but I was dreadfully thirsty and finished my gallon of water without thinking about how I would replenish my supply. Every half hour I had to stop and take off the ticks that had become attached to the calves of my legs, after stabbing them individually with Severina's knife. During most of the afternoon I forged ahead, not knowing exactly which way I was going; the important thing was to keep moving. It rained again that evening, which offered some relief, and I was able to refill my container. Hanging my hammock and climbing into it were almost insurmountable tasks. I fell asleep with the certainty that I was feverish. Somehow, the thought that I might not make it through the night didn't occur to me. I fell into an unsettled sleep.

Strange noises keep awakening me. Monkeys, perhaps, or birds with green, blue, and white wings and long pink beaks; I can see them clearly in the surrounding darkness. I can also hear the deafening croaking of frogs from a nearby pond; as I approach the pond's edge, the sound suddenly stops, and silence reigns, except for a single, tentative croaking from here and there on the other side. I take a step, this time in complete silence. A light from the other side is reflected on the surface of the water, and with time it grows in intensity but not in brightness. There must be a swarm of mosquitoes swirling around my head, to judge by the sound. I cover my ears with my hands, which are wet with perspiration.

It is now completely dark around me, and I am aware that my breathing is short and difficult. It is not easy to get through the underbrush, which I am clearing with my hands as I walk. The brown leaves are blowing in the gusty wind, and there is the smell of burning leaves. If I can only get to where the smoke is coming from to warn the native. I wonder what language he speaks. A man and a woman are holding rakes and watching the fire. He leans down and removes his black hat in order to blow on the fire. Ah! I know who that is, it's Pastor Bob, and the woman is my mother. She is listening to him as she always does over coffee and cakes while Johnny and I sit and listen in the kitchen. He is talking about the thick vegetation in the Garden of Eden and about how much Adam and Eve enjoy their life there. The vines become more and more thickly intertwined so that I am forced to hack at them with the hatchet, which breaks suddenly, leaving the empty handle in my hand. I am unarmed when I see the anaconda at the edge of the pond, its body half-submerged. It is preparing to strike an animal leaning down on its forepaws to drink. It opens its jaws, exposing pointed teeth and a darting tongue, and if you look carefully you can see a fruit on the ground near the drinking animal. Eve comes up to the animal, pets it gently, points to the danger, and lets it escape. She is naked except for a string around her waist; her dark skin and face are painted with complicated decorations. She takes the fruit and disappears into the jungle in search of Adam and other men who are carrying torches and spears. A loud roar startles me, and I look for the snake, but all I see is a pair of soft brown eyes gazing at me from within a face covered with fur. It walks around my hammock, sniffs me, and then lies down. Everything is quiet again, except for Pastor Bob, who has trouble coming to the end of his sentences, stringing new clauses one after the other, making himself gasp for air. Johnny is egging me on, grinning; I can't hold myself back. But Reverend, don't you remember? In the Bible knowing somebody is naughty, isn't it? Mother can't keep from laughing, and she chases us out. It is pitch dark; I can't tell if my eyes are open or shut. Johnny must be lying on the ground beneath me, there with the big cat. The torches scare them away as they come closer. A big black face, all painted with white and red stripes, is peering, very close by. There are others, too, holding torches and spears. Adam and his friends, looking for the snake. I point to where I last saw it and try to explain that it is dangerous. It must be Braulio's party, with the torches reflecting in the water. Rose is trying to make me drink, and I hold my mouth shut because I already feel sick. The water on my face and body feels cool and refreshing, but it brings back the pain that seems to be everywhere, even in the words that are being spoken around me. The floating sensation makes me dizzy, yet I can't get up to dispel the nausea. Then as the words become slower and softer and the rhythmic sound of paddles in water more monotonous, I begin to wonder if after all dying isn't quite easy.

I HAVE JUST lived one thousand years. Maybe a little more, maybe a little less. I lived through different epochs and had several lives. I think I was different people, too. It's all gone now; I've forgotten everything, except for flying over the jungle. I am that bird again soaring, high above an endless undulating surface of green. My outstretched arms are feathered wings that glide ever higher into the light . . . Now I see the lights . . . They are burning in concentric circles going upward as they become more distant. Now they are closer, moving in different directions. Then everything is black until I see the face.

A dark human face, pensive, without expression, just concentrating in all that water. Now it has sunk beneath the swirling surface, yet it is still there, blurred, covered by mist. There is a strong odor like leaves rotting in stagnant water. A cloth is wiping the water away; it feels rough as it scrapes my eyelids, and I see the face again, watching me intently. When it turns away I can sense that everything is brown. Ceiling, walls, light. In the open areas, green. I am in a hammock. There is movement somewhere, but all I see is water, flooding everything. The cloth again on my eyelids. The movement is a fan, moving slowly up and down, held by a pair of small hands, attached to a small naked body crouching on a dirt floor. The hair is cropped in a ring around the head. This face is expressionless, focusing on the movement of the fan.

Suddenly, as the water returns, I feel the air moving around my face, and once again there is pain in my legs, in my arms, and in my chest. My entire body is burning, and I feel that my eyes are filled with sweat or tears, or both. I am vaguely aware that I am. A hand brings a wooden bowl with steaming liquid to my face. The vapor infuses my nose and lungs with a coolness that rises and spreads through my head. The pain is gone. Or is it I who have gone? I no longer see or feel anything. I am searching for something very important. It must be in the back room of the old garage behind the house in Arkansas or somewhere along the crest trail in the Sierra Nevada, or there in that shade next to the cool spring. If I could only reach it, drag myself out of the scorching sun. Breathing quickly, I slip into the icy water. I must have left my body, or parts of it, in the sun. The essence of the water, like a woman, caresses my body and with the sweetest voice whispers into my ear about dying and being born.

There is the regular beat of a drum and the sound of a stringed instrument close by. The color brown is everywhere. Now it is red as well, right there, where a fire is burning on the ground. It is dark. The light of day is gone, and the acrid smell of damp burning wood is all around. The child is still there with the fan. Or is it a different child? This one smiles at me. It looks like a girl; her two upper front teeth are missing. I try to return the smile. A scrawny dog is lying next to the child. There is the deep, almost asthmatic sound of a crude musical instrument with a hollow tone. Now three men come into the light of the fire. They hold a long bamboo cylinder, which they play as they sway and lean forward. Their hair is cropped just above their ears, and oil or perspiration shines on their brown faces and bodies. They wear a narrow white cloth band around their necks and arms just below their shoulders and other bands around their knees and ankles. A band around their waists supports a loincloth. Facing in my direction, they play their instruments in unison standing and looking into the distance. They continue playing while they walk in a circle around the fire; then they leave. The drumming sound has been there all along. I try to see where it is coming from. A tall figure is crouching with his bony knees around a drum. His face is painted, and he is beating a constant rhythm, singing a monotonous melody. As the drum beat increases in intensity and tempo I feel my body responding, as if the vibrations are traveling through me. Then the sound rises with the smoke through a hole in the top of the hut. Now it is the sound of rattles that someone is shaking over my head and chest.

The tall figure performs a kind of dance behind the girl with the fan. A mass of long dry grass hangs from his head down to his torso; his face is covered by a mask, which rises and falls as his tall figure bows and straightens up to the sound of the drum. Around his waist hangs a grass skirt. He is barefoot. When the drums stop beating, he removes the mask with the long rustling grass and reveals a face, chest, and arms brilliantly painted. He makes the sound of various birds; then he imitates the calls of wild animals, and finally the roar of a wild cat, all the time shaking rattles and dancing in front of me. He stops and comes close to me. I recognize the same face that watched me earlier. He gives me some sweet-tasting juice, then passes a bowl in front of my nose, and I smell the acrid fumes. I see him drink from the bowl. Slowly the image vanishes as my mind drifts away to the beginning or the end of time. I open my eyes and see him again. He is on the ground, writhing in what looks like extreme pain, his arms beating the ground and his face contorted into a series of almost inhuman expressions. All this time the child continues waving the fan in my face, paying no attention to the extraordinary events taking place.

When I look again, light is coming into the hut. The child is sleeping next to her fan; the man is still on the ground. I am shivering. The shaking vibrations rise from my feet and get stronger as they approach my chest, causing my shoulders and head to shake violently in the hammock. I try to rise in order to find something to cover myself with. But all I am able to do is swing awkwardly back and forth. I am again drawn into a spinning vortex. Suddenly I feel myself being covered with something heavy. It is like the fur of a large animal against my skin, and it warms me.

I must have fallen asleep. When I open my eyes the sense of who I am and where I am slowly dawns on me. It still seems as if I am dreaming, but the impression that I am alive comes to me with considerable force.

Now there are women in the hut, squatting on the ground near me, busy doing something with their hands. Some are preparing food. Others are weaving a kind of cloth on small looms held between their knees. They are naked except for colorful bands tied around their arms and legs. Some of the faces are old and wrinkled; others are young. They are talking animatedly, paying no attention to me. I look at them and see two or three sets of earrings hanging on each earlobe and necklaces made of beads or other objects. One woman has a necklace that looks like a set of teeth. There are lines painted in complicated patterns on their faces and arms. The older women have a rough patterned cloth over their shoulders. When they notice that I am watching them they look at me, and then as soon as they meet my gaze, quickly turn their eyes away. One is nursing a child who cries every time the mother tries to disengage herself. A few children, all naked, are playing outside the door of the hut.

A young woman with black hair reaching almost to the tips of her full breasts comes over to me and, smiling, offers me some sweet juice, which I drink with pleasure. I, too, smile and mumble something. My voice, so weak and trembling, surprises me, but what is more surprising is the response of the women, who start talking to me all at the same time in a language I have never heard. We seem to be communicating something; maybe it is that I am alive, that we are human, that they want to take care of me. Certainly the animation in these faces conveys goodwill toward me and something like a wish or desire for me to be healthy. Soon I find myself talking to them in English, realizing that it doesn't really matter what language I use, since I feel they understand my intentions rather than my words. When I finish, they all chime in to tell me something, which makes me somehow contented.

The tall man who is taking care of me (healer, witch doctor, shaman?) returns and chases the women out with angry words and gestures, as if they were violating some unwritten law. They calmly pick up their belongings and children, dodge his swinging arms, and leave, shouting back at him in a teasing voice, as they offer me a last smile. The witch doctor looks at me attentively. I can see his thin arms and shoulders, his haggard face with deep natural lines running contrary to the painted ones. He approaches with a bowl which he sets on the ground, dips his hands into it, and slowly begins to rub my body with a bitter smelling dark red oil. It is then that I realize I am naked. The man seats himself on the ground next to me. After uttering some words of preparation in a deep voice, he takes out a long cigar and shows it to me while describing it at length. He motions to an adolescent, perhaps his assistant or apprentice, who takes a coal from the fire with his fingers, brings it to the shaman, and offers it to him solemnly. When the cigar is lit, the shaman sits and smokes quietly, letting the smoke pass by my face, rise upward, and escape through a small hole in the straw roof of the hut. Once again I experience the sensation of floating and of traveling to realms I have never before visited. When I wake up the shaman's apprentice offers me something to eat, a kind of warm mush with vegetables and leaves.

The next morning I felt stronger and stood up. The assistant was there; he gave me food again, and then offered me a string for my waist, like the ones he and the shaman wore, and a band to put around my upper arm and two more for my ankles, helping me attach them. After I ate, sparingly, he communicated to me that something important was about to happen. Almost immediately there was commotion outside the hut, and a young man entered. He was painted with brilliant red and orange stripes and wore a headband with long white and green feathers. He started speaking, and only after a number of declarative sentences did I realize that he was trying to talk in English. What made his speech peculiar was that in addition to the difficulty he had producing the sounds, it was colored by a strong Australian accent.

After a while I learned that he was the chief's younger brother, and that his name was Kota. He went on to tell me that I was better now and that in a while (later today? in a week?) I would be moved outside to recuperate. Then I was to have my own hut, the hut of the . . . (here his words completely escaped me) where, according to him, I would learn how to be an Indian. Once I accomplished that the chief himself would pay me a visit and bestow tribal membership on me. In the meantime I was to give Kota lessons in English so that he could translate the chief's speeches to me. At that point he went to the door where he gave some orders. Presently the shaman's assistant, whom he addressed as Tior, and another adolescent entered and held me up as I stumbled to the outside. There a hammock was tied between two trees. Once I was installed, Kota and Tior sat nearby on the ground, while the women began their activities in a circle around us at a respectful distance. Kota showed me that he could count up to three and said that beyond that it was just "more." He could also say A, B, C and at the same time drew the letters in the dust with a stick. Tior, for whom this was apparently a first lesson, tried to imitate him. For me it was immensely enjoyable to watch and feel able to communicate with someone. During the next few days I taught them some phrases, which they repeated over and over, but mainly I just talked to them, slowly, with gestures, repeating often so that they could understand, and soon we were able to exchange some rudimentary ideas and even joke a little. Nearly always there were some boys nearby practicing with tiny bows and arrows made of delicate pieces of wood. The tallest one was wearing several strings of beads around his neck, shoulders, and upper arms; his body was painted black, contrasting with the front half of his head, which was shaved and covered with a white chalk. His mouth was a brilliant red.

One afternoon the shaman came up to us carrying a large cloth bag of leaves, berries, and shrub clippings. With Kota interpreting, he explained that with the medicines he had collected in the forest he would be able to cure me completely. He diagnosed my illness thus: my soul had been sucked out of me by evil spirits or by a shaman of darkness so that all I had left in me was pain and fever. Fortunately a jaguar had saved me and protected me in the forest from further invasion by evil spirits and had delivered me to the tribe's hunting party when the moon was full. The hunters spared the jaguar and brought me to the village. Does this story confirm in a way vague memories of events that took place in the forest after I had passed out? Or does it, just by coincidence, run parallel to the hallucinations I experienced during my fever? I have given up trying to know. I am just happy to be alive, whatever it was that saved me.

Soon I am strong enough to sit with the villagers and eat some roasted meat that tastes a little like ham and that they seem to cherish. It is served with mush and a bitter beverage. I don't understand much of what they say. Kota seems to be the tribe joker, for he is always talking and making the others laugh, and he takes pains to translate for me his own jokes. After the meal he takes me to a hut at the edge of the village where I am surprised to find a stack of human bones, including the skull, some khaki clothes, and a pile of what were once someone's belongings.

"This will be your hut," I think he said. "You live and sleep here. My brother/chief visit you soon (tomorrow? in five minutes?). Here is where white guy live. He dead. Those his bones. Cleaned off by piranha. Men make funeral soon. Grind bones, mix with food, and eat. You have his soul now. Jaguar keep it for a while then give it to you. That's why you are healthy. You look at stuff."

He started a fire in the center of the hut so that I could examine the belongings. Kota handled everything as I put it down, as if to verify my inventory. The clothes were nearly all eaten by ants or termites. Inside a small metal trunk I found some cooking utensils, knives, a machete, a pistol, a mirror, razor, soap, pencils, pens, an oilskin portfolio. The last item included some Australian and Brazilian money, a permit in Portuguese allowing one Elliott Todd to "travel unimpeded in the upper regions of the Tapajós and Madeira Rivers for a period of one year." The document was signed and dated, but since I had no idea of the current date, I couldn't tell if the permit was still valid. Passport. Visa. Brazilian identification. Driver's licence. List of inoculations. Some photographs. There was a manuscript, too, much of it devoured by insects.

Kota set up my hammock and then invited me to follow him. We descended a winding path and came upon a small river. There we swam and soaked in the dark water. After returning to Todd's hut, we sat by the fire and chewed some leaves while Kota told me what a fine fellow Todd was and that since I had his soul I would also bring happiness to the people of the tribe. After Kota had left, as I lay in my hammock listening to the mosquitoes buzzing around me, I thought how strange it felt to be another person. For the Indians I had inherited the soul of the Australian, and that was sufficient reason for them to treat me well. For me, at least at present, I have assumed his identity and have his passport and other documents. Is this what shamans mean by saying about the sick that they are born again into health?

I have decided to write this diary in English from now on, without code or mirror. It is unlikely that anyone, friend or foe, will find and use it, and the ants who come across these pages one day won't really care what language they are digesting.

ELLIOTT TODD, TO judge from what is left of his papers after insects, mold, and humidity have taken their toll, was an anthropologist. He had come to this area to study the customs, religion, language, and social organization of a village in the Amazon basin on a grant from a university in Australia. His manuscript is both personal and scientific. On certain pages he writes mainly about himself—his feelings and his physical well-being, or rather, ill-being, which occupies him more and more frequently toward the end. On other pages he compiles organized data and writes short descriptions of customs and ceremonies. Todd gives surprisingly little information about his past life. He refers to somebody named Maud rather often, wondering how she would react to the Indian customs he is describing "if some day she is willing to accompany me to this area." The last pages of his writing are devoted to his illness and how much he suffered from the pain he had to endure. Indeed, he seemed in his last words to welcome the thought of dying soon and being spared further misery. He had woken up one night with horrible abdominal cramps and was unable to keep any food down from then on. At one point he wrote: ". . . if only I could vomit my guts out it would be a relief." Apparently the same shaman who was leading me back to health was unable to cure Elliott's disease. He wrote further: "If I have a parasite or a bacterial infection, there are no drugs here that can cure me. If on the other hand my body has been invaded by a foreign object, as Surupuven [the shaman's name] says, or my soul has been stolen by a spirit, I lack sufficient belief in his cure to benefit from it." After his death, his belongings were left untouched by the members of the tribe. To judge from his passport photograph, he was a big man with a bushy head of hair and beard. If I ever have to use his papers to get myself back to civilization, I hope that my beard will look enough like his.

How Todd happened to stumble on this particular village, which he called Xantupá, is included in his notes. He came into the interior by river on a boat piloted by natives he had hired in Santarém. They abandoned him when they thought he had no more beads or trinkets to pay their return trip down river. The first Indians he encountered were "too westernized" for him, which induced him to work his way a distance farther upstream. There he discovered a tribe called Paumadi, which he felt had been less influenced by the outside world. He was befriended in their village by a North American missionary who was bringing "the word of God to these savages" of Paumadi and teaching them to read and to cover their genitals. This alone made the tribe unsuitable for Todd to study, but the missionary helped him out by suggesting that he visit the Xantupá people, who were, in the words of the missionary, "unspoiled indigenous natives that he might be able to observe and even help to civilize."

He was brought here, to Xantupá, by two Indians newly converted to Christianity. The trip through the jungle was extremely difficult and took a number of days to complete. The people of this village treated him at first with indifference, letting him set up camp in the vicinity but otherwise ignoring his presence entirely. After days of waiting and many attempts to win them over with gifts, he watched the children come each day closer to his tent. Then it was only a matter of time before the adults became friendly, too. Finally the shaman and the chief accepted him, and he was given this hut, where I am now reading his notes.

How many pages of Todd's notes have been devoured by paper-hungry ants? I can't find any indications in his notes of where this tribe is located. I assume it is within the borders of Brazil, for Todd's permits and visa are in Portuguese, although this does not rule out his having crossed an unmarked border. There is no indication left of the particular river system this area belongs to, nor are there comments which might help identify which one of the larger ethnic or linguistic groups the Xantupá Indians belong to. Their neighbors, the Paumadi, the tribe that the missionary had converted, share the same language, customs, and rituals, according to Todd. The two groups were driven apart by the arrival of the missionary, who tried to convince them that their shaman was ignorant as well as evil, that they needed modern medicine to cure their illness, and that they would surely be damned if they continued walking around naked. As this had coincided with an onslaught of new diseases and the awareness that wildlife to hunt was becoming ever scarcer, the missionary's talk of plague and famine fell upon ears that were ready to listen. After a good deal of bickering, the chief's brother, the shaman, and half the tribe split away and settled in this location. The tribes are still on friendly terms and often get together for celebrations and the exchange of marriageable women. Many of Todd's observations relate to a comparison of the two tribes, the one corrupted, according to him, by foreign ideologies and customs, the other more at peace with itself and following its own traditions. But he recognizes that both tribes are threatened by extinction in one way or another, first by exposure to intruders— including missionaries and anthropologists—and then by settlers burning the forest to make place for pasture and by developers seeking to become rich from mining or drilling.

How this tribe and others came to such an isolated location and managed to remain so long relatively free of the influence of western civilization is a question that Todd reflected on at length. His belief is that the history of the Amazon Indians has for centuries been a matter of weaker tribes being forced by stronger ones ever farther into the interior and to less amenable, less fertile lands. The pattern kept on repeating itself when the Dutch, French,

English, Portuguese, and now the North Americans began encroaching on their homelands, continuously uprooting them. "The only safety is in remaining small and keeping isolated," he concludes. Then he asks: "But for how long will yet another move be able to preserve them?"

He includes long descriptions of the diseases both tribes are subject to: monstrously deformed feet, bacteria from stale meat, viruses that are carried and transmitted by certain birds they eat, respiratory illnesses that cause continuous coughing and spitting of blood, dysenteries of many kinds. He does not know, he adds, how many of these diseases are caused by contact with outside carriers who are immune to them, but he feels this to be the greatest threat to the survival of the Indians. He goes on to mention various crusts, scabs, lesions, and wounds that never heal, as well as insect bites that cause huge swelling. None of this provides entertaining reading for me right now when I am just recovering from a sickness. Among the diseases suffered by the members of this tribe, Todd takes pains to point out that some are psychosomatic and can be cured by a shaman. He notes the prevalence of illnesses inflicted by spirits and those brought on by the spell of an old woman or an evil shaman. Often a malady is brought about by the loss of a person's soul or by the insertion of an imaginary foreign object in the body. But the other illnesses are real, in his view, and can be successfully treated by modern pharmacology. I wonder if this isn't oversimplified, especially after my own healing experience.

Much of what Todd learned seems to have come from his friend and my healer, Surupuven. He writes about the world of the spirits and how great its influence and power is at all times in the mind of the Indians. "Gods, spirits, demons, the souls of ancestors, the dead, mythical animals, these are the unseen companions of the Indians, lurking everywhere behind trees, under the surface of the water, always helping or getting in the way of human endeavors. Their appetite for sacrifice, gifts, favors, and ceremonies is insatiable, and when they go hungry they make sure that humans pay the price. The shaman serves as intermediary and interpreter, both to the high gods and to the lower spirits, placating them on behalf of the tribe. He makes noises that sound like different animals, invoking the spirits to enter his domain, relating to all the divinities through his own experience of ecstasy. This is something that Ogg [apparently the name of the missionary in the neighboring village] will never understand."

The remaining pages of Todd's notes pertain to the language spoken by the Xantupá and the Paumadi and consist mainly of simple lists of words with English approximations. These will be very helpful to me, I am sure, once I have a chance to study them and try them out on my new friends. Whatever he wrote about the structure and syntax of their language and its classification among the Indian languages is lost. His remarks on the social and economic conditions of the tribes are few and far between, but they are disturbing. The natives nearly starve for half of the year, because during the rainy season it is impossible to hunt; but in recent years there is so little game left to hunt that the season of famine extends almost throughout the year. Sometimes they are forced to eat dirt to appease their hunger pains. He points out that he has read as many books about the Amazonian Indians as anyone, but that he is still mystified by them, even after studying this tribe and living with them day in and day out. "Will these people," he asks, "ever cease to bewilder me? Just today Juva drowned her deformed baby in the river and brought the little body back to the village holding it by the foot and in her other arm she carried a load of a certain kind of leaf that the natives consider to be a wonderful treat; she had found the plant while she was holding her baby's head under water. She gave the leaves to the other women on her way to the shaman's hut, where she made arrangements for escorting the little soul to the other world. A few minutes later she was seated with the other women, busy grinding the leaves into a fine pulp in a stone bowl between her knees."

Elliott Todd meditated at length on the natives' nakedness. For him it was a signal that the tribe was relatively untouched by the outside world and could teach him their ways unsullied. He also had an esthetic interest in their bodies. He found the men strong and handsome and quite remarkable for their posture and general bearing. Above all he admired the women; starting out by describing the intricate designs painted on their faces and torsos, he ended up concentrating on their bodies, describing the size and shape of the breasts, the natural posture with slightly protruding stomachs, and the absence of bodily hair, which he surmised had been removed in some ritual. He ended his description with a comment on the "winning smile" of the women. He related at one point that the chief wanted him to join the tribe officially. He would have only to go through a naming ceremony (which included dances, rituals, and a large feast), live henceforth without clothes, wearing only a penis sheaf. Then he would be able to marry one of the adolescent girls and go hunting with the men.

I found Elliott's final pages quite moving. His suffering was enormous and his mind wandered frequently, even in his writing. But at one lucid moment he wrote that he felt that his friends, the Xantupás, had done everything in their power to save him. His illness had become an issue in the community; he had heard about long speeches concerning his condition made by the men at night when they gathered to discuss important matters. The chief had even come to his hut to inform him that the spirits were in agreement that he would continue to live. The shaman had exhausted himself with dancing and singing, fasting and going into ecstatic trance, day after day. "If the power of their belief and of their will for me to live cannot save me, nothing can. I know I am ready, wanting to die. Yet I seem to be weeping so much of the day. My tears are not for me. Nor are they falling for my friends in Australia, for any grief they may feel when I am gone, even though I know that each of them has a particular affection for me, as I do for them. I believe my tears are for this

Indian tribe, for each one of its members, and for their children. For they are like Juva's baby and like me in that nobody can save them. They are doomed along with the rest of the tribes in the vast Amazonian jungle; their destiny is to perish from the onslaught of civilization. Disease, poverty, prostitution, exhaustion, alienation are all waiting behind the next tropical tree that is felled or burned. When the Indians are finally separated from the spirits that inhabit the forest around them, they will vanish. That the rest of us may not be far behind is a consequence that comes to me almost with indifference."

Kota woke me the next morning, inviting me to eat with him outside his hut. During a breakfast of manioc paste he informed me that his brother, the chief, had decided not to visit me until I became a real member of the village.

"How do I become a real member of the village?"

"You see," was his answer.

"Was Todd a member of the village?"

"He only here. Not real Xantupá."

"Wasn't he here long enough to be a Xantupá?"

Kota gave a long answer, mostly in his own language, so that I understood only a fraction of what he said. His main idea was that although Todd was a good person and gave many nice presents to members of the village, he was still only a visitor. You could see this because he continued wearing his hot clothes, even in the forest. Because he was not a member of the tribe, he could not come to the men's house in the center of the village to talk about hunting. Nor could he give a speech at night, hunt with the men, have his body painted, or take a Xantupá wife.

"What about me? I don't give any presents. How do the Xantupá feel about that?" This question had been bothering me.

"You have no presents to give," was the answer. Then he went on: "You have no things. You didn't even have a soul when you came. When you become a member of the village you will help us improve our life. And you will give us many strong babies."

On that subject he said no more. Instead, he told me that the chief, most of the men, and the older boys were about to embark on a hunt to gather meat and food for a ceremony. They would not return until they had caught enough game for a fine feast that would last a whole night. The women would be gathering roots and leaves and finding wood for the cooking fires.

In a few days the village did indeed seem empty. A few children played in the areas between the huts while the older women were busy cutting and peeling vegetables and young women walked to and from a garden situated outside the village carrying heavy loads. Kota remained in the village with plenty of time on his hands for talking and telling stories. I asked him a question that had been teasing me for some time. Why, I wondered, did the men have no beards or hair on their chests? Why did neither men nor women have pubic hair? Unable to make him understand that question, I pointed to the white sheath shaped like a pointed shell that he and all the grown men wore on their penis. "What is that?" I asked.

"You get it too. At feast."

The next day Surupuven and Tior walked by the hut while Kota and I were talking. They were followed by a woman carrying a large basket piled high with leaves and roots on her head. In a sling hanging from her shoulder a baby was sleeping peacefully with his cheek against her breast. The three of them disappeared into the shaman's hut, the site of my recent recovery. Suddenly a boy came running into the village. He stopped in front of Kota and paused to catch his breath. Kota offered him something to drink. The boy then let go a swarm of words. He was obviously excited, and his eyes flashed continually as he gestured with his body, arms, and hands. He acted out shooting with bow and arrow, then crawled about on all fours, grunting and squealing, before he finally crumbled to the ground with an animalistic death rasp. Then he jumped up and began his story again from the beginning. By this time some women and children had gathered to hear his narrative, commenting on it vociferously and repeating the sounds of the dying animal. Finally the child skipped into Surupuven's hut, where we could hear him retelling the same event.

"He says they have made a successful hunting trip and that they will return soon. They bring monkeys, armadillos, and a big peccary, which Chief Jotuven himself shot with an arrow. That means we will have the ceremony soon and you will have a name."

During the next few days the activity around the village was more animated. The women were occupied going to and returning from the gardens with baskets heavy with bananas, manioc, leaves, and the like, or else sitting in a circle in front of some of the huts chatting and singing as they peeled, hulled, pounded, and ground various leaves, vegetables, roots, and vines. The dogs were scurrying around and begging. When the men returned there was great exclamation from the villagers as four of them carried in the great pig and others brought monkeys and fish which they had caught on their return trip. The armadillo was brought in on a leash since it was still alive; they closed it into a cage for a later date. After some time the men went to the men's building where, according to Kota, they would retell the events of the hunt, each one describing to the others his adventures.

I wasn't able to watch as much of the preparation for the feast as I would have liked, for I was ushered into the tribe's meeting place, where I was lectured for hours on end by what must have been all the elders of the village. I think they were talking about the history of the tribe and the village and probably their myths of origin. Whatever they were telling me was of considerable importance, to judge by the amount of vehement argument certain statements provoked from members of the audience. When the old men had finished their discourses, the chief, Jotuven, came in, talked at length to considerable approval from the audience, and then left. Upon which Kota told me it was time for me to address the group and describe my achievements; this meant, according to him, my forebears, my hunting exploits, the rivers I had traveled on, the wives I had, and finally all the children I had produced. It didn't take me long to cover those items; I spoke in English in a loud voice and with many gestures. They all listened attentively, not understanding a word. When I thought I was done they insisted I continue, not letting me go until I had talked for at least an hour and a half. Finally, each elder came and greeted me, flashing a toothless smile, and left.

Later Surupuven, who appeared more or less in charge of the ceremonies, and Tior led me to my hut. On the way I saw Kota handing out thin pieces of bamboo, about six inches long, to anyone who wanted them, which appeared to be everyone. He demonstrated how to hold the sticks, a little like the way one grasps chopsticks, to a cheering and laughing group of people standing around. When I arrived two women were waiting with red and black paint, which they proceeded to spread with their hands in vertical stripes on my body while I stood, naked, in the middle of the hut. Kota came to tell me the women were both wives of the chief, which showed how highly the village regarded me.

"Now you stay here. No eat."

"Why?"

"Part of *bojná*, naming ceremony."

"How long?"

"Soon."

"When will we eat?"

"Right away."

That turned out to be the next day, toward evening. Until then I was captive in my hut, for Kota had installed two guards outside the opening, big bruisers, each holding a spear. At one point, when the need to urinate became pressing, I approached the door only to find the two glistening spears pointing at my chest. I gestured to the forest and then to my crotch to show that my intentions were legitimate and necessary. Minutes later I heard Kota call from outside: "Piss on ground." Surupuven was my only visitor during this time; he came in from time to time to smoke and go into a trance. A pet monkey came as well to sit on a bar between the vertical support beams and look at me with his sad eyes. Then he jumped up to the rafters and busied himself catching and eating spiders.

The next morning Surupuven returned with two women to prepare me for the event. This meant shaving my forehead, painting my face black, attaching colored feathers to my torso and thighs with some kind of gum, and providing me with a crown bedecked with long white feathers. The naming ceremony began at dusk, continued all night, and resumed the next evening.

I remember in particular the eating, which was non-stop because of the abundance of meat on this occasion. Much of my prestige in the eyes of the villagers was due to the success of the hunt that preceded the feast held in my honor. To them the meaning was clear that my spirits were strong and would insure successful hunting in the future. At intervals during the meal there were speeches, concerts played on long recorder-like instruments, drums, and rattles. The men, with the women in back of them, danced all decked out in painted designs, feathers, and costumes made of grass and vines. I had to do a solo dance two times, jumping around more or less to the rhythm of the drums, to enthusiastic approval.

All of this was great fun for me, and after a day of fasting I was extremely hungry and ate with real pleasure. But the horrendous part of the ceremony was to come: my involuntary depilation. At a signal from the chief, when my second dance was finished, to the accompaniment of drums and instruments, six villagers, both men and women, took hold of my arms and held me down while the others, with the little bamboo sticks I had seen earlier, pulled out the hairs of my body one by one, from my armpits down.

"No fight," Kota warned me. "We finish soon. You keep hair on face, to look like Todd."

I'm not going to try to describe what this felt like. They worked on about four areas at a time—one person doing my torso, another my thighs and legs, and two concentrating on my crotch, one on either side. This appeared to amuse them greatly, for they all chatted and laughed constantly; the ones holding my arms smiled and gave encouraging words that I couldn't understand. Sometimes a great cheer would go up, the reason for which I never understood. Each person was able to pluck for a few minutes and was then replaced by another, with the result that I had no reprieve for the time it took them (an eternity, certainly) to make a clear-cut of my surface, including all the hills and valleys. When they started inspecting their work and looking for hairs they had missed, I figured the ordeal was over and that I could wake up from this nightmare. But my hopes were dashed when they all cheered and turned me over in order to start on my back.

Eventually the torture came to an end. When my tormentors finally released me, Surupuven approached with Tior and, after invocations to the spirits, they began to fit me with a penis sheath. This is a white cone-shaped wooden object that covers the penis but nothing else, making it look as if one had a constant white-colored erection. The only difficulty they encountered was my circumcision: there was no foreskin for them to attach the sheath onto. I was too dazed to figure out how they resolved the difficulty; I only know that they did so to the accompaniment of great cheers from the onlookers.

After that I was decorated once again with red and black paint; the feast continued, and everybody seemed happy to smile at me and give me more food, especially roasted peccary meat, which was quite tasty. Then Jotuven came over to me and, after a short speech, gave me a bow and a half dozen long arrows. Then he loudly pronounced the word "Kojutowen," at which everybody shouted as they started to dance around me. This was the climax of the ceremony. Some of the older villagers retired. Then, one by one the others faded into their huts, and at the end only the chief and his two wives, the shaman, and my friend Kota remained by the fire, talking, telling stories. I felt somehow elated to know that I had a name and an identity, a community standing, some friends, a bow with arrows, and a penis sheath. Perhaps it was the beginning of a new life.

FROM THE NEXT day on, Chief Jotuven became my devoted friend. He taught me to use the long bow and arrows that the men of the village take on their hunting forays. We went out several times in the area within a day's walk of the huts, and he showed me how to track, use dogs, make monkey sounds, and aim with precision. It didn't take me long to overcome my aversion to killing animals when I myself felt the hunger that is the daily experience of the villagers. He also trained me in the art of making arrows, from finding and shaping the wood to sharpening the point and making and applying poison. Another project was building a new canoe from the wood of a large tree that had fallen about three miles from the village. Here my training as an apprentice builder helped me devise tools to aid in scraping out the hull. The evening was often spent in Jotuven's hut with his wives and Kota, who continued translating for us, since my progress in learning their language was painfully slow.

"You need wife!" the chief told me solemnly.

"Tell him I already have one."

An exchange in their language followed.

"Only one? No believe you."

I went to my hut to get your picture, Deb, which had miraculously survived Braulio's ransacking henchmen and the ants. My remaining possessions were hanging on a string from a rafter: clothes, boots, sun hat, blanket, tent, and wallet, which was empty except for the color photograph showing you smiling and looking up from a suitcase you were packing just before we left for Brazil.

"Here is my wife, you can see her. I don't need another."

Jotuven looked at your image for a long time, showed it to his brother and to his wives. He had a long discussion with them. Finally Kota interpreted:

"My brother say you need wife anyhow. We go get girls soon, from Paumadi; Tior and Jubulá need wives. You come along. You see Paumadi chief and the missionary guy."

The chief continued talking to the interpreter.

"Then one day you go down the river and get wife in picture and bring here. Jotuven want her for his wife. He trade one of his for her. You take pick. He say this one, she eat better."

I already suspected that the same word is used in Xantupá language for eating and having sex. The wife he referred to seemed to understand the conversation, but showed no visible concern; if anything, she seemed to concur with the proposal.

In the meantime, Surupuven, the shaman, began teaching me the medicinal values of the foliage growing within walking distance of the village. Since he had already explained his kind of medicine to Elliott Todd, he must have thought it only natural that a white-skinned person would want to know what leaves were used to cure what illness. Maybe he had learned from teaching Todd how to organize his knowledge by taking one leaf at a time, pronouncing its name distinctly, and telling how to prepare it for each one of a number of different ailments. Often Kota was not there to interpret, so Surupuven would say the name of the leaf several times in a loud voice, go through the preparation with gestures signifying "build a fire," "boil," or "chew and spit." Then he would describe the sickness by scratching his leg, pretending to be hot, running to the forest to defecate, or being invaded by spirits. My notes on what he told me are rather confused.

Preparations for the trip to Paumadi took two full days. The entire village was busy getting food ready and making gifts for the Paumadi chief to distribute to his tribe. Kota was to lead the trek, and Tior, Jubulá, and I, those in need of wives, were to follow him. Once our bodies were painted in complicated designs, special ceremonies were held in our honor, and we had to listen to speeches by the chief, the shaman, and the oldest of the elders. When we left early one morning, the rest of the village accompanied us for about two hours, and then, one by one, they fell back and returned the way they had come.

The trip was a long one. Penetrating farther into the forest than I had done since coming to the Xantupá, I became aware once more of the mystery of the forest. The deep echo of silence that inhabits every corner of the space overflowing with foliage, the heat, so often unbearable, the coolness of the path in thickly covered areas, the sudden sounds of insects and monkeys, the smell of leaves baking in the sun, the rustle of the wind, starting miles away and coming closer to cause the heavy branches to sway far above us, all that blends into a single experience that I can not grasp in any meaningful way with my mind. Kota went ahead; I followed, stumbling, sweating, cursing when I wasn't fully absorbed in feeling myself swallowed up by the surrounding green immensity; then came Jubulá, and finally Tior, whose main function was to see to it that none of us lagged behind. Each night we cleared a little area, made a fire to prepare a sparing meal of dried meat, leaves, and manioc bread. Then we sat around the fire while Kota told stories and Tior imitated animal sounds and movements. Jubulá was the handyman, tending the fire and the cooking. My main function, I found, was to practice on Elliott Todd's harmonica while the others listened and dozed. Whatever I played, be it scales, arpeggios, or simple melodies, they listened in deep silence.

We walked for two days along the banks of a river; I was unable to find out why we had not taken a canoe. We frequently ran across monkeys and other edible animals, which we hunted when we needed to. We saw no humans. I was walking barefoot, which made it easier for me to keep up with the others, and every night the four of us busied ourselves removing insects from each other's feet and rubbing them with leaves that made our skin sting and feel cool.

The first Paumadi we saw were women tilling the gardens located farthest from the village. I was surprised that they were covered with loose hanging cotton print dresses and that their hair was cut short, not hanging long and straight like that of the Xantupá women. They greeted us, smiling, and then sent a child scampering away to tell the other villagers. After talking about matters I didn't fully understand, we continued our way, leaving the women to their work. We were met, just before the first huts, by a portly white character in short khaki pants, leather shoes without socks, and a wilted safari hat, holding pieces of cloth on his arm. He smiled—a few of his front teeth were missing—and then gave a mock military salute.

"Aha! Private Parts, I presume," he said in a jovial North-American English, laughing and handing us each a large piece of cloth. "I am trying, you see, to teach these savages to dress decently, to observe decorum, to conceal their asses, and here you come, spoiling my good work. Put these on please, for as long as you are here. You can tie them shut with this rope. After you leave, do as you please!"

He went on to talk in the native language to Kota and the others, who appeared to have no objections to covering themselves. It was apparently not a new experience for them. Then he led us into the village, which had almost twice the number of huts as Xantupá, and took us to meet the chief, who was a good deal older than Jotuven, and explained the purpose of our visit. After we listened to a short speech from the chief, the whole village went to the men's building in the center, which had been made over into a kind of church, with two wings built in the form of a transept, and rows of pews in which we all took our seats. The American came in, dressed now in a long white priestly gown and wearing on his head what looked like a fake crown of thorns.

He walked ceremoniously to the altar, looked carefully at his audience, smiled knowingly and then proceeded to give a sermon, alternately in English and in the local Indian language. While he was speaking some of the natives walked in and out; others were sitting or kneeling. The sound of talking, singing, and even snoring provided a continuous background for the reverend's monotonous voice, like the echoes in a stone cathedral.

"We can give thanks," he intoned, "for the unexpected visit of our pagan friends, in the hopes that they may one day see the light and open their eyes to Jesus and to the gifts of the almighty Lord, to the workings of the Holy Spirit, and to the forgiveness of our Holy Mother . . . They come in need, and, God willing, we shall do everything possible to . . ." A large insect with a curled tail was creeping toward my bare foot, and watching it prevented me from hearing the rest of the good man's homily.

After the service we were invited to view a soccer match between two groups of young unmarried men. Tior and Jubulá joined in after a while, striving with difficulty to kick and run while holding on to the pieces of material they were unused to wearing. Next, the village members sat in the open to eat a light meal. A feast would be prepared for the next day in our honor. I was to be a guest in the hut of the white missionary.

"Ogg's the name. You can call me Jack; after all, we can be informal in this godforsaken place. Seeing a white man around here is a rare thing, a rare pleasure indeed. So let us celebrate!" He went over to a trunk located at the edge of his hut, unlocked it with a key, opened it, and after rummaging around a while, emerged with a bottle and two glasses. "We have to take it neat; there's no ice and the water tastes putrid. Nevertheless, here's to you! I dare say you haven't tasted good Scotch for some time. What brings you here? Are you looking for Elliott? What a shame, he was such a fine fellow, albeit damned opinionated."

I related briefly how I happened upon Xantupá and that I only knew about Elliott Todd from reading what was left of his notes.

"But good heavens, my good man! Why in God's name are you parading around naked with your Indian companions? You aren't obliged to, you know. Just declare your wishes and expect the natives to honor them. Elliott was bad enough about forgetting his proper place, but I hate those anthropologists who come around thinking they can become Indians by taking off their clothes and painting their nipples. Don't tell me you let them strip you and give you one of their names! At that rate white men will lose what little respect they have left."

I didn't even attempt to explain to him what had happened to me at Xantupá and how I had ended up naked, barefoot, and seeking a wife I didn't want. An hour earlier my story made a kind of sense to me, but now, in Ogg's imposing presence, it was considerably less plausible. Even though he understood my words, this man would never be able to fathom how I had gotten into this mess.

A young woman came in carrying a wicker basket with a few things to eat. She wore a dirty plain dress, an apron, and tennis shoes. Jack and I sat at a table where the woman served us without speaking or smiling.

"This is Daisy; she's my servant and companion, if you know what I mean. She is happy because she is the best dressed woman in the village. Her rivals are furious because she is from another tribe and has no husband or brothers or sisters, that is to say, no status. But I am showing them all that God does not recognize castes, that we are all equal in His eyes, and that this poor creature can outclass them all when fortune smiles on her. But back to you, Hank. Of course you are anxious to return to civilization, since you have no pious vocation to help these natives cope with the rigors of life here in the wilderness. Let's see . . . a boat should be coming up the river next month. If you come back in, say, three weeks from today you can stay with me here and hitch a ride downstream and be in Santarém a couple of weeks later. From there it is easy as pie. I've done it often."

Did I really want to go back to civilization? The thought had not occurred to me since it hadn't been in the realm of possibility. I took it for granted that I was eager to return to paved streets and elevators. But now that a real vision of towns and traffic was beckoning to me, I hesitated. I had three weeks to decide, but there was no way I could explain to my reverend friend that I might have reason to want to stay here, at least for a while.

"What's your vocation, Jack? It must be strong to keep you here so long."

"Make no mistake about it! I'm in the wilderness because I like being here. Not that I particularly enjoy nature in the raw or fire ants or piranhas or these devilish mosquitoes," he answered slapping his face furiously. "Or the Indians, either. They are fine, don't get me wrong, they're affectionate in their way, and very appreciative of what we do for them. And Daisy takes care of my worldly needs so that I can concentrate on my higher calling, which is to prepare these souls for the day when they are no more and can enter into the kingdom of our Lord and live in celestial huts and enjoy the everlasting rain forest, while playing harps like the rest of mortals who have become immortal."

"But what is that in everyday terms? What have you in mind for this village who have entrusted themselves to you?"

"First you have to realize how they were faring when I arrived, with my baggage of illusions and ideals. I'm a realist now, and do you know who taught me? Daisy did with her blank eyes; so did the chief, with no thought behind his painted face other than survival and screwing his four wives, so did the shaman who took off with half the tribe to escape my influence on their traditional values and rituals. I realized that these people suffer because they are backward, to put it crudely. They are back in the Cro-Magnon age, relatively speaking, where life means eating, fucking, and putting off dying as long as possible without modern medicine. They lack social skills, to begin with, and education— that's it in a nutshell. My function is to teach them Civilization 101, a course I invented, which brings them forward from barbarism and primitivism to somewhere around the time of the

Old Testament. That is to say the rudiments of civilized life. The rest is up to FUNAI, the Mormons, and the prospectors, who will give them all they need until the time they have to settle in a slum of some city and work their way up in society. Don't laugh when I say prospectors. The people who come here to make a buck by slashing and burning forests for pasture or to dig up the earth to create a mine are the ones who bring modern life, health, and prosperity, what we could call good fortune without stretching the notion too far."

"I once taught a beginning course in some language. I remember starting with the alphabet. Which alphabet do you give them to learn?"

"Faith, peace, non-resistance, trust. The old conquistadors got it wrong, don't let anyone fool you. They arrived here with the sword and the cross, but the sword always came first, that's why so many Indians were slaughtered, often unnecessarily. Nowadays we bring the cross, and once it has been accepted, there is no need for a sword, only a shovel, or a tractor, or a jet."

"What about the Xantupá? Why did they flee you? And why did the others remain?"

"That's simple, if you take time to think about it. Humans are divided into those who accept and those who resist. Accepting God's will and accepting progress are about the same. That means that these good Paumadi Indians will eventually come into the twentieth century, where they belong, while the Xantupás will end their days fighting and fleeing, avoiding the inevitable, and will soon perish from cholera or famine."

"While your disciples live in slums, eat garbage, and beg their way into our century?"

"What can you expect? It's a fact that the different races are miles apart in adaptation and ability. The good Lord had His reasons for creating inequality, and it isn't up to us mortals to question them. All we can do is ease the burden of the poor while progress makes its way and takes its toll. However you look at it, the church's main function is helping people die in peace."

He paused a while. He was sweating from the heat, the amount of whisky he had consumed, and the expense of energy. He added:

"Not many of my colleagues would put it as bluntly. But I'm a realist, don't ever forget that. For centuries theologians didn't realize that God favors progress. He created it, after all! Original sin is the wish to remain behind, in the garden of the past. I teach freedom, the freedom to choose between keeping up or staying behind and perishing. My students—don't ever believe they are anything but savages—are the most recalcitrant there are. My vocation, Hank, is to jolt them into God's twentieth century."

He went to his cache and brought out another bottle of Scotch.

"Just think a little. It was a brilliant idea of the Conquistadors to come with the sword and the cross, with a little help from the Jesuits. I know I'm repeating myself—it's a professional tic. They taught respect and love; in those days the two belonged together. Nowadays, things are different. The sword has been put back in its sheath, and we missionaries arrive in the forest with the cross and the handshake. Soon afterward someone sends in a ballot, and everyone ends up smiling. You see, if we don't pacify the Indians, they will flee to the back country, way upstream, and one day they will riddle a prospector with poisoned arrows. What then? Two weeks later the whole tribe will be massacred, including the naked women and children, with a little torture and rape thrown in for good measure. No one will know who did it; the settlers, the prospectors, the police, the thugs from Santarém and Manaus, the foreign investors, all of them have valid excuses. 'Couldn't have done it , I had a miserable hangover that day.' We teach the Indians to love their neighbors, including the settlers and the fat São Paulo businessman who sits with a rifle between his knees on his launch for a vacation. After a bit of preparation, our natives learn how to make a deal with the newcomers and everyone comes out ahead, no exceptions."

Suddenly Jack became animated. He got up to throw more wood on the fire, which was almost out. His woman was already breathing heavily in her hammock, and the sounds of the forest as night approached seemed louder as I listened to this man, who needed so desperately to talk.

"Hank! I gotta tell you this. You won't believe it, but you're going to have to stay awake long enough to listen."

He sensed that my mind was wandering, giving in to the need for sleep, that I was forcing myself to keep awake after the arduous walk through the forest.

"Here. Have another little bit of schnapps, as my Lutheran colleagues used to say when they were feeling ecumenical. That will keep your thinking alert long enough to hear this bit of naughty narrative. But it's all true, I swear to God, I do, every word."

"Don't give me too many words to believe, Jack, or I'll doze off and start believing my dreams.

"Listen to this now. When I first came to this part of limbo . . . wait; there's something else I have to tell you, if you haven't already guessed. For fifteen years I was a priest; went to a seminary in Phoenix, was ordained, tonsured, the works! I even had a little flock of my own in the hinterland of New Mexico, where I did all the sacraments strictly according to hoyle. Until that day when one of my sheep came to me to confess how he had mounted the wrong ewe out there somewhere in the pasture behind a thick hedge. At that very moment, looking the poor jerk in the face as he simpered, I was reborn; I went to my Bible and just the right chapter and verse for him popped up, I forget which one it was— it doesn't matter anyhow. I read it to him and he repented then and there with great sincerity and feeling. No more hocus-pocus, just the pure word of God as He said it did the trick and set me free to go in the direction of righteousness.

"But be patient, Hank! I'm getting there. I arrived one day on my first mission in a village in the vicinity of the Orinoco, up

north. I don't know what got into the administrators of the church
to send me to a tribe that was just barely out of head hunting
season. They had seen a few missionaries and other whites, and
they were fairly peaceful. But there I was, fresh out of a stint at
LETA, that's the Language and Evangelical Training Academy,
funded by the Associated Ministers of Christ, the State
Department, and a grant from the Wall Street Journal. My mind
was still fresh with memories of sin and abstinence, obedience,
and poverty. So I show up in this village where everybody cries
from joy at my arrival and puts on all sorts of ceremonial ritual in
my honor, where all I can see is the work of the devil and his in-
laws. We ate dog meat, can you imagine? They even had me eat
ground, that's it, dirt, soil, whatever you want to call it, mixed
with fragrant leaves and the rancid fat saved over from the last
tapir they had cooked. It nearly killed me, I assure you. It made
me realize that the first thing I had to do was teach them to treat
me with respect. That worked for a while, but then they started to
take me for a god, since I was always talking about Jesus. So the
chief calls me into his hut and tells me that not enough babies
were being born in the village and that since I was a god with a
rugged look they expected me to impregnate the women of the
tribe. I mean all the women! As I was telling him that was out of
the question, two big guards with poison-tipped spears and fiercely
determined faces appeared, wearing those disks in their lower
lips that made them even more convincing, leading an eighty-
five year old hag. They dragged me out to an isolated part of the
forest and left me alone with the ancient granny, making it clear
that we were to copulate before they would take me back to the
village. My choice was clear: it was either lay this creature or try
my luck with the ants, crocodiles, and vultures.

"I looked at her. She had no teeth, the lines on her face were
deep and dark, her eyes had been made dull by cataracts, and
what little hair was left on her head was stuck together with some
kind of gum and made to look like spikes pointing in all directions.
She was dressed in something resembling a burlap bag. Her bare

feet were misshapen by disease, reminding me of the Yanomani children I had seen with feet twisted by the mercury the gold miners had left behind. When the guards were gone—thank God they understood my need for privacy in all this—she smiled at me and said quickly in her Carib language: 'I've had many men during my long life. You may want to think again before trying to eat with me'—you know what that means, right? Her implication was that I would not measure up, and I was ready to agree with her wholeheartedly. 'Tell me about them, Old Mother. I wish to hear.' So she started with the ecstasy she experienced out in the forest with the chief from another village who had just killed her husband in battle. He was himself killed a few days later, in an ambush. The next time was with a 'god who had fallen from the sky.' It took a long time to explain this, but in the end I understood that a small aircraft had grounded in the forest and that this pilot, who had survived with a few scratches and bruises, came upon her and other women working in a communal garden. She remembered specifically his leather skull cap and goggles, which were signs of the divinity of the god who flies through the air and comes down to earth in fire. 'He chose me from all those women, and I stared at those godly eyes when he came into me, and I felt the earth tremble and the waters roar.' Her next lover was a mainline Protestant missionary, who made her cover her behind with a cloth whenever they had sex. Either he couldn't bear the sight, or he feared that evil would overtake him if he ever did take a good look. It—the cloth cover—became part of their ritual and assured them a satisfying sex life for some time. As she talked I could see that she was giving into the sweetness of the reminiscence and had practically forgotten my presence. I quietly took out a piece of charcoal from around a fire that had burned there a night or so before, and I drew a pair of goggles around my eyes; after that I took a handkerchief from my pocket and showed it to her. She fainted then and there, and when she came too, she thanked me profusely and made her way back to the village.

After that the guards returned to accompany me, apparently satisfied with my performance.

"In about three days they came to get me again, taking me out to the forest with a woman about ten years younger, but still old enough to be my grandmother. This one looked daggers at me when we were alone and started to run away. The guards brought her back. They tied her to a tree and suggested they hold her while I did my thing. I told them I didn't need them, that I had a way of doing it without her even knowing that it happened. They thought this was immensely funny and went off laughing. Once they were out of sight I started to dance around the tree she was tied to, singing loudly, making obscene gestures, and yelling nonsense phrases, mostly Latin. She covered her eyes and began to moan quietly. After fifteen minutes of this routine, I cut her bonds and went on dancing. She eyed me and quietly crawled away without attracting my attention; as soon as she was out of sight she bolted. Again the guards came back, laughing as soon as they saw me. Three days later it was a fifty year old wife, quite fat; apparently they were descending the age ladder to be sure that I got to them all before any died. She told me she had borne fourteen children, didn't want any more, and considered herself too old for that kind of stuff. Then she suggested that if we faked it she would make me special food and tell the chief, who was her husband, what a fine fellow I was. So we sat there, and she gossiped about her friends and neighbors in the village for a couple of hours until the guards returned and accompanied us back to the village.

"Now you should have seen the next one. She was about thirty, had a perfect figure, and swayed with her hips as we walked into the forest. When the guards left and she turned her face to me . . ."

"Jack! How many are there to go? I'm falling over. Can't you tell me the rest later sometime?"

"But Hank, now the good stuff starts. There were fifteen of them, ranging from this last one to the youngest who had just started developing breasts. You've only heard the beginning, the dull stuff where nothing happened! The fact is that I actually made all the rest, every one of them, and I'll die if I don't tell someone who can understand what it was like. But okay! I'm willing to put off the rest of my story until tomorrow. You know, by the way, that you will be expected to choose a wife at the ceremony. You won't marry her for a couple of years since they are all too young. But you will take her back to Xantupá; it's part of the deal the two tribes have. I think it is abominable, really, that young girls are traded like that without being consulted. Oh, they will take good care of your bride and send her through all the pagan wedding ceremonies you can imagine, including shaving her head and having her hug a cloth full of biting ants to give her lessons in pain! At least they have given up the custom of gang raping the women before their marriage. But after all I have done for these children to turn them into good, obedient Christians, they get whisked back into the barbarism and squalor of another tribe. Promise me, Hank, that you at least will continue to instruct the one you choose in the wisdom of the word of God! If you promise that I'll send my blessing. She will certainly miss the hymns and country music I play for the village in the evening and during services. Tomorrow I have to show you my loudspeaker system. It runs off a generator I arranged to have brought upriver on a barge a couple of months ago. When Christmas comes I'll make it play carols all day so that the natives get in the proper spirit, if those corroded wires last long enough. It will sound like downtown Houston!"

The next day's feast and celebrations were nothing compared to the ones in Xantupá. There was little in the way of dancing, and the music was all supplied by Ogg's loudspeaker system blaring out sentimental songs and old-fashioned hymns recorded by a congregation in some church, all interspersed with interludes of reggae rhythms and religious rock. Jack gave a sermon, changing his robes a few times to present different sections of his service.

Since he did it in English and then in the local language, the whole affair took rather long. I spent the time daydreaming about Deb. The choice of brides was a simple affair: seven girls had been prettied up by their families with lipstick, curled hair, and something that resembled new dresses. They stood there looking scared; their mothers were behind them, fussing like proud owners of pedigreed dogs. There was no way for me to back out of this now, so I picked the one I thought had the nicest smile and the most joyful eyes, with the thought that whatever happened she would be better off living the traditional life of the Indians than the bastardized Christianity Ogg was forcing his tribe to swallow. Tior chose a cross-eyed one, perhaps because that gave her a more spirit-like, otherworldly look, and Jubulá wanted the fattest one. The most moving part of the celebration was the wailing of the parents, which went on for hours and continued even after our departure.

That night I returned to Ogg's hut and had to endure the rest of his story about the Herculean labors he had performed with the women from the tribe near the Orinoco in the north.

Our group, plus the girls, left the next morning after accepting gifts and food. As soon as we had passed the outskirts of the village, we took off the pieces of cloth we had been wearing and left them hanging like ghosts from the branches of low trees. The girls watched with interest. They followed the men, carrying their meager possessions in slings over their backs and their worn tennis shoes in their hands, which made walking through the brush easier.

Along the way Kota explained to me that my bride's name was Meelú and that we would be married after she grew breasts and became a woman. She would learn the ways of the Xantupá by playing with the other girls, working in the gardens, and helping the older women in their tasks. Although she might help prepare my food, Kota made it clear to me that she would sleep in a special hut for girls and that I wouldn't have any sexual contact with her until she had become a member of the tribe and received a name, with ceremonial feasts and ordeals. Then he told me that one of his wives was eight years old and spent her time with girls her age. I had never seen him with her.

OUR RETURN TO Xantupá was met with the wailful sound of the Indians expressing their joy. At first the tribe members seemed to pay little attention to the newcomers, but soon the word got around, according to Kota, that our choices were fully approved of by the elders and the chief. All three set up hammocks in a hut that was reserved for adolescent girls who do not live with a family. Occasionally I see them running with the village children, playing or taking part in the preparation of food. My time for the moment is taken up by training in hunting and making weapons with Jotuven and by the lessons the shaman continues to give me in healing and in medicinal plants. It is a little difficult to explain what my situation here is. The villagers certainly have a plan for me; they expect some kind of contribution to their community, and they must feel that I am likely to be successful in providing it. For them my future is already determined, although I am not quite sure what they have in mind. At the same time, Jack Ogg's suggestion that in a few weeks I make my way back to his village and hop on a boat headed downstream toward civilization keeps returning to me. At the time I dismissed the idea, but it is becoming more and more appealing. What bothers me most is that the uncertainty of my position in the tribe seems to be satisfying to almost everyone except me. If only I could express myself to them, tell how I am torn between two ways of living, two sets of allegiances; if I could only understand their expectations of me . . .

At night I stay awake for hours writing in this diary and studying the Xantupá language. I review the sounds and expressions I have heard during the day and reread the notes scribbled in my tiny notebook. How difficult it is to learn a language without textbooks or teachers, the way children do so easily. Kota is a good language informer, but he is limited since he can't get it through his head that the words he says to me in his kind of English are different from the Xantupá words he uses to say something to his brother. Elliott Todd's notes are finally becoming useful. I am able to understand simple declarative sentences now, and I am making a collection of a large number of words pertaining to spears, archery, fish, animals, and plants; but connecting them together so that my friends can understand me is another matter.

Observing Meelú has become a real pleasure. I see little of her, since she is usually busy with other girls or working with the women. She brings food to my hut in the morning and evening, most often without saying anything. Whenever our eyes cross and she looks at me directly, she gives that appealing smile of hers. After I have eaten the evening meal, she searches my feet for jiggers, extracting them with deft fingers whenever she finds any. When it hurts and I grimace, she smiles, as if to make the discomfort easier to take. She is also learning how to pull out ticks without tearing them and to find and destroy lice in my hair and beard. Two times now she has painted my body for some ceremony; when she is done one of Jotuven's wives comes in to check out her work and gruffly points out mistakes in the design, all the while I am standing naked in my hut. What thoughts can be taking place in Meelú's young head? What kind of idea does she have of her future? What can she possibly know about me, with whom she is presumed to spend her life? I have never sensed in an adolescent so great a feeling of acceptance, even of resignation as I do in this child. What great trust she must have in the old folk, in the "system" of her tribe to decide her fate. And what blows me away is that for her what happens is neither good nor bad; it just is, and she accepts it with her knowing and plaintive smile. Sometimes, when I watch her at some simple activity, I feel the fragility of this small creature and the dangers she faces in the jungle and from encroaching civilization. I forgot to mention that after two days in Xantupá, Meelú took off her flimsy dress and adopted the nakedness of the tribe.

Last night Kota led me to Jotuven's hut for some talk. The chief, in the presence of his wives and an elder, informed me that the he wanted me to leave soon to go to the "big place" to fetch my wife and bring her back. It would be important to leave very soon to avoid the rains, which were just around the corner; it seems that once it begins to rain it is impossible to travel anywhere. Then, after the rainy season, I am to bring her back, she will become a tribe member, and an exchange of wives will take place. "Your wife is very strong, she knows healing, and she will give birth to next chief." As he said this, he held the snapshot of Deb I had given him, waving it up and down for emphasis.

There was no place for discussion. The chief had spoken; that we had become friends and spent hours together each day did not seem to make any difference. Kota and I talked about it afterward.

"It is all figured out how we get you to the big place."

"By river?"

"By road. You see. We take you there."

"When?"

"Soon. After feast and dance and you get ready. Everything start when sun rise."

"Kota, tell me. What if something happens to me on the way and I don't come back?"

"Nothing happen. You come back."

"But if I meet a crocodile and get eaten, fall in a river with fierce fish. Maybe another tribe captures me. What will happen to . . ."

"That can happen. Then your spirit come back and help us just the same. You come back."

"But suppose something like that does happen to me. I'm not worried about me but about Meelú. What would happen to her in the village?"

"She find other husband. You put your things together, take clothes along for big place. Surupuven make you safe trip."

At dawn three days later, Kota and four men with spears and arrows came to my hut, and we left for a cross-country trek. Dressed as I was when I left Braulio's in khaki shirt and shorts, long socks and boots, and a safari hat for the sun, I found crossing the forest much more difficult than before when I walked naked and barefoot. We went rapidly, without talking. After a day we came out of the forest to a dry area which almost seemed a desert. There were shrubs with sharp thorns everywhere, and along the dry tan earth, a hissing snake often dodged between stones. The heat of the sun was unbearable, yet it didn't seem to trouble my companions. Kota's only comment was: "Trees gone. No people here." He meant, I think, that the Indians had moved out of the area when it was deforested. To judge from the ruins of wooden shacks here and there and remnants of barbed wire fences, the area had been a pasture before the heat of the sun and erosion had rendered it useless.

After two days of sweating in the savanna we entered the forest again, but it was as hot since many trees had been cut, and the rays of the sun could reach us on the ground. There was no wind. At one point we heard rustling in one direction, and immediately my companions crouched and prepared for skirmish. It turned out to be two male Indians, dressed in blue jeans and baseball caps, carrying rifles. We let them pass by before we continued. We skirted a tiny village of wooden shacks and large road making equipment. Half an hour later we came to a break in the forest; it was a road with trees cut back twenty-five feet on either side. It went perfectly straight in both directions as far as my eyes could see.

"Here you get ride. We wait for car."

"Oh! That's called hitchhiking; you stand at the side of the road and hold your thumb out like this, and maybe a car will stop. Maybe not."

"Car stop."

The spontaneity of this whole procedure made me uneasy. If I did come back, and I half expected to, how would I ever find the village again, which for all I knew could have moved to a different place.

"Kota, how will I find my way back to Xantupá? I'll surely get lost."

He seemed nonplussed; perhaps the thought had not crossed his mind that there would be any difficulty for me to find my way back. Finally he understood.

"We meet you right here after rains. There tall dead tree. You know where," he said pointing to twisted branches reaching high above the foliage on the other side of the dirt roadbed.

At that point one of the warriors touched Kota's shoulder and pointed up the road. All listened. Kota motioned to one of the men, who proceeded to lie across the ruts of the road, and the rest of us retreated to behind the closest trees. Soon a jeep came in our direction in a cloud of dust, with its radio blasting forth a popular Brazilian tune. The startled driver came to a quick stop, pulled on the emergency brake, and stepped out to inspect the body. He had barely time to approach it before he was surrounded by Kota and the others holding their spears ready to throw; the body in the road quickly revived and pulled out a knife. The driver wisely held his hands up and was quickly relieved of the revolver he had hanging from his belt. Kota motioned to me to approach.

"Take to big place," he said in English.

The man, his face dark from years of exposure to the sun, answered him in an Indian language, slowly, as if searching for words. Some conversation ensued.

"He want papers."

I took out Elliott Todd's permit and handed it to him.

"Australian," he said in Portuguese, looking at me. "Okay, let's go." In a voice filled with anger he said something to Kota and then headed for the driver's seat. Before I climbed in next to him, Kota slipped the revolver into my pocket while giving me a bear hug. As we started off I could see my friends retreating in the dust into the forest.

"Lucky you have the permit," he said in halting English. "Without it we could both get into much trouble, even though I think this one is fake. So what!"

I answered in English, not letting on that I could speak Portuguese.

"Where are you going?"

"Rio."

"I'll take you as far as Brasília. You can catch a flight from there. Do you have money?"

"Yes," I answered, feeling the wad of Brazilian bills that Todd had stashed away in his portfolio.

"It'll take a couple of days. I hope you don't mind sleeping on the floor at the government post."

When I gave him back his revolver, he thanked me, and told me how difficult it was for a mine inspector to do his work. He had an area with 500 mines to visit each year. Since he had time to visit only half that number, he forged documents for the ones he skipped, especially those where the miners were hostile and threatening to government agents. When he went to the mines where he could expect at least a neutral reception, he would explain the regulations, look around, and leave, suspecting that the miners would ignore his recommendations and tear up the sheet where he listed the changes he ordered them to make.

"What do you look for when you inspect a mine?"

He must have felt that he could trust me. "First I check out the sanitary and safety conditions of the workers; then I take samples of the soil and look to see what is done with the chemical runoff; finally I am supposed to ask about how the managers treat the Indians living nearby and the ones who work for them.

All that is reported to the central office in Brasília; you can see in the back seat the boxes of files I am taking there now. What is hard is when I find outrageous violations of the rules and write a strongly worded report recommending that a particular mining permit should be rescinded, I know that it will be filed in a big drawer and forgotten. But what the heck? I have a family to feed; they hardly have enough to eat even when I am paid. Can you believe that two years ago I received the department award for being the most conscientious inspector? That means that I didn't receive any bribes from the miners' association, as far as the department knew. What they don't know is how much I make from gifts from the miners who want me to write a favorable report on their operations. That pays for my children's shoes and a room for my father, who . . ."

Here Hank's diary breaks off. It would be difficult to reconstruct the rest of his return trip or to know how long it took him to reach Rio. He phoned Erik from Brasília. A few hours later Deb, Erik, and Maria met him at the Aeroporto Galeão.

The meeting was a little extraordinary. Maria was crying loudly, Erik wanted to take charge of the baggage (there wasn't any), and Deb, who was afraid to react too strongly to her first sight of Hank after so long a period of waiting and worrying, fainted when she saw him with his unkempt beard and looking like an emaciated, flea-bitten hostage with a wild pattern of black and red lines painted on his forehead. That gave Erik something to take care of. Hank consoled Maria, and after Deb came to, with the help of Maria's smelling salts, Hank was whisked off by his friends in Erik's car before there could be any trouble with the authorities over his papers or his identity.

As Erik drove from the airport toward his house with Maria at his side, Hank held Deb tight in his arms in the back seat. She was calm now, having convinced herself that this phantom was Hank and that he was alive. Now it was Hank who was in shock, breathing heavily, shivering in the humid 98° heat, unable to say anything more than:

"I'm glad to be back."

"Don't talk. Just relax, my love! You'll feel better soon."

"I'm glad to be with you all, glad to be free, and especially glad to be me again!"

"And you're safe, too; that's what I'm thankful for; in one piece, although you do look a bit peaked."

"Maria's cooking will take care of that," Erik joined in. "You can begin your rehabilitation as soon as we arrive."

At lunch, in the garden under the shade of a jacaranda tree, Hank told briefly where he had been and what he had been through, including his trek across Mato Grosso do Sul, the sojourn at Braulio's, the experience at Xantupá, and his return.

"I've read about this Braulio Souza e Rego. Seems to be rather influential politically, but no one takes him seriously. But say! Hank. You were in Petrópolis all that time, only an hour away! Had you been able to escape, you could have walked from there!"

"I can tell you more, Erik, when I get a chance to look at my diary to remind me of what happened. I wrote everything down just after it occurred, so I could afford to forget things along the way. It is all there, but it's in code so I'll have to translate for you."

"Take my advice and hide your diary. You will be politically suspect to some people, and what you wrote and thought may be of value to someone who wants to do you in. Sr. Braulio certainly has agents in this city who would be happy to oblige their employer by making incriminating evidence disappear. I would lay low for a while, if I were you; you can also ask for protection from the Consulate. Is your diary here? May I see it?"

Hank went into the house and with some difficulty extricated his notebook from a pocket inside his shirt. The pages, no longer holding together, had yellowed from the sun and abuse and were damp from perspiration.

"Here," he said handing it to Erik. "Maybe we should leave it out to air for a while."

"It has the suspicious look of a document that might get someone in trouble, make someone else rich, or both. Your code will excite the curiosity of any snooping eyes," he said, looking at the first few pages. "I know exactly how we can conceal it. Maria, my dear! Would you put this somewhere where you will be sure to find it?"

"Erik, don't make fun of me! You know I never lose anything."

"That is exactly it. When Maria puts anything away only she can find it; I can't, and certainly no thief or secret agent would think of looking inside an old cookbook on a shelf with fifty other cookbooks. Here, dear! Take it now."

Maria took it, walked briskly into the kitchen, and immediately returned. "Just tell me when you want to see it."

"By the way," Hank asked. "What day is it today? What month are we in? I want to start right away settling scores with the people who sent me on this insane goose chase. They owe me money, too. SOD was supposed to send a check months ago. Did it come, Deb?"

"Nothing came from them."

That night Deb moved from her room in the house back to the little cottage. She finally felt in tune with Hank as he took off his clothes and showed her the painted patterns on his body and explained the meaning of the long wide black and red vertical stripes running from his shoulders to his buttocks and the intricate labyrinthine patterns on his neck and chest. He put off telling Deb who the artists were until sometime later when . . . when it would be easier to explain, but he did describe how he had ended up without pubic hair.

"I think you look fine like that; it goes well with the artwork," she laughed, caressing his balls. "It will be a shame to wash off the colors; I'll feel like I'm destroying a cathedral or desecrating some symbolic relic. May I take a picture of you? Just for us to see, no one else."

Deb went to the house to find her camera. When she returned Hank posed for a series of snapshots that would display his decoration from all sides. Then he climbed into the tub where Deb slowly and lovingly sponged away the dyes that clung stubbornly to his back and chest. She was wearing a terry cloth bathrobe tied loosely at the middle and revealing one of her breasts. Hank felt how deeply he loved her. When he was dry, Deb cut his hair short and gave him a lindane shampoo, efficient nurse that she was. While Deb bathed, Hank shaved his beard, which by this time was full and bushy, and then the two of them, in their familiar bed, talked and loved each other throughout the night.

The next morning Hank was feverish, but since it was Saturday the U.S. government offices and subsidiaries would be closed anyway. Eating Maria's food, loving Deb, and taking long walks with Erik cured Hank of his fever, and by Monday morning he felt healthy and aggressive.

He headed for the SOD offices in a cab. The fourth floor of the building where he had been interviewed months ago was deserted; the furniture was gone, the rugs were torn out, the doors ajar, and dust was everywhere. Down at the concierge's booth, Hank learned that the offices of Southern Overseas Development had moved to "somewhere on the Rua Alfredo Gamba, near the Hotel Restaurante Europa." Hank instructed the cab driver to cruise the area but found nothing. At the hotel the people behind the main desk hadn't heard of SOD.

Hank returned home in the afternoon. Deb was at work, Erik out on errands, and Maria resting. Hank called the Consulate, asked for John Webb, the cultural attaché's assistant who had introduced him to Kater months ago. Webb had been transferred to Iceland.

"Then can I speak to his secretary?"

"I'm sorry, I wouldn't know who that is."

"Her name is Delgado, Pilar Delgado."

"Delgado . . . She left at the same time Webb did. We wouldn't know how to contact her."

No one seemed to know anything about SOD. Hank called a phone number he had written somewhere among his notes taken during his interview with Kater.

A secretary answered in English and claimed not to be able to give out information of any sort. She asked for Hank's name and address and then suggested he check with the Rio branch of the Chamber of Commerce. It was closed.

That evening Erik invited Deb and Hank to dinner at a restaurant overlooking the bay.

It was dark when they returned. They did not notice until Maria was preparing tea that during their absence the house had been entered and searched.

"Yes. Someone has been here." Erik strode across the living room. "That chair was next to the window when we left, and the painting over there is crooked. Let's see . . . yep, the papers on my desk have been moved around. The drawers have been messed up, the room has been searched. Go, Hank, and check the cottage. Here take this along just in case." Erik handed him a revolver.

The cottage looked as if it had been pillaged by the Huns. Chairs lay broken on the floor, the exposed entrails of the disgorged mattress were strewn about, the clothes had been torn from their hangers in the closet, and all of the cabinets and drawers of the kitchenette had been emptied. Hank could see that the rugs had been yanked up and the wall hangings pulled off. In a closet the locks had been torn off empty suitcases, and someone had opened the trapdoor to the subfloor space.

"It's a total mess," Hank reported. They peered around the courtyard with flashlights and found that someone had probed with a shovel as if searching for a lost treasure.

"My medical supplies are gone, Hank. Mostly bandages and tape, but there were syringes and painkillers, too. Do you suppose they were looking for drugs, Erik?"

"Maybe. But even if they weren't they wouldn't pass up something worth selling."

"What else is gone?" Maria asked looking anxiously in all the corners. "My sewing hasn't been touched; the cookbooks are safe!"

"The TV and video are okay. It must be something other than an ordinary break-in. By some miracle we haven't been burglarized before; but you hear more and more often about Rio residents coming home to find nothing left in their apartments or houses. I'll call and report it to the police." Erik found that the lines were cut.

It was three hours before an *inspetor* arrived, followed by two assistants, chain-smoking as they looked around. They sealed off the cottage so that no clues would be lost before a full-fledged investigation could be initiated, with a warning not to touch anything. If Deb or Hank needed a toothbrush or a pair of shoes, they would have to buy them.

"Three out of five houses in the neighborhood have been vandalized in the last year, so this is nothing unusual. The fact that almost nothing has been taken makes one think that the perpetrator was either drunk, stoned, or had a grudge against someone living here or against someone he thought lives here. It is also possible that this was done by a gang out for the kicks more than the loot. At any rate, it is lucky you weren't home— you could have been hurt or killed."

"How long will it be before the investigation?"

"Hard to say. Sometimes two weeks, sometimes two months. You have to understand; we are up to our ears at the station. A quarter of the force has been laid off because there's no money. Some of the guys have been transferred downtown to protect the tourists from being mugged. Two of my agents just got fired for taking bribes. Another was shot last week and won't be replaced. If you are in a hurry, come to my office tomorrow after three; maybe we can work something out."

When the police had departed, Erik calmly removed the tape that they had used to seal off the cottage.

"Unless I go and bribe them tomorrow, they won't come to

investigate at all. And if they did come it would take them years before they decide they can't come to any conclusion. Anyhow, they knew this wasn't an ordinary break-in; you could tell by their pinched faces as they looked around. That means that if they ever find who broke in they would cover it up."

"Oh! Erik. Shouldn't we move to where we can be safe?" Maria's voice and eyes were pleading.

"It's too late to be safe anywhere."

EARLY THE NEXT morning Erik visited his neighbors to ask what they had seen or heard. The ones living right next door to either side hadn't noticed a thing. One of them did think, though, that the area may have been a little more noisy than usual. Someone else exclaimed at length about the riffraff and "different people" moving into the neighborhood. Only the old Italian who spent his time sitting outside the main entrance to his house leaning his chin on his cane and watching life and vehicles go by, had noticed something unusual. From what Erik understood of his garbled Portuguese, about nine o'clock an unmarked, closed truck had pulled up in front of Erik's house, followed by two Fords. He was sure they were Fords, for he could identify any car on the road without making a mistake, so take his word for it, they were Fords. Some men rushed in, turned the lights on, remained inside for an hour or so, then rushed out and drove off at top speed. What did the men look like? How were they dressed? The informant wasn't able to see well, you understand, his eyes are getting feeble and it was already dark. They were men, just like most men around here, stocky, curly hair, hatless, open shirts, in a hurry.

"They weren't children, then."

"No. They were just like you and me, only not so tall as you. The kind of people you see walking on the street, not *ladri, no, non sono ladri.*"

Erik returned to report to his friends what he had found. Deb had gone out in search of a phone to call the clinic and ask for the day off. After returning she consoled Maria, who seemed to be the most affected by the break-in. Hank sat glumly in a corner.

"From what you say, Erik, I gather that this was no ordinary burglary, and it was not performed by abandoned kids, homeless bums, or street gangs. I've got a funny feeling it has something to do with my return."

"But nobody knows you're back, Hank. And who would be interested in you or your belongings?" Erik asked, forgetting what he had said the day before.

"I think I know who might be interested: the same people who made sure I couldn't reach you or Deb by long distance. The same ones who turned me over to Braulio and then told him to get rid of me. The same ones who couldn't give Deb any help when she was inquiring about me, and who are doing their best now to keep me from seeing anybody."

"Oh, darling. What connection do you see?"

"Maybe, Hank; everything's possible. But I have found that the only way to survive in this climate and city is to avoid paranoid thinking like the plague. If it doesn't kill you it will drive you nuts."

"Somebody does know I am here, and I kick my damn ass for telling her over the phone."

"Telling who over the phone?"

"A receptionist at some number I called yesterday. When she asked for my name I told her, and I probably gave her this address, too. I think it was some business affairs bureau, or intelligence office. If only I could see Kater soon and get my name off their books! I won't feel free until I do."

"Once your name is in someone's books," Maria broke in, "it is never erased. We saw that during the military rule after Goulart. My uncle Christino Peixas, when he was young, wrote some articles critical of Vargas. Then he settled down and made a lot of money and stayed away from politics. Twenty years later, for no reason, he was arrested and tortured. It broke his spirit; he couldn't work after that."

"Maria is right, Hank. By looking at the way they dance and play music all night you would think everyone lives for the present moment here. But memory is a beast with long tentacles that never let go. I hate to say this, but you and Deb should go back to your country. You can stay in the cottage as long as you want, and we will miss you terribly when you do go. But my gut feeling is: leave now."

"I'm still under contract. I don't see how l could let my friends at the clinic down. We are absolutely swamped; I even feel guilty for staying away today."

In the afternoon Hank took a cab to the U.S. Chamber of Commerce. There in a business directory he found the new address for SOD—just off Rua Alfredo Gamba. He hailed another cab in the street. The driver sped off, taking a route that went by the beaches.

"How about going across town rather than around it? It's worth a good tip if I get there soon."

"If you want to go directly, add two hours to the trip in this traffic. Senhor, enjoy life! Look at the girls! You can't be making money all the time. You will die young."

Eventually the driver found the location Hank was looking for. It had a modest exterior but was solidly built, like those quiet buildings in the shade of tall trees that house insurance companies and stock brokers. An old uniformed guard accompanied Hank into the elevator, pressed the third floor button, and said that he didn't believe anyone was there.

The elevator door opened directly into the offices of SOD. Things looked no more promising there than they had in Erik's cottage after the raid. Desks, filing cabinets, tables, chairs, typewriters, computers, boxes of files and invoices were strewn around the floor or stacked in corners without apparent order. Pieces of plywood and wooden ladders leaned against walls covered with chicken wire in preparation for replastering. Paint cans, one on its side in the middle of a yellow puddle, and spray-paint equipment gave off the acrid smell of unfinished remodeling. Two men were sitting at a table close to an open window, going through files.

"Sorry. We're closed. We won't open for at least another month," one said in English.

"Can I ask a question? It's really very important."

"If you want a job, forget it. We're cutting down our staff drastically. Hard times."

"I don't want a job. I already have one . . . With SOD."

"What?" the other asked. "I haven't seen you around."

Hank explained as briefly as he could who he was, that he wanted to quit his job with SOD and pick up his check. He added that he wanted very much to see Herb Kater.

"Kater is on vacation in the States. He won't be back for a couple of months. Smart guy, getting out while we are relocating."

"Then I want to see his assistant. I've forgotten his name. A handsome guy with a square chin and wavy hair."

"Beats me. What division was he with?"

"Kater was in charge of Special Missions before he moved to Operation Administration," the other chimed in. "That office has been discontinued; I don't think anyone is left, certainly no one who would know anything."

"Then who is Kater responsible to? There must be someone around here who has some authority to deal with cases like mine."

"Right now there is nobody around except us, and the only authority we have is to look through these files and decide what to toss."

"And we'd better get tossing fairly soon; if we don't we will be tossed ourselves . . . and shredded, too."

"By the way; how long have you been moving? Every time I phoned from the field all I could hear was a recording saying my call would be taken as soon as someone was available. Was there something wrong with the phone system?"

"We just started moving a month ago."

The other young man went over to the phone, picked it up. "It's working fine now."

"Before you go back to work, just tell me this. Where can I go to get this business cleared up? Surely there is an office somewhere where one can resign."

"Hard to say. Have to go to the Consulate for that. Personnel, I suppose; that's where I'd go."

"Wait! He should go to Infocord; you know, the Office of Coordination of Information. They were probably overseeing your mission. You could talk to, let me see . . ." he paged through a directory, ". . . Hassleton; he's the chief there."

"Where is that?"

"In the basement of the Consulate Annex. But you can't get in there without prior clearing."

"Rudy, you know he won't be able to find the Annex anyhow. Here is what we'll do. It's closed now, but we'll call first thing in the morning, to make things easier for you, and let Hassleton know you are coming. Give us your phone number and we'll make an appointment for you."

"I'm not sure where I'll be. Let me call you. What time?"

"Eleven."

Hank wrote the phone number and left.

When he phoned the next morning, he got through right away.

"You have an appointment with Hassleton at three this afternoon. He said he wants to see you. Come to this office at two; there will be a car and a driver to take you to the Annex."

Hank had two hours to eat lunch and gather his thoughts. To clear his mind he walked through the streets in the vicinity of Rua Alfredo Gamba. "I like these people," he thought as he watched the flow of the crowd in the afternoon heat. "Although it feels strange to be back among city dwellers—to see the secretaries, shoppers, business people, all intent on getting somewhere or doing something—the best part is no one seems to notice me. It's been a long time since I've felt as anonymous as I do right now." He made his way to the SOD offices. A young guard put him on the elevator. Once again he got off on the third floor. No one was in sight amid the boxes and the furniture. He cleared his throat, wandered around looking through open doors into the various rooms: offices, meeting rooms, a library, storage closets, rest areas. One door looked like a safe; another was locked with a huge padlock. Finally he returned to the open area next to the elevator and walked to a desk with a telephone and what looked like a government directory. As he paged through the headings in the directory, he vaguely sensed a presence nearby. Was somebody moving behind him? Suddenly he felt an excruciating pain in the back of his neck; he slumped down as he realized he was losing consciousness.

When Deb returned from work at seven she found Maria and Erik resting in the courtyard after having spent the day clearing away the mess in their house. They chatted for a moment; then Deb went back to the cottage. She returned to the courtyard after a moment.

"Have you seen Hank? He isn't in the cottage."

"We saw him go out late in the morning. He didn't say where he was going, but just before leaving he made a call to that Southern Development outfit. I think he went there."

"Thanks, Erik. I'll shower and wait for him before eating."

When Hank hadn't returned by eleven, Deb realized that she was worried.

"Here he survives being lost for months in the wilderness, and I'm all anxious when he is an hour late for dinner, in a town where no one arrives anywhere on time."

"Oh, you know men, Deb. They need some distraction. And he hasn't been in a city all this time."

"Yes, Maria. I know men. But I also know Hank, and I'm worried."

By midnight Deb was feeling frantic.

"But where could he be, Erik? What could be keeping him? Nothing makes sense. The thought constantly goes through my mind that something has happened to him. I feel like screaming, rushing to your car and driving around to find him somewhere. I have to know where he is!"

"We are as worried as you are, Deb. I have to tell you this. Maria told him just this morning not to go anywhere, to stay here, to forget about any obligation he may have to tell those people what happened to him. He said: 'It is a point of honor for me. I have to tell them what happened, what they did to me. Then there is the money they owe me. I didn't go through all that experience for nothing.'"

Erik started calling everywhere he could think of. All the United States offices were closed. He had Hank paged at the Bar Luis, where they had all gone several times. In the meantime Maria brewed some chamomile tea.

Deb went to work as usual the next morning, distraught after a sleepless night. Early in the afternoon Maria phoned her.

"Deb, I'm sure everything is alright, but Erik just received a call about Hank. It seems he was hurt somewhere last night; that's all I know. Maybe he was hit by a car or something. Erik doesn't know anything, either, so he went to find out what the situation is. We'll call as soon as we know something. At least Erik knows where he is, so you can relax."

"But where is he Maria? I need to go there right away!"

"Erik didn't say. He just said to phone you, and then he left. I'll call the first thing I hear."

"Maria, what does your intuition tell you? How is Hank? What do your spirits say? I need to know something."

"The spirits say he is not suffering. They also say he is alive. They don't tell me anything beyond that."

An hour later, Erik called Deb.

"I'm with Hank at the Public Emergency Clinic. He's alive, so don't worry."

"What happened?"

"It seems he was mugged yesterday afternoon. They found him in a gutter this morning in some favela, and he was brought here in an ambulance."

"How does he look? Is he in pain?"

"He looks like they gave him a real workout. He suffered several blows on the back of the head and he is massively bruised. They say he is okay. There are a few broken ribs and other bones, but his breathing and heart are normal. Only he is comatose, so I haven't been able to talk to him. Here is the address. Can you get over here? Maybe you can bring him out of his coma."

Deb managed to remain cool enough to get herself driven by a colleague to the hospital, where she found Erik sitting next to a bed in a large and noisy ward. In the bed was Hank, bruised and bandaged almost beyond recognition, attached to a primitive heart monitor and a bottle for intravenous feeding. She looked at his face for as long as she could before her tears obscured her sight. The expression on his face was relaxed, at peace, almost smiling.

Deb phoned the Consulate and SOD. No one knew anything. Finally she got through to Hassleton's office. There the secretary put her on hold. After five minutes another secretary came on and announced that Hank hadn't shown up for his appointment in the afternoon and that they were wondering where he was. That was all.

Three days later, when Hank came out of his coma, the only visible change was that his eyes were open when he was not sleeping. A flock of physicians, including the best neurologist in Rio, made extensive tests and declared him vegetative. Since any change in his condition was dubious, they advised Deb to "learn to live with it."

Summoning up all the energy within her, Deb requested an official inquiry into what had happened and engaged an American lawyer to do a private investigation. After a week, when nothing more could be done for Hank in the hospital, she accepted Erik's offer of a large loan to pay for airline tickets and asked him to drive Hank and her to the airport. She thanked Erik and Maria for all they had done and promised to keep in touch. She flew first class to Seattle seated next to Hank's litter. During the flight she kept his inert hand clasped in hers and stared blankly in front of her. She hadn't slept for four days. Only occasionally did she become aware of the activity of the flight attendants and the conversation of the other travelers around her. Voices saying words that made no sense drifted in and out of her consciousness. "Can I serve you a cocktail? . . . No problem . . . Increased productivity means . . . There has been a veritable invasion of Brazil by American brand names: Pizza Hut, Arby's . . . The captain has announced that we are going through a turbulence; please fasten . . . First they have to eliminate virtually all restrictions on the participation of foreign capital . . . If there's no privatization and zero inflation, then most state banks must be liquidated . . . The cheap stocks are making Brazil's markets boom . . . We're seeing another economic miracle . . ."

III

Portland, Oregon:
Deb

D EAR ERIK AND MARIA,

It is now two months since I arrived in Seattle. As I mentioned when we talked long-distance, I am living with my mother, at least temporarily, waiting to decide what to do with my life if there is anything left of it. We found Hank a place in a convalescent hospital where he can stay until I discover a nursing home I can afford. That may be difficult, perhaps impossible.

I feel bad for not having answered your letter sooner. Your offer to forgive the loan for our tickets from Rio to Seattle overwhelmed me with emotion. What can I say, except that some day I intend to repay you in full, however long it takes.

The return trip can't be described; it was misery and suffering from beginning to end. I went without sleeping or eating and survived on a few cans of pop; even that nauseated me. Installing Hank in the first-class cabin of the 747 required two mechanics and medical personnel. One stewardess helped me while another kept telling the anxious passengers that everything would be okay and that they could look forward to a wonderful trip. They were clearly put out to find that they were to fly in a kind of air-ambulance instead of the usual luxury and the anticipated fun and games. How can you flirt properly with the stewardess if you are sitting one row from a comatose passenger being fed intravenously? Well, they found a way: they got completely skewered on booze and loosened their inhibitions as much as they could hope to. After an hour aloft Hank and I were forgotten, and I could cry my eyes out without being noticed. One of the stewardesses was very helpful, and the passengers did their best not to notice Hank lying there or me sobbing away. Soon instead of feeling embarrassed for causing a spectacle I had the impression I was invisible.

After an endless flight to Miami, Hank had to be unloaded from the jet. At the airport we were put into a special room reserved for handicapped people and nursing mothers with their babies. There I could feel more alone with Hank during the hours we waited for the flight to Denver. That jet was packed and much more uncomfortable.

I have some dear friends in Denver but couldn't bring myself to call them and explain. Instead I sat in the special room staring through the window at the planes landing and the others taking off. The jet for Seattle couldn't take us because that model wasn't equipped to install Hank. So we were shipped off to Los Angeles and from there via San Francisco to Seattle. I'll spare you the details of the rest of the trip; it was uninterrupted misery. What strikes me now is that no one talked to me or asked any questions. My situation must have seemed bizarre to anyone who saw us. Were they all honoring my right to privacy? Or have I become too accustomed to Brazil where everybody talks to you? When I left Rio, I dreaded having to talk to anyone, but after a several hours of silence I longed for human contact and a few kind words. I remember thinking that the gates of loneliness were opening to me and that I had no choice but to enter.

My mother met me with one of my sisters and a paramedic ambulance, which could transport Hank, who is really too much for us to handle. Mother is taking care of me as best she can. She is getting me to eat a little, and I sleep in fits and starts. Each day I take walks to get the feeling of being in Seattle once again. Then I spend the afternoons with Hank, sitting in a narrow courtyard, looking at the surrounding brick walls. He is strapped in a wheelchair so that his head faces straight ahead, and at times he almost looks the way he used to, only quieter and as if lost in thought. I spend hours talking to him, explaining things, telling him what I am doing, even reciting a little poetry I had learned in high school. The only poems I remember seem to be about death, and I suppose I get a strange sense of comfort from that. Hank still doesn't give any signs of recognition or mental activity, but he looks as he always did. I daydream sometimes that he understands everything I tell him, that he senses my kisses and tears but is simply unable to respond in any way. Maybe he is having profound thoughts inside his head; he has plenty of spare time for that and no distractions. Then when I look again at his empty expression my dream shatters like glassware hurled against those brick walls, and I feel even more alone. At least he isn't suffering; his face shows no pain, and at times he almost seems to smile, as if at some distant, vaguely humorous idea. That's when I remember that the pain is all mine.

Thank you for all the information you sent. I am going through it slowly because it is still hard for me to concentrate on anything that requires mental effort. I wonder why that American lawyer in Rio pulled out of my case. As you said, he has had time to familiarize himself with the issues and has done some investigation. But why was he so enthusiastic at first?

Just before I heard from you, I attended a legal seminar here in Seattle on problems of litigation involving foreign governments and companies. One of the presenters was an attorney from Portland, Oregon. He sounded quite competent, so I talked to him after the seminar and explained briefly Hank's situation. He said that if American companies or the U.S. government is at all involved a suit can be filed here. What I will need is a contact in Rio to do the legwork. Since I no longer have an attorney in Rio to represent me, I plan to phone for an appointment with the Portland lawyer as soon as I feel strong enough. Are you still willing to help me out, Erik, to be my contact, as you offered? I can't imagine anybody anywhere who would make me feel as secure as you do.

My mother continues working as a nurse on night shift in a big hospital located around the corner from where she lives. She is almost sixty and was considering retiring soon, but now I believe she is too worried about me and Hank, particularly the financial aspect, to think about it seriously. How are we ever going to pay for his care? Currently I have no money. I know Hank's parents have nothing. My own father disappeared when I was ten, so he won't be of any help. Maybe Social Security can help; my sister's husband is checking into that.

I have been going on and on. In a way you are my real parents, my real human connection, and I am so thankful that you exist. I think often of my other friends in Rio, and I also wonder what has happened to all my patients. I wrote Bernie to get things straightened out with him. If Roger calls—he should be back in Rio by now—tell him what happened.

One of the reasons I am rambling on so is that I don't really know how to sign off. The two of you must have been sent to me by my guardian spirits, who knew ahead of time how much I would need the kind of loving support and generous help you seem to have an endless supply of. If anything good came out of the whole misadventure, it was surely knowing you. Please write again as soon as you can. In the meantime, give my love to your daughter, to Carlos, and their children.

Fondly, Deb.

P.S. I know that there are a lot of our belongings scattered around your place. Bernie will want to retrieve the medical equipment. I would like you to give what is left of Hank's travel gear to someone who can use it, maybe your grandchildren. The desk I used is full of old letters, notes, and agendas that you can mail me. Keep Hank's diary, which you hid somewhere, Maria. I couldn't bear to touch it now, but maybe in a year or two my eyes will be able to focus on it without filling up with tears. D.

In time Deb's tears dried up. She went to a counselor, a friend of her sister's, who listened attentively to her woes and made suggestions she couldn't possibly follow. One was to focus on the tragic side of life in order to realize that she wasn't alone. Instead, Deb began going to every comedy Seattle's movie theaters had to offer. She started exercising and running regularly to get into better physical shape. In a stroke of genius, she cut her visits to Hank in half.

One day the next week Deb drove to Portland for an appointment with Steven Thornton, the attorney she had written about to Erik and Maria. He explained to her that he would do the research for her case and once all the information was in hand, another member of his firm would take over to do the court presentations.

"That kind of specialization helps us win more often," he told her.

It turned out that he knew a good deal about the care of handicapped people and was able to suggest ways to finance Hank's care. He was also acquainted with a home in Portland where Hank might be very well taken care of, if Deb was interested.

As a result Deb herself moved to Portland, made friends there, installed Hank in the Friendly Lawn Home, received a grant from an endowment for his care, and concentrated on the preparation of her case.

Deb found an apartment on a hill north of Washington Park. The neighborhood reminds me of Berkeley, she thought as she climbed the five flights of stairs to look at the empty rooms once again. A living room with a narrow balcony jutting out over the street and a view of the Willamette River in the distance flowing under the Fremont Bridge. On one side of the fireplace, a door opens into the bedroom with a tiny bath. On the other, a small kitchen harbors a two-burner gas stove and a refrigerator. Deb sat at the kitchen table and wrote a list of food, staples, cleaning supplies, and furniture she would need. Then she signed a copy of the lease, wrote a check, and walked downstairs to the landlady's apartment. There she asked for directions to the Goodwill and Salvation Army stores. It needs work, she thought as she strode down the hill toward 19th Avenue, but it will be a neat place when I am done.

The Friendly Lawn Home was an old building located some four miles to the north, across the river, on a busy thoroughfare near the University of Portland. Fortunately a city bus line went from her own neighborhood directly to Hank's new home; the trip took less than an hour. Deb went to see him in the morning twice a week; on rainy days she would sit with him in a large living room where other residents sat talking to no one or rocking aimlessly; one adolescent boy spent his days in a wooden bed built into a corner of the room, turning and moaning at five-minute intervals. The place is clean, Deb told herself, Hank is being taken care of, and I can afford it if I find a job. Still, she knew she would feel depressed after leaving.

From her flat, Deb could walk to most of the other parts of the city she needed to frequent—stores, theaters, laundromats, her lawyer's office—even when it was raining, which seemed most of the time. Not having a car parked on the street appealed to her, although it meant she couldn't drive into the country on nice days or explore on her own the parks, campuses, and suburbs she longed to see when she studied a map. She would have to postpone her desire to drive along the banks of the Columbia River as it flowed north toward the Pacific.

Instead, she plunged into the life of the city, as much as her means permitted. Neighborhood movie theaters, she found, were cheaper than the ones downtown. Shopping without buying was no problem for her; she learned how to try on expensive dresses and sweaters and then explain that they weren't exactly what she wanted; after that she would take a bus to a thrift store to look for something similar. She went to the museums on the free entrance days and took a bag lunch to the noon faculty and student concerts at Portland State University. To mitigate her loneliness, she sat in the cafés in her neighborhood, reading or talking to people at nearby tables. That is how she landed a job as photographer.

"There's no way I'm going to be a nurse again!" she said to herself as she read the classified ads in *The Oregonian*. "That part of my life is over. I have torn those pages out. Or do counseling, either. Nothing related to health." She made some phone calls. Most of the positions that appealed to her were already filled. The ones still not taken were located way out somewhere, paid barely minimum wages, or were night shift only. A tall, black fellow saw her reading the classified ads and asked her what she was looking for.

"A job."

"Need it bad?"

"Real bad. Do you know of anything?"

"I just quit myself, so I'm looking, too, or will be."

"What was wrong?"

"They changed the rules. I was selling cameras. Then they wanted me to take pictures, but I didn't want to. It's not what I'm good at. I'm better at talking. Gimme an espresso, please. A double. You want one? I still have a paycheck coming."

"No thanks. I have too much caffeine in my veins as it is. Have you been replaced?"

"I could care less. They can take their job and shove it." He looked at Deb. "Want to apply while it is still open? If you can take pictures, go for it. I'll write the address here."

"Thanks. I'll try right now," Deb said picking up the napkin he handed her.

"Tell 'em Josh sent you. Then come back and tell me how you made out."

When Deb returned to the café in the afternoon, Josh was still there talking with friends, at the same table, in front of the same crumpled classified section.

"Get hired? It took long enough. These are my friends here."

"Glad to meet you all. My name's Deb. The man at the Shutterball said he'd hire me provisionally. Guess I'm lucky. I don't have much experience, a portfolio of my work to show, or a résumé. The worst is that I don't even have a camera to my name. So I had a lot of explaining to do, like I left my camera in Rio, which is true, and my portfolio is still sitting in Seattle, which isn't."

"How did he react when you said my name to him?"

Deb paused. "The guy was sort of complaining about you when I went in. So I just said I had heard they needed someone."

"Sort of complaining? Must have been bitching. The guy hates my guts and cooked up a way to get me to quit, and it worked."

"Know why he didn't fire you?" one of the friends put in. "Since you quit it means he don't have to pay no unemployment for you now that you ain't working. You got screwed, man."

"How are you going to take photos without a camera?" another of Josh's friends asked Deb.

"I don't know. I have until Monday to figure that one out."

"Want to buy mine? It's a little Korean camera I got secondhand that's easy to use and has lenses and filters, you'll see. You got your job, Deb. Now what about me?" Josh showed her the newspaper. "They want somebody to help clear out clogged sewers. And here is an ad for a maintenance person in an apartment house. When they see my skin will they hire me?"

"You could always push. Money in that, man!"

"None of that shit for me. I wanna be serious."

"You know, Josh, they are always hiring in big hospitals. They need people to do all sorts of things, and the pay isn't bad. Get some application blanks and let me help you fill them out. I've had experience with hospitals!"

As Deb walked home along Glisan Street, a sign announcing an exhibit of local photographers caught her eye. Pisces Gallery, second floor. Deb went up the stairs. It was a large one-room affair with screens and triangular constructions for hanging items on display. Two women were talking together behind a table with flyers and art magazines spread in neat piles.

"Can I be of help?" one of the women asked. She was tall, thin, with black hair cut short serving as a frame for an angular face. She was dressed in a Japanese gown that coordinated oddly with her features. "We usually have paintings and pottery, and sometimes sculpture. These photographs will be here only for the rest of the week, so if you want any of them, you should purchase them now."

Deb walked slowly around the room examining, with what she thought was now a professional eye, the styles, techniques, subject matter, and lighting effects that were currently in photographic fashion. What attracted her most was the nature scenes and the shots of black and Hispanic children playing in inner-city streets.

"Bye, Mary," the woman behind the table said as the one who had addressed Deb walked out the door, holding an umbrella and a bag with a French bread peeking over her shoulder.

"See you, Bev."

When Deb had looked enough, she went up to say good-bye and take her leave.

"Are you from around here?" the woman asked.

"I just moved from Seattle."

"That's where we want to go. The art market is too slow here. The real action is in Seattle, and a gallery needs action to survive. We are trying to locate there, but it's expensive and it won't be easy to find the right layout. What do you do?"

This woman is all questions, Deb thought. At least I have an answer today.

"I'm a photographer."

"Interesting. How did you hear about this show? I am curious to know what you think of these shots. I'm not much into photography myself; I'm more a painting person. We all know photography is a great art, capable of conveying real feeling. But we didn't sell much; it wasn't worth the bother hanging this exhibit. I'm sure we would have sold much more in Seattle."

"Will you move there?"

"Mary and I both have families here, so we expect to commute. It's an easy drive, and we will have the best of two cities to enjoy."

Deb looked at this woman, who, unlike the one who had left earlier, had no distinctive features. In her forties, dark-brown hair tastefully arranged, suit and silk blouse with a scarf around her shoulders, high heels. But engaging, seemingly interested, listening to Deb despite her jeans, tennis shoes, and her hair still damp from the rain.

I'm learning how to talk to everybody, Deb thought as she walked down the narrow stairs to the street. Sure sign that I am on my way to recovery.

MINUTES AFTER DEB went out the door of Pisces Gallery, Bev, one of the gallery's co-owners, packed up to leave for the day. She let down the Venetian blinds and closed them to keep the morning sun from shining on the exhibit. She turned the lights off, set the burglar alarm, shut the door after her, and locked the dead bolt. Instead of going out the street door, as Deb had done, she continued down the stairway to the basement where her Lincoln was parked near a concrete pillar. Unlocking the car, she sat in the driver's seat, looked at herself in the rearview mirror and fixed her hair. She started the car, let it run, pushed a button on the dashboard, and drove out through the automatic door that had just opened for her.

City traffic; rush hour. Bev knew she was relaxed as she arranged her speed to make all the green lights on the one-way street. After seven blocks, she entered the freeway heading south, going at the same speed as the other cars. Once in the ebb of traffic, she turned on the radio, which was preset for peaceful music; she couldn't tell if it was country or new age.

"Gosh!" Bev suddenly heard herself exclaim out loud. I didn't even find out that photographer's name. I must be losing my touch. A connection is always useful in the art world, she went on to think. Of course that woman can't have much talent, really. How could someone dressed in sweater and jeans, getting wet in the rain and no umbrella in sight, come to a gallery and believe she might be of interest to the owners? Come to think of it, she didn't ask anything about the gallery. She probably wasn't interested. Well, too bad.

It started to rain. Bev turned on the wipers as the freeway entered into a curved area. I wonder how that new cook will turn out. She doesn't look like much, but she did have good references, and she arrived on time this morning. I'll find out soon. Diane will tell me what she thinks if I ask her. And of course Steve will have an opinion about the meal whether I ask him or not. Such a gourmet! I have never seen anyone enjoy food as much as he does. And so fussy; he would rather go hungry than eat meat cooked a little too long. I'm thankful for that, though, because it relieves me of the chore of cooking for my family. Let someone else who enjoys doing it prepare the food. I have better things to do with my time.

Mary is so much fun to be with. People can't imagine how sharp she is. I thought I'd die this morning when she described the president of the Portland Central Bank after he walked out of the gallery. Then at lunch, while we were having our manhattans, she seemed to know how to read everybody's mind as they walked by our table. What a good idea it was to go into business with her! We agree on everything, it seems. But what is her home life like? They haven't invited us over once! Of course the one time we did go to her place to deliver a piece of sculpture, Steve couldn't get over their living room, calling it a "tropical forest of bonzai trees." What an idea to grow them commercially in their home! And her husband with his enigmatic smile! What can he be thinking? When Steve checked them out before Mary and I started the partnership, he learned that their nursery business was thriving.

Bev entered the off ramp and turned toward Lake Oswego. It was raining harder now, and the narrow blacktop full of curves caused her to slow down. She went into a driver's daydream as she followed the twisting pattern of the road, which shined as her headlights reflected on its rain-drenched surface. A number of subjects popped up that evening in her stream of consciousness.

One was that Steve, her husband, was becoming so busy in his legal practice that he came home later every night. Sometimes he arrived after she had eaten and was already looking at TV in their bedroom. Then she reminded herself that she had a beautiful home, one of the finest in the elegant suburb where she and Steve had it built, and one that lent itself ideally to their social life. What she did not mention even now in her interior dialog was that the house owed its existence to the tragedy that had befallen them five years earlier outside of Boston. She had been driving on an icy road with their fifteen-year-old son Scott, taking him to or from some sports event, when another car lost control and forced her to jump the curb and smash into a roadside oak. She sustained only minor injuries, but Scott landed in the hospital and after several weeks of spinal surgery and rehabilitation, came home in a wheelchair he was never to leave except to go to bed at night. Steve took the matter to court, sued some insurance companies and municipalities, and came out five million dollars ahead, half of which will pass on to Scott when he reaches twenty-one in a few months. They pulled up stakes in Massachusetts and came to Portland where Steve joined a large and prosperous law firm. They bought a lot on the shore of an artificial lake isolated from the surroundings, where they built a house according to specifications to meet all the needs of a family with an adolescent handicapped child.

As she drove she visualized her house. Concrete paths make it possible for a wheelchair to have access to the entire lot, even to the boat house where a bridge leads directly into the cockpit of the speedboat. Bev saw in her mind the ground floor of the house, the country-style kitchen, the spacious dining and living rooms, den, study, family room. Then she saw Scott's apartment with its heated swimming pool, exercise gym, living room, bedroom, and study of his own, plus an attatched apartment for the live-in person who takes care of him, currently a young Canadian woman named Diane. Upstairs is Bev's masterpiece: an oversize bedroom with a balcony and view of the lake and a large bathroom with a built-in spa. There are sitting rooms on each side, the one for Steve with a library, comfortable armchairs, old-fashioned lamps, an ornate desk, and a fireplace. The one for Bev is large enough to store her extensive collection of clothes and shoes, a table for doing gallery business, and dressing tables with mirrors. A long private driveway, which curves through a dense forest of fir and pine, discourages the curious from coming too close.

Bev pulled up under a roof that sheltered the entrance. Steve's car was already parked on the left hand side. She ran up the brick steps to the main entrance carrying her attaché case. Inside she could smell that dinner was almost ready.

"What a day!" Bev sighed as she rushed to the closet to hang her coat. "Steve!" she called out. There was an answer from somewhere in Scott's area. Bev walked into the dining room and pushed the swinging door to the kitchen. "Hello, Melissa," she said as she caught sight of the cook. "How was your day? Everything certainly smells good. What did Scott have for lunch?" She went over to the stove, lifted a lid, and watched the steam escape upward, sucked by a fan into a copper hood. "When will dinner be ready?"

"In about a half an hour. But I still have to set the table. It's hard to get used to where things are."

"Don't worry, Melissa. I'll send Diane to help."

As she walked back to the living room she saw Steve crouching in front of the fireplace with a match in his hand.

"Hopefully it won't smoke like last night. It's the gusty wind that makes the chimney do that. Once it is warm all the way up it won't happen. Hello, Darling. How was your day?"

"Busy, busy, busy! Make us a drink, will you? We eat in a half an hour. Anything happening tonight? No, I don't think so. I'll wash and say hi to Scott."

Bev went through a wide door on the opposite end of the living room. Scott was in his wheelchair reading the *New York Times* his father had brought home from downtown.

"Diane, please go in and help Melissa. You can tell me later how things went today. Hi, Honey." She leaned over and kissed Scott on the cheek. He lowered the newspaper and blinked at her.

"Hi, Mom," was the standard greeting.

"Dad and I are going to have a drink next to the fire. Come join us if you want to."

"I'll come in a few minutes. There is some interesting stuff here in the second section. Apparently the art market is picking up in the East. Maybe the recession is over and you won't have to work so hard to convince people to buy paintings."

As Bev sat in front of the fire briskly burning in the marble fireplace, Steve brought in a tray with two martinis. She thought he looked fine in his light blue button-down cardigan. He was still wearing his tie from the day, and his dark hair, with undulating gray strands, as usual gave her a sense of stability and continuity. And for a lawyer, his face was not at all unpleasant, really. Too bad he didn't do trials. With his thin build and clear voice he could be spectacular.

Steve kissed her on the lips and gave her one of the glasses.

"We aren't doing anything tonight, are we? At least I hope not," he said. "We can enjoy a quiet evening at home, doing what we like and maybe even get to bed at a decent hour. How does that sound to you?"

"Very good drink! To our health! Does what you say mean we go out too often for your taste? Actually we were home two nights last week. That's pretty good. What can we do? We are both professionals, and that gives us obligations to fulfill. And admit it: if we stayed home much more often, you would find it pretty boring."

"It would be nice to have more time with Scott. I was talking with him just before you came home, and it seemed to me that he was somehow more distant, more interested in his own activities than in connecting with us."

"He's the last person I'd be worried about. For one thing, he can't get into trouble, even if he wanted to. For another, he has Diane to be with. She is a wonder. Not only does she take care of all his needs, but she gets interested in what he is doing and tries to learn about it herself. She reads the books he reads, and she had him teach her how to use his computer. Plus that, she is pretty, don't you think so?"

"Well I noticed that you are very good-looking tonight."

"Do you know what she did as soon as she came three months ago? Maybe I told you this already. She came to me and said that if Scott started to bathe himself he would feel more independent; so she asked for my permission to help him get him into the tub and let him do the rest. Now she wants to have him dress himself."

Scott wheeled into the living room.

"The fire feels good. Some day I'm going to learn how to split wood, Dad. Why not? People do all sorts of things from a wheelchair, like mountain climbing and parachuting. Do you want anything? I'm going to get a beer."

He wheeled into the kitchen.

"Since when has he been drinking beer?"

"See what I mean? I didn't know about his bathing routine, and you don't know about the beer. We need to be with him more. He will be wheeling up Mount Hood before we know it."

"Dinner is served," Scott said from the dining room door, imitating the nasal voice of an imaginary butler.

Bev and Steve sat down at the large dining table. Diane pushed Scott up to the other side of the table and sat next to him.

A normal American family, eating dinner, Bev thought as she surveyed the table and its occupants. Nothing unusual about that. We're comfortable in our surroundings and with each other. No real elegance here, no stiffness. It's sort of quiet. Of course with Diane at the table we can't talk freely as we used to when Scott ate in the kitchen. It was Diane's idea to have him eat with us. I wonder if it was in order for her to eat with us, too? It's true he eats quite well now. I used to lose my appetite just seeing him try to hold a fork and drool. He's managing better now in general; when he receives just a little help in eating you hardly notice his handicap. But Steve used to talk about his clients at dinner time, I knew them all by name, practically by case number. He says he wants to protect their rights by not talking about them when someone can overhear.

"There is a new model wheelchair coming out that will make it possible for me to use the public bathroom without the kind of problems I have now. They talked about it on the Internet. Costs a chunk, but I think it's worth it. What do you think?"

"Do you really need it, dear? You haven't complained much about this one."

"Well, it's not really the most polite table talk, the kind of thing one wants to bring up all the time."

"You are perfectly right, dear. Let's talk about it later."

"We don't have to talk about it at all, actually. The question is whether you want to buy it now or wait until my birthday when I'll be able to take care of the transaction."

Bev surveyed her family again, deciding to change the subject. "I have been asked to give a lecture on *itijame* at the Portland Art Museum in a month or so. Do you remember that complicated process of triple folds and dyeing? It will be one of those noon lectures. It's one of my best subjects since I've done so much research on it. You are all invited, you too, Diane. I hope the talk will be well attended. Also Mary and I are still thinking about relocating to Seattle, but that will take a lot of preparation. What we have in mind is to spend two to three days a week there, staying overnight, of course. We would have a full-time person always there. That way I wouldn't have to be at the gallery all day like now. I could be home much more. By the way, a strange woman came in just before closing time today. She is a photographer, not interested in showing, just looking. Has a sad, brooding expression on her face, as if she's not quite with things."

"Be careful with walk-ins," Steve started to admonish her.

"There are a lot of psychos around that corner of town, almost as bad as East Burnside . . ."

"Don't worry. I can take care of myself, and we have a good alarm system."

"You need a watchdog, a miniature dachshund, or a fierce old cat sleeping on a chair," Scott suggested. Then he turned toward his father. "How about teaching me to drive again. It has been six years since my last driving lesson. I need to have my wheels, as they say, and be independent. That will free Mom and Diane from taking me everywhere. What do you think? Don't forget my sterling record as a wheelchair pilot. Not an accident in five, no, six years, unless you count the time I forgot the parking brakes and swooped down into the lake."

Melissa came in to remove the plates.

"How was the meat, Steve?" Bev asked. "Was it rare enough for you? Mine was a little too rare, Melissa. The cauliflower and the yellow sauce were just right."

"I thought everything was fine, I enjoyed it all."

Diane got up to help remove plates and bring in the desert and coffee and then remained in the kitchen.

"Tell me, dear. How is work? Any new cases? How are the old ones getting along? I'm really not up to date."

"I drove to Salem again today, to teach that seminar in criminal law to the inmates at the State Prison. Those guys are quite smart. They are quick to see how the laws I describe affect them and where to find loopholes. You should hear them ask questions about the parole laws! One of them would make a first-rate cross-examiner."

"But what new cases do you have? You know what I mean, the kind that enhance your career. You don't get paid for going to Salem, do you?"

"Well, there are the usual wills to draw up and probates to settle. Don't forget that we are always doing corporation work, which gives the firm a steady source of income. But there isn't much excitement in corporation proceedings; not much to talk about."

"Any new divorces?"

"I'm trying to steer clear of them as much as I can. I'm more interested in cases involving a small guy and a big guy. You could say I represent the first or the second little pig, not the third one or the wolf."

"First pig v. wolf. Dad, that case would go down in history! Did you win it?"

"Several times. I'm working on one right now where a woman is seeking damages from the government and an American firm for what happened to her husband while he was working for them in Brazil. It's a matter of obtaining redress for a victim, almost of defending the deer after it has been eaten by the lion."

"How is it coming? Are you able to gather evidence without going down there?"

"I think so. I have good connections in Rio and the evidence is piling up."

"Maybe you should arrange a trip; I could use a vacation."

"Don't take this wrong, Dad. But the law is one profession you won't ever see me involved in. How anyone can bear to read more than one paragraph of legal prose is hard to comprehend. In the meantime, please accept my petition to be excused from the table. I will challenge anyone to chess tonight, if that isn't too adversarial. Or just come in and rap for a while."

"Admit it, Diane. Have you ever in your life had to endure a more boring conversation? I felt like dropping a glass of milk on the floor to bring it to a sudden, disastrous end. Tedious talk should be banned from the table just like discourse on excrement and ancient history."

"If you listened a little you might find it more entertaining. How much of it did you hear?"

"Hardly any, how did you know?"

"When you sit there and forget to eat, when your eyes gloss over, then I know you are miles away. Where did you go?"

"Is that why you nudged me? Actually I was listening to music."

"How do you do that?"

"I turn on a built-in stereo in my head."

"Do you want to swim, or is it too soon after eating."

"Right now I want to ask you something, Diane. I need your opinion. I am going to write a book some day, don't laugh, I've written half of it already in my head."

"I assure you I'm not laughing. Go ahead."

"You will find this stupid, for sure. Let's go swimming."

"It's unfair, Scott, to say you are going to ask me something and then shut down like a baseball game that has been canceled because of the rain. Either ask or don't ask. I'm ready for the question or for a swim."

"Okay. Here goes. What I know the most about is the family since I've lived in one for twenty years. I also observe my friends' families when I am invited to dinner or to their cabin in the summer, and I see strange situations and interactions. Now back to tonight's conversation. Was that a normal dinner conversation for a typical American family around the table in the evening? Or is every family different?"

"Do you want to know if your family is representative in any way?"

"That's it, Diane, you got the idea! Can I write the great American family novel using the idiosyncrasies of my own, at least as a starting point?"

"Scott, you might do well to wait a bit before writing that novel, maybe forty years. The book will be much better. Don't you know more about other subjects?"

"No. I don't want to write about being a handicapped teenager. That would be even more boring than my parents' conversation. It was enough for me just to accept that I was a cripple and that my life would be like an amputated limb. Writing about it now would be like suffering from prolonged phantom pain."

"If it is any help, Scott, I'll tell you that family life for me was never anything like what you find so uninteresting. It wasn't a family at all; it was a madhouse. Have I ever told you? No, I guess not. My parents were always fighting; I had to keep peace and take care of the younger kids. Their talk was mostly about where the next meal would come from. Or the trouble my oldest brother was in."

"Diane, you're making me feel guilty. You should write my novel! How did you survive?"

"I went to a high school run by the diocese where the nuns took interest in me and encouraged me to learn. After graduation I left. I took a bus for San Francisco and worked as a nanny in Mill Valley. In the evening I went to a community college. Then, when the man of the family started fondling me as I walked by him in the corridor, I saw your mother's ad and came here. You can use my story if you want to. I can't help thinking I have been very fortunate."

Steve came in.

"Instead of playing chess, Scott, I'd enjoy a swim with you. Diane can rest a little."

THE NEXT MORNING Scott and Diane ate breakfast, as was their custom, in the kitchen before his parents came downstairs. This particular morning, however, was different since it was not Diane who prepared Scott's meal, but Melissa, the Thornton's new cook. Theirs was a difficult household for a cook to perform her duties to everybody's satisfaction. Consequently Bev had been obliged to hire a different cook every two months or so, and she found the breaking-in period to be distracting from the attention she usually spent in other activities. Greta, the last cook to leave, explained to Diane as she folded her aprons and packed them in her bags that it wasn't feeling sad from seeing Scott in a wheelchair all day that made her want to leave. It was because when food was delivered from the store she couldn't be sure of the quality of the fruit and vegetables. Harder yet for her was to take orders from the lady of the house, who went over shopping lists and menus in the greatest detail, specifying how everything was to be seasoned and prepared, and who then lost all interest in the results except to nibble from her plate and make short comments.

Melissa had graduated from a respected Portland gastronomic academy that taught the preparation of foreign cuisines, and she came with the most laudatory written recommendations. Thus Scott found not ham, eggs, and toast set in front of him that morning, but a cheese omelet, *café au lait*, and a fresh, warm croissant.

Scott looked at Melissa from across the table. "Mom told us

about the school you went to and the references, but that's all. What would you like to tell us, Melissa? I think knowing the cook improves the taste of food."

"That's new to me! Where did you learn that one?"

"Excuse him, Melissa. Scott is just curious. He wants to know where you lived before coming to Portland, I guess."

"Malheur County, in Southeast Oregon. Ever hear of it? It's on the Idaho border."

"I've seen it in pictures and on the map, which is the easiest way for me to travel. When I think of Malheur County I imagine sagebrush, gullies carved out of rock, grazeland, and rolling flat-topped hills. Little towns, too, with a highway going straight through and on each side churches, a movie, a bar or two, and a grange for entertainment. Is that about right?"

"That's it. But you forgot the filling station, the feed and seed store, the new motel, and the diner where I was a cook. Everybody knows everything about everybody else, and on Saturday nights some Indians come in from the reservation to get drunk."

"But why do they call it Malheur? It sounds like a dangerous place to me. That means misfortune or disaster, doesn't it, Diane?"

"Oh, we don't think of it that way. It's just another place to live, one where there is plenty of room. But it's true what you say about the name. Some trappers lost their equipment and their furs along the river, and people have called it that ever since."

There was no time to go into how Melissa happened to leave home and end up in Portland. She had to prepare breakfast for Bev and Steve, who, to judge from the flushing of toilets and running water of showers upstairs, would soon come down. Scott and Diane got out of the way.

It's like having breakfast in a busy restaurant, Steve thought, eating his omelet while Bev gave instructions to Diane regarding Scott's activities for the day. Next it was Melissa, who stood at the table and took notes while Bev outlined the week's menus.

"At about ten-thirty or eleven, when the rush is over, call Grossmeier's on the phone and give them the order you have on the list. It is best to talk to Lewis, because he is the most conscientious clerk and gives us the best choices. I told him you would be ordering from now on."

"Yes, Mrs. Thornton."

"Tomorrow, Mr. Thornton and I will not be home, so the three of you can eat what is left of the roast. Thursday we have guests, so we will talk about that later. There will be someone here to help with the serving and cleanup. Friday we are going to the theater, so you will have to be ready earlier than last night, say six o'clock. Saturday is something, but for the moment I forget what it is. Then you will have Sunday off, isn't that nice?"

"Yes, Mrs. Thornton."

"Bev, excuse me. I'm going upstairs to do the work I brought from the office. I don't have an appointment until eleven."

"I am leaving as soon as we are done with the menus, Steve. See you tonight. By the way, I will need all the bills to pay by Friday at the latest. Has our tax refund already arrived? Here, Give me a kiss."

Steve walked upstairs to his study where the desk was cluttered with files he had brought from the office. He looked through them. New material from Rio for the Myers case. Deb will be happy when she sees how much there is. Maybe she will smile, as I have seen her do only once or twice.

An hour later Steve went downstairs to say good-bye to Scott, whom he found dressed in shorts, trying with immense effort to walk between parallel bars with Diane holding him up from the front, encouraging and steadying his movement.

"Damn! This is hard! Just try walking on legs made out of noodles sometime. At least my sweat glands are getting a workout. Give me two hundred years, I might be able to take a step on my own."

"Once Scott has learned how to be patient, Mr. Thornton, he will make more progress. He can already stand holding on to the bars without getting tired; he couldn't do anything like that when I came."

"Diane's making my life pure misery, Dad, forcing me to do so much hard work. But there's one good thing about her; she agrees on scratching the schedule Mom set up for us. There's no way we are going to that handbell concert at the Episcopal Church or have tea at Sadie's. Instead, it's Tower Records this afternoon and then watch a swim meet at Portland State."

Steve drives to his office. Behind the building there is an open public parking space where he leaves his car every day. He enters through a back door, waits for an elevator. Seventh floor. It looks quiet inside as he opens the door to Suite 718. That turns out to be an illusion.

"Morning, Grace."

"Good morning, Mr. Thornton. Deb Myers is in your waiting room. Minerva called and asked that you go in there right away. Your client took ill, or something."

Steve strides down the hall to a small waiting room attached to his private office. There he finds Deb sitting on the edge of the couch, holding her head between her hands and breathing heavily. Minerva is kneeling in front of her, holding a glass of water.

"Mrs. Myers was waiting for her appointment and suddenly began feeling weak. Then she fainted on the couch. Feeling better now, Honey? I think so. Mr. Thornton's here, see? He will take care of everything."

"Thanks, Minnie! Bring us an herbal tea. Some ice in a plastic bag, too, please."

He leaned down and put his hand on Deb's shoulder.

"Oh, Steve! It must have been a panic attack. I was just sitting here and it happened."

"What happened, Deb?"

"I'll tell you in just a minute. After I have some of that tea."

Minerva brought in a tray with two steaming mugs next to a bag of crushed ice, which Deb took and placed against her forehead. They both sat in silence while sipping their tea.

"I feel better now. I'm not sure what happened. The day

started out pretty well, with all sorts of resolutions, like eating regularly and getting more exercise. I had all the information ready to bring to you, and I felt good walking over here. I arrived much too early, so I sat down to read your magazines, those ones on the table. I landed on this article "The New Faces of Terrorism: The Areas of Danger Need to be Redefined." See this map of South America? The authors red-flag Colombia and Peru, marking them as 'alert.' Now here Venezuela, Ecuador, and Bolivia are yellow, which means 'deserve watching.' What about the rest of them? Look! They're gray, that is to say 'safe.' I wondered how anyone could say Brazil was safe, and that got me to daydreaming. Here I go on and on, and you're probably in a hurry."

"No. Go on, Deb. Tell me."

"First I saw myself walking on a trail at the base of Sugarloaf Mountain, looking out over Copacabana. Then I started to climb up the steep paths of the Tijuca National Park along with pedestrians and joggers. The sweet scent of jasmine and honeysuckle along with the odor of wet moss was so strong that I got lost in them and really believed I was there. I saw clearly the different types of ferns that grow in the shade of the trees, and the sound of the birds grew louder and louder in my ears, so loud it became unbearable. Then I saw Hank walking slowly up the path. Since I was running I caught up with him easily and embraced him from behind and started to kiss him on the cheek. But it was someone else who turned and looked at me in fright, pushing me away, and then I came to, sitting here and sobbing. Steve! I don't know what happened. What could it mean? Am I going crazy?"

"Well you certainly don't look crazy now. You never have to me."

"You are very kind. And I do feel quite sane whenever I'm with you. Did you learn how to treat your clients' hysteria in law school?"

"I wish I had. Legal training isn't that advanced, even now. That reminds me to suggest to you that you go see a friend of mine, Norm Blumer. He's a hypnotherapist, and he might be able to help you clarify your memory of the last days you spent in Rio. He is also a psychiatrist. He can give you a prescription to keep this from happening again. Are you ready to work now, Deb? I don't want to hurry you, but . . ."

"Okay. Let's go."

Steve led her into his office. He paged through the documents and letters he had brought from home, explaining to Deb the relevance of each. Then he took the pads of yellow-lined paper Deb had carried in. They were covered with writing in longhand; many pages had been crossed off and rewritten, and inserts of various length were stapled to the sides of some pages.

"The narrative you asked for tells everything I remember from my stay in Rio. It will bore you to death, I'm sure, but there it is. I'm sorry it took so long to prepare. I will be glad to elaborate on anything you think is important."

"Let me look at it a little now; I won't try to read all of these pages until later when there is more time."

Steve started reading on the first page. Curious to see how he reacted to the anecdotes in her story, Deb watched him read. His face registered interest but not surprise. His eyes moved rapidly from one side to the other as he read. Gray eyes. Maybe they had been blue and were dulled by reading so many legal documents, Deb thought. The hands are clean and soft, used to holding and turning pages; they haven't done hard work, at least not for a long time. The hair is plentiful, wavy and graying. How old can he be? Late forties? It is comforting to be around him. Even little mannerisms that Deb is familiar with by now, like bringing his hand up to touch the side of nose, add to her sense of security. What kind of life can he lead, away from his office and the heavy furniture? Does he always wear dark three-piece suits, striped shirts and conservative ties?

"It will take me a while to go through all this," Steve admitted to her. "I am going to take this home and read it in front of the fire, like a good book. I have a meeting, so let's call it for today.

In a day or so Minnie will phone you to set up another appointment."

Deb walked home. After stopping for a bowl of soup and tea at a lunch counter a block from her flat, she checked her mailbox (nothing there) and walked up the stairs. Two hours to kill before Jennifer comes home from work and knocks at her door for their daily run. Enough time to take pictures? Not really. Deb put a tape in her cassette player, picked up a magazine, and lay on the couch looking at the cracked plaster ceiling. Sambas she had learned to enjoy with Roger beckoned her back to the side streets of Rio. Deb remembers the hillsides where wretched shacks, piled up upon each other like endless carcasses, stretch out as far as the eye can see. Above it all, like in a surrealist painting, the white shining statue of Christ offers thanks for the wonders of God's creation.

When Deb woke at the sound of knocking at the door, she was shivering. Clouds had covered the sun while she was asleep, and her entire room was growing dark.

"Jeez! it's cold in here," Jennifer bolted out as she entered. "Must be ten degrees warmer outside. You don't have storm windows; do you have heat at least? I don't see any curtains. Let's get going. A good run will warm us up."

Being cold wasn't new to Jennifer, Deb thought, as she put on her running pants and shoes. She must have known cold nights during the years she was living on her own, after deserting her foster home when she was seventeen. Now at twenty-two she was in a group home where she had been hired to oversee the rehabilitation of girls her own age in an independent living program funded by the state. Strong, optimistic, resourceful, she was the ideal running companion for Deb on those cold April afternoons that are so conducive to melancholy.

After running two miles through Washington Park, they arrived at Moonflower House, the old yellow frame building where Jennifer watched after a dozen young women, taught them social skills, and helped them through the anxieties of job interviews and the disappointment of being rejected. She often invited her friends to dinner as part of a training program in social adjustment for the girls. That night her guests were Deb and Liz, a retarded woman of twenty-one. Deb looked at her face, which appeared much older with its deep lines, sharp features, and the piercing expression of her dark eyes. She was barely five feet tall. Her speech was difficult to understand at first, since she seemed to speak mainly in grunts and monosyllables. "You will get used to her soon," Jennifer said. "She has a terrific sense of humor. Once the girls understood her way of talking they began to enjoy everything she said. She's my best resource for teaching the girls manners, because they all take it on themselves to give her lessons on how to hold spoons and forks and carry on pleasant chit-chat. They have to be careful, too, for Liz seems to understand what they say about her."

After dinner Jennifer told Deb more about Liz while the others cleaned up and did the dishes.

"Her mother, Glenda, is a doll. She is a free-lance seamstress working out of her apartment on Quimby Street; let's walk Liz home after dinner and you can meet her mom. The two of them have always been real close, and I love them both. Liz has an older brother, but I haven't seen him; I think he's in jail for something or other."

Later that evening, Jennifer, Liz, and Deb walked down the dimly-lit streets toward Glenda's apartment. Liz, in the middle, held her two friends by the hand, encouraging them to sing along with her as they strode through the cold night.

Glenda and Liz lived on the second floor of a six-unit apartment building. Her front door opened onto the middle of a wooden balcony cluttered with flower pots still bearing the ghosts of last summer, and various bowls set out for feeding neighborhood cats. As the three women approached, the door opened and let escape an angry female voice.

"God dammit to hell! No! you stay here, Dearie! But don't you dare go anywheres while I'm gone! And watch your goddamn language! I ain't gointa take no shit from you, neither. Git! More of that kind of talk and you'll get a whippin when we're home."

A stout woman in her thirties rushed down the stairs from the balcony.

"It's Flora an' she's pissed!" Liz said as she walked in, still holding Jennifer's hand; Deb followed. There they found Glenda standing in the middle of a tiny living room with her hands on her hips. Short, wearing glasses, her dark hair curling down to just below her ears, dressed in black with a tape measure hanging from her neck. She was visibly in the midst of a project; cut patterns pinned to cloth lay everywhere, and a large piece of fabric was waiting in the jaw of an electric sewing machine. The room was warm and smelled of cigarette smoke. Next to Glenda cowered a blonde girl of about thirteen with almost transparent light skin that gave her what Deb could only depict as an angelic look despite the fear still lingering in her expression.

"Boy, hope you didn't hear all that garbage! Come on in," Glenda exclaimed. Jennifer introduced Deb. "Pleased to meet you. Don't look at the mess. I was trying to get this job done. Here, let's go to the kitchen. How about some pop? Or juice, maybe. You can go look at TV if you want, Sylvie, or come sit with us."

Liz joined Sylvie in front of a comedy show while the three others squeezed around a kitchen table.

"That was my niece who just went out in such a tiff. She brought her daughter to be with Liz, saying she had to go shopping. She got angry when she found Liz was gone, but she left Sylvie here anyway. She probably wanted to be alone with her boyfriend, and her daughter is old enough now to ask questions. 'What are you doing there in the bedroom, Mommy? Are you coming out soon?'"

"I don't say that, Glenda! And I know what they are doing, anyways," Sylvie, overhearing, complained.

"That's probably true," Glenda said, turning to Deb and Jennifer. "I have three nieces living in town, and all three of them heap their troubles on me." Now she was speaking in a voice low enough to be covered by the television. "My niece, Flora, sleeps with someone different every three weeks; but she wants to keep her daughter away from the boys in the neighborhood who might fool around with her. And Sylvie is so pretty she attracts them all. Flora is on drugs, too, and Sylvie knows it. Just watch: if she isn't on them yet she will be tomorrow or the next day. She told me just tonight," Glenda was whispering now, "that she's pregnant."

"Who's the dad?" Jennifer asked.

"She thinks it's that boy García, the bagger at Marvin's Market. Nice looking boy, but a high school dropout. The problem is telling her mom. You heard what happened tonight; that will be chicken feed compared to the next eruption."

"When you are sure, I could talk to García, you know, about responsibility and all that," Jennifer said. "His sister is one of the girls in my group."

"I can hear everything you are saying!" Sylvie complained.

"Well then come on over and talk with us."

"Want to see the show."

Glenda went on. "I think Sylvie wants to keep the baby. You can guess who is going to bring it up."

"Flora?"

"No, me. That's why those three nieces of mine came to Portland. They knew they couldn't trust my sister, their mom, to take care of their kids since she's always drunk or stoned. So the three of them moved up here to be around me. That's okay, but I get tired sometimes. One day I'll tell you about the other two, when there's time."

"Hey, Glenda!" Jennifer said. "I was over at Deb's room today, and it's freezing there. Is there any way to make curtains to keep the cold out?"

"You could ask the landlord for storm windows. Is there any heat, Deb?"

"I live on the fifth floor; the windows are large and the view is great. None of the windows on that building have storm windows. There is a wall heater. The trouble is I am used to a warm climate, and the cold goes right to my bones."

Glenda thought for a few minutes. "There is a kind of thermal material you could cover with a pattern, which would look real nice. If you measure your windows I'll tell you how much material you will need, and you can buy it on a special. You can pay me for my labor; if you help with the measuring and cutting that will save time. I'm pretty busy, but we could start right away."

By the time Deb left, she had agreed to return in two days to begin work on her curtains with Glenda.

That night, after Diane had gone to bed, Scott wheeled over to his computer, turned it on, and wrote the following:

"Dad is under the weather. He looked washed-out when he came home tonight. His gut, he says. Told him to have it checked out, but he prefers to let it run its course.

"It is important to separate myself from what happens around me. I knew this instinctively after the accident; it was a matter of survival. Now if I'm not careful, I risk getting swallowed up. All one has to do is look, the situation is pretty obvious. Take my father and mother. They hardly talk to each other, yet they believe that they are playing out their respective roles normally and that their cohabitation is just like that of any loving couple. In the past they stuck together in their concern for me. Now they are moving beyond concern, replacing it with routines that prevent them from feeling any kind of real emotion, anguish or joy. Shall I awaken them? How?

"I also have to separate myself from what is left of my body. The first step is to cease talking or writing about it, act as if my body simply didn't exist. My body and I can become estranged or simply drift apart, a little like my parents, who live in the same house and avoid each other as well as they can. It's true that thinking almost exclusively about my body for a couple of years helped me get the use of some of it back. My hands would flap around grotesquely when I tried to make them do anything; now they do fairly much what I want. But my legs are still so uncooperative that I really have to get away from them. It would be great to have them amputated, and yet perfectly futile. Let me amputate the past instead, the accident, and all the suffering and self-pity that came my way and burrowed into me like some underground rodent looking for roots to devour.

"There is something else that bugs me. Why did Diane stop bathing me and tell Mom I should do it myself? Over the years I have been bathed by so many hands that left me perfectly indifferent! Now, just when I am beginning to enjoy the sensation under the touch of her hands, it is gone. Perhaps my enjoyment was a little too evident. Or is she just trying to make me more independent? But now, get this! I've become modest like a fourteen-year-old girl. After years of being moved, wiped, and poked by nurses and attendants, I send Diane far away when I go to the can or piss. Not that it is easy to swing myself around alone, hanging on to ropes attached to the ceiling. But my biceps and shoulders are developing; I would be the envy of high school wrestlers if they could see me!

"Oh, well. There are still joys in life for the maimed. Sleep, for one."

DEB AWOKE THAT morning feeling different, as if something in herself had changed. She exercised, ate breakfast, and planned her day: measure windows and shop for material, visit Hank, go to the Reed campus to take pictures, run with Jennifer, and work with Glenda in the evening. Her schedule collapsed when Steve phoned.

"Deb, I've tracked down Kater; talked to him just now on the phone. Can you come over?"

She found him in his office dressed casually, turtle-necked sweater, corduroy pants, zipper jacket. He was pale, leaner.

"The flu, I think. It's been feeding on me for a week now," he said.

"What are you doing to take care of yourself? Have you seen a doctor?"

"There's not enough time or energy for that. If I don't feel better in a day or so I will."

Deb surprised herself by instinctively going over to him and putting her hand on his forehead.

"If anything, you feel cold. Promise me you'll take care of yourself. I need you. You know that, don't you?"

"Now listen to this. Herb Kater quit his job in Rio way back in October, long before Hank returned from Amazonia. He is now employed as lobbyist in Washington for various Christian organizations. It sounds as though he is a newborn Christian himself. I have to call him again in twenty minutes—he's in a meeting now. He seemed in a fairly receptive mood, although he didn't remember anything about Hank when I talked to him an hour ago. Also, can you tell me the approximate dates when Hank went to see him? And where was it that . . ."

Deb ran back home to catch the 11:30 bus. At least she didn't have to excuse herself to Hank when she was late for a visit or even when she missed one; he always greeted her with the same blank smile, never asking where she was or what kept her so long. She missed the bus. Out of breath, she slowly climbed the stairs to her apartment. There in front of the door she found Jennifer, sitting on the floor, waiting.

"Deb, I need help. Can I move in with you for a while? I've got problems, big ones!"

"Come on in, Jenn. I'll make some hot cocoa. Have you been here long?"

"About an hour. But that's alright, 'cause I was able to get away from it all. How life can be turned upside down in ten minutes! Catch your breath. Have you time for me to tell you what happened?"

"Go ahead. My day is topsy-turvy already."

"Did I ever tell you about Russ?"

"Not that I remember. As a matter of fact, you haven't told me much at all about your life."

"What happened is that this old flame of mine . . . I don't really know where to start."

"Start with what this old flame of yours did just now."

"He showed up."

"Where?"

"At Moonflower House. When I got there this morning, he was in the waiting room. He looked worse than ever: black bristle all over his chin and cheeks, hair matted down, eyes sort of wandering here and there, smelling awful of cigarettes. So he goes: 'I gotta get back with you, Jenn. It's my last chance.' So I go: 'No way, Russ. We've been through ever since you faded after my abortion. Now you turn up and expect me to rescue you from yourself.' So he makes a fuss, lies on the couch, and then he goes: 'I'm not moving until you come too.'"

"Jennifer, that's awful. What did you do? Leave him there?"

"No. I didn't want the director of Moonflower House to get involved, 'cause she would have been really pissed, mainly at me. The only way I could get him to move was take him to my place, and that's where he is now."

"How did you escape your own room with him there?"

"I ducked out while he was in the john and came here. What should I do, Deb?"

"Don't go back until he's gone. You can stay here as long as you want. What do you need? "

"Nothing, really. Just a couch and a blanket. I've survived on less. But I can't go back to work, 'cause he can bug me there any time he wants. If I leave him at my place he'll either smash my stuff or sell it to buy the car he wants."

"Sounds like this Russ is slightly off. What's with him?"

"Coupla years ago, he was the first guy that didn't treat me bad. Actually helped me a lot. He used to sit with me under the trees on Park Avenue and look at me real quiet, and he'd go: 'Jenn, come out of it. You deserve better. Get away from those weird people.' I used to think he was jealous, but now I know he was caring for me, in his way. We had fabulous sex together, but he wouldn't do it until I was sober, and I hated that 'cause I had to choose. But it got me off drugs. After we made love and I was reaching for a needle, he'd say: 'Wait, Jenn; if you stay off we'll do it again in the morning. Sleep now.' And he'd go on talking real gentle, like a soft song, until I fell asleep, him holding my arms. I think he stayed awake all night to be sure I didn't sneak. But it turned out he had his own kind of weirdness. He had come here from Montana. He said it was too warm in Portland, so he gave his coat to a friend who didn't have one. That was just like him. But it wasn't like him to start walking around alone all the time, or spending the whole day in a second-hand book store leaning against a shelf reading. When I told him I was pregnant, he really shaped up, got a job at a parking lot, started talking with people again. We decided I should have the abortion because of the drugs I'd had. But when it was over he got weird again and then one day he wasn't there. I still don't know what happened. Once he had talked about committing himself, but at the time I didn't understand. A lot of what he said went over my head anyway."

Jennifer finally fell asleep on the couch. Deb covered her, then phoned Steve, who was not at work. She remembered that one day he had given her his home number in case of an emergency. Where had she put it? She found it in her purse. A young man answered. Could she talk to Mr. Thornton?

"Yes, certainly. Hold on."

She explained Jennifer's predicament and asked him how best to get rid of Russ.

"Give me the address, Deb. I'll call and have one of the young lawyers go over there to handle it. They know how."

Deb walked to Moonflower House, explained to the director that Jenn was ill and offered to sub for her, adding that she was a social worker and had met the girls already. Soon she was sitting at the table with them for a belated lunch.

"Tell me, Scott. What were you like before the accident? You don't have to answer, of course, but I am a little curious."

"Imagine a tall gawky kid with pimples: vain, conceited, lazy. Get the picture? A harder question to answer would be what I am like now. I haven't the vaguest. You would know better than I do. For the ancient stuff, ask my mom; maybe she can remember that far back."

"What's changed the most since then, beside the obvious?"

Scott and Diane are resting in the pool after a workout. Scott can stand if he lets the water support him and helps a little with his hands and arms. The water comes up to their chins. Their voices echo in the pool gallery.

"The pimples are gone. That's progress."

"Were you as flippant then, Scott?"

"Maybe not. That's what is difficult now. Taking myself seriously is too risky. The big change was that Dad began talking to me, as if he suddenly realized I was there. Before that I don't think I really existed for him. I remember the day I woke out of the coma. He was the first person I saw; he was there, looking at me intently, and he didn't get up right away to leave. He said some things I've forgotten, but I'll never forget the look on his face. He hadn't shaved for a couple of days, and he must have been exhausted. There was a kind of terror in his eyes I had never seen, and a kind of softness, too, that I hadn't seen, either. Then he leaned over and kissed me on the cheek. I was frightened at first, because it was such a surprise. But then I realized something big had happened, and that it wasn't all bad."

"Seeing the two of you now, I would have supposed you were always close."

"From the time before the accident I mostly remember Mom. She was the one who took me places, gave me stuff, and taught me most of what I knew. For Dad, I had to invent all sorts of antics to get his attention."

"What sort?"

"First, I became a jock. I went out for all the sports and did my best to succeed in every one. I was pretty good at some of the swimming strokes and at tennis; for the rest I came in second or third. I got letters in high school and sported them proudly around the house so he would notice. Then I realized that he couldn't care less about my athletic prowess, since he never watched games on television. Next I went into acting, debating, choir; I even studied like mad and got the best grades imaginable. Nothing worked. So I became nasty, hung out with a punk crowd, and started on grass and alcohol after school. It was the accident that put a stop to that. Good thing."

"What stroke in swimming were you best at?"

"Backstroke. I would push real hard with my legs at the start of the race and lunge into the pool ahead of all the others."

"Race you over to the other side and back! I won't kick, to make it even."

In a fury of splashing and thrashing in the water, the two of them finished two laps, Scott in the lead.

"No fair! You let me win."

"No way! Your arms are stronger."

When they had finished puffing and laughing, Diane went on:

"Do you know how your parents met? I'm curious to know how they could get together."

"Do I sense from your tone that they are an oddly assorted couple? There is nothing closer to the truth. Let's go out. I'll tell you when we're dry."

By the time he wheeled back, Diane had brought cold juice and was waiting for him at a poolside table.

"Thanks. That will hit the spot. Is anyone home?"

"Your dad is upstairs, still nursing his flu. You mother told me this morning she wouldn't be home until six. And to bring you up to date on everyone, Melissa is in the kitchen reading another one of her books. This must be her second or third this week."

"Cookbooks?"

"No. It's a fat romance, about five hundred pages of love and longing. She was half way into it at noon; now she's getting near to the end."

"She must be a genius to read so fast; or maybe she skips the parts where nothing happens. Is this the book I saw on the kitchen table with the cover showing a Victorian lass with her clothes falling off swooning in the arms of a dashing officer on some tropical island? I wonder on which page that event occurs."

"That was *Tropical Passion*; she finished it two days ago and offered it to me to read."

"I hope you accepted her offer and read the book so you could contribute to my education about those matters."

"Sorry to disappoint you. I'm busy enough as is."

"Tastes good after the swim. You were inspired. Just now I was inspired, too. You asked about my parents, then we talked about Melissa's novels. Why don't I write a book about my parents' courtship and turn it into a gooey romance? Keep them separated and lusting for each other for hundreds of pages, throw in a bit of sex here and there, transport the action to the South or the wild West in the 1880's, add a host of secondary characters, and end it all happily ever after. Trouble is, I would have to read one of Melissa's novels to learn the tricks of the trade. Once I tried, but the first few pages discouraged me from reading the rest."

"Try a soap on TV. That would be a quicker way to find out how it's done."

"At that writers' conference I went to last summer there was a seminar on writing and publishing romances. Too bad I didn't attend that section; it was the most crowded affair of the weekend."

"Want to tell me about your parents now? There's still time. I'm curious."

"On a cold winter's night in the 1960's, in a train—coach class—. . ."

"Tell it straight, okay? You can add the ornamentation later, when you are writing."

"Can I help it if it was a winter night? The 60's and the coach class are also true. I am assuming that it was cold. All that is essential to the story, even if it sounds corny."

"Sorry, Scott. Go on."

"Dad, that is to say, Steve, was a prelaw student at a university in Boston. Since he was on a scholarship and lived at home during the school year, he needed to get away when Christmas break came around; so he was on his way to Providence with a friend. They were horsing around with a bunch of students from different colleges, drinking beer, flirting, talking politics and Vietnam, and singing at the top of their voices. There weren't nearly enough seats to go around, and many were standing in the aisle or sitting on suitcases, all of them a bit hyper after finishing their exams. Get the scene?"

"Yes. Sounds as if you were there."

"I've never even been on a train! But no matter. Mom, Bev that is, climbs aboard at a station south of Boston. She goes to Wellesley and is on her way to Providence to visit an aunt; her home in Maryland is too far away for a vacation that lasts less than two weeks. A little put off by the general hilarity, she tries to make herself small so no one will notice her. Steve gallantly offers her his suitcase to sit on. 'Thank you very much.' Steve's friend asks her where she's going. Discovering that all three have the same destination—you see, it was providential, of course—they become friends fast, especially when the train lurches and Bev lands on the lap of Steve, who is sitting on the floor. She remains there until the train lurches in the other direction and sends Bev to the opposite side with Steve sprawling at her feet and his friend on top of him. The remainder of the trip is fun, and when the three disembark at the station in Providence they have collected each other's addresses and other vital information. Bev offers to have her aunt drive the boys to the home of Steve's friend, and she even entertains the thought of getting together with Steve while they are in Providence, but she abandons the idea when she sees the expression in her Aunt's face as they drive up to a ramshackle house near the fish market. That's how they met. Do you want to hear the rest?"

"Of course. What interests me is how they got together and stayed together."

"I don't know if I can answer that . . . I do know that they didn't see each other in Providence. Bev was busy being shown the historical sites of the city and visiting relatives. One was her age, a distant cousin in his third or fourth year at Brown, who went to great pains to appear interesting. He drove her to some young people's parties and told her how disgusting it was to see college kids protesting the war in Vietnam when they should cooperate to stem the spread of communism. 'Worst stuffed shirt I ever met,' Mom told me. Wherever she went she kept an eye open for Steve, thinking he would miraculously come around a corner. Actually he was helping his friend's father fix fishnets and going out in an unsteady boat early in the morning to haul in a catch. The rest of the time he and his friend were planning how to avoid the draft if and when it came their way."

"So that's how they met and lost each other. Now tell how they found each other again."

"But that would leave out what is most interesting, the part each one lies awake at night thinking about the other, wondering, longing, aching, discovering emotions hitherto unbeknown."

"Sounds promising yet a little worn out. How much do you know about what they felt? Did your mother tell you all this?"

"No, I am inventing it. If I left the interim completely blank, it wouldn't make much sense, would it?"

"It would leave me free to imagine how they felt about each other, and my imagination is as fertile as yours. Go on."

"Well, they met at the railroad again, but this time it was on the tracks. At the time college kids would sit on the rails to stop freights carrying supplies for Vietnam. It was spring; Bev and the Wellesley contingent had their sleeping bags, sandwiches, and thermos full of hot coffee. Steve had come in an old pickup someone drove. They parked it right on the tracks so that its lights would be seen by oncoming trains. When Bev saw him sitting on the tracks strumming a ukulele she realized that she would marry this guy some day. It had started to drizzle, and he was chilled to the bone. She offered him coffee, and they started singing songs together, this time songs of solidarity, and someone recited Martin Luther King speeches. When they had all been arrested, carted over to a courthouse for arraignment, and released, Bev and her friends drove Steve to Wellesley where he spent the night in the cottage of the woman who did Bev's laundry and ironing. From then on they invited each other to dances and picnics, and after they graduated they got married in a big church ceremony in Baltimore. Through college connections she landed a job in Boston and he went to law school. I've had enough of this story . . . I must have heard it twenty times."

"I'd really like to know more about the woman who did Bev's laundry."

"I would, too. But that is all she ever does in this story, so I assume she spent the rest of her days ironing and laundering. There is no picture of her in Mom's album, which has hundreds of snapshots from the Wellesley days. Ask her to show you her old photos; she would love to, and she'll describe the Wellesley buildings to the last brick and tell you what each and every one of her classmates is doing and who each is married to."

"Are your parents living happily ever after?"

"What does it look like to you? American life is like a roller coaster, as countless people have said. It has its ups and downs. But most often it rolls for a while and then coasts the rest of the way. After the marriage and Dad's law degree my parents started coasting right away. Mom worked her way up the ladder, and Dad joined an important firm. They let the wind blow their dreams and ideals away while they made money and secured a position in society. Their private future displaced the future of mankind in their plans. Then I was born, which was a big investment, only it bombed when I flew out the door of the car and landed paralyzed on the asphalt. But making millions out of my misfortune got them rolling again, and now they are running on the momentum."

"But still, are they happy?"

"I don't know quite what to tell you, Diane. We are getting somewhere in me that I don't want to explore much further. They are probably what is known as happy, but separately. Mom might make a career out of her gallery; I sincerely hope so for her sake and for the sake of all of us. Dad has started to float. Aside from a few of his clients his work doesn't interest him, yet he never questions the necessity of going to the office every morning. I'm afraid that I provide the only emotional outlet he has right now."

That brought a slight smile to Diane's face.

"Why afraid? Couldn't that give him a way to step out of himself and go somewhere?"

"It wouldn't lead him far. The way I feel now I can be only part of people's past. They have to go beyond me."

Diane watched him, studied his eyes and his expression.

"He may. But you can, too. Let's talk more about this later."

When Deb returned to her apartment after dinner, she found Jennifer talking to a young man. At first she thought it was Russ, but when she saw his well-groomed hair, dark suit with tie and vest, she felt even more disoriented.

"This is Tim, Deb. He's from your friend's law firm. We've been talking since five-thirty when he came. Look how late it is! Oh, yes! Glenda called. Got any food?"

"Glad to met you, Deb. Steve gave me your address so I could let you know what I was able to do. I really must go now. It is late, as you say."

"Stay a little longer, Tim! We would feel safer with you around. And you must be starved after listening to me so long!"

While Deb fixed vegetables and spaghetti, Jennifer cued her in.

"When Tim got to my appartment, Russ was tearing everything apart looking for cash and things to sell. But seeing Tim calmed him down, and he let himself be taken over to a precinct office, where he was booked."

"But as I told Jenn, they released him on his own recognizance, so he is as much a menace as ever. I got a court order to keep him away from Jenn's place and from Moonflower House, but since he hasn't any address I couldn't deliver it. I've been telling Jenn to stay here a little longer, if that is alright with you. Then I can come over tomorrow evening and check things out. I'll also consult with Steve about what to do next . . ."

Deb phoned Glenda, told her briefly how she had been detained.

"Can I come tomorrow? Maybe our luck will be better in the morning."

When they had finished eating, Tim took his leave, and Deb described her day at Moonflower House. Wrapped in a blanket, Jenn fell into a deep sleep on Deb's couch.

AFTER REREADING THE most recent letter she had received from Maria, Deb took out a writing pad and a pen and started to write:

Dear Maria and Erik,

I was happy to learn that Erik is out of the hospital and on the mend after surgery. Maria's cooking will be the best therapy in the world. I often think about you both. Sometimes it seems that all of my experiences in Rio are far, far away; then at other times it feels like they only happened yesterday.

It was the end of winter when I last wrote. Now it is June already, and I can go out without a coat and feel closer to the wind and air. The weather is warm enough to bring out many beautiful blooms.

Providing my attorney, Steven Thornton, all the information he needs to prepare Hank's case is what keeps me the most occupied. With Erik's help from Rio, Steve has most of the documents he needs to go to court. Being at this stage in the process gives me a sense of closure and lets me hope that one day I can stop grieving and begin to live.

Did I tell you that Hank is in a convalescent home in Portland? It is an old building with well-kept gardens. I try to visit him at least twice a week. When the weather permits, a nurse wheels his chair to the gardens and we sit in the sun. I make myself believe that he enjoys sitting outside next to me. At times I hold his hand in mine while I talk to him, and I feel a deep sorrow for him, for me, and for all the people who are suffering like us.

Whenever I visit Hank I'm completely there for him. Does Hank feel that I am there so fully with him? Maybe he does, at some unknown level. At times I wonder whether he is not in the best of two worlds: his body is still with us, alive, without pain, yet his spirit is free and can dwell in other spheres. I don't think too much along these lines; who knows where they might take me.

Thank you so much for mailing those photographs Hank and I took in Rio. Right now I am sorting and arranging them. I think they are good enough to be put together in a book called "The Many Faces of Rio." Instead of dedicating it to Hank's memory, I thought I would have him be coauthor. Now all I have to do is write a text and do some touching up and editing. I wish I had my own darkroom; it's hardly convenient to use the one in the shop where I work.

How is your daughter and her family? If her husband is transferred to another city, as you say, where will he be going? How soon? It won't be easy for either of you to have them leave Rio, I would think. I hope they won't have to move very far away.

Two weeks ago I went to Seattle for my mother's sixtieth birthday. She is healthy and in good spirits. In two years she plans to retire after thirty-five years as a nurse. My two sisters Julie and Ruth were there with their husbands and children. It is hard to believe that the youngest child, Rob, is already nine and that the two oldest ones are in high school. I'm enclosing some pictures I took of them; you will see how handsome they are.

> I wish you and Erik the very best. Please give my regards to your daughter and her family.
>
> Fondly, Deb.

She wrote the address on an envelope and sealed it. It was already late. She would have to hurry to make her appointment with Steve by four o'clock. After gathering the folders she had prepared, she left.

Deb checked in with the receptionist and went into the waiting room that led to Steve's office. It looked different. There were new paintings on the walls, fresh flowers on the table, and the rug had been changed. She remembered Steve mentioning that a new attorney was joining the firm. There were nine partners now, according to a flyer on the table.

After a while a secretary called Deb's name. She found Steve sitting at the end of the conference table, finishing a phone call.

"Hi, Deb. Ready for work?"

"Here is the material you wanted," she said as she handed it to him.

He glanced quickly through the papers.

"These will help, certainly. It will take about an hour to complete the forms that have to be filed with the court by Monday."

"I'm ready whenever you are."

Steve pulled out a wad of papers from a drawer.

Some time later Minnie knocked and peeked through the door.

"Do you need anything else? It's five o'clock, and I'm about to leave."

"Did you finish the letters for Wilson?"

"They are on the desk for you to sign. See you Monday."

"Have a nice weekend at the coast!"

It was hard to conceal a feeling of satisfaction later when they finished filling out the last form.

"We did it! Why don't we celebrate at a restaurant nearby; one can't go anywhere at this time with the freeways packed with cars and RV's."

They got into Steve's car and headed for Le Pavillon, a French restaurant close to downtown.

They had to wait to be seated. He looked at Deb. She smiled at him, enjoying the activity around them. He smiled in return. Maybe she enjoyed being with him, in anticipation of a pleasant meal. Her face was relaxed, and he could appreciate for the first time the smoothness of the skin of her cheeks and forehead, the serenity of her expression amid the hubbub surrounding them.

When they were shown to their table, Steve was about to ask for a larger, more comfortable one; then Deb thanked the headwaiter who was seating her, saying that the table was just right. As a waitress lighted the single candle in the middle of the table and took orders for drinks, he realized that he would be able to continue looking at her face, from the front now. He discovered what he had not noticed during the months he had worked with her: that she was quite beautiful.

They had not spoken since entering the restaurant. Steve decided for some reason to keep their conversation on a banal level.

"Here we are, after almost three month's work, and your case is ready to be launched. It looks good to me, and I think you'll win. But you can never be sure, and I always warn clients not to be overconfident. As soon as I find out who in the office will represent you in court, I'll let you know. You will have to meet with him a couple of times." That was the right thing to say under the circumstances, but Steve felt a bit pompous saying it.

"Like in life, maybe: you don't know what will happen until it's happening."

"The trial won't be easy, you can be sure of that. Filling and filing forms are a pain; but the waiting and the anxiety can be really stressful."

"Do you feel that strain, too? Or is it just routine stuff you have done over and over?"

"Do I feel it, personally? Yes, I guess I do. I was saying this for your sake, because I know what to expect. But it's true I dread court appearances, and I'm not very effective when I speak to a jury. That's why we have someone else do that work, and I am thankful for that."

"Is that a common practice among law firms? It is new to me, but it seems very sensible that each partner would do what he or she is best at."

"I don't think it is that common. But since it is sensible, as you say, distributing work according to particular talents may be catching on."

"Thanks for telling me. It makes me feel more secure. The only problem is that I'm used to you, and I'll have to learn how to be comfortable with someone else."

"Just remember that the more unbearable and egotistical he is the better chance you have of winning. Does that make you feel better?"

"I'll tell you when I meet him. When will that be?"

"As soon as I can arrange it. I'll be with you. Don't forget, too, that after it's all done, after you've won—or lost—and if there are no appeals or further complications, you will be surprised at how easy life is outside of courts and law offices and wonder why you spent all that energy. And then we will be done, and you will begin a new life."

"And you will continue with similar cases and other clients like me?"

By now they had been served an attractive entrée on elegant china with enough glasses and silver to crowd their tiny table.

"I have to admit I haven't had a client like you before," he said looking at her face again. "It's curious to see you in a new context. You look different in the light of the candle from how you appeared under the fluorescent light of my office," he added, slightly unsure of his syntax.

Deb looked up from her plate, and laughed. The compliment, awkward as it was, struck her as amusing.

"And there is something else I should tell you, even though it may not be necessary. I have never had any relationship other than a professional one with a client. I may on occasion play squash or tennis with a corporate client, or even go have a couple of beers. It is important to keep that in mind with female clients."

"Of course. I imagine that is part of an ethical code."

"One that my colleagues don't always observe. When you think of the trust our clients have in us, it is really a slimy thing for someone to suddenly think he's above morality and try to make out."

"You feel strongly about that, don't you? I like that. You are committed to your profession, and that's what makes you a good lawyer."

"That may be true, but it's not the whole story. I haven't told you about my family, have I? I know all about yours, but for you," he paused, wondering where to go next, "I'm just a symbol, sort of, one of help, of authority, of strength. But that's hardly how I appear to myself; actually I don't even know how I appear to myself," he concluded, realizing he was getting nowhere.

It was easier for him, after they finished their wine and broke their bread over a salad with an oil and vinegar dressing, to tell her about Bev, Scott, the accident, and how he was trying to care for them and do his work at the same time. Deb felt her eyes moisten as he described his attempts to make Scott's life bearable and the guilt he felt when he did not succeed. She looked at him; in the light of the candle he was pale, as if exhausted from the continual expense of effort.

"I have no energy left for anything else. Certainly not for any kind of emotional involvement, which would be another drain on my time, on my life."

Dessert was Camembert and another half bottle of red wine.

"You may not have told me any of that before, but somehow I knew it all along, and you should know how much I have been aware that you, how shall I say it, are carrying a heavy load with no relief in sight. I did the closest thing I could to praying for you, and not just because I wanted to win the case. I felt you needed help, and I didn't know where it would come from. Now it seems to me that you will find what you need somewhere, perhaps inside, inside yourself. You could look for it there when you have time."

They ordered coffee, and she continued. "I appreciate your telling me this, even if it wasn't really necessary in my case. You know me enough to realize that I am also emotionally overloaded, with going to see Hank, trying to communicate with him, and not knowing if there is any spark there. His eyes, once so expressive, are now blank, yet without losing any of their beauty. I stare into them and feel a kind of emptiness overtake me. One day in the future I won't be able to feel this pain any more. I fear that day, but I know it is the only thing that will save me."

As they finished coffee, they agreed that they could be most useful to each other as concerned and caring friends and that this would be the most satisfying way for them to continue enjoying each other's company.

With that agreement, they began to relax in each other's presence.

When Deb returned home that night, she had two calls on her answering machine. One was Jennifer, telling her that Russ had hung himself in his room in the psychiatric ward where he was waiting for a permanent placement. The other was Glenda.

"I wonder if we can work more steady so we could finish the curtains soon? My son is getting out of jail any time now, and I'll need to keep an eye on him. I really hope he don't get himself into the wrong crowd again. It could be the same story all over. Is tomorrow night okay?"

She called Jennifer at Moonflower House. She wasn't there, and no one knew where she could be found.

The next night, while they were cutting and sewing the larger curtains, Glenda told Deb, in her direct way, about her son, Darryl, who was about to go on parole after spending a few years at the

State Hospital in Salem. He had been locked up for selling drugs. He had also been charged with abusing his retarded sister, but that count was rejected by the court.

"I don't really know what to believe," Glenda told Deb. "Maybe now Darryl will tell me what really happened. He's a good boy, but he sure knows how to get into trouble!"

A FEW WEEKS later Deb is at her breakfast table writing to her mother when the phone rings.

"This is Steve, Minnie has unearthed more papers for you to sign. The ones you did sign are already filed at court. Do you think you could come over sometime today, like the middle of the afternoon?"

"Sure! I'll be there about three."

Deb looks at her agenda: Morning—work with Glenda. Meet with Jennifer for lunch. Afternoon—finish the Jones family portraits at the studio. See Hank.

Steve won't take long, she thinks; there's plenty of time for everything. I may be a little late for Hank.

Steve lifted his eyes as he saw Deb come into his office. She was dressed in a blue skirt and white blouse, and she felt refreshed, refreshing. I must have changed radically in the time he has known me, she thought, from the haggard woman who first walked into this office. I feel like myself now, self-assured, even attractive.

"Nice to see you, Deb."

I wish I knew what that means. How do I look to him?

"I'm happy to be here. I brought a gift for Minnie. She has done so much for me, she deserves recognition. I can give it to her on my way out."

"You can give it to her now. She is about to bring in the papers."

Minnie came in shortly after, handing a stack of papers to Steve, who shuffled through them.

"Minnie, I thought you would enjoy this. It is a way of saying thank you for all you have done for me and for Hank's cause." Deb handed her a jar wrapped in red paper.

"Thank you very much, Mrs. Myers. What is it?"

"It's strawberry jam. There is a patch at the Friendly Lawn Home. I picked these last time I visited Hank."

"My boyfriend loves jam, and I have no talent for doing anything in the kitchen. We will share this for breakfast."

"Minnie. There is a paragraph missing here on the second last page, where I made an insert mark. You will find it on the original. How long will that take?"

"Half an hour, Mr. Thornton. I'll get to it right away."

"Do you mind waiting, Deb?"

"Not at all."

"There are some magazines on the table by the fish tank."

"Thank you. I'll find something to read. By the way, I'm applying to serve on a committee; it is about housing for the homeless. Can I use your name as a reference?"

"Yes, of course. That will keep you busy now that there is nothing more to do until the trial."

Deb sat next to a built-in fish tank along the back wall. She was fascinated by the almost motionless large black oscars drifting slowly back and forth, their big round eyes looking at her while their thick-lipped mouths opened and shut at regular intervals. What a hypnotic sight, she thought. Only after looking closer did she notice their fluorescent colored spots, like sequins on dark velvet, intermittently changing from orange to red. In contrast, the miniature bala shark fish, dashing back and forth, were patrolling the waters in the vastness of the fish tank; while the iridescent scales of the diamond and rainbow shark constantly changed the hues of their subtle colors. In a corner of the tank a long silver arrowana rested quietly like a comic mermaid, waiting. Innumerable smaller fish added depth to the tank: the black spot barb, the jumbo severums, and the deceiving pink convicts looking like innocent goldfish, but actually quite ferocious. All these iridescent changing colors reminded Deb of the thousand city lights reflecting at night on the surface of Copacabana Bay.

"Where are these fish from?" she asked.

"Brazil."

"I don't remember having seen this tank before. It's wonderful!"

"It was installed earlier this week. The last time you came in it wasn't there." With a smile he added: "These fish will always remind me of you, and Brazil."

"Is that why you picked them?"

"I liked them and was amazed to learn that they are from the Amazon."

Deb finds a magazine and begins reading. From time to time she looks up at Steve who is working at the conference table. He is an intelligent man, she thinks. We have worked steadily together, and I'll miss coming here and seeing him.

It takes Minnie nearly an hour to return with the stack of papers. Deb goes over to Steve's desk; he shows her with his hand where to sign.

"You see how much I trust you; I don't even read what I am supposed to sign in this office. Hopefully the person who is to take over the case will be as dependable."

"That reminds me, let's see if he is in."

Steve ushers Deb out into the hall and precedes her past several doors, around a corner, to an open door. He leans in.

"Mike. Have you a moment? There is somebody I'd like you to meet."

They enter a large, well-lit office with a table full of athletic trophies and, in a corner, contraptions which Deb identifies as exercise and weight-lifting hardware. She feels as if she has just entered a gym.

Sitting with his feet on his desk, a man in shirt sleeves, his tie hanging down loose, is talking on the phone. Nevertheless, he motions to Steve and Deb to enter.

"... that way," he says into the phone, "your ass will be covered. Mine, too, for that matter. At any rate don't forget to make the transfer of funds, and right away! Okay. Bye. See you."

Turning to face Steve and Deb, he stands up, smiling.

"This is Deb Myers. Mike Hoffman, who will present your case in court. He is like those fish from the Amazon that devour human flesh within minutes. In the courtroom that is a virtue, at least for the person he represents."

"Glad to meet you, Deb. Steve is so kind; he always chooses the most ingratiating qualities to describe in people."

Steve describes Deb's case briefly to Mike, reminding him of a discussion they had held earlier. Mike looks at her, intently, she thinks. She finds him rather short; his hair is receding.

"You are lucky, Deb," Mike explains to her as if confiding something. "Whenever Steve prepares a case we win. It's inevitable." Mike looks at his wrist watch. "Time to quit, isn't it? Let's all go to dinner at my club so I can get to know Deb, and you can have a decent meal, Steve. I hear Bev never cooks for him, did you know that? So we have to fatten him up when we get the chance. What do you say?"

"Very kind," Steve answers. "I have to be at home."

"How about you, then, Deb?"

"Thank you. Another time, maybe. I do have a prior engagement."

Steve escorts Deb back to his office.

"I think we have everything in order now," he says, and in a gesture of friendship, places his hand on Deb's. She looks at him.

"I'll miss not seeing you. I am so used to our weekly appointments that I look forward to them. It sounds funny but it's true."

Steve looks at her and smiles. "Come to think of it, I feel the same way. How about celebrating over a nice dinner? Are you free this evening?"

"Aren't you expected at home?"

"Sort of, but it isn't all that important. It is just that I didn't want to hear any more of Mike's hunting stories."

"My prior engagement isn't important, either. It can be canceled."

Steved reaches for the phone and calls for a reservation at Chez Nous, an elegant establishment for those in the know.

"*La cuisine est magnifique chez nous!*" announces a deep voice that greets us as we enter. Through the tall windows we can see the terrace where drinks are being served. A relaxed maître d'hôtel leads us to a round table in a wood paneled room with a view of the gardens. After the waiter opens a bottle of white wine and pours into tall goblets, we toast to the success of our case. I feel overwhelmed by the beauty of the place and the exquisite food. We hardly talk as we eat, and I look in the candlelight into his eyes and notice their warmth and depth.

It is still early when we leave the restaurant and decide to drive to Washington Park. We walk through the Rose Gardens, enjoying the colors and scents. The long shadows of the evening cast a strange light on the gravel surrounding the beds in profuse bloom. From the lookout point Mount Hood appears above the outline of skyscrapers, the snow on its crest shining like gold in the setting sun. We take a hidden lane up the hill to the Japanese Gardens. It is cool in the path, and we feel refreshed after the first hot day of summer. Except for the sound of rustling leaves, the chirping of birds, and a squirrel busily crisscrossing in front of us, everything is quiet. Halfway up the hill, Deb pauses to catch her breath, turns, and smiles at Steve, who is coming behind her. He continues climbing and takes her arm in a gesture of helping. To see him better in the growing darkness, she pivots her face toward him raising her eyes and mouth, where he places his lips, first cautiously, then gently, then with more pressure. She ceases thinking and with her hands invites him closer. Soon one of his arms is around her waist, a hand caresses her hair, and they forget where they are in the darkness of their closed eyes. This kiss of yearning and joy lasts until it is interrupted by the sound of approaching footsteps and heavy breathing.

"Passing on your right!"

Two runners in shorts streak down the path, leaving behind them the debris of the moment scattered on the ground.

Deb and Steve continue their climb slowly through a forest of trees and ferns. Suddenly they find themselves in a clearing where the oblique light of the setting sun filters through the leaves onto a bare area with rocks set amid the ripples of carefully raked sand. Without words, like initiates in a new dimension, they sit quietly and contemplate the stern, bare patch. Deb takes Steve's hand and holds it in both of hers.

They follow a path leading back to shaded vegetation, where moss seems to cover everything except the shiny surface of gray protruding rocks. The sound of gurgling water draws their attention to a bamboo bridge. They cross onto a tiny island surrounded by connected pools fed by a slender waterfall. It is still light enough to perceive a splash of intense blue and purple flowering iris set against different shades of green. There is a stone bench where they sit while the light continues to fade, remaining strong only at the top of the trees where it reflects against the leaves.

"Is there anything real here?" Steve asks, as if to himself.

The soft sound of water mingles with the silence; there is no movement, except when he leans over to finish the interrupted kiss, his arm on her shoulder. This time their lips remain pressed together, half open, for as long as they can hold their breaths. Then, without a word, they stand up and continue to follow the water as it curves its way along different levels of terrain, surrounded by pale bamboo groves. Japanese lamps discreetly illuminate the path shrouded in shade. The stepping stones finally lead them to a tiled-roof gate where they exit onto the road.

Saturday morning. Scott is explaining to Diane that Bev is in Seattle again looking for a location for the new gallery she plans to open with Mary: a place that will attract a larger population of art and crafts consumers than the one they are currently serving. If all goes well she will be home by Monday noon. Meanwhile, Steve gets up early, walks the quarter mile to the road for the newspaper and returns in time to join Scott and Diane for breakfast on the patio.

The sun is reflecting brightly on the birch leaves surrounding the lawn that lies behind the house. The day will undoubtedly prove to be beautiful, especially later when a wind from the ocean will pick up and cool off the afternoon. The morning is quiet except for a concert of songbirds that blends with the muted sound of bees already visiting the flowers in the large pots that surround the breakfast table in the sun. Diane serves, letting father and son talk about whatever seems important. Steve appreciates her devotion to Scott and her willingness to help Bev. Such an attractive and intelligent young woman and yet content with this work, he thinks as he watches her wait on Scott.

"Dad, if you have time, you might enjoy going to Powell's Books this afternoon to hear Conrad Levine. He will be autographing copies of his latest book and I understand he will give an informal talk. Should be real interesting."

"The name sounds familiar. Who is he?"

"A poet who is just now getting recognized. He is known mainly for his pieces on the oil spill in Alaska, where he shows the destruction and the plight of the birds; it's almost surrealistic when the description turns violent. I have the book so you can see it whenever you want. Actually it was Diane who told me about the poems; she came across them somewhere. How was it that you learned about them?"

"I happened on that book on my way for the interview with your mom a couple of months ago. I was waiting for a Greyhound bus in San Francisco, and the book was lying on a bench. It was obviously poetry, so I started reading, and since no one came to claim it, I took it along."

Steve said something about being surprised to learn that she read poetry.

"You'd be surprised at what she reads; more than I do with all the time on my hands."

"How do you manage to find time to read with everything you have to do around here?"

"Both you and Mrs. Thorton let me have enough free time to read. Hope you don't mind if I delve into your library on the second floor sometime. I'm really curious to see what is there."

"You won't believe what an efficient research assistant she is! Whatever I need to know she finds out in a jiffy."

"Aren't you afraid, Scott, that I might need a good research assistant at the office and hire Diane away from you? She may consider it more exciting than here in the wilderness."

"If you do, I'll disinherit you, for sure, Dad. Anyway, Diane always says she's glad to be away from the bustle of downtown."

They all laughed, recognizing incongruity. Steve wondered why he so enjoyed talking with Scott and Diane when Bev was out of town.

"Seriously, Dad, try to go to the reading. Then you can tell us about it tonight."

"Couldn't I take the two of you there; you must both want to hear . . . what was his name?"

"Conrad Levine. Thanks, but I can't. Chuck is coming over this afternoon with some of his friends; they'll bring their instruments and practice here, maybe on the patio if it isn't too warm. Diane is anxious to hear what a string quartet sounds like up close, in the flesh."

"I've only heard recordings, not the real thing. And Scott's friends will need refreshments, so I'll be useful, too."

Later that morning Steve drove into town. He turned on the radio to help him avoid thinking about the previous night—about what had happened and where that might lead. He went straight to his club for a workout, a game of squash, a swim, and a massage. He felt relaxed, free of concerns when he walked into Powell's. There he picked up Conrad Levine's newest book, a collection of prose poems. He bought a vegetarian sandwich on sourdough bread and tea, sat down at one of the round tables where people were eating, playing chess, or reading magazines, and began paging through the new book while he waited for the poet to arrive.

"Well, hello!" It was Deb standing in front of his table, smiling with obvious pleasure at finding him unexpectedly.

It was a surprise for him, too, and at the moment he was at a loss for something reasonably intelligent to say. He did, however, manage to invite her to sit with him.

"I came to see Conrad Levine," he said. "Have you read anything of his?"

She had read a good deal, adding that she also had a personal interest. "He was one of Hank's writing teachers at college, sort of a mentor; Hank talked about him often."

By now Steve's wits had returned and he was able to chat merrily with Deb until the poet arrived to give a short and enthusiastic reading of some recent work. He was tall and a bit awkward in public. After his presentation, Deb waited in line and eventually spoke with him, introducing Steve to him as "Hank's avenger."

Steve and Deb went out together and walked south toward where he thought his car was parked. Deb suddenly interrupted whatever Steve was saying to ask:

"Are you busy this evening?"

"Not that I can think of, really. Why?"

"I just wondered if you would like to come over for a snack with me. I miss you, especially after last night. That was pretty intense, and I am wondering how you feel about it. Would you like a gourmet snack at my place? It's the newest French restaurant in town, called Chez Moi! Open by appointment only, and exclusively for special guests! What do you say?"

"I say let's go for it! And you know what I would enjoy? You could read some of Levine's poems for me, with your wonderful voice. As for how I feel, I don't know yet; the intensity hasn't quite worn off."

"Agreed. I also want to show you my album of Brazil photos. Let's walk. There is a little market on the way, if you don't mind stopping. You can push the shopping cart, but be careful in the narrow aisles."

They continued this banter as they walked briskly toward the market, unaware of the Saturday night crowd on the sidewalks and the honking of cars stalled in the streets. At Merlin's Market and Deli, Deb picked out salmon steaks, a variety of cheeses, lettuce, and a French bread; Steve watched and then made a detour to the wine section, pondered for a while, and finally selected a Mâcon Blanc (already cold) and a Dão he had never tasted, admitting to himself that he was taking a risk. But isn't living a risk anyway? He hurried back to Deb before starting to think further along those lines.

Deb's building was on a quiet side street; the main door, hidden in the shadows of a tunnel-like brick entrance, was already locked, and Deb was obliged to give her package to Steve in order to extract her key and insert it into the lock. They climbed the five floors to her apartment in silence, pausing at landings to catch their breaths. Her apartment was cheerful and light, in contrast to the rest of the building. Her living room suggested to Steve a simple yet intense life full of subdued femininity. Deb went into another room to freshen up and change clothes, and returned comfortably dressed, smiling, as if happy to receive Steve finally in her own surroundings.

There was just enough room in the kitchen for them both to stand. She prepared the fish and the salad; he cut the bread and the cheese. They spoke little, but he could sense her presence right at his elbow. He wondered if she could read his thoughts when she explained where something he needed was without his having asked. He paused to look at her as she spread herbs and poured wine on to the fish, and he realized how his perception of her had shifted from the kind of sympathetic indifference he initially felt for all his clients to a form of wonder before a particular kind of beauty he had never known. Did she seem different because he desired her as she stood there in her silk-like pant suit, completely absorbed in preparing the meal? Had she actually changed? Or had he?

While the fish baked, they drank wine together looking at the view from the balcony outside her living room. A cool breeze was already circulating, and the clouds were beginning to show the effects of a summer sun about to set. The muffled noise of the city rose to them from the narrow streets below where the crowds still pursued their boisterous activities. Steve listened to what Deb was saying, but he was more focused on his sensation of being intensely alive. She was saying that he was probably right to think that her building wasn't the safest. She added that she knew how to defend herself, having taken courses in self-defense when she was in Brazil. On the other hand, she added, "these days you aren't safe anywhere. Even in the best neighborhoods you can be mugged. Anyway, I like it here. And now that you have seen it, I like it even better."

They talked on, ate at a table with candles in the living room, laughed, listened to music, and took turns reading Levine's poems out loud. Time stood still and passed rapidly by as Steve thought he should soon help clear dishes and take his leave. Instead, he turned off the lights, placed the burning candle in the unused fireplace, and invited her to sit next to him on the floor.

"Wait," Deb whispered, as she went to a closet, found a bedcover, and spread it on the floor. Then, without either of them being fully aware, they slowly undressed each other and were caught up in a vortex of passion and poetry that neither fully understood until later.

W ELL, ACTUALLY, IT wasn't as simple as that. Life gets more complicated the closer you look at it. Take Steve, for example. He wasn't really ready for this to happen; he walked into it blind and almost made a complete mess of it. The fact is, he was perfectly inexperienced as far as these things go. This was no secret, except maybe to him. What was his life like, up to then? All his friends will tell you that it wasn't the greatest, if they are being honest. For that matter, he didn't have many friends who could tell you much about him. What about the guys at his office like Mike Hoffman or Benny Brooks? Benny is the one who brought him into the partnership and became his habitual squash partner, probably because Steve didn't feel he had to win all the time. A little overweight, always cheerful, and moving his jaw to keep his chewing gum moist, Benny was everybody's fraternity brother, during and after college, always there to help, ready to join in for a good time. Big on corporation law, he had climbed the ladder fast and then settled down with a drab wife and three daughters, now in college. Benny's vocation for friendship found its natural expression when Steve arrived in Portland with an ambitious wife, a crippled son, and a determination to make it as a lawyer. They played squash in winter; in summer and fall it was tennis or jogging, and in December they went Christmas shopping together to buy presents for their families. Once at a party, after too many drinks, Benny confided in someone that he thought Steve would be best described as a lifelong "virtual virgin in search of fulfillment."

As stupid as the remark was, it made you ponder. Steve's early life was difficult and businesslike, almost ascetic. He married right out of college, and set his compass on a career that was manageable. That marriage produced one son and a series of overcooked meals, until his wife decided to entrust the needs of his nutrition to hired help. She kept to herself his other needs, but from all appearances didn't put them to much use.

The next morning when Steve finally came down to breakfast, Diane and Scott had finished theirs and were at the table deep into the Sunday newspapers. Steve looked a little tired.

"I hope you aren't getting the flu again, Dad. It's unusual for you to sleep so long."

"No. I'm okay. I went to bed late."

"Did you go to the poetry reading? How was it?"

"I loved it. Thanks so much for telling me about it."

"What did he read?" Diane asked. "His own work, I suppose."

"Yes. I marked down the ones he read in the collection of his poems I bought at Powell's before he arrived. I'll show you. I wonder where I put the book. Did you see it? Could I have left it somewhere?"

"It depends on where you went. What did you like the most?"

"It's not so much particular things he read or anything he said. But I think the experience changed my life."

"How's that?"

"Tell you later. I've got to sort things out. How was the quartet? Did you enjoy it, Diane?"

"It was fabulous. It felt like taking a steam bath in sound. Scott told me there were a lot of wrong notes because the music was so hard to play, but I didn't even notice. After they finished we all had sausage and cheese on Melissa's fresh bread and drank some beer."

"We were too tired to wait up for you, Dad. Sorry. What did you do?"

"I saw a friend at Powell's and had a bite afterward."

"Benny?"

"No, someone else."

"Hope you had fun. When is Mom due home?"

"Tomorrow, if they are successful in finding a place. Otherwise it will be next weekend. Who got the papers?"

"Diane and I raced. She jogged, and I put the new wheelchair on overdrive. I had to wait for her where the road curves and divides, you know, where that big cedar is growing in the middle."

Fifteen minutes later Steve went upstairs to his study and shut the door.

"Where?"

"Right there, on the floor."

"No!"

"See the candle he put in the fireplace? I left it there, as a reminder that it really happened . . ."

"Did you stay on the floor all night? I mean! That's romantic!"

"It was more like, cold! You know I haven't finished doing those curtains with Glenda. So we went into the bedroom and got warm together, and then we fell asleep. He left about three, and he's coming back tonight."

"Deb! It feel good?"

"Yea it does. But there are still problems, and I need you for that. Thanks for coming, Jenn. I'll make tea."

"You know, Deb, I've never seen him, even from a distance," Jenn shouted to Deb in the kitchen. "Tim likes him a lot, but says he's too gentle to be a good courtroom lawyer."

Deb brings in a tray with mugs and a few leftovers from the previous evening.

"I'm not worried about Steve or anything like that. I feel he's just right. He's obviously in love, maybe for the first time. He is awkward enough, and you should see how nervous he was when we were alone together for the first time. But he learned a lot already last night."

"He's married, I guess."

"That's true. But it's me I am concerned about right now. It's not that he has a wife, but rather how do I feel about intruding into a family, disrupting a relationship that may be more or less okay? Know what I mean?"

"Or that may be more or less awful."

"There is something wrong in that family, I have sensed it somehow since the first appointment I had with him. He looked like an unhappy man, and yet last night he was absolutely glowing. I met her once, Steve's wife, that is . . . you are the first person I've told, other than my mother. When I first came to Portland I walked into a small gallery to look at an exhibit, and there were these two women running the place. It happens that one of them was Mrs. Thornton; she was polite, well dressed, very professional. I didn't put the two together until he told me last night that his wife co-owned Pisces Gallery and was away in Seattle looking for a location where she wants to expand her business. Once his wife had a face, it was harder for me to deal with disrupting a family."

"I wonder if anybody else has ever had this problem . . ."

"But then there is Hank, too. It may sound silly, but I feel I have betrayed him, and it makes me want to cry every time I think about it. If I could only tell him, he would forgive me, but he can't, and that's what hurts. I have also betrayed the friends who supported Hank and me for so long down in Rio, through the worst of times."

"When will you tell them?"

"As soon as I know it will work."

"What will they say?"

"You are right; they will say it's great, that I had to do it sometime, the sooner the better."

"I don't know what to say about Hank, Deb. You will get the answer when you least expect it. Maybe by talking to him you will know how to get his forgiveness. You may have to go deep inside yourself to find out that you received it. I know I'm not making much sense, but you know what I mean. It's just like when you knew Steve was unhappy without him saying anything."

"I could try that. But there is something else, too. It's me. I wrote my mother about a month ago that I wasn't interested in a relationship any more, that I can do without men and the problems they bring, even when they are decent and caring. You know how it is, Jenn, after Russ and all the suffering you went through."

"I know the feeling, but I can forget it, too, Deb. That is where Tim helps me a lot, just being around, wanting me to feel good. Nothing has developed there yet, but I'm sure something will."

At noon Glenda phoned.

"I can't work for a while. Darryl's due home the day after tomorrow, and I have heaps of stuff to do to get ready. Plus I'm real nervous about his coming. After he's been home for a couple of days we can start again. Don't worry, we'll finish the curtains before next winter."

Deb took a bus to the Friendly Lawn Home. On the way she wrote on the back of an envelope what she wanted to tell Hank. This shouldn't be a confession, she thought. Rather, it's a matter of information, of telling him what she is doing, like sewing curtains or joining a committee to help the homeless. What else can you tell a person who can't understand? At the beginning Deb had tried to talk about important matters, like her political convictions or how the case was coming along. After a month as she sat next to him, she began to relax and ramble on about how she spent her days, from getting up in the morning to going to bed at night, including what she ate for each meal. He seemed to enjoy that better maybe because she no longer paused to formulate a sentence or an idea but simply let her voice drone on and on until it was time for her to leave.

This afternoon Hank was supported in a special chair in the

side yard next to flower beds in full bloom. Deb kissed him and held his hand while she described her day. The only difference from the last time she had told the same story was that at the end she went on to say that she slept with Steve, who will now take care of her as she knew Hank would want. Deb then invented a dream she could have had during the night and described how Hank came to her, forgave her, and wished her all the happiness he was capable of bestowing on her. Once she finished she held her breath and let the tears stream down as she watched Hank's face for any signs of understanding. What she saw was a pair of white butterflies fluttering around his head. As she leaned forward to kiss him good-bye, one of them came to rest on her shoulder.

When Deb returned home late in the afternoon, Steve was sitting on the floor outside her door. Next to him was a large plant and a few packages.

"Steve, how wonderful!"

"This is a friend for you when I'm not here," he said, motioning to the plant.

They kissed before going in. He opened one of the packages and took from it a down sleeping bag with a light blue cover.

"This is supposed to be good for below zero weather, Deb. We won't shiver tonight!"

They went shopping for dinner at the same market and stopped for a cup of coffee on their way back.

"I hope you aren't awfully hungry. I just got home from Hank's, and I need a shower."

"May I join you?"

"The shower stall is only a quarter the size of the kitchen, but let's try."

The following morning Scott and Diane are sitting at the breakfast table.

"We'd better wake Dad. He should have left for the office by now."

"Is it possible he hasn't any appointments today?"

"I suppose it is. But it isn't like him to sleep this late. Would you go up and wake him, Diane? He will be furious with himself for oversleeping. Just knock at his door and then go in and shout his name in his ear. That's what Mom does."

Diane went up the stairs and returned right away.

"He's not there, Scott."

"Really? How was his bed? He may have gone out already."

"It hasn't been touched."

"Hey, Dad. What are you up to? Can't be playing squash all night."

At that moment the sound of Steve's Jaguar pulls up in front of the house.

"Let's not say anything. We'll see what he says."

Steve comes in the front door and heads for the stairs.

"I'm going to shower. Don't wait for me."

"Mom's due home at noon," Scott shouts at him. "She called last night while you were out."

After his shower Steve drank a cup of coffee in the kitchen. Melissa informed him that Mrs. Thornton was expecting Mr. and Mrs. Fukuda for dinner. Would he please see to the wine? Steve left without seeing Scott; he was already late for an appointment. That means Bev and Mary found a location for the gallery in Seattle, he thought. They will want to go over the legal questions at dinner. Wonder how much refurbishing it will need. Going up to Seattle to pound nails and paint walls is something I'd rather not do right now. Maybe Milton Fukuda will want to do it himself since he is so handy with tools.

When Bev drove in after lunch she was too wound up with her trip and her new gallery to ask how her family had fared during her absence.

"It will be just perfect," she explained to her husband over the phone. "It is a fabulous location, and the rent is affordable. It doesn't need a thing; you won't believe how beautiful it is going to be. We bought some of the furnishings already in Seattle; they will be delivered next week. That means I'll have to go up again next Monday and spend the week there, I hope you won't mind. You can come along if you aren't busy and help us settle in. But we can really do it ourselves since there is so little to do. You see, it was a gallery that went bankrupt, and we arrived there just at the right moment to save the owners a lot of money and effort. I am so happy! All the walls are painted white and only need touching up. We bought the screens and sculpture supports that were about to be advertised for sale. There is a little apartment in the back where Mary and I can stay, and we will save a lot of money that way. All we need is beds and stuff for the kitchen, some chairs and desks. I have a whole list; you can help me shop at Moynehan's. They are expensive, but what can you do?"

"How soon do you think you can open?"

"We are aiming for August. The main problem is promotion, but if we start our advertising right away we will be able to draw a respectable crowd for the grand opening. The one thing still to be decided is what to exhibit. Tell me what you think: how about a show of Northwest artists? We could ask for submissions, hire a jury to judge them, and get a lot of free promotion from all of that. Not a bad idea, is it? Otherwise we could take artists we have shown in Portland and hang their stuff in Seattle where they aren't known. That would be less exciting, but it would work."

"Go for your first idea! It will take more energy, but you will attract lots of attention that way."

"I'm thinking we'll have the opening before Scott's birthday. That reminds me: have you decided about his present? What do you think about my suggestion?"

"You mean the car with controls he can manage? I checked with Volvo. They have a model that includes its own motorized wheelchair. You can wheel in and lock the chair in place, without any help. Costs a fortune, but I ordered one last week anyway, knowing you would go along with the idea. This model needs to be put together on Scott's specifications somewhere in the East; after it is shipped to Portland it can be stored at the local dealer's and delivered here on his birthday. Will he ever be surprised!"

"What color did you choose? How about extras?"

"I ordered extras galore. I chose red, his favorite color. It's a four-door and has a fairly large trunk."

"Great, Steve. Now, I have a lot to do this afternoon. Can't spend any more time with you on the phone. Come home as early as you can. Mary and Milton are coming for dinner, and we have a host of decisions to make."

Steve dialed Deb.

"Darling. Bev's home, and I can't come tonight; I'm hooked and booked. But the future is looking up because she will be practically living in Seattle for the rest of the summer. I suspect she will close down the gallery in Portland, and that means many changes are about to take place, domestic and otherwise."

"Could you stop on the way home? Just for a few minutes?"

"Yes, love. For a few minutes."

The intercom rang.

"Scott, dear. I need Diane for a couple of hours. I'm in my room upstairs. Tell her to bring a pad of paper and a pencil, and my calendar from the kitchen. Then you can go and see if Melissa needs help."

Melissa did not need Scott's help. "I work better alone," she told him. "I could use someone to run and fetch things like onions or flour, but you don't quite fit the bill. Better go find something else to do. I'm already behind from jabbering with you all morning."

He wheeled to his room, turned on the computer, booted up the word processor and wrote.

"Mom's home. She's a whirlwind of activity. Energy to burn.

"What's Dad up to? There are all sorts of plausible hypotheses, and I am unwilling to choose any one of them. Let him choose. He will tell me when he is ready. But it's a shame he doesn't share the process of sorting things out instead of keeping them all to himself. I wonder if it wouldn't make him feel less vulnerable.

"Family life has become decidedly more interesting around here. Just imagine the conversation at dinner if everyone suddenly decided not to hide what is on his or her mind! If I get the time, I'll write out that conversation.

"The nights are cool, but the days are decidedly hotter. I notice it especially in my exercise and pool room, where there is no air conditioning. When I practice rope climbing, a sport for which I am ideally qualified since I can't cheat using my legs, I drip with sweat. The trick now is to change from one rope to another somewhere near the top and then slide down. Soon I can start swinging from one to the other like my hero, not Tarzan any more, but one of the apes, who was much better at it than he was.

"I am sidetracking here. The true reason for writing is this. After our swims in the afternoon, Diane puts on a bathrobe and gives me a rubdown. It is a time I always enjoy. Yesterday, when it was so hot, she wore a loose tunic, and when she massaged my shoulders and chest, I could see her breasts. Just for a moment, really, and I looked away to avoid embarrassment for either of us, and probably also to make the event more likely to happen again. But the vision was absolutely clear, like the sight of Mount Hood rising out of the clouds on a winter morning, and when I shut my eyes I can remember it as if it were the most detailed color photograph. I doubt that anyone can adequately describe the sight of a pair of breasts without becoming wordy, mawkish, or disgusting, and I certainly won't try. Let me put it this way: these are the first breasts I remember seeing outside of pictures, so they looked a little different from what I expected. They were small, and although she was leaning with both arms outstretched, they did not seem to be separated from the rest of her chest. Yet they belonged to a different world, perhaps to a different dimension. Their skin was almost transparent, and the tips grew out of that transparency as if effortlessly.

"Here she comes! It's time for our swim. Anyway, I am getting frustrated. Not with the image, which is still vivid, but with the words, which are about to smother it."

When Steve left Deb's place, he should already have arrived home half an hour earlier. Deb closed the door and took the phone.

"Glenda? This is Deb. Can I come over for a few minutes? Not to work on the curtains . . . I would just like to bring you something."

"Of course, Deb. You can stay as long as you like. Liz and I are just finishing dinner. Come and have some dessert with us."

Fifteen minutes later Deb presented Glenda with a jar of strawberry jam.

"It's as if Hank and I had made it together."

"How sweet! Sit down. I'll make some decaf. Mind if I try it now, on toast?"

Later, after Liz had gone out to a movie with a friend, Deb told Glenda about Steve.

"No big deal, Deb. Either you like a guy or you don't, and if you like him you might as well shack up together. Really, why not? It's natural, isn't it? I just keep my eyes on Liz, because someone might abuse her, like it already happened a couple of times, like just last week with that stupid Bud Portsny down the street."

Glenda caught her breath. "But we're talking about you, Deb. You did the right thing, and you've got nothing to worry about. Seems every time I get laid there is hell to pay. I can't understand why but someone always learns and gets pissed at me, like my nieces, and just look at them! It's a different guy every night almost!"

Deb went on to tell Glenda that Hank and Steve's wife were both innocent, that they had done no harm, and how guilty she felt for taking something away from them, from their modest claim to happiness. Glenda looked at her.

"I say screw that kind of talk! That's their problem, not yours. Think about your happiness for once. They can take care of theirselves, Hank, too; he's alive, what else can he ask for? Look! I've got Darryl coming home tomorrow, in the afternoon. He just spent two years behind bars, so you can imagine what kind of a mood he's gonna be in. Not happy to be a free man, no! Just pissed because he lost all that time and has to report to the parole officer every other week. I know him! Look around, Deb. The place is a mess; he hates anybody else's mess, even though he don't never see his own. I haven't had a minute to pick up for his homecoming or have a party for him. And I get worried he might get ugly when things go wrong for him. Anyhow, like I say, that's his problem. I've got my own to take care of before I start thinking about him."

"Do you think he has changed while he was in prison?"

"He's getting let out early for good behavior. And he took courses there and got training and counseling. Every time Liz and I visited him, he treated us real nice. His case supervisor told me he's become a Christian in the last months. So I'm hoping he's improved. Come over some time while he's here, you'll see, and you can tell me what you think. Once he's settled, we can go back to working on these curtains; maybe we can finish them."

When Steve rushed into the living room over an hour late, the guests, Mary and her husband, Milton, were already sitting by the empty fireplace pretending to enjoy drinks Bev had been obliged to prepare hefself.

"I'm so sorry! Between the office and the traffic, I just couldn't get here any earlier. I even took a different exit from the freeway so that I could escape all those stalled cars. That slowed me up even more and made me lose my way in those little streets south of the country club."

Bev was peeved. "When I called your office they told me you had left long ago. We wondered if you would ever arrive."

As an act of repentance, Steve went on his knees to set a fire, which he soon had burning briskly. Then he gathered the glasses and made everyone a new version of whatever they had been drinking. At dinner the meat was overdone after being kept warm so long.

"We think we have a reasonable plan," Mary explained to Steve and Milton. "Actually, we figured it out while we were driving this morning. For one thing, we won't need to worry about money. We are both old hands at borrowing and at obtaining grants. Besides, closing Pisces will give us extra cash. The nice thing is that we can do it all ourselves, without any help from our husbands. Don't you like that idea, Milt? You can work at the nursery all you want."

Milton, who seldom says much, smiled enigmatically and moved his head in consent.

"It only means we will be gone quite a bit in the next few weeks," Bev added. "We have to finish setting up and start the promotion to make this gallery take off. Figure it this way: we'll be gone off and on for the rest of the summer. Now is that so bad? But I'll be home for Scott's birthday," Bev looked at Scott, who was not listening very carefully to all this. "That's important!"

"Wouldn't it be less inconvenient if you opened later, maybe toward the end of August, after the birthday?"

"Steve, Honey. Where is your business sense? We have to open as soon as possible to take advantage of what's left of the tourist season. That's when the sales will be. Then for the rest of the year things can slow down and we can spend more of our time at home, until next summer comes around."

Bev and Mary's plan was unanimously adopted. The next morning Bev sat with Scott and explained to him her expectations for the new gallery, attempting to soften whatever resistance he might have to her being away for so long. She wanted him and Steve to be present for the opening and to remain in Seattle long enough to enjoy everything the city has to offer. They could all take a trip to Victoria or Vancouver and visit some friends on the San Juan Islands before returning to Portland. "Then we'll be home and relaxed for your birthday. Won't that be nice?"

Later Steve joined Scott for a game of chess. Scott tried every trick he could invent to help his father win, but nothing worked.

346 | CARLOTA LINDSAY

"Dad, you're playing worse than ever! Do you have things on your mind? Or are Mom's plans getting you down?"

Steve started putting the chessmen in their wooden case.

"Both. I need to talk to you sometime, Scott. Soon, but not right yet. I've got to figure things out beforehand."

"Don't wait too long. You might forget what you had to say."

"Are you going to be able to keep busy while your mother is gone?"

"I doubt that will be a problem for me, or for you, either. I haven't enough time as it is, not even enough to look after my dad."

THE SKY WAS overcast at noon when Darryl walked out of the State Hospital office building in Salem, the paperwork required for his early release having been completed. He had refused the offer of a last free lunch, thus advancing his freedom by twenty minutes. He lit a cigarette, protecting the flame of his match with his hands, and headed toward Center Street where he suspected his long-time buddy Asco Derm would be waiting for him in that beat-up Plymouth of his. During his stay at the Penitentiary and later at the State Hospital where he had entered a social skills rehabilitation program, it was Asco who had supplied him with the pot he needed to sell in order to maintain a style of living that somewhat resembled what he had been used to before his arrest. Good guy, that Asco, Darryl thought as he caught sight of the rusted green vehicle, still looking low and sleek in its old-fashioned way, waiting at the exit from a parking area. Let's see how cooperative he can be now that I really need him. The words of the final paragraphs of his release were still ringing in his ears: by order from the parole office, it was strictly forbidden for Darryl to use drugs or alcohol, he could not use or possess firearms or any other kind of weapon, and he would not qualify for a driver's license. He was to report to his parole officer every two weeks and was expected to undergo counseling on a regular basis. He was further required to actively seek employment. He would certainly need the help of a friend.

"Hya, buddy. Glad ya could come. Let's split."

CARLOTA LINDSAY

Asco's car took off with a roar from its broken muffler and souped-up engine, showering the surroundings with sooty exhaust and the acrid smell of tires burning against asphalt.

"Wanna go to the coast? That's where the best crack is, if you want any. Nothing doing in hometown. Might as well forget it."

"Go for the coast. It'll be okay if I get to Portland by tonight. Mom is expecting me, and she probably has installed a direct phone line to the parole board just in case I don't show up on time at home. Hope she doesn't drive me nuts. She is so virtuous it makes you wanna spit. I could use a rock right now!"

They head for Lincoln City at something near eighty miles an hour. Asco skillfully slows down for speed traps and is alert to the radar detector's beep.

"Hey! Asco, old bud. I gotta tell you something. Now don't get me wrong or think I'm off my rocker or something. But I tell ya, I seen the light."

"So what. There's pleny of it around. You go blind or something there in the bin?"

"No, you turkey! I seen the light of Jesuss, that kind of light. I'll skip the details. I just wanted to let you know that I've been saved, and if you wanna be saved, too, just stick around me an I'll show you the way."

"Quit bullshitting me. If you ever see that light, it'll be when you're ready to croak, not a second earlier. You're gonna keep on boozing and abusing and whoring it up until they come to shut the curtain for ya. Maybe then you'll see the light of day through the haze, I mean, if you ever get sober enough."

"No shit! Asco. Don't worry about them things, for me seeing the light don't change nothing really. I just know that when they come for me it will be the angels with their harps and boring music for all eternity, and that'll be okay, because until then I'm going to live it up. I gotta make up for lost time right now. Two whole fucking years in that hole!"

"How di't happened? Musta been a miracle, one of them walking on water tricks, or some phoney cure: they glued your leg back on after chopping it off, right? And you walked away thinking the Almighty was some carpenter."

"They had these young people at the hospital, interns or something from some religion college, where they learn how to preach and console people, how to talk to them when they done something bad and make them feel guilty and promise not to do it again and believe it, too! But they really figured out what made me do it, and told me they even felt that way sometimes, and one of them had been a street kid for a couple of years, and you should have heard his stories! Anyhows, these interns would talk to us for as long as we wanted. I liked it because it was in a nice sort of chapel, away from the cells and the razor wire. The guys were handsome and looked at you direct. But the one I liked best was this fat babe with thick glasses, a loud voice, and a laugh you could hear from acrost the recreation yard. We'd go into that chapel and joke and laugh and then all of a sudden we was talking about the meaning of life. She said hers didn't have no meaning for a long time, and then she decided to go out and help jerks like I who needed to be set straight, and that's what gave her life meaning, just like that! And we went on talking until finally I go: 'Okay, is He some big mean parole officer in the sky who's going to keep me from having a ball when I get out of this pigpen?' Then she goes: 'Not really, but you may find Him somewhere when you don't expect it, like in a tavern or a whorehouse when your rope comes up short.' I figured that was pretty cool, it sort of lets me do my thing and get saved, too. So when the intern left to go back to school, there was this preacher from a church who would come every Sunday afternoon and tell us stories about Jesuss up in heaven, and sometimes about that dirty devil down in hell, and he gave me a free Bible. I always have it on me, right here. Where are we going? You better decide quick."

They were entering Lincoln City. They stopped at a diner for a snack then went to a marine repair shop where Asco asked for an acquaintance, who, upon seeing the two of them, put on a jacket. They all went outside in back of the shop for a smoke. They talked for a while and made plans to meet again after work. Then Darryl and Asco walked down the main drag, visiting an adult video shop and a gun show; they went to a sheltered part of the beach to have a joint. Later Darryl phoned his mother to tell her he would be home at noon the next day and she shouldn't worry, cause he was okay and being very good.

The next morning, after Asco's friend went to work, Darryl wanted to go fishing. He had his "severance pay," as he called it, and arranged a boat rental. It was cloudy and cool; no breeze rippled the gray water's surface as Asco steered toward the open sea over long silent swells. They unpacked their rented tackle and began the ritual of seeking food from the depths, catching a few bottom fish as the time passed. In the meantime, Darryl talked and talked, dispelling the two years of silence that were still haunting his mind.

"You're a great guy, old Bud. Better'n I'd have thought. And you're going to help me get used to being free again. It's tough to be free, to be with people who don't have to watch every step they take. They are all walking here and there, without thinking about where they put their feet. If they step in a puddle or on dog shit, no big deal; they just wipe it off on someone's lawn or a towel. But me, I have to be careful and look everywhere I go. I might stub my toe on somebody's shoe, bump someone and have to say I'm sorry. I can't even look hard at people; I have to look down, at their shoes, not in their eyes. Did you ever look at anyone in the eyes, knowin' you're as good as them, knowin' they can't do nothing to you because your ass is as clean as theirs?"

"I donno, Darryl. Never thought about that."

"It's for sure you haven't. You're scared shitless, like the rest of us. You think you're free, but inside you know damn well you ain't, because any minute you can get kicked in the ass by one of them fuckers you get in the way of. I been thinking a lot in my extra time, and that's what I've come up with. Life is getting your ass kicked. You can go on like that if you want, but not me. I'm going to come out on top, walking down the street looking anywhere I choose. And you can too if you stick with me, I'll show you how it's done. You're a neat guy, and I'm going to make it worth your time to stick with me. First, I'll make you my lieutenant, my first assistant, my agent, my seeing eye. Look around, observe everything I tell you to watch. It'll make you alert. Here's what I'll do: I'll give you a special name, a name for the people we trust and who take our orders. I'll call you Che (Daryll pronounced it Kay), just like Fidel Castro's right hand man. You'll be Che Asco! What do you think of that? Great, huh?"

"What'll we call you? Fidel?"

"Not a bad idea. But I've got something better in mind. Just wait and see."

Darryl went on in this vein until it was time to return the boat and try to get him back to Portland by noon.

Che Asco took the longest route to Portland. On the way to Tillamook, Darryl indulged in the pleasure of talking and not having to listen. His friend obliged by uttering grunts of assent from time to time.

"I tell ya, society's gotta change. Here we are in your crate that's about to fall apart, wondering if it will go another ten feet, and we gotta be in Portland by an hour ago. There's no reason for that when all the rich bastards take their time and stop whenever they need to piss. It boils down to they have the good deal and we got no deal at all. That's what they call the shitty end of the stick. We'll always have that end no matter which end we grab, and that jerk over there with the shorts and long socks, looking like a kangaroo, will always get the clean end. The rich don't wear gloves no more, it's a fact, because their end of the stick's always clean and smells like perfume. Just tell me if that isn't right! Right?"

"Uh!"

"The next point is . . . Before long you could do a little hard work and look in your rearview mirror. A cop's been on your ass for ten minutes."

"I seen 'im; don't worry. Here's how we get rid of pests. Watch!"

Asco started to slow down gradually so that soon, in addition to the patrol car, there were two RV's and a pickup hauling a long boat, not to mention four impatient cars bringing up the rear. Presently a turnoff appeared to the right, and Asco put on his turn blinkers and exited, waving his hand to the relieved drivers as they drove by, still wary of the police vehicle.

"Now he'll wait again in a trap two miles down. I know this guy. Caught me twice. He'll wait a long time. What's the next point you were gonna make?" Asco said as he turned into a gravel road in a cloud of dust.

"I don't know. What was I talking about?"

"Beats me. Some kind of stick with perfume on it."

"Forget it. Anyways, before life can be worth living around here, everything's gotta change. It's not just the rich guys that bug me, it's anybody who thinks his feet don't stink because he can change his socks every day. You walk down the street and look into a restaurant and you can see 'em sitting there eating frog's legs and snails and sipping wine by the drop because it's more polite that way. The waiters treat 'em with respect and bow and hold the ladies' chairs and talk like their mouths are full of broken glass. The same waiters, when they see us come in, cuss like truck drivers and throw us out on our asses . . . And those snail-eating bastards get the babes after dinner, believe me; they can't hardly wait to get home but do their humping right in the car driving down the freeway, and the cops never stop them, they just look the other way or salute."

"So how you gonna change all that? Shoot the bastards?"

"No. You gotta be smarter than that. You gotta educate 'em. Teach'm street skills, let'em know how it is to live a day in the gutter, and they'll come around quick to our point of view, and pretty soon they'll invite us to dinner and offer us the ladies. Just wait and see."

"Wake me up when it happens!"

"Something else I gotta tell you. While I was there in the State Hospital, they was trying to educate us. That's where I got the idea. One cute babe gave reading lessons to the real dumbbells. Someone else tried to tell us about table manners, and a guy would come once a week to show us how to paint mountains and rivers."

"So what did you learn? How to sew and knit?"

"No. I was too smart for that. I learned about the law; you know, courts, judges, trials, depositions, all that muck. This Portland lawyer came down once a month to tell us what our rights are and how to insist on them. The wardens hated him, you can believe that! Because he told us just what to say when they wanted to frisk us and how to get them on unlawful seizure. And we got First Amendment rights all over the place. And there's something called due process which I can't explain to you because it would take too long and I'm getting hoarse anyways. But you better learn about it, to save your ass."

Darryl waited a moment for Asco to grunt.

"So this lawyer comes down once a week and the class got smaller because those lazy bastards wanted to learn something easier like how to shine shoes, so I was the only student there at the end and I listened to every word. I forget what his name was. Fartbaum or something like that. After a while he would just talk to me, and he gave me advice on how to succeed and stay out of trouble when I got out, and he asked me what I thought about this or that, what I wanted to do with myself. He actually listened to what I said! First time it's happened that an older guy took me seriously enough to . . . to converse with me, if that's how you say it. I really looked forward to seeing him, and I was pissed when something kept him from coming."

"Does he eat snails?"

"I'm not bullshitting you. I never knew my dad. My stepdad beat me up each time he got his paws on me. Then it was teachers, the police, the wardens, and the therapists, all of them against us, afraid of something, I could see it in their look. This lawyer knew something they didn't. If I see him again sometime I'll thank him for what he done for me."

Darryl wakes up late in the morning. The warm sun is showing through at the edges of the closed Venetian blind of the only window in the room he is occupying in his mother's flat. He feels out of place in a twin bed with shiny brown veneered headboard and a worn crocheted spread. The pink pillow case with its factory-made lace under his nose, smelling vaguely of perfume or herbs, bugs him. His mother's sewing projects, commissioned by various Portland women, hang from temporary clothes bars and on the backs of chairs. The only sign of his own presence is a pile of dirty clothes and a pair of boots blocking entry through the door and an ashtray filled with stubs.

"Shit!" His first word uttered today expresses his feelings about being home. When still an adolescent, he had moved out of the surroundings dominated by his mother and become accustomed to living in cheap hotel rooms, nearly abandoned rental houses, or in the apartment of some waitress he had temporarily attached himself to. Even living on the street and sleeping under bridges, as he had sometimes done, was preferable to this crowded, feminine, shut-in atmosphere.

If I'm gonna stay here any amount of time, all this crap has to go! Talking to himself is a habit he picked up in prison. First I gotta figure out how to satisfy the parole officer that I live here and then sleep somewhere where I won't go crazy in two weeks. I need a headquarters, anyways, a center for operations. They can't keep me here during the day, and if I'm busy late at night, there's no use in disturbing everyone when I come home, is there? I'll call Asco in a little while; it's for sure he can find a pad for us to operate from.

When I find that new pad, what am I gonna do there, a free man, like they say? First I gotta do something to get meaning in my life, like the fat intern said. I gotta give myself over to a cause in a hunnert percent, total involvement. Nothing else matters except that cause. The way I see it now it's gonna have something to do with making people realize things and come to their senses. They gotta see things like they are, as bad as they are.

Okay. First I'll need to hang out around town for a while, on East Burnside maybe, and meet some cool guys and teach them all this stuff. Asco can help round up useful characters, smart ones especially. Being tough isn't enough to survive these days. When those clever cons I knew at the State Hospital come out I'll recruit them.

"Daydreaming never gets you nowhere. I'm outa here," Darryl says as he heaves his already dressed torso out of bed and heads for the door with a: "See yas, Mom and Sis, sometime," without waiting for a response.

The next evening Deb is walking to Glenda's. Despite many interruptions their curtain project is progressing, and at this stage Deb's main function is to watch Glenda sew, hold the fabric when necessary, and keep her company during the dreary hours it takes to do an ambitious undertaking well. She enjoys the walk, especially after standing long hours at the camera shop, where she is trying to put in extra time so as to make up for the days she has missed recently.

Glenda is already at work with the half-finished curtains spread on couches, tables, and chairs. Even the fishbowl is covered with a bright flowered design.

"Hi, come on in. There is more of a mess than usual. Darryl has come home, so I can't use the room he is sleeping in any more."

"Is he here now?"

"He's out looking for a job. You can see him when he gets back."

"Is there room for all of you here?"

"Not really. He has to sleep in Liz's room; we put up a cot in mine for her, which isn't all that convenient. Liz hates having to give up her room, and she lets him know how she feels. They are typical brother and sister, fighting all the time but actually loving each other down deep. Then my nieces and their kids are always coming around, in some kind of trouble as usual, needing me to get them going in the right direction. And all that shouting before they're ready to settle down and listen to me. Last night I was still up at three talking with Myrna getting her to admit that her man isn't going to quit drinking just because she loves him and sticks with him through thick and thin."

Through this entire monologue, Deb marvels at Glenda's calm and her ability to weather the worst storms without anxiety, with her hair unruffled, so to speak. Every time Deb works with her she hears the recital of another series of heartbreaks and betrayals, like a soap opera of the underprivileged, without commercials. And now Glenda's son is back; who knows what further trials he will bring shouting and screaming to her door.

Liz comes in with her usual complaints about a friend's boorish behavior at the movies and at the coffee shop where they stopped for a snack. As often happens, her anger gives way to humor as she gets farther into her narrative.

Loud steps coming up the stairs and on the concrete landing announce the arrival of Darryl, who bursts in and is about to cross the room without greeting anyone when he catches sight of Deb, and he pauses to say "Hi."

"Asco phoned about an hour ago, from the carwash. He said he didn't know where he'd be later on tonight but that he'd call again. If you ask me you should stay home and get some rest. Any luck?"

"Nah! No one needs help, so I don't even have to explain to them where I'm from. Right now I've got a lead: some contractor needs a hod carrier, which would suit me fine, being outside and building myself up."

Deb couldn't see much need for building up Darryl's strength. He was sturdy, about six feet tall with well-developed arm muscles covered with tattoos. She was surprised by his direct look, the stern, almost disapproving, expression she encountered in his eyes, which seemed to watch her intently.

"This is Deb. She comes in sometimes; we're working on curtains together."

"Hello!"

"How do you do, Darryl."

"Hope you get this junk out of the way by tonight when I come home. I can't find my way in this warehouse. See ya later!"

Darryl went into his room and after five minutes walked swiftly through the living room and out the door without comment.

Darryl has found a means of independent transportation; he is riding the dirt bike he used in junior high, unconcerned that the small bike can barely support his current two hundred plus pounds. His evening is planned. First, he will have coffee and a sandwich at Herb's Eatery, next a couple of beers at the Grouse tavern, and finally some serious drinking at O'Gorman's Bar, downtown. I'll have to watch out; it would be just my luck to be busted for not having a bike light!

At Herb's, he sat at a table on the sidewalk, watching the people walk by as he read a motorcycle magazine and finished his sandwich and a doughnut. Three old acquaintances stopped at his table and congratulated him on his release, saying that it must feel great to be free again. What was he going to do with himself now that he was out? Where was he staying?

An hour later he was sitting at the bar in the Grouse, talking to a waitress he had known some time ago. She told him news of his friends and acquaintances and added that if he wanted to move in with her for a while he could stay at the apartment she shared with two other girls. They brought guests, too, so it would be okay. Darryl said he would think about it and let her know. Right now she should probably get back to serving tables; her clients were looking impatient.

By midnight when he left the Grouse, Darryl had found a job. A man with a loud voice standing at the bar needed someone dependable to deliver letters, documents, and small packages by bike in downtown Portland. If the customers liked him and he avoided being hit by rush-hour traffic, he could begin taking in a reasonable amount of money in tips in a couple of weeks. He was to report to work the next morning.

At O'Gorman's, Darryl joined Asco and his friends around a pool table. He made his way back to Glenda's at two-thirty and, unable to navigate into Liz's room, fell into a deep sleep on the couch.

T HE WEEKEND HAD been hectic. Bev and Steve spent all of Saturday shopping for furniture, comparing prices, trying out chairs, asking to see that carpet lying on the bottom of a heap of other carpets, and rushing back to the first store they had visited before it closed, since after all it did have the best prices. This was somewhat abstract for Steve as he stood by listening to Bev ask questions and verify quality. He felt superfluous. Furthermore the image of Deb's face kept passing through his mind, inviting him to think about her and wonder when he would be able to be with her next. In the basement of the Mall they bumped into Flo Hoffman, the wife of Steve's partner, which provided Bev with an opportunity to burn off some energy talking. Despite the limited time at her disposal, Bev told Flo all about the gallery and invited her to come up to Seattle as soon as she could.

"We go there all the time. Mike has a marathon of some kind at least once a month in Seattle. That gives me a chance to shop, and I'll stop in on our next trip. By the way, Steve, Mike told me about that cute chick you introduced to him. He's real eager to get going on her case."

Steve muttered some kind of response.

"What was she saying about a cute chick?" Bev asked as they hurried up Morrison Street.

"That must be Deb Myers. I handed her case over to Mike for the trial. It's not the way I would describe her."

Which was true, not so much because saying so would help

Bev return her attention to the shopping, but because it didn't do justice to Deb. Flo's remark left an unpleasant taste in Steve's mouth, as if he had just eaten stale deep-fried potatoes with cold coffee. He wanted to go to Deb, see her smile, remind himself what she was really like.

Back home, Bev sequestered Diane after dinner for more work on inventories and forms, and on Sunday she asked Scott to enter them on his computer and give her a printout. Finally, before retiring, she asked Diane to draw a bath for her and give her a massage.

Bev spent Sunday going through her clothes, trying everything on, showing each garment first to Diane, who was appointed to help with the wardrobe, then to Steve, in his study, and for final approval to Scott. Bev finally decided that her wardrobe was dreadfully out of date and, further, that it no longer fit her with the extra pounds that weeks of eating in Seattle restaurants had wrapped around her waist. Her favorite stores weren't open, so she postponed further purchases until after she arrived in Seattle. A pity Diane wouldn't be there to help. But Mary had excellent taste that could be depended on.

Mary came early Monday morning to call for Bev. Eager to arrive at the gallery site before the truck from Moynihan's did, they drove off quickly in a shower of waving hands, wishes of good luck, and warnings to drive carefully and take care of yourselves.

"Come, Scott. Let's have an extra cup of coffee and relax. I'm pooped. How about you?"

"Come to think of it, yes. It will take a while to catch our breath."

"I know how we can accomplish that. If I can arrange to take off today and tomorrow, let's go to the beach house. We haven't been there since fall, and I suspect it will need a good cleaning and maybe some repairs. We can also lay in supplies for the rest of summer."

"How about trying out the boat? It's been ages since I've felt the swell of the sea. What about Diane and Melissa?"

"Let's take Diane along. Melissa can have a two-day vacation. I'm thinking of hiring someone local to come and help with the heavy work."

Soon they are driving northwest toward Seaside. As Steve drives, Scott is describing to Diane the perils she will encounter at the shore: long vistas of firs bordering the sandy beach, sea otters sunning themselves on the rocks, and whales spouting as they swim within sight of land.

"Where are they headed?"

"I forget where they are going in this season, but it's either south or north."

"North," Steve says. "They are on their way to Alaska."

Steve and Bev's beach house, which is more than a cabin but not quite a house, smells of being shut-up for months. Mice have found their way in and made comfortable nests out of cotton gnawed from mattresses, and remnants of last summer's wasp nests still hang from the rafters. After two hours of sweeping, dusting, airing, and washing, the house is transformed into something quite inhabitable. The three of them go outside to eat the picnic lunch Melissa had prepared. They sit at a metal table beneath shade trees where they can see the afternoon sun reflecting on the waves. Scott watches Diane, still wearing the apron from the morning's work, her hair held back by a colored handkerchief. He senses disappointment and asks her what she is thinking.

"It is beautiful and elegantly furnished with those leather armchairs and the long drapes. But I expected something more primitive. I must be used to the cabin we sometimes went to in Québec. It was in the woods, near a tiny lake where the mosquitoes were fierce in the evening. We were at least ten miles from the closest settlement, and no one else lived on that little lake. There was only one room for everybody; my parents had a curtain around their bed. There was no electricity or plumbing; we kept the food cold by lowering it on a rope down into the rocks below the floor. I was extremely happy when we went there and used to spend hours just breathing the air and looking at the clouds in the sky. For me, the TV and VCR don't belong."

Steve and Scott exchange a glance and decide to unplug and hide every electronic gadget on the premises, including radio and stereo, and replace them with plants that Steve would buy in town later in the afternoon. However, he would keep the phone plugged in, since he had to stay in touch with his office.

It took more than an hour to force open the rusted lock to the boathouse door, clean the carburetor of the motor, and bail out the water that had collected in the boat. Finally Scott and Diane were able to steer out into the bay. Steve went up to the cabin and dialed in a call to Deb.

"Hi, sweetheart," he told her answering machine. "I'm at the coast, cleaning up the place. It will be presentable, and you'll love it. Let's plan to come Friday, if you can. Leave me a message. Love you." Then he drove to town in search of food, plants, and some tools.

At three ten on a hot, muggy afternoon, George Lewis sits in a faded armchair, two springs in the seat of which are pressing against him uncomfortably in the rear. This new client is either late or a no-show; in either case, I am stuck for an hour in this heat until my next appointment at four. While waiting I might as well look over the information the court sent on this fellow.

George is a novice counselor in one of the agencies that offer next to free therapy to people off the street, some of whom can barely afford the four-dollar fee to get their lives straightened out or to be heard and understood by someone who takes them seriously. Working part-time at minimum wage, he benefits from free supervision and an occasional feeling that he is succeeding in helping a victim of social injustice crawl out of a pit of self-blame or self-deception. Burnout is lurking around the corner waiting for George, and he vaguely recognizes its familiar face.

Let's see: Darryl . . . last name and Social Security Number on file. No known aliases. Caucasian male, 28 years old. Release on this date from minimum security based in part on good behavior. Completed detox, rehab, social skills, correctional treatment, etc. George reads quickly; he knows more or less what to expect in these reports: a psycho-social profile, psycho-sexual assessment, medical and educational test results, opinions by psychiatrists and psychologists. If he doesn't come, I won't need to know all this. How long was he in? Two years. Behavior: cooperative in group work and fastidious in ward cleanup duties. A loner: kept to himself; no close friends on ward. What was he in for? Possession and distribution of a controlled substance and assault with dangerous object (a two-by-four). History of petty burglaries, armed theft, and motor vehicle violations (including four major accidents in one year—one involving involuntary homicide, dismissed). Consistent alcohol and drug abuse. In the course of group therapy he admitted having molested a retarded younger sister, later denied it. Subject is court-mandated to continue counseling for anger and violence. Counselor is to report regularly in writing to parole board.

"Your client is here," the voice of a crisis-line operator interrupted George's reading.

"Thanks, John." George took a file folder and a pencil and went to the waiting room. There he introduced himself to a man six feet tall, wearing baggy military slacks, boots, a baseball cap, and, despite the heat, a torn red flannel shirt with the tails hanging out. He led his expressionless client to the narrow nook where he had been reading and invited him to sit in either one of the two armchairs.

"This is where we will meet in the future, Darryl. Perhaps if you can arrive a little earlier next time we will be able to make progress."

There was no answer.

"Maybe you could tell me a little about yourself and we could get to know each other, sort of to break the ice."

Still no answer.

"Anything. It doesn't have to be really important. Like what you enjoy doing, where you hang out . . ."

"Look. Let's cut the shit. I gotta come in here, you've gotta listen and ask stupid questions. We'll save a lot of time if I just tell you what you're expected to put down on that report you're supposed to write. Look. I'll tell you everything. Don't ask, I'll tell you everything you'll ever need to know about anybody. But first I gotta know where you're coming from, know you're not gonna tell a bunch of lies that'll get me in more trouble. Nobody needs a hassle. Everybody should mind their own business, keep their noses out of what doesn't concern them. "

"What will it take for you to trust me?"

"Nothing you can do. You'll know when I start talking."

"What would you like to do until that happens?"

No answer.

"I notice your hat. You interested in baseball?"

"Naw. No good at it. Never could hit the fucking ball. Usedta think it would be less stupid to use baseball bats for bashing heads. I practiced on a basketball once. Got suspended from school for that."

"How did you feel when you were a kid and couldn't hit the ball?"

"Let's forget that crap! I know you are paid to get me talking, but it ain't going to work. If you want to know me, let's talk about politics and all them crooks in Washington, or Salem, or at city hall. They're the ones who tell you what you can't do while they are raking in the dough with their shady deals and kickbacks from lobbyists. Go over to the capitol some time and look around the halls to see those mealy-mouthed fast talkers all dressed up with suit coats and ties waiting around for a politician to walk by and when one doesn't come they go in the offices and kiss-ass the secretaries to get a word in with the boss. It's enough to make you want to puke. But I'll tell you why I wasn't any good at baseball—here, write it down, you can tell this to anybody, to the parole board if you want to. My dad never taught me, that's why! D'you know what he was doing instead? He was beatin' the shit out of me, with his belt, with a baseball bat even, you better believe it. That's when he was drunk. When he was sober he was trying to get me to smoke pot. 'Jes try it, you little bastard, it's good for you,' he'd say, and then he'd start pounding me when I said 'shove it.' Mom turned him in finally. While he was in for abusing me and my sis they found he'd murdered someone back in Texas, so now he's got at least twenty years to cool off. Serves 'im right, the dirty bastard."

"How do you feel about him now?" George asked automatically, before he realized the absurdity of his question.

"That's it for today, buddy! See ya next week. Won't be more than half hour late." Darryl stood up, shifted the visor of his baseball hat to face backward, and walked resolutely out.

George was better prepared for Darryl's next appointment a week later. He had read the prison release report thoroughly and had devised a strategy with his supervisor. He began by asking him about his prison experiences.

"It was a gas most of the time. Me and Larry stuck together until he almost escaped and got removed from Correctional Treatment and poked back in the black hole, where he's still staring at a blank wall, probably. He was in for raping a child, the dumb shit; he was so smart he never should have got caught. After he was gone I stayed away from the others and minded my own business. They were a bunch of wimps, kissing up on the therapists, trying to get out on good behavior so they could go back to their old dirty habits. Do you want to know the truth? I'll tell you. Once you got a habit, like doing . . . burglary, mugging, hot-wiring cars and trucks, screwing, flashing, doing hard dope—nobody can change you; you're stuck for good. Those therapists are a joke. Larry sweet-talked them and right away they figured he was getting better and would become a real angel, teacher's little helper. Then every night we laughed ourselves sick remembering the stupid stuff we said in therapy during the day. Larry's friends and one of mine smuggled in dope for us, and I fiddled with the TV set and managed to get porno programs every

night. Boy were they pissed when they found out! But they didn't
know who did it, so I still got merit badges for good behavior.
What a laugh!"

"What do you want to do with your life? You are bright, you
have ability, you could fix TV's or maybe even go into selling,
since you talk easily."

George felt Darryl's eyes looking at him. Those eyes are
distrustful, defiant, he thought, taking note of them in order to
add a comment on the chart.

"You're too fucking innocent to do me any harm, so I can
talk to you. But don't never let me down. If you tell lies about me,
you're in deep trouble. Get it?"

"You have made yourself sufficiently clear."

"This is what I want to do with my life. It's not worth a shit, so
I can risk it for anything. This is what I'm gonna do: make the
world a better place for decent people to live in. You know what
I mean by decent people. Me, maybe you, other cool cats. One of
the things I'll do for sure is gun down a couple of politicians,
catch them in the act of stealing our tax money. That won't be
hard because they do it all of the time. Next thing I'll do is take
care of any black, Jew, or chink who screws a white woman.
When I see them walking together on the street I feel like shooting
them both right there in the open with a semiautomatic. I can get
one any time, no problem. But I'd rather stalk them, torture them
slowly so they know what they done, leave them to die by
themselves. Maybe you haven't guessed yet, but I'm a very
religious person, I'm a Christian. God made us white and black
and other colors for a reason, so we'd stay apart—each on a
separate continent. That's why He created four continents, they're
for the four races. I'm a religious person I tell you and I can't
stand seeing adultery all around, people screwing in every nook
and cranny, under staircases, on the elevators, in the back seats
of cars while guys are changing the oil! Fornucation! That's what
it is! Forn-you-kay-shun! It's a sin, and what I'm gonna do with

my life is shoot all the fornucators in the world, then it will be a better place to live in."

"Go on; tell me more."

"No. It's better when I don't talk. I mean I'm a man of action; words don't mean nothing. It's a waste of time to sit here talking nonsense since it's all bullshit anyways. And better not forget that words can get you in trouble, especially you if you think you can get away with telling anybody what I said today, big trouble."

George tried again to explain what confidentiality meant, that only if he thought Darryl was a threat to his own or someone else's safety would he reveal anything said to him in "this room." Then he went on to explain how one of his clients (he was making this up, by the way, maybe to let Darryl know how important he was) threatened to commit suicide, forcing him to contact the fellow's nearest relatives and the police.

"They should just let the poor jerk do it. If he wants to kill hisself, why shouldn't he? That would be one less slow driver on the freeways, one less asshole waiting in front of you in the supermarket check out line. Get this straight, Buster, life ain't sacred. We are no bigger than flies or sow bugs eating turds. God created us to be eternal, but ever since that bitch Eve listened to the devil's sweet talk, we're here to die, that's all. Better to do it sooner than later. Life's a messy place, and it needs to be cleaned up quick or it won't be worth living anymore."

"I can feel where you are coming from, and I can understand that you really believe that people are pretty corrupt. What about the people who are close to you?"

"Forget that. There ain't nobody close to me. My mom's a case in point. She's a basket case if there ever was one. I gotta get away from her or she'll drive me nuts. I hafta live with her, 'cause I got no money. I can work, no problem there; I'm strong as a horse. What can I do in that hole? She's there smoking and sewing on rich women's fancy clothes while she ain't practically got nothing to wear herself. When I try to smoke a little pot, she gets on my case and says she'll call the

police or the parole board to get me to stop. Or she yells at me
to keep my paws off my sister when all I want to do is show
her she's neat. She's 'tarded, you know, doesn't really know
much about anything although she can cuss like a trooper
when she's pissed. All girls should be 'tarded, then you could
lay 'em without them talking back all the time. But it's Mom
what's bugging me now. Trying to teach me stuff I don't want
to know. Crap like taking a bath, wearing clean clothes, being
presentable, like she says. That's for when you're a kid, not
when you weigh 220 pounds and could throw her out with
one finger, she's such a shrimp! That's why she's such a bitch.
No flesh on her bones, an she's a real midget. But she's
supermouth, she is! Tell me: how do I get her to shut up? As
long as she's sounding off at me I can't live. Oh yea! I forgot to
tell you I got a job. Started a couple of days ago doing bicycle
delivery around town. Some day I'll bring ya a letter."

Darryl began to stand up, then sat back down.

"But there's another problem. It's the kind you can help me
on. Mom's got this customer, a babe in her early thirties who
comes in the apartment sometimes when I'm there. Mom and her
have some kind of project making curtains or drapes or whatever.
I'm having a beer or something and turn on the TV or some music,
and Mom tells me to turn it off so they can concentrate. They are
so quiet, and I can't get used to no one talking or belching or no
TV, just the hum of that sewing machine. Drives me crazy. So
what can I do? So I start eyeballing the babe to make her nervous,
so she'll go sooner. So then I discover that she's real cute in those
tight jeans and the way she moves! I mean, I can feel every muscle
in her body under my hands, in my mind, you know what I mean.
She don't pay no attention to me; she says 'hello, Darryl' in a
milky voice when she comes and then they start to work, her
leaning over the sewing machine and me looking at her behind.
I gotta have that babe, one way or another, you'll see, I'll tell you
when."

"That babe, as you call her . . ."

Darryl puts his hands up to his face and rubs his cheeks, signs of agitation that George takes note of as Darryl interrupts: "Her name is Deb, and after she goes home Mom tells me to leave her alone, to quit staring at her because she's a nice lady. Nice lady, my ass! From what she said talking to Mom, she's got this guy, a lawyer, on her hook, and she's about to land him. Maybe she has already because last night when the phone rang and I picked it up, thinking it was my friend Asco on the other end, there's Deb telling Mom she can't come to sew on the weekend because she's going to the coast. Mom goes: 'oh-oh! you going with you know who?' And Deb doesn't answer right away, but then she's all: 'Yea; he just called and invited me,' in that voice of hers that goes straight to my crotch. 'Where will you stay?' 'In his place, near Seaside.' 'Great! Hope you'll be alone with him,' you can see Mom's a real bitch. 'He didn't say, but I think we will be.' What about that? Is she there right now, in the cabin laying her lawyer until he cries for help? I got to find out; I'll let you know what's what next time. These rich bastards—lawyers, accountants, wardens, stock agents—they're out for themselves and no one else. That's why they put me in jail, to get me out of the way so they can get all the money and privileges and screw all the babes. But I'll show them. That Deb's going to have to choose between I and her lawyer, and it's me she's gonna pick, just watch. Once I get her under me she'll send him packing. They didn't call me Long-Dong Darryl for nothing, back in high school while I was still there. Lawyers haven't got it any longer than six inches, its a known fact. I'm out of here. See you sometime."

Darryl walked out through the waiting room where a flea-bitten worm was sitting chewing his fingernails. Must be George's next appointment, Darryl thought. I should talk to him, I'd fix him up good, make him into a man. He continued through the office full of people answering telephones and writing at typewriters. Once outside he sauntered along the sidewalk past the Greyhound station, looking in to see if he knew anyone. He continued along the same street, examining the window displays of an adult bookstore, then jaywalked across the street and entered a video arcade.

THIS IS A blast, Darryl thinks as he rides his bike down Burnside Street, slithering between cars waiting at traffic lights. All them poor jerks sitting there waiting for something to happen. And when the light changes you can be sure one will stall and nobody will move and everybody starts honking and it's pandemonium everywhere, with guys opening their car doors and getting out and yelling at each other in this heat. They ought to just sock it out and leave each other lying in the street; that would be worth stopping to look at. As he peddles by a long blue Cadillac waiting at a corner, he kicks it with the side of his boot just before turning against the light into the cross traffic. The well-dressed driver honks in fury at him, but Darryl knows that's all he can do, and he laughs out loud as he approaches a tall office building. Three more deliveries to make. This one must be for a lawyer, he thinks as he locks his bike to a lamppost and walks quickly through the posh copper entrance toward the elevator. The more names an outfit has the more important and rich the lawyers are. This one has nine names, and the envelope is addressed to one of them. Too bad it isn't a bomb. I might go up with it too, but it would be worth it.

"Thank you. Do you want me to sign?" a receptionist in a miniskirt asks, standing next to a desk.

Long legs. Darryl has to collect his thoughts to answer.

"No, thank you, ma'am. It isn't necessary for this type of delivery. If there is a yellow sticker on the envelope, then you need to sign. When the sticker is red, then it has to be hand-delivered to the named addressee," Darryl says, quoting from the handbook he had memorized.

"I learn something new every day. Nothing to go out. Someone picked it all up at four."

Darryl lost track of what she was saying as he recognized the attorney who had given him lessons in legal rights at the State Hospital. The lawyer walked past him, paying no attention, conversing with another person dressed in a suit and tie. Darryl stood watching them walk down a hall and disappear through a door, which then closed.

So this is where he works, in one of them nine-name firms, Darryl thinks, wondering how the same person can seem so relaxed and friendly as a teacher and then become stiff, too busy to notice anything or to remember someone. A nice guy sometimes, then just another rich bastard the rest of his life. Too bad. I could use him when things get tough. Now I have to find me one of those dirty shysters, probably a Yid, to keep me out of hock.

But Darryl is intrigued to see this man in his own world, looking somehow unsure of himself, under stress maybe, not so much in control of events as you would expect from a highly-placed individual. In the days to come Darryl has more deliveries to the same law firm, but he does not see this lawyer again.

After two more stops, he heads home, this time without stopping for a beer or spending time with friends. That can wait. He knows his mom is going to work with Deb this evening, and he wants to see her again, shoot the bull with her, maybe.

As he comes in he sees Deb sitting at the table, eating with his mom and Liz. They all seem happy. "Come on Darryl," Glenda says. "Have some tuna salad; I can fix some more in a jiffy."

"Thanks, I'd like that. Let me wash up first." It is important to be polite, just like at the law offices. Lucky they taught me manners at the State Hospital; you never know when you'll need them.

"You just sit, Glenda. I'll open another can of tuna for Darryl. You're tired, and he must be hungry. Liz can show me where it is."

That is the first time Darryl has heard his name pronounced by Deb. It sounded like soft ice cream looks as it pours into a cone at the Dairy Big Orange, and he felt for the first time that his name was not the disaster he always thought it was; it suddenly became a mysterious entity with a beauty of its own. Darryl sits down with the women and begins to eat, trying hard to sit up straight and use his knife and fork correctly.

"Your mom tells me you are working now. What is it you do?" Deb asks.

"It's no big deal. I deliver stuff around town on a bike. I take envelopes to different places, sometimes small cartons like to drugstores, sometimes it's stuff that rattles, like false teeth to dentists' offices. Yesterday I had to deliver something with Dangerous written all over it. Never did find out what that was. The day before there was a nasty looking snake in a cage that I took to a pet shop."

"You'll have to be careful," Glenda warns. "I don't want anything to happen to you now."

"I can see that it could be interesting work. You are outside, getting exercise, it's probably very healthy. Does the exhaust of the cars bother you?"

"Don't notice it. The best part is figuring out how to get from one part of town to another in the shortest time, and when I do it without having to stop at all I give myself special points for doing good."

"How many points do you have so far?"

"I lost count, but it helps pass the time."

Darryl senses that Deb is listening. Is it what he says she finds interesting? Or is it he who is . . . fascinating?

As he leaves the table to go to his room, he is sure that he must have this woman. Maybe not right away; a sudden move can frighten her away. He'll play it cool, and then he'll have her on his own terms.

"Who is this Deb, anyhouse? How come she's always here, like eating dinner and making you work?"

"Well, she's not always here like you say. And for your information, she is my friend. She started coming over a while ago to make some curtains according to a design she made with thermal stuffing to keep the cold out of rooms in winter. It's a great idea, especially now with the cost of energy and everything."

"But who is she anyways? She must be somebody. Where's she from? She can't come out of nowhere?"

"I told her to get a patent on the idea, she said all she wanted was to keep her place warm for herself and that if anybody wants to do the same they're welcome to it. But I insisted and she wrote to a company. They didn't even have the courtesy to answer."

"Dammit! I don't give a shit about those curtains or any fucking company. All I am asking is who this Deb is and why she hangs around bugging you when you have other things to do, like picking up around this dump so I can see where I am going at night."

"Cool it, Darryl! It's none of your business who she is or what she's doing. She's my friend, that's all. And you better keep your paws away from her if you know what's good for you. The way you look at her! Thank God she hasn't noticed your big sheep eyes moping at her."

"Look, Mom! I'm simply interested in this person like a human being. Can't I do that? She's a human being, so are you, and me, too. Get the idea? I learned that a year ago. Ya gotta take interest in other human beings, God said that; I'll show you where if you really wanna know. We all belong to this world, and if I ask you about her it's because I'm always seeing her around here making you work your ass off. If it was someone else I'd be asking about someone else."

"Okay! Okay, you're right. But she's paying me my regular fee, and she has brought food and nice stuff a lot of times, so you shouldn't complain. I'm happy to have her here, because she's my friend, like I told you, and she's very nice, really thoughtful. She takes an interest in Liz, and even took her out to go roller-skating once. More than you've done!"

"Great! Now tell me who she is."

"She has a pretty long story, and it's a sad one, too. She grew up in Seattle; then she went to college. Next she married this guy and got a job as a nurse somewhere in South America, doing stuff to help the poor. While she's there her husband gets this job where he's supposed to find out who's shipping drugs up here. And so the drug lords capture him and nearly beat him to death, with the result that he had a stroke or something and is a vegetable now. She has to watch this happen to the man she loves! She's lonely now and needs friendship; that's where I come in."

"So where's her dude now? Still alive?"

"He's in some special clinic in town where they take care of those cases. Must cost her a fortune. That's why she needs to save money. Gives him the best she can and then goes without herself."

"She must do something other than take care of her vegetable and make curtains. What does she do with herself?"

"She works all day at a camera shop. She's also a volunteer helping fix up old buildings. And she does other stuff, in her spare time. I think there's a boyfriend somewhere, too."

"But she's still married to her vegetable! How can she have a boyfriend? Who is he?"

"Well, how should I know? She's got her own life, and I don't judge what she does. She knows what she is doing, and that's her business, not mine, or yours, neither. Remember that!"

The phone rang. Asco wants to come over with a friend. They could go and hang out somewhere.

"You'd better forget about her, Darryl. I'd be happy if you found a nice girl to live with or marry, someone who could handle you better than I can. But Deb's not for you. She's serious about Steve, her boyfriend; he's a lawyer, and he's real nice to her. She deserves all the happiness she can get."

Darryl grabbed the phone book and took it into his room. While waiting for Asco to come, he went through the listings under Attorneys in the Yellow Pages. Searching the columns of the names of local lawyers, he found only one whose first name matched: Steven Thornton. Is that the fellow who came to teach us about law at the State Hospital? Darryl checked the address. There it was: same building, same floor where he made the delivery that afternoon.

"Asco's here!" his mom shouted to Darryl, still in his room. He took his wallet and walked quickly through the living room, slamming the front door behind him. "Well, you could at least say good-bye!"

"This is Ralph," Asco said, pointing to a man of medium height who looked about twenty-five years old. He had light curly hair, pale skin, and a smiling expression, someone you could trust. Ralph had a red Mustang, in which they all drove to an amusement park that had been set up in the parking lot of a department store. There they threw darts at balloons, baseballs at dolls, guessed the weight of the fat lady, and took innumerable rides on electric cars and fast-moving roller coasters, while all the time razzing the girls and trying to cheat the operators out of entrance fees. Ralph proved to be a good guy, ready for anything, not afraid, like Asco is sometimes.

When it was dark they went to O'Gorman's Tavern for some billiards and beer. Darryl asked Ralph what he did.

"I'm a seed and fertilizer pilot, but most of the time I spread pesticides. I operate up and down the valley, wherever they need me. There are lots of farms with big fields, and if I don't try to be too careful I can finish a field faster than any other pilot in the business."

"What's the secret of your success?"

"For one, I don't worry about the regulations. I mix the stuff, five gallons here, five gallons there. If you work fast you get done before the wind picks up and spreads the poison around too much, like in the next fields or pastures."

"Couldn't you lose your license?"

"Who said anything about licenses? Never could get one because there's a felony on my record."

"Ya! Ralph spent time for stealing his own little daughters from a foster home! And they call that justice!"

"Must be rough. Miss them?" Darryl asked.

"Tell you about it some other time. Right now not having them around suits me fine."

"Who hires you to fly then?"

"I've got a reputation for being fast and efficient. I do what the farmer says and don't ask questions. Only if I break telephone wires, the farmer's got to do the explaining and the repairs. I don't stick around."

"Tell Darryl about all the crashes you've been in."

"Well, not really that many. My record is sixteen last year. Having no insurance helps me beat the competition, but it's a mess when I break a leg or an arm. Usually I'm able to walk out of the crash with a couple of bumps and maybe a sore back. Sometimes I break something, and then I'm out of work until I'm mended. My girlfriend, she's is a nurse's aide, she takes care of me. And I have to find another plane, too, if the old one is too mangled. A new one costs a bundle if it can fly."

"Did you ever do any bombing?"

"Sure did. During the late summer when there is a forest fire in the mountains; they pay me to drop sacks of water. That's a real sport. Wanna come along next time I go? You can learn the ropes."

"How about doing a favor for me now, Ralph? Asco's not right for this kind of work, but I think you could do it. It hasn't got nothing to do with flying, but your mustang will help. Here on this sheet of paper is the name of a lawyer and his office address. What I want you to do is find out whatever you can about him. Where his home is, does he have wife and kids, what he does with his time and money. A little detective work. Sounds like you could do it?"

"No problem. But getting information is as far as I go. What's in it for me?"

"What's an afternoon of your time worth? Plus the gas. We'll work that out when you deliver. Asco'll tell you about me, won't you, old buddy?"

Then Darryl told Ralph about his stint at the Penitentiary and the State Hospital. They kept on drinking until the tavern closed. Darryl spent the night at Asco's after a harrowing ride in the red mustang with Ralph at the wheel.

The next time Glenda expected to work on the curtains with Deb, Darryl made arrangements to be home. Once again he was agreeable at the table, explaining the humorous things that happened on his job, how he was nearly "runned over" by a concrete truck, and how he was in an elevator between floors with an important looking executive when the power went out. Glenda as usual was full of stories about her relatives and friends, to whom the most dreadful things always seemed to happen. Deb told anecdotes from her stay in Brazil, including the time she, too, was stuck in an elevator in Rio and how she and Erik managed to escape. She spoke simply, looking at Darryl along with the rest, cueing him in on what he might not understand about a foreign country.

Someone had to take Liz to a friend's house. The neighbor wasn't home to help out. Darryl's license was suspended. Glenda had to drive her over. So she gave Deb some sewing to do, mentioned to Darryl she would be back in ten minutes, and, watching his eyes intently, told him to be good.

Darryl knew it would be at least twenty minutes before his mother could possibly return from her destination. He sat down where he could see Deb's eyes as they focused on the careful work of her fingers.

"Want me to turn the TV on? Might be something good on."

"You don't need to turn it on for my sake. But if there is something you want to see, go ahead; it won't bother me."

"What kind of programs do you like? Sitcoms? Soaps? Movies?"

"It is hard for me to say. I don't have a television where I live, so I don't see it much."

"No TV? What kind of a place do you live in? A big house somewhere?"

"Oh, no! Just a small flat."

"Where abouts is it?"

"I don't know the names of the neighborhoods in Portland yet, so I really can't say."

"It has an address, doesn't it? All apartments have addresses."

"Perhaps. But I don't give mine out, I'm sorry. Really, Darryl! I have to sew this, so why don't you go ahead and turn on the television. Don't let me prevent you from doing whatever you have in mind to do."

"I doubt you'd like what I have in mind to do. But now that you mention it, here's what I'm thinking. Deb, why don't me and you get together? You're just right for me, you're good-looking, you got a cute ass . . ."

"Please, Darryl, I don't know what you are saying, but I don't like the sound of it. I would rather you were quiet, or went somewhere else."

"Hear me out, babe. I don't say this to all the broads I meet. I never said it to nobody for that matter, so you should be honored. I gotta have you, I gotta live with you, I gotta touch you all over. And I'm asking you real nice, because I'm a good, peaceful person, the kind you like, I can tell."

Deb did not answer. She pursed her lips, looked furtively around the room for a means of escape.

"You better answer and say yes. Because I could come stay in your pad; that would solve where I live. You could cook for me like you did with that tuna. It was real good! I'll get you a good TV, with a VCR and we could rent movies, maybe some hard porn flics and watch them together and then do the same stuff they do in . . ."

"Darryl, stop this right away! I don't want to hear any more! You must be crazy to talk like that. You have certainly misjudged me."

"You mean you're saying no?"

"I'm saying NO in capital letters."

"So that's how it is. You keep that cute little body all for yourself, eh? Whatcha saving it for? Some rich bastard who won't do nothing for you but get you knocked up and then says 'tough shit, babe' and splits. Or maybe some rich lawyer named Steven? What's he giving you. Fifty dollars a shot? You better change your mind quick, babe! Darryl don't like to take the back seat!"

As he shouted this, Darryl stood up slowly, as if gathering his energy. He realized that he was smiling, confident in his strength and determination.

Suddenly, Glenda came up the stairs and pushed open the door.

"Sorry; I got delayed in the traffic. Leave us now, Darryl; we have work to do."

"Glenda, I can't stay any longer. I must go right away. Perhaps we could finish the work sometime at my place." Deb ran out through the door.

"Darryl! Come here! What happened?"

Steve and Scott are driving home after having dinner together at a restaurant across the Columbia River in Vancouver. They have been talking, especially Steve. Now they are silent as Steve skims over the bridge and follows the curves of the freeway through Portland. It is the kind of silence neither one knows how to break tactfully. Both concentrate their gaze on the speeding cars and bright lights.

"Nice dinner. Thanks," Scott finally says, with immense effort.

"It was nice, wasn't it? We'll have to go back there again."

"Who will *we* be, from now on? Things are going to be different with Deb around, and I'm having difficulty figuring out just how much. Can you foretell where we will be just three weeks from now?"

"The important things don't have to change, Scott. Like the way we feel about each other or what you and I do together. I intend for that to stay the same no matter what happens. Now that I have told you all of this the hardest part is over. Right now I feel much closer to you than I did this afternoon."

"But the important things, which you say won't change, will continue in a completely different setting, with different people, and maybe far away from here."

"This is hard for you, isn't it?"

"The worst part is I feel lonely, like after the accident. In a way I wish this had happened back then. I could have gotten accustomed to all the disasters at one time. Having them spread so far part gives me the impression there are more to come."

"Are they both disasters of the same magnitude?"

"More or less. The accident took away a future I was counting on, and that's how I feel now, too."

"I'm sorry, Scott. What do you need in the way of a future? What were you counting on?"

"I was counting on things staying the same, at least for a while. I can understand Mom's need to go to Seattle, and it doesn't bother me because she's basically still around. But your thing is different, and I'm afraid it will take you away."

When they drove up the driveway of the house at Lake Oswego they found it dark.

"Everyone is in bed, Dad. Let's go down to the lake for a while. I don't need light to wheel down the path. We could take a couple of beers."

Soon they are sitting on the pier, looking across the narrow lake at the reflections of the well-lit houses fluctuating on the surface of the water. They drink quietly, each lost in his own thoughts.

"It's your future we should drink to, Dad. After all, you can find happiness with Deb if you try hard enough. She has already done a lot for you; I can feel it in your expression and in the way you move."

They touch mugs and drink.

"Now I hope you will bring Deb over soon so we can meet.

Right now she's no more than an abstraction for me, and that's hardly a satisfactory way of thinking about the woman your dad loves."

"I'll arrange that as soon as possible, Scott. Should it be here or somewhere else, neutral territory, so to speak?"

"Here, by all means."

They watch the windows across the lake grow dark.

"Thanks, Dad, for telling me. I couldn't have waited much longer. I'll leave you the burden of telling Mom, whenever you are ready."

"You don't think you'll need to tell Diane, do you?"

"I won't need to tell her anything. She will simply read it in my mind. But she'll keep it to herself."

Once Scott is in bed, Steve phones Deb. She asks him to come to her place. When he arrives he finds her fully awake, high-strung.

"What happened?"

"Nothing that involves us, or me either, for that matter. But it makes me nervous, and I need to be with you."

"Can you tell me something? Can't I help?"

"Not really. For the moment I'd rather forget it. I'll tell you when it doesn't bother me any longer."

To soothe her nerves, Steve talked about his dinner with Scott.

"It's a tremendous weight off my chest to have told him. Bev is next. I'll tell you when that happens. For now, Deb, let's get away from everything, at least for a week, what do you think? I have something planned, something magical, with primeval forests, a quiet lake, a cabin with a fireplace, seclusion."

"Back to your cabin in Seaside?"

"Farther away than that, Deb. More exotic, more secluded."

After Deb finally relaxed, they made love and then slept in each others' arms until the sun woke them, shining through a window into their eyes.

Ralph's Mustang was waiting in front of Glenda's apartment when Darryl came out.

"I got what you want. You know, about that lawyer."

"I was going to work, but that can wait."

"Here goes!" Ralph did a U-turn from the curb between two moving cars, then drove through a stop sign.

"You drive your plane like that?"

"Even better! Wanna get Asco? He's free today."

As the three of them were driving toward Lake Oswego, Ralph explained:

"Your man is a partner in a law firm, one of the big fish. Probably rolling in cash, they all are. Married. Wife's name is Beverly. One kid, stuck in a wheelchair. We're headed for their place now; it's an estate set in the woods on a small lake. Hard to find, and there are no markers. I was there yesterday and went to the door pretending to sell magazines. A good-looking chick came and then went to call the missus; she left the door shut so I couldn't see much, but I could make out that the place has an up-to-date security system, so that if you're thinking of breaking in it'll take some precautions. When the lady came she was pleasant enough, although she wouldn't let me make a phone call, which is natural, I guess. There is a pile of loot there, you better believe it. They have a place at the coast, too. What else do you want to know?"

"What does the lawyer do for fun?"

"Not much. Sits around at home, works late, goes to concerts, takes walks. Spends a lot of time with his crippled kid."

"I mean women. Does he screw around? Does he do drugs?"

"No clue about women. He doesn't use crack or anything. None of the dealers I know has heard of him."

"That means he covers his ass good."

"See that little barn on the left? We turn right into the next driveway. Then there is a long ways to go up to the house."

Ralph turns and, for the first time that day, proceeds slowly up a single-lane blacktop driveway lined by trees. After three sharp curves they come to a fork in the road where Ralph pulls off to the side. They get out and Ralph leads them to an opening in the trees through which they can see a large house set in the middle of a lawn with shade trees spreading out on all sides.

"I got a picture of this," Ralph added. "Always carry my telephoto camera in the car. Wanna see anything else here?"

"Have you seen their place on the coast?"

"Haven't had time to go there. But I know the address."

"Let's shove."

They speed off toward the coast.

"What's eatin' ya, Dare?" Asco asks. "You're sour like one of them whorenado clouds. No one knows where you're goin' ta strike next."

"Don't you bother with me, Che! I got problems and I'll tell you when I'm good an' ready."

"What's this lawyer business all about, anyhows. The guy got something on you? Sounds like an ordinary rich bastard to me, just like the rest of them. Tough about his kid, though. I allus feel like crying when I hear about some poor crunched-up little child, like when they get borned with fins instead of arms and legs. That's what happened when Margo saw her kid all deformed for the first time. D'ya hear what happened to Margo?"

"Who the shit is Margo?"

"The broad you used to screw in high school, remember? The red head with them freckles all over her puss. But this was later, so you didn't have nothing to do with that kid, 'cause you were behind bars, and unless you was the original flying fuck, as they say, you was innocent of . . ."

"Aw shut up, Asco. We got serious things to do at the coast. If you're yacking all of the time we can't think nohows."

"No, but I gotta tell youse this. I just learned it last night on TV. Down in the rain forest in South America or somewhere they got these natives, sort of Indians the way they look, an they walk around naked all the time. You shoudda seen them. The men wear a string around the middle an they have these lines painted on their faces and bodies; their balls just knock around when they fight each other or hunt. The women haven't nothing on at all, and they're something to look at, some of them but not the old dried-up ones! We oughta go there sometime, the three of us. It would be a bash! Only you have to watch out; they're all cannonballs, so we could get eaten up alive!"

"Cannibals, you idiot!"

"An' have our heads paraded around town on the end of a stick. Ralph would be tender and juicy with that blonde hair of his. Know how it would feel to be chewed on by one of them cute naked babes? I can just guess where they would start their meal."

Ralph pulled over at a gas station, took out an address, and asked for directions. The attendant drew a map on a piece of paper and added:

"It's in a real remote area, so follow this closely or you can lose your way."

At first the route took them away from the ocean; then it climbed over the side of a hill where it became a gravel road with a strip of grass in the middle; later it entered a wood. After a half mile they came to three mailboxes, the middle one was marked Thornton. They followed the middle driveway and came to a vacation house overlooking a bay. There was no car or other sign of human presence. They scouted around, joking and making fun of the kind of people who would live in such a place. Behind the house was an outside Jacuzzi, some lounge chairs on a deck, and a path leading down to the shore, next to a contraption that looked like rails. They figured that was for pulling a boat up on dry land.

After they sat in the lounge chairs smoking and enjoying some beer they had brought along, Darryl examined the surroundings and told Asco and Ralph to clean up the butts and bottles and to follow him. They walked through trees and undergrowth to a slight incline from where the back of the house and the hot tub were visible.

"Let's see if we can get to the road from here."

After some difficulty, they arrived at the mailboxes. "Ralph, I want you and Asco to come here and stake out this house. Do it from that spot where we could see it. Stay as long as you need to find out who comes here. Bring your camera along and see if you can get pictures of people getting in and out of the tub. Don't get caught; if you are careful and crouch down nobody from the house can see you. Let me know as soon as you have a couple snapshots."

On their way back to Portland, Ralph had more to tell Darryl, if he wanted to hear it.

"Of course, I do! What are you holding back?"

"Nothing about the lawyer. I didn't know if you wanted to hear some stuff I learned about your mom."

"The less I hear about her the better. But it's not going to bug me if she's up to something, though, the bitch."

"She's seeing some guy, I'm sure of that."

"Tell me more."

"She went out the other night after I took you home. She was in her bathrobe, with her hair in curlers. She wasn't going to no social reception. She went into a door on the first floor of your building. Then this morning when I was waiting for you she comes out of the same door, wearing the same getup and traipses back up to your place. She must like it there! You aren't pissed, are you?"

"No, but thanks for telling me. These are things I gotta know. Don't talk it around."

That afternoon, when Darryl showed up for work complaining that a headache had kept him home all morning, he was told that he had been fired.

So Mom's laying that Harding oaf! Can't picture that one. She's so little, and the guy has to weigh a ton. He ain't got no middle, so his pants are always hanging on to his hips. Must have lost 'em dozens of times, his pants that is. Probably has to tuck her head under his chin to make out. If she's on top—how else could she do it?—she's gonna slip off and bust her ass. I'll bet they just fool around; he can't fit nohows. And the way that guy talks! They don't have no time for screwing because he never shuts his mouth; she'd have to shove a couple pairs of socks in it. But I'll show her. No broad in my place is gonna play around with strangers. Who knows, he could be part Chink, you can't never tell. If they have a kid it'll be a Mongolian idiot, and that'll make Asco cry buckets. What'll people think of me? She's going to stop that stuff quick. Liz don't mess around. Deb won't neither when she and me get together and that punk lawyer is past tense.

These were Darryl's thoughts as he stood in front of Glenda's building, wondering what he would say to his mother. Since he couldn't find the words to tell her what he wanted to, he decided not to say anything for a while. He turned around and walked down the dark street. He wasn't seen by his mother or his friends for four days.

When he returned, his mother told him she had been about to turn him in and that the next time he acted up she would call the parole officer. He did his best not to listen to the rest of her oration until she mentioned that someone called Ralph had been trying to reach him on the phone since yesterday.

Darryl took the phone into his room.

"Got your pictures. When do you want to see them?"

"Tell me what you saw."

"Well, we hung out there for two days, even slept in the woods overnight. Asco was worried we were going to be eaten by bears and raccoons. Day before yesterday up comes this Jaguar with the lawyer and a babe. It wasn't his missus because I woulda known her, and it wasn't the chick from their house neither. Someone else. It was getting dark. They went into the house and right away came out to go to the hot tub. We could see they were both bare-assed, and he was pawin' her while they climbed in. You couldn't see them in the tub, but I took some telephoto snaps as they came out. One picture shows everything, them standing there with nothing on. You can see their faces real clear. Then they came out in pajamas and ate a meal right there where we drank beer the other day, with candles and wine and everything. After they went inside we figured we'd better stick around for more, so we had another night of mosquitoes and Asco's bitching. They left in the Jaguar early in the morning, so we packed up and came back. Where the hell you been? We been trying to get you all day!"

"You did everything just right. That's all I need for now."

"Sorry I didn't get anything on the woman. I could work on that if you want me to, but not for a couple of days. Gotta fly tomorrow."

"No. Once I see the snapshot I'll know if she's the right one. Won't need anything else on her. Thanks. Here's what we'll do. When you're through flying, pick up Asco and bring a couple of baseball bats, a crow bar, and some spray paint. We're going to have some fun in that vacation house! How soon can you do it, Ralph?"

"Gimme another week. I'm flying in the lower Valley for three days. Then I'm gonna see my kids over the weekend down in Medford. Say a week from today."

"Just get the pictures to me before you take off, Ralph. Finding me another job will keep me busy while you're gone. I'll tell Asco."

After the receptionist called Steve on the phone to tell him that Deb was in the waiting room, he found it increasingly difficult to pay attention to what his client was saying. Steve listened some moments longer and then suggested that he go over the documents first and advise her later of the options at her disposal.

Deb did not come to his door immediately; perhaps she stopped to talk to Minnie on her way down the corridor. Steve hadn't seen Deb since their night in Seaside, ever since Bev had returned from Seattle to spend time with her family. He went to the window and looked out. It had stopped raining, and the first clear sunlight of the day reflected its pastel tones on the drenched leaves of the trees lining the avenue in front of the building. The air was clear, and if you were outside you could probably inhale the scent of damp dust and smell the drying raindrops. Could Deb and he go out into the streets and walk, hand in hand, through the city until they grew tired enough to find a place to sit quietly together for as long as they wanted? During the last three days his idle moments were full of such thoughts. She would appear to him, enticing, loving, beckoning him with her elusive smile, her soft, intimate voice, and her gentle, caressing gaze. Each time Deb entered into his daydream through a kind of side door which was always open to her and invisible to everyone else, she was dressed in the summer frock he so loved, and her hair reflected the light around her face. His vision of her drew him back to the center of his being, which he had neglected to visit for twenty years at least, and there he had the sense of rediscovering a self abandoned long ago at some turn in the road. Which part of him was this? It felt strong, and demanding, and nourishing. A part of him that believed that dreams could still be fulfilled.

When five minutes later Deb appears in reality, she is wearing a light brown jacket, blue jeans, and a scarf over her head.

"I was going by and just had to see you. Can we?"

"Yes, we needn't worry about anybody coming in" he answers, closing the door. They embrace for a long, passionate kiss, standing in the middle of his office.

"It's lucky you don't have a couch here. Who knows what might happen? When are you going to tell me, love, about the trip and the cabin and I don't know what else you have planned for us?"

"If you can, we'll leave Monday. I'll take the entire week off; it's a time just for us."

"Can you tell where we will be going?"

"I'd rather it be a surprise."

"Give me a hint at least so I know what to wear."

"Dress for the most beautiful weather imaginable, with cool mornings, warm afternoons in the sun, dinner outside, and nights cold enough to enjoy a fire. If it rains, we'll be together all the more . . ."

The phone rings.

"Mr. Thornton, Mrs. Thornton is here. Shall I show her to your office?"

"Thank you. She knows the way, but I'll come for her in a minute."

Steve turns to Deb. "Bev is up front. Two unexpected visits at the same time! I'll take you out and receive her." They kiss briefly.

"Who was that?" Bev asks when they were inside Steve's office. "I've seen her somewhere before."

"That's Deb Myers, you know, the one with the husband who was injured in Brazil."

"I thought you were finished with her. Isn't Mike Hoffman taking her on?"

"I think she was with him just now. She stopped in to say hello . . ."

"It is almost time for lunch. Are you going to invite me? Or do you have other plans?"

"Will you deign to have lunch with me, Madam? We could go to the club, or maybe you would prefer Palmer's, or the new restaurant in the Mall."

In ten minutes Steve and Bev were seated next to a window at one of the favorite lunch spots for tired shoppers, where men and women discuss business over abundant salads and tourists wonder what to visit next.

"Shall we have a little drink? A new bartender came shortly after you left for Seattle, and he's first rate."

"Not really. I have a lot to do this afternoon and I want to stay alert. Look! There is already a line of people waiting for a table. It's fortunate we came in before twelve. Don't look now, but isn't that the Myers woman we just saw? She's standing in line there, with a black fellow. They seem to be together. Then we won't have to invite her to our table, will we?"

"Of course not," Steve answered, peering out of the corner of his eye to see if indeed it was Deb. Yes, there she was, standing just as he had seen her half an hour earlier, next to a tall black man, talking quietly, looking straight ahead and smiling absently, as Steve had so often seen her do.

"The best would be for us to focus on the menus and not see her. Then we won't have to talk," Steve said, wondering who Deb's friend was and why they were having lunch together.

"Who is her friend?" Bev asked. "Are all of her friends like that?"

"I don't usually inquire much about my clients' personal lives; it doesn't really concern me at all," Steve replied, dying to know the answer himself.

"Now I remember where I saw her. It was in the old Pisces Gallery one afternoon. She came in and looked around at the exhibit we were showing. I remember she said she was new to town and that she was a photographer. I didn't think much about her, she was sort of drab, worn-out. I can see she is much prettier than I had thought. Why didn't you tell me? Well, maybe she is in love with that man next to her and that brings out the beauty in her, although I don't really think he is a good choice for her. She needs somebody more settled, somebody who can take care of her. That man looks like he's wearing working clothes under his jacket. Just think! Coming into a restaurant dressed like that.

Oh, good! They have been taken to a table at the other side of the floor. Now we can talk about something else."

Steve felt immensely relieved.

"Can you believe it's August already?" Bev continued. "The time goes so fast while I'm busy in Seattle that I can hardly catch my breath. Sometimes I wonder what you can possibly be doing with yourself alone here in Portland. How do you keep from being bored to death?"

"I manage pretty well, actually. There is Scott to talk to, work at the office, and now that summer is here I can get outside. Did I tell you we went to the cabin to make repairs and tidy things up? Diane went, too."

"It must have been back in April that I saw Deb Myers in the gallery. I doubt that I would have recognized her without your telling me who she is."

"For now let's talk about something else. When are you coming back again?"

"In a week or so, to get ready for Scott's birthday. I want to invite all our friends to his party. His friends, too, of course, although some of them look pretty disreputable, as if they haven't taken a bath for a week."

"What can you expect? They are still young. Should we ask them to bathe for the occasion?"

Back at her apartment, Deb phoned Glenda.

"By the way, I'll be leaving Monday for a short vacation. It will feel good to get away."

"Does that have anything to do with Darryl? Something, for sure."

"Nothing directly. It's true he upset me terribly, and I never want to see him again. But it's not because of him that I'm going away."

"Well, you won't see Darryl again, I can guarantee that. At least not at my place you won't. I didn't see him for four days after that business. Then when he came back I told him next time it was the parole officer he'd have to explain that to, not me. That made him knuckle down. He even cleaned up all his stuff. He did lose his job, though, and that bugs me a little, but I'm sure he'll find another, as strong as he is. But you can forget Darryl; he's out of your life, I told him just that. Where are you going, if I may ask?"

"Steve is taking me somewhere; he hasn't told me exactly where, but I suspect it will be nice and that we will be alone. Do you know what happened just this noon? I met Pete from the homeless project, and we went to lunch in a restaurant in the mall. While we were waiting in line I saw Steve and his wife sitting there at a table. I'm sure they saw us, and they must have been talking about me. I was so embarrassed I didn't know what to do, so I just stared in front of me while Pete was talking."

"What's there to be embarrassed about? Everybody eats lunch, usually around noon."

"Well, I can't greet Steve's wife, since we haven't been introduced. I just saw her once, before I knew who she was. And it gives me goose pimples to think of greeting him while she's there next to him."

"You make things so complicated, Deb! There's always an easy way to handle those things. Just go up and introduce yourself, like I would, or run away if you don't want to face her. Whatever you do, don't just stand there and squirm like a jellyfish."

"And I also wondered how Steve would react, especially since I was unable to tell him why I was with Pete. I still don't know how to handle that one."

"Let him stew for a while. A little jealousy is the best medicine for a man, because it keeps him from taking you for granted. Have you checked your answering machine yet? You probably have a message from him already asking who that fellow was. Don't answer right away. The longer he frets, the better. Hey, Deb! Someone's at the door. Can we talk later? Bye."

Deb looked at her answering machine. There were no messages. She dialed Steve's office.

Asco is driving slowly toward the coast. It is important to avoid the police, since he and Darryl and Ralph each have an open beer can hidden between their knees.

On the way, Darryl explains to his friends his theories about fornication and the dangers it poses to society as a whole. He is holding one of the photographs Ralph had taken of Steve's hot tub.

"You see, them people in this picture are fornucators, and that's wrong! They ain't got no right to do that. The Bible says so like ABC. I'll show you where when we get home. What we're gonna do is smash that place up and then leave this picture on what's left of the bed. It's gonna show them they shouldn't be doing that stuff and that they better repent. It's obvious to anyone who thinks about it. As long as people are fornucating and getting away with it, society can't enforce other laws like it should."

"Yea," Ralph put in, "but how's that different from just screwing? Can't tell me you never done that."

"In high school, his nickname was 'Don One,' the number one guy who made out with the most babes, wasn't it Darryl? He used to keep score in his social studies book. You shoudda seen the filthy pictures of screwing he'd draw in the can. An when he wasn't screwing he was jacking off. The guys would tease him by saying 'what a jack you are' where everybody could hear."

"Ralph, you gotta use your head. There's a big difference. Old people get married; they screw or they don't, that's up to them. Now with you and that nurse, that's okay, too, because she's your woman, that is until you decide she ain't anymore. Then you find someone else to be your woman, and then you're just screwing, nothing else, which is okay, too. You see that babe in the picture is my woman, and she's getting screwed by the lawyer, and that's fornucation, and it's gotta stop. So he's gonna get killed in the end, somehow. What's going to happen is his wife will see the pictures we're gonna leave there and she'll shoot him when she sees proof of what he's up to. She's got a right to, 'cause she's his woman."

"How do you know she can shoot?"

"It doesn't matter, Asco. She'll get him somehow, that's all that counts. Same thing for that guy who lives downstairs at home and fucks my mom. I don't want nothing to happen to her, so I'll get them apart a different way. Just wait, you'll see."

Asco parks his Plymouth behind some branches near the mailboxes. They walk down the driveway toward the cabin.

"I'll take care of the security system first; that's my kind of work. Then we break in and demolish everything. You start in the kitchen, Che Asco; Ralph can do the rest while I do some research in the desk, if there is one, and in the bedroom. I hope there's a safe to bust open. When we're done, these cans of spray paint will make the joint look real pretty. After that, we'll retire to the beach. I've got some crack on me."

"Here we go," Asco shouts. "It's going to be a blast, a real holycost!"

On MONDAY MORNING Deb began a dream. In her dream she was floating west, away from Portland, toward Seaside. Steve was in her dream, too, seated to her left, driving a car. She had the impression that he was dreaming the same dream. Their dream took place outside of time, and they felt their thoughts merging between them in a kind of song without words. Later, however, Deb did retrieve a few words and set them as well as she could to scraps of a melody she remembered.

Soon we leave behind the geometric patterns of lingering neighborhoods and suburban filling stations to find ourselves in a world of tall trees and dense vegetation. We continue along corridors through endless groves of fir and pine forming at times a thick, dark forest. Occasionally as we look down at the side of the road we see a stream gushing among ferns of all sizes and rocks covered with moss. We pass open farmland where black-faced lambs seem to stare at us with curiosity.

When we arrive at a beach, we park the car in a parking lot full of pot holes near the road. A gust of wind blows my skirt way up and fills our nostrils with the peculiar salty seaweed smell of the ocean. We remove our shoes and run on the sand toward the waves, where the surf hits against rocky outcrops and bursts into spray and foam. Standing on a bluff we gaze at the deep aquamarine and turquoise colors of the water reflecting brilliantly where the haze lets the midday sun come through. Gray, long-winged gulls glide like oriental kites in the airstream, crying out their plaintive call. A pelican makes a swift vertical dive into the waters and reappears with its beak overflowing with fish and water.

We are free and we laugh and shout raucously into the wind, calling out each other's name at the top of our voices. Holding hands we run back to the car, put shoes on our sandy bare feet and head north. We drive through a landscape of hidden meadows dotted with daisies and buttercups and watch dairy cattle pausing to graze in lush green pastures as they move slowly along a fence. We enter Astoria from the south after crossing a short bridge over Young's Bay. Elegant Victorian houses hang precariously on the hillsides and beckon us to admire their acrobatic skill. We find a restaurant perched even higher on a terraced hill. There we hardly taste the salmon we order, concentrating as we are on the view through wide open windows and gazing tirelessly at the Columbia River hauling its glittering waters for miles as it fans out longingly in search of the Pacific Ocean.

We cross the Columbia on the Astoria Bridge, which feels like a tightrope high above the glistening water. On the route toward Aberdeen muddied tidelands huddle around oyster farms, and we coil through small processing and lumbering towns. Aberdeen passes us by with a polite nod as we continue north through a contrasting scenery of ancient forest groves and desolate clear-cuts where emaciated tree trunks lie like masts of abandoned ships.

Later a sign on the road announces:

Olympic National Park. Lake Quinault.

"We are almost there," Steve says, turning toward me to see my reaction.

"It's like a secret wish come true. I have always longed to come here. Something must have prevented me until I could do it with you."

Steve turns into a narrow road flanked by the trunks of giant spruce and hemlock trees. It feels like entering an imposing cathedral with a gigantic nave. We pass by a group of small buildings crowded together—the park headquarters, a tiny post office, a general store, a few houses. Steve pulls up in front of a log structure, goes inside, and returns a few minutes later carrying a bunch of flowers, a picnic basket, and some keys.

After a half mile the road turns to the left toward the lake. It comes to an end in a clearing where we park the car. We breathe deeply to fill our lungs with the fir-scented air and feel our legs regain contact with the earth. Our cabin stands by itself in a wooded area on the edge of the lake. After Steve unlocks the front door and we step in, we look around briefly and open the windows to let the fragrant air permeate our cabin. He beckons me toward an open window where the lake lies before us bathing in the late afternoon sun.

"It's magnificent!" We embrace and start kissing, realizing that this is the only adequate language to express our joy at being together and alone in this deeply moving landscape.

The time to be practical comes. We walk back to the car, unpack it, and haul in the clothes and the food we have brought along. On a small table we spread out a cloth. We discover that we are hungry as we start digging eagerly into the picnic basket, taking out the bounty it contains and placing each precious object one after another on the table. Soon we sit in front of a colorful array of food: chunks of Swiss and cheddar cheese, a loaf of French bread, a bowl of ripe pink peaches, sensuous looking green grapes, and bright red apples. There is just enough room on the table for a bottle of Burgundy and a wild blackberry pie. We begin eating in silence, watching the quietly moving opalescent waters of the lake reflect the evening light. A breeze rustles through the pines and firs, cooling the air.

Steve pulls the cork and pours some wine. "To you, and to our love!" he says looking into my eyes.

"There is no time here," I say after I take a sip. "May it disappear altogether from our lives." We now drink from the same glass, and I feel Steve's arm around my waist.

After eating we go for a walk along the lake and watch the mist hovering on the surface, already obscuring the distant shore. Sitting on a large smooth rock, we see the light of the moon beginning to reflect its pale light on the motionless surface of the now gray water. Two birds fly rapidly across the expanse. Cries of other birds emanate from all directions—from the nearby forest, from across the lake. Suddenly we notice, toward the shore to the north, the shadow of a person standing in a boat silently drawing in a net. Soon the mist moves toward us and envelops the boat.

We are cold and walk back to the cabin. Steve sets and lights a fire. After watching the flames lick around and ignite the fir logs, we take off our clothes and step into the shower, where we have to joke about the intermittent hot and cold water surprising us from one moment to the next. Now with our hands we lather and explore each other's bodies and feel like young lovers just discovering forbidden sensual pleasures. We dry our bodies in front of the warm fire gazing at each other in the orange light. We slip into bed. Under the down comforter I can feel drops of water still on Steve's back as he starts to warm my thighs with his hands and lips. The windows are wide open, and the light of the moon reaches across the floor into a corner. Only the sound of frogs croaking along the shore and night birds singing in the nearby trees remind us that we are of this world as we talk, kiss, touch, and caress, making love far into the night.

The next morning, while still in bed, Steve begins to talk about himself. He claims to have never before spoken on the subject at much length, and I think he feels awkward.

"You need to know who I am, Deb, and if I am long-winded enough about it, I will start to understand, too."

"Perhaps you are less complicated than you think. Would it be more interesting over morning coffee?"

"No, I think this part should be taken on an empty stomach, if you can last."

It is as if Steve wants to uncover his life with Bev and expose it to the sun and the light so that it can heal. How can he explain his involvement with her without grounding the story in his drab, joyless childhood in a lower middle-class area of a North Boston suburb?

Steve pauses to hold me close to him, as if he wants me to reassure him before he continues. Then he looks at my face and traces the features with his index finger.

"I think I'm already beginning to understand, so I'll go on. Our neighborhood was not particularly wholesome, so my mother took pains to keep us off the street and out of trouble. She succeeded so well that the three of us became bookworms and overachievers at school, which led to scholarships and college. I went to Boston University, where I immediately felt . . . marginal is the best word for it. I commuted from home and had no skill in coeducational banter. Soon we learned my father had cancer, and I spent whatever free time I had helping out at home. One of my sisters, Phyllis, was just married and expecting, and Susan was still in high school, so neither one could be depended upon."

"That must have been rough. Did you keep on at school?"

"Doggedly. Dad died two years later, at home, in my mother's arms. She was a strong woman and never complained. I think you remind me of her."

"Thank you, Steve."

"He had been doing chemotherapy regularly and suffering from it. I remember helping him into and out of the tub and seeing his wasted body. But he didn't complain, and his mind was still sound."

"Did he finally start talking to you, toward the end?"

"Not really. I think he considered himself so unimportant that he didn't want to impose such a trivial subject on anyone, especially his son."

"Are you like your father in some ways?"

"I probably have his patience, but that is hardly a useful character trait in the long run. As a matter of fact, I am becoming impatient now; maybe it is time for coffee."

"You can wait here. I'll prepare something. Just tell me how his dying affected you."

"It brought me a sense of liberation, even though I suspected I would have to support my mother from then on. But studying prelaw and working nights was invigorating, and I finally started making friends."

Steve watches me as I comb my hair in front of a mirror and as I draw a frock over my body. While I prepare breakfast in the kitchen, he lies there with his eyes shut, but I can tell he is concentrating.

"Bev was a lot of fun to be with. Just now I was trying to reimagine my meeting with her on the train to Providence," he tells me over coffee and toast. "What I liked the most was her laughter. I remember how she would move her head when she was amused; her long hair would swirl around and touch my cheek. Like many other students she was against the war in Vietnam and expressed her convictions with eloquence and a good deal of humor. That was fun for me, and it gave me a release from the silence of home; I realized I could say whatever I wanted, and Bev would cheer me on. Soon my mother remarried, and Susan got into optometry and became self-sufficient. All that made it possible for me to begin enjoying life. Consequently I got married and went to law school, as my parents had always hoped I would do."

We finish coffee and clear off the dishes. Then we start walking along the lake shore, toward the town and the little grocery store, reacquainting ourselves with the landscape from the night before. It is a roundabout way that takes us along densely planted trees and then turns outward following the shore of a narrow peninsula. There are driftwood logs lying on the coarse sand, providing us with a place to sit and contemplate the lake as it shines in the morning sun. The lone fisherman from last night is gone; in his place blue and red dragonflies skim over the surface of the water in the sun.

"We were married in a big ceremony in Baltimore." A light

breeze sends ripples along in the reflected sunlight. "Her family was quite well off and conservative, but they accepted me in spite of my modest background. They were convinced I would make it as a lawyer. And I liked them, so they liked me in turn."

"How did getting married change your life?"

"You can hardly say we settled down, since we were living the life of married students while I finished my degree. I crammed my head with legal briefs, she worked to support us, and we hardly saw each other, yet we were closer than we have ever been since. We went to concerts and lectures together, and we played lots of tennis. Those were the years when Bev got started in business. To support us she had taken a job as copygirl in the advertising department of an art magazine. To everyone's surprise she became indispensable and worked her way up fast."

"Did you ever settle down like professionals are expected to?"

"That happened when I graduated and started work with a law firm. Then Scott was born. He was the only child Bev was able to bear. She had two miscarriages after him."

"I am sorry, that must have been hard for you both."

"It was. But I think that what really affected our relationship was his accident. The car accident he was in . . ."

Steve falls silent. We remain quiet while the path we are following veers away from the shore into the forest. Squirrels run up and down the trees in a constant chase, and the air is full of the chirping of insects and the songs of birds.

"How life keeps on!" Steve says, interrupting his silence. Clearly he has come to an event that is difficult for him to describe. He doesn't quite know how to start, but he feels he has to say something. "Just look at the trees around us . . . even the birds tell wise stories about life and its struggles, about having and letting go."

We finally arrive at the settlement, and in the general store where people pick up groceries, mail, and gossip we overhear a conversation about a dispute going on over fishing rights on the lake.

Walking down the narrow road that twists its way from the town to the highway, we look for an entrance to the rain forest. When finally we find it, we go in, overcome by a feeling of reverence, as if we were entering some sacred abode in a distant culture we barely understand. An overabundance of vegetation is everywhere, growing in confusion, twisting next to, under, above and around itself.

"You could call that cooperation," Steve says, pointing to a mass of intertwining trees, vines, and branches. "Or interdependence, or maybe love."

The air has become warmer and more humid. Somehow the strenuous energy of growing is communicated to our senses.

"I like that. It is hard to imagine that right next to the road there is this world of variety and richness hidden out of sight. Yet it is so close to the industrial world of buying and selling."

As we walk we look down to see our feet moving amid a profusion of lichen, moss, tiny trees, ferns, and ground plants growing everywhere, even on the ghostly remains of decayed trees. Above, lacy vine maples and moss-covered tree limbs stretch out in a canopy in search of light. We pass under trees that are centuries old. At the end of the path we cross a rope bridge suspended over a small ravine, and the rocking movement under our feet communicates to our bodies a feeling of insecurity that conveys to me the fragility of the rain forest and the natural world.

We slowly make our way back. It is midday, and we are hungry. We stop at the only restaurant in town and sit down at an outside table in the sun next to a grove of trees. The single waiter approaches with the menu and recommends the catch of the day. Waiting for the food to come, we hold hands, and I sense Steve looking at me. It feels as if he wants to memorize every line of my face, my light brown hair encircling my features and half-covering my ears. I feel his gaze as it follows my brow, gently curving toward my nose, lingering on the hint of a smile that I feel playing around my lips, and coming to rest on the lightness of my blue eyes. Through the intensity of his eyes I discover, in a brief moment, my own beauty, realizing to what extent my lips are sensuous, my expression soft, my ears delicate.

We eat slowly, saying hardly a word, continuing to gaze at each other. I know how deeply in love I am, and Steve's eyes are saying something about a lasting passion.

We walk toward our cabin along the somnolent surface of the afternoon lake. On the way we sit on a low rock and let the gently lapping waves that reach the shore cool our feet. Steve bends over and kisses my wet toes, and I let my fingers run through his hair.

When we arrive at the cabin, Steve sets and lights a fire and then sits next to me with his arm around my shoulders. Soon the flames fill the cabin with a cheerful crackling sound.

"I love, you, Deb," he says. "I didn't know that our love would mean so much to me, that it would take over my life with such sudden intensity."

We stare into the fire, wondering if it will spit a spark out on the rug.

"I still need to tell you more about myself and my life with Bev. It's a way of working through the only other love I have experienced, one that didn't last."

He gets up to stir the fire, which doesn't need stirring since it is burning briskly. Then he sits down again and takes my hand.

"Scott was severely injured in a car accident when he was fifteen. I still remember the evening when the phone rang to tell me what had happened." Steve describes the accident, how Scott remained in the hospital for months, and how he will have to spend the rest of his life in a wheelchair. "Once he was a teenager like any other; then suddenly, when he needed it, he summoned up tremendous courage in order to adapt to a new, restricted life. Every day I grow to admire him more, it seems."

"You will allow me to meet him, won't you, Steve? For you it must have been an awful experience to have only one child and see his life almost destroyed." Deb looks at him, then gets up to make tea. After she pours, they sit together in front of the fire watching the flames, and Steve continues.

"I'll skip the next part of the story, the personal injury litigations, which went on for a long time. Briefly, we got a lot of money out of the accident, which permitted us to move to Portland and start a new life. It also made it possible to build a big house designed to fit Scott's special needs; he actually owns half of it. I joined a law firm in Portland, and we made new friends. Bev said she wanted to restrict her interests to her immediate world: Scott, me, and the house. But I think a change had already begun in her before the accident back in Boston when I got a secure job that paid well."

"Were you ever happy with Bev?"

Steve pauses and searches back in his mind for an answer. "I guess I was happy with her, or with our life, while I was a student. Afterward she became more and more involved with her work, and so did I, for that matter. We forgot to talk about politics, went to parties instead of lectures, gave up tennis. Then she started going to church again; it was the same denomination she knew as a child, and she became active in committees and activities. I had to go to church with her and sit through the long pretentious sermons, the sound of the organ, and the pious smiles. Bev changed politically, and supported Reagan and Bush with the same energy she had denounced our involvement in Vietnam. The result was that since neither of us liked to argue we had less and less to talk about. My own personal contribution to our drifting apart was to work harder, thinking that by being successful we would be drawn back together again. The opposite happened. The more I succeeded as an attorney, the higher Bev believed we could go in the social register, because success came to mean wealth and prestige. I remember one night in Boston thinking that happiness was like dry sand slowly slipping between my fingers. Then Scott's accident suddenly jolted my hand, and it was empty."

Deb tightens her hold on Steve's hand, and he squeezes hers in response. "When we moved out here, I devoted my energy to work. Bev went into art as a form of self-achievement, of doing something that belonged strictly to her; she also expanded her circle of friends." He throws more wood in the fire and pauses for a while. We watch the renewed flames shoot upward reflecting a reddish glow on our faces. They seem to be consuming a dark, uncomfortable past that both of us wish to free ourselves from.

"I don't know what our family looks like from the outside, but from the inside it's a comfortable prison cell where I have everything I could desire except an interesting life. Scott's accident was a life sentence for me; I knew that from then on I was the primary emotional support for Bev and for Scott and that I had to stay with them. But now that is changing. After all, I was the architect and general contractor of my prison, so it shouldn't be impossible for me to remove at least some of the bars."

"Or to pick the lock, if the door was ever really bolted."

"For a long time my identity came from being responsible and working hard. I figured nothing of importance would ever change in my life. Just as the doctors had told Scott that he 'would have to learn to live with his injuries,' I must have told myself something similar. I ruled out anything like loving another woman, which I thought would lead to nothing more than a string of fleeting relationships." He pauses and looks at me. "Now I think I was simply afraid of loving because I sensed it would be so overpowering I wouldn't be able to handle it. And I was right: it is affecting every fiber and cell of my body."

"Is it a transformation?"

"I think it is more like a dance; the steps always lead us toward each other and back to ourselves, and they tell us what we are capable of doing."

I remember that there is a guitar in an otherwise empty closet. Fortunately all its strings are intact, but it needs considerable tuning. Then I sing for Steve a song I learned from someone when I was in the Peace Corps. Maybe he will understand the words more clearly than I do. It is a ballad in Spanish that goes something like this. "Many years ago in a kingdom by the clouds there lived an enchanted horse who roamed the mountains. One day a blue heron landed on his back and together they crossed a wild river. When they reached shore, they came to a hut where they lived through the cold, long winter." That is all I remember of the verses; perhaps the song ends there.

"As you were singing I remembered the walk we took this morning. When we were sitting on that driftwood log, looking at the lake, I watched your face next to mine reflected in the water. I could see through your features the pebbles and leaves lying at the bottom as if they belonged somehow to your face. Then a breeze came and wiped out the reflection, and all I could see were the ripples on the surface."

"Did the image return?"

"I don't know; by then we had moved on."

We look at each other and then sit close together as we watch the fire turn into vibrant coals, and we feel their heat penetrate our bodies and spirits.

The week goes by swiftly. On Friday morning I wake up early; a ray of sun is shining through the window and floods the bed with light. Against the big pillow, Steve's face looks relaxed. He keeps his eyes closed, perhaps seeking to prolong a fleeting dream or in search of a few more minutes of sleep. I see a smile lurking on his lips and gently kiss him on the shoulder. I get out of bed and stand naked in front of the open window, feeling the freshness of the early morning bathe my body, accepting nature's offer of energy collected in the coolness of the night. Out at the lake ripples barely disturb the pale aquamarine waters. Suddenly the penetrating shriek of a lonely crow breaks the morning quiet. I come back into the room, look at my body in the mirror, and realize that it is beautiful.

I decide to make pancakes for breakfast. I slip into a dress and enter the kitchen. The smell of freshly brewed coffee fills the cabin. "I'm coming!" Steve calls from the bedroom.

We eat and joke about our simple life. No newspaper, television, or radio. Commuting is out of the question. Weather conditions are irrelevant. No mail for the past five days, no phone rings.

We go for a final walk along the shore. We watch the mist slowly rise from the water as the sun comes over the jagged treetops and reaches the lake with thick warm fingers of light. We say good-bye to our cabin, the lake, and the noble trees that have witnessed the unfolding of our love and thank them for allowing us to be guests in this regained paradise.

We pack our suitcases and load them in the car. Steve pulls out a map and spreads it over the hood. We will head north around the Olympic National Park toward Port Angeles and then go up Hurricane Ridge. For the night we will stop at Port Townsend and on Saturday catch the ferry for Seattle.

Arriving at Port Townsend in the late afternoon we find a quaint town, as if turning backward to look into another century. We have a room reserved at what resembles a stone castle perched on a hill overlooking the Sound. The next morning we walk on the grounds at Fort Warden, feeling the warmth of the sun as we loiter on the pier and watch families fishing. It is a peaceful spot, despite the cannons still guarding the strait. We return to town for lunch at a restaurant close to the harbor. After leaving our car in line for the afternoon ferry, we walk around the downtown looking at store windows and Victorian façades. In one antique store, Steve sits at a large rolltop desk that once belonged to a famous judge and assumes the stern look of a man deep in thought as he decides matters of life and death. I try on a hundred-year-old long ruffled dress complete with wide-rimmed hat, sequined handbag and matching parasol. Steve laughs as I curtsy, and he beckons me to sit on his lap. Then we visit the New Age Boutique and admire a display of rocks and crystals. In a corner of the room at a table a tarot card reader sits next to an oil lamp shuffling her cards. Steve looks at necklaces and insists that I try one he has picked. It consists of turquoise beads and semiprecious stones cut to resemble stars, moons, and suns. "A cosmic necklace," the clerk says as she hands it to Steve. He puts it around my neck and whispers in my ear: "For you the stars and the moon . . . you are the keeper of my universe." I look in the mirror and see his face shining with pleasure from behind my head.

We board the ferry and go to the upper deck. We hold hands as we look at the gleaming water of the Sound and listen to the calls of the gulls.

"I wonder what it would be like to quit everything in Portland and come to a place like Port Townsend to live. I could be a small town lawyer and help people draw up wills and set up tiny corporations." He looks at me. "There are so many different things you could do here, with me."

"The first one would be to enjoy life. I'm willing to try."

With that brief promise of a future, we see the skyline of Seattle appear bathed in the orange light of the evening. We take Interstate 5 to Portland. Steve stays overnight at my apartment. Early on Sunday morning he heads for Lake Oswego.

SCOTT WAS THE first one to hear the roar of Steve's Jaguar as it pulled up to the front door. He and Diane had just finished breakfast and were on the living room floor reading the Sunday papers, Scott lying on his back, Diane leaning on elbows and knees, absorbed in world politics, local news, sports, and comics. Melissa was still gone, having decided to take the week off when she learned that there would not be enough people around to keep her busy in the kitchen.

Steve came in, looking refreshed and healthy. Diane went to brew coffee.

"Were you with Deb?"

"We went to Lake Quinault and around the Olympic peninsula. The weather was superb, and we got to know each other."

"Was it a honeymoon?"

"So to speak. And it was good, all the way through. Eventually I'll have to live with Deb."

"How about bringing her around some time, so I can give my approval. You know that a man can't live happily with a woman unless his son judges her to be worthy of his dad."

"Of course! As soon as I can. Mom home yet?"

"No. She called and said she can't make it before Wednesday. So if Deb is available bring her over for lunch, and we can spend the afternoon together. Diane will make one of her concoctions, which no one will be able to find a name for ... or resist ..."
This last was added as Diane came in with coffee and toast.

"Welcome home, Mr. Thornton. I hope you find everything in order."

"Steve!" Steve said.

"You will have to be patient with me. Calling someone your age by his first name isn't easy. When I was a child in Québec all grown men were called Monsieur; the only exception was my father, who was Papa."

Scott could see his dad blanch, slightly but surely. "Times change, Diane," he said. "When you were a kid, all men over twenty-five must have looked ancient, venerable, worthy of respect. My dad is different. Look how young he looks! Especially this morning. I don't mean to be disrespectful, of course, but you will have to agree that he isn't 'of a certain age,' as you say."

"No, Scott. Your father isn't *d'un certain âge*; he's *entre deux âges*, between two ages, and that is the most interesting time for a man, as they say. Is that better . . . Steve?"

"Before I forget, Dad, a day or so ago the sheriff called from Seaside. It seems someone broke into the cabin and made a mess of things. He didn't give details other than to say that he had sealed off the doors and that we should come to check things out. There wasn't much Diane and I could do about it, so we didn't go over. Anyhow, you were due home in a couple of days."

"I'll ask Bev to go and inspect the damage when she returns on Wednesday. I'll be plenty busy after taking the week off. It sounds as if the sheriff wasn't in any hurry. I'll phone Deb now to see if she can come for lunch."

An hour later, Steve was holding Deb's elbow as she walked up the stairs to the front door.

"I must say, I'm impressed," she was telling him as they paused to look around. "It's really elegant with the driveway making a circle, all those trees, and this house. Wow!"

"I don't really want you to be impressed. It is something else I need from you."

Scott, on the veranda, beckoned them to come up.

"Welcome to our humble abode. You must be Deb."

"And you must be Scott."

"Let's not pretend we don't know each other, Deb. I understand Dad loves you; that's enough for me to love you, too. Come in and meet Diane, wherever she is."

"Thank you, Scott. That helps me relax. You must have understood that meeting your lover's son for the first time can be a harrowing experience. Lead the way. Do you need a push?"

Steve breathes a sigh of relief as he watches the two of them go inside together laughing. They find Diane on the patio with a tray of cheese, crackers, and beer. Seated at the table they can see the little lake resting in the sun between shade trees, lawns, and pretentious houses. First they talk about the trip Steve and Deb have just completed. Scott asks Deb for her impressions; Diane wonders about the people who live in the old depressed logging towns. Steve listens to their voices and relaxes, hardly hearing what they are saying. After lunch Steve and Diane clean up the kitchen while Deb and Scott make the rounds of the property together.

"I wonder what they can be talking about all this time," he says when the dishes are dried and put away.

"They are talking about you," Diane says as she and Steve return to the patio. "It is their common interest. But now they are beginning a philosophical discussion. Can you see? You can tell by the way he is gesticulating over there on that bench."

"Do you know what they are talking about, Diane?"

"He is asking her about the nature of love."

"How do you know?"

"It is as if I could hear them. And the subject has been on Scott's mind lately. I can't really answer all his questions. You need to hire someone other than me to educate him on those matters. Or better yet, you can tell him yourself; that would make him happy."

"I suppose he thinks I am an expert, an authority, after what has happened. But there isn't really an awful lot I can tell him.

It's a matter of feelings, and it's not easy to find the right words to express them."

"You could start with that. He will ask for more, of course. By trying to answer him you can learn more about yourself."

"What are they saying now, Diane? Telepathy isn't really eavesdropping, is it?"

"Deb is telling him how she felt when she first knew she loved you, how it affected her thoughts, her feelings, and her body. What she is saying is really beautiful. If she hasn't told you all this, you should ask her; you will get to know her better."

Steve shuts his eyes and tries to imagine what Deb is saying.

"Deb is crying now," Diane says, interrupting his efforts. "It is something about losing someone and about feeling helpless."

Exhausted from the stress of bringing two disparate parts of his life together, Steve takes a pillow from the couch, throws it to the floor, stretches out, and falls asleep. He awakes to the sensation of Deb leaning over him, kissing him on the eyes and forehead.

"Scott and Diane are swimming. He and I had a wonderful talk."

"Shall we go and swim with them?"

"Let's just stay together."

"Tell me what you told him, Deb, out there on the bench. The two of you looked so deeply involved in what you were saying. It must have been important."

Deb answers, and then she and Steve walk around the little lake.

"Our love needs a real lake for a setting. Let us go back to Lake Quinault soon!"

Steve and Deb return to the house, where they have a light supper with Scott and Diane. Then, in front of a blazing fire, they listen to Scott's new CD of Monteverdi madrigals. Steve drives Deb back to her apartment and on his way home realizes that since noon no one has mentioned Bev.

That evening Scott wrote the following in his computer:

"What do I think about Dad's affair? What role I am playing in it? Is it my duty to say 'Dad, you're a cad'? That rhyme alone would prevent my saying it. Tell Mom? That's for him to do, not me. But still I am an accomplice to the destruction of my family, betraying Mom by remaining silent. Not only that: I am encouraging my father to . . . let's face it, to wallow in licentious, lustful, and lascivious behavior by politely receiving his mistress, knowingly bestowing hospitality on somebody depraved enough to want to corrupt him. Words, words, words. None of that is true. How to avoid this kind of role-playing monologue? It's as if the words and the generalized sentiments, none of them really mine, keep me from knowing how I feel. Shit!

"Let's start again. Dad is happy, beaming from ear to ear. His hormones have undoubtedly been reactivated and are cruising through his veins; they will probably prolong his life by years! I have always thought of him as a quiet, somewhat melancholic individual, who kept his thoughts to himself because they were never really cheerful. That has changed overnight. It is the first time I have ever seen him enjoy being himself. We all owe Deb our gratitude for bringing out of him someone who had been hiding inside for so long.

"Furthermore, I liked her immensely. When she told me this afternoon about her husband and how much she still cared for him I started to cry, me, the tough guy in the wheelchair! Some day I will try to describe her, as an exercise in using words to depict something so ephemeral that it flies away before the words can settle down on paper. I am referring here to the softness of her hair as the sun shines through it, and her eyes, which give the impression of being here with you and at the same time thousands of miles away. It must drive Dad nuts; it would me. Oh, Hippolytus! Ancient brother! Am I falling for Deb? Shit!

"What about Mom? She is the hardest one to account to. Does she suspect anything? She is surely too innocent to conceive of such perfidy. I don't have a clue how she will react, and I'm not enthusiastic about learning, either. Perhaps this means that beginning now I will have to take care of her, emotionally, just as she has taken care of me since the accident. Or maybe not: she has already started a new life for herself, up there in Seattle, and if her gallery is a success she has it made. Just think how happy she will be selling paintings and sculptures to the rich and rubbing elbows with the famous! That's got it all over being a self-sacrificing lawyer's wife with a crippled kid to look after. And she's a handsome woman, no question about that. She will find someone else right away. Maybe she has already; wouldn't that be a surprise! 'Oh! Steve, I meant to tell you . . .' Furthermore, she gets on so well with Mary . . . there might be something going on there. Well why not?

"Where am I in all this? I'll soon be twenty-one. What an initiation into adulthood! Most boys my age leave home, or get booted out, and they are glad to fend for themselves, raise a family, or ride the rails with a bottle of booze in their pocket. I would do well to think fast about what I am going to do . . . with myself. There's the rub: to do anything I have to drag one hundred and forty pounds of myself along. That's why I have never contemplated any change in my routine. Sit around here, be taken care of, think about life. Jesus! What a worthless, parasitical existence!

"Wonder where Diane is. Has she also found someone? 'By the way, Scott . . .' she will say. 'See you around some day.' That is why I need to get my butt out into the wide world, if not to seek my fortune at least to do something useful. I have to talk about that with Chuck; he will come up with some ideas."

At that moment Diane came in.

"Did you call me, Scott?"

"Not that I know of. But I was wondering where you were."

"Upstairs in the library. I came across this, which you might find interesting," she said, handing him a book which looked like a collection of essays.

"Thank you. I've been thinking about Dad and his adventure, from every possible angle, and I can't come to anything that possibly resembles an opinion or an attitude. May I ask you what you think?"

"Ask again when you decide how you feel, and then I'll answer. You can take your time, Scott. I'll not be going anywhere."

Bev returned elated, enthusiastic.

"We had a wonderful time in Seattle promoting our gallery. As you know, we hired a mover to bring up a number of paintings by Portland artists. We hung them and held receptions in the hope of meeting some of the local artists. They came running, you can be sure, most bringing along slides of their work. You can't tell much from slides, so we made arrangements to visit the studios of the most impressive ones. We were wined and dined, I'll tell you! I must have gained five pounds. Some of them are fabulous talents. They have no exclusive gallery contracts, so we can give each an exclusive show this fall. We sold four paintings at those receptions. The place looks just great! I hope we can all go up for the grand opening."

Bev, so full of Seattle, her gallery and her expectations, had little time or breath to inquire how her family had fared during her absence.

"By the way, since you were gone, I invited Deb Myers over for lunch on Sunday to give Scott some diversion. They got along fine."

"That's nice. Oh, did I tell you about Mary's run-in with the director of the gallery at the university? It was funny . . ."

"And also, I had about a week of traveling to do while you were gone. North along the coast. Didn't get to Seattle, though; I would have dropped in on you."

"Come up as soon as you can manage it. You'll just love it."

"One more thing. While I was gone the Seaside police department called to report that the cabin has been broken into. Since they talked to Scott I don't have any details. At any rate they want us to come to check things out and estimate the loss."

"Oh, dear! We didn't need this, just when everything is coming along so well! When shall we go there? It'll only take a couple of hours . . ."

"I'm up to my neck in work, Bev, after being away last week. Could you go and have a look around? Maybe tomorrow or the next day? Take the inventory along to see what if anything has been stolen."

"Sure, Steve. That's no problem. Mary's taking care of the gallery in Seattle, and I'm home to take it easy and get ready for Scott's birthday."

When Bev arrived at the beach house, two policemen were waiting to remove the seal and show her around.

"Be prepared for what you will see," one of them said. "It's pretty nasty. The whole house has been trashed."

Bev unlocked the front door and saw what looked like the scene of an earthquake. Turmoil and destruction lay everywhere. The windows were broken, and the living room looked as if it had been traversed by two opposing armies. Long slashes in the dark leather couches smiled mockingly over a floor covered with scattered pieces of smashed vases and cut glass. The VCR and hollow television set had been sent clear to the other end of the room where they leaned against a big mirror, which now reflected a distorted image of Bev amid big red paint splashes on the white rug. The kitchen was a mixture of broken dishes, cans, and bottles lying fragmented in a large puddle of salad oil and white and red wine. It was as if a gigantic angry arm had shoved everything off the shelves in one stroke. The bathroom had been assaulted with a sledge hammer which left gaping cracks in the toilet bowl and tub. The medicine cabinet lay on the floor, its cracked mirror still bearing the muddy imprint of a large boot.

Bev felt tears running down her cheeks as she contemplated the remains of her favorite place in the cabin, the master bedroom, where she used to rest on warm afternoons while Steve and Scott busied themselves with the boat. She saw her beautiful raised king-size waterbed with its velvet padded headboard and the ceiling-high lace pleated curtains all twisted, torn, slashed, and piled together in three inches of stale smelling water. Black and red paint had been sprayed over the walls in obscene patterns that represented, when Bev looked at them carefully, leering, dancing hunchbacks with long dripping erections. Bev muttered to herself as she walked through the house again, feeling the wind blowing through the broken windows. What kind of a nightmare was this? If she could only wake up in a sane world!

Next to the desk she stopped to examine a heap of crunched papers. A sense of order seemed to emanate from two photographs placed neatly, one next to the other, on top of the mess of torn papers and envelopes. It was as if they were intended to give meaning to the chaos that lay everywhere. Bev went down on her knees to look at the photographs. They were enlargements, one showing a naked man and a naked woman stepping out of the hot tub, smiling at each other. On the other one, which showed the same two people dressed and eating at the table that overlooks the shore, the faces could be clearly seen. Bev felt short of breath, and her heart began to beat wildly as she recognized Steve. Who could the other be? It is . . . it is that Deb Myers, that's who!

Bev thought her eyes were playing tricks on her.

"It can't be Steve. It must be someone else who looks like him."

She rubbed her hand against her forehead as if to erase the image from her mind.

"This is crazy. I must be dreaming." She held her eyes shut for a while to force the image to disappear. When she opened her eyes, the photographs were still there in their naked truth. She felt dizzy, and a strange weakness took over her body . . .

She opened her eyes and saw a smiling face above her.

"You are okay. You just fainted. It's all over."

What was all over? Bev recognized the two policemen, and then she understood.

She got up and walked out of the house in search of fresh air and peace of mind. She looked at the beach and the surf below.

"Do you want us to call somebody to take you into town?" a hoarse voice said from above her shoulder. She looked up into a policeman's big mustached face.

"No, thanks. I'm all right."

"You know, I've seen houses a lot worse than this, especially in cases of arson. There is nothing left but rubble. Your building is still solid."

"Here more is broken than you can see."

She remained on the steps while the two police cars left. Then she turned around, went in, walked through the living room and entered the bedroom. She bent down and picked up the photographs, which she carefully placed in her handbag. She locked the doors and drove off.

I'd better get myself a cup of coffee, she thought. She stopped at a roadside diner. It was toward the end of the afternoon and the parking lot was already half-full. She drove past some partly rusted cars and trailer trucks and parked next to a fancy new car.

The smell of fried food and burnt tomato sauce struck her nostrils as she entered the restaurant where loud chatter and smoke filled the air. She made her way to an empty booth next to a window and began to stare out at a dog sleeping in the sun. She picked up the menu and started to look at it. Two unshaven men in sleeveless undershirts and muddy boots stood close to her.

"Mind if we sit here?" one of them said as he sat opposite her. The other took a chair and sat at the end of the table. She looked at them in surprise and decided to keep on reading the menu. A waitress in a short black tight skirt and high heels came to take orders.

"Look at her sway!" one of them said whistling as she approached. She smiled broadly.

"You don't look so bad yourself," she said. "What'll you guys have?"

Soon she came back with hamburgers, fried onion rings, French fries, and beer.

Bev felt uncomfortable, sitting next to the two men, forced to smell their sweat and see their underarm hairs move back and forth in front of her face every time they reached over the table for salt or mustard.

"Pretty cozy, eh?" said the one across the table, revealing black spaces between his teeth, currently filled with ketchup. "Ain't this pretty much of a dump for you to be eating in? You slumming? I'm free after five." Both men laughed.

Bev rose without a word and headed for the door. She ran to her car, unlocked the door, climbed in, and began to sob as she drove toward Portland through the rush hour traffic.

It was evening when she arrived home. She turned on the lights in the living room, kicked off her shoes, and felt the plush rug under her bare feet. She sighed deeply.

"This is my world, my real world. I'm home, with my things, and, after all, my family."

She drew a hot herbal bath and spent an hour in the tub, listening to soft music, relaxing her aching muscles and overwrought nerves. As she dried her body and changed into a silk nightgown, she wondered where Steve could be. She went into the kitchen, fixed herself hot chocolate and toast and glanced at a note on the refrigerator door: "Missed you for dinner; went back to the office. See you in the morning. Love, Steve." Maybe it is better this way. I am not strong enough yet to handle this. She wasn't even strong enough to go to Scott's room and greet him.

When Bev got up the next morning, Steve had already left.

Steve opened the front door late that evening. Bev was lying on the couch with a book in her hands, keeping her eyes on the door and her ears on the driveway. Melissa once again had decided to spend the evening out. Scott and Diane were off somewhere.

It will be best to confront him with the truth right away, while everybody is gone. Maybe he will repent and ask to be forgiven. Then life will be normal again. After all, he has never done anything like this before. It really isn't like him at all.

To Bev's surprise, Steve was calm, relaxed, and controlled, as she had always known him to be. There were no signs of anxiety or guilt; he looked at her no more or less than he always did.

Let him have his dinner first. Then when we retire to the bedroom all hell will break loose.

Steve fixed himself a drink while Bev heated something to eat. He ate, cheerfully, without hurrying. He wanted to watch the late news before retiring, which was unusual for him. Bev agreed to join him. They sat together on the couch and even joked occasionally while the TV screen displayed its usual flashing menu of international terrorism and local urban violence.

It was midnight before Bev and Steve went into the master bedroom. The lights are dimmed, and fresh pink sheets smelling of fabric softener bring a sense of peace and continuity to the room. Steve is standing on his side of the bed, Bev on hers.

"As you know, I went to the beach house."

"Yes, that was yesterday, wasn't it?"

"Yes."

"How did it look."

"Awful, simply awful!"

"I talked to Jones at the insurance company. Somebody there will file a report."

He shows no special concern or distress. He is used to taking things in stride; life is too full of stress anyhow.

"The insurance forms were in the mail today."

"I'll fill them out this week."

"Steve, I need to talk to you about something really important."

"What's that?"

"Well . . . I was really upset at the beach house . . ."

"Of course you were; it must have been a real shock."

"There was a photograph there."

"A photograph?"

"Yes, of you and Deb Myers!" She takes a picture from the top of a chest of drawers and throws it across the bed at him. It falls next to his feet. Picking it up, he stares at it for some seconds. His face grows pale.

"Aren't you going to say something?"

He looks at her and then says, softly: "I've been meaning to talk to you about this for some time."

"For some time? How long?"

"I don't know what that picture is all about. But that's neither here nor there. The fact is that I want to move out and live with Deb."

"Are you out of your mind? Do you think you can walk out of our marriage just like that?"

He remains silent, staring at her. His silence makes her even more enraged. She turns, picks up a Venetian glass paperweight, under which she had placed the incriminating photograph, and without thinking, throws it with all her force at Steve's head.

He ducks, and the heavy glass strikes the floor-to-ceiling mirror behind him with an ominous crunching sound. Large cracks spread from the center outward in all directions. Steve leaves the room.

Bev sees a fragmented image of herself and all her possessions.

A muggy morning. It felt warmer than it actually was. Bev disliked the stress the weather always seems to bring in August with its long stretches of hot, humid days.

Bev finished her last sip of coffee, picked up the phone when it rang.

"Hello. Oh! Hi, Mary. Where are you?"

". . ."

"I'm so glad you came down. I need to talk to you badly, Mary. We may have to postpone the grand opening. Can we get together for lunch today?"

" . . ."

"Yes, please cancel it and join me at The Gables."

The restaurant was crowded when Bev and Mary arrived. They had to wait an hour for a table, so they went to the bar, found a quiet table in a corner, and ordered drinks.

"You look pretty strung out, Bev. What's up?"

"I feel just miserable. Life is giving me a rotten deal right now."

"How rotten is rotten?"

"Yesterday I had to go to Seaside to check out the beach house which had been vandalized."

"When? Was anything taken?"

"Well . . . The house looked awful, an utter mess . . . the windows and mirrors were broken, the furniture was smashed, and there was spray paint all over."

"I'm so sorry, Bev. But you're insured, aren't you?"

"Of course. The insurance will take care of everything. But there's something else . . ." Bev chokes up and starts to cry.

"What is it? Must have been pretty bad." Mary takes Bev's hand.

"At the beach house I found some photographs. One shows two people coming out of our hot tub, naked. Can you believe it? It was Steve and one of his ex-clients!"

"What? Are you sure?"

"Yes. I brought the photograph. Here it is!" She takes it out of her handbag and hands it to Mary.

"Wow! Who could have taken the picture?"

"No idea. It was on the floor with another just like it."

"So Steve and this woman take hot-tub baths together, or so it seems."

"But they are having an affair, obviously. I confronted Steve, and he didn't deny it. He just said he wanted to move in with Deb."

"Who?"

"Deb. That's her name, the one in the picture."

"Move in with her?"

"Yes. Move in with her, and all the rest."

"Sticky business."

"I was demolished. Steve never did anything like that in all our married life . . . he was always the devoted husband."

"What can I say, Bev? I feel terribly sorry, of course."

Bev starts sobbing. "Why would he want to give up our beautiful home, our social life?"

"A mid-life crisis, maybe? How old is he?"

"Forty-seven."

"Probably just a fling, and he will come to his senses in a week or so."

"I don't know . . . I hope so . . . He's my whole life. Ever since Scott's accident, my life has revolved around the two of them. There is the gallery, but that is not a vocation, it's just a career."

"I know how devoted you are to your home and family."

"Why would Steve do something like this to me? What is he looking for in her?"

"Did you ask him?"

"No. We really haven't had time to talk. I just blew up."

"Something tells me a long talk would be helpful."

"I intend to try. But I know I will never give him up. I can't live without him." Bev is still crying.

"How about an open marriage? It is very fashionable, you know. The best families do it. That's what Milt and I have."

"I didn't know that."

"You weren't looking. We never kept it a secret."

"But I know I would never want to share him, either."

"It's a way of keeping together."

"Yes, that's true but . . ."

"How has your marriage been lately? You know what I mean, in bed."

"Come to think of it, it hasn't been much to brag about for a couple of years. We're like partners, roommates. Not much sex any more. We've both lost interest."

"That may be the problem. But Deb doesn't look all that sexy, either. I mean, you know. What does Steve see in her?"

"I wish I knew. She's pretty much involved in social causes, maybe that's it."

"Nonsense! No man loves a woman because she cares for the poor."

"Steve was into that social responsibility stuff when we were in college, going to demonstrations and writing manifestos. That's why I fell for him; he was intense, and I admired him immensely. But after Scott's accident I saw through that stuff and got busy with things that mattered, real-life things like special education and schools and taxes."

"Then he's a leftover from the sixties. But you're right that he is too old for that kind of nonsense."

Bev looks at Mary, her eyes wide open. She suddenly sees the photograph again on the table and begins to cry once more.

"There is still time, Bev. You can do a lot with your life, with him or without him."

Bev keeps on looking at Mary, tears rolling down her cheeks.

Mary takes her hand. "I never told you about my divorce, did I, Bev? It was awful, but not half as bad as when later someone who was very dear left me. I wandered around town like a zombie until I looked seriously down at the river one night, then I decided that it represented not death, but life. When the water flows around a bend or through narrows, it flows a little more frantically, but it keeps on. People can learn from looking at the river. Of course there are floods, and droughts, and . . . engineers build dams . . ."

"Oh, Mary, what can I do now?"

When Steve came home that evening Bev was waiting for him. She had sent Scott and Diane to a play, put on a new green dress, and prepared a special meal for two, with candles. After dinner she said she wanted to talk about Deb. They sat at the table, the gentle light still reflecting on their faces.

"When did this all start? This thing between you and Deb."

Steve tried to think back. "When I first saw her, I guess. I felt sorry for her in her plight. She was different from other clients, interested in things beyond herself."

"Did she talk about changing society, achieving great things, being a champion for the poor?"

"No. She doesn't talk like that. She gets involved in small things, where she can make a difference."

"Yes. I can hear her saying you should get involved in changing the world, too. Things like 'we're all in this together,' or 'everybody shares the guilt,' and so on and so forth."

Steve didn't answer.

"Why didn't you tell me earlier? . . . About this involvement."

"I don't know. I guess it just happened without my noticing it. All of a sudden it was there."

"But when the affair got far enough along that you couldn't help noticing it, why didn't you say something then?"

"I didn't want to hurt you."

"Hurt me! Do you realize what you are saying? Let me tell you that you have hurt me terribly!"

Steve looked at Bev with an expression of grief in his face. He was turning around to leave when Bev stretched out her arms and held him back.

"Steve! I can't let you go. I can't live without you. I need you! Don't leave me!"

Later he called Deb and explained that he wouldn't be able to see her for a couple of days and that there were many difficulties to iron out before he could begin a new life with her.

DEB WAS STILL in bed when she heard a knock at the door. She hesitated before opening. A young man was waiting with a large bouquet of red roses and an envelope. She tore it open and read:

"My dear love. Sorry I was so brief on the phone last night. Bev was in the room sobbing. I'll be at your place early tonight. Love you, Steve."

She held the flowers and the note against her breast, closed her eyes, and let the strong perfume of roses go through her body. It was as if his arms were holding her.

The sun was still bright in the sky when Steve arrived. He glanced at the red roses in a vase above the fireplace and smiled. He bent one off its stem and placed it in the opening of Deb's blouse. He kissed her lips, running through her hair with his hand. Then he kissed her cheeks, her eyes, and her neck, down to where the single rose was resting. As he loosened her blouse the rose fell to the floor. They followed its lead, at first kneeling while she took off his lawyer's jacket, tie, and shirt, then sitting while he removed her blouse and loosened her skirt.

Deb suddenly stood up and went to lock the door. "Just a precaution. I'm getting superstitious."

Walking back to him she kicked off her shoes and skirt, kneeled again, undid his belt, zipped down his fly. When they were both naked Steve placed the rose on Deb's belly button and began making love seriously with his hands, his lips, his whole body, and Deb reentered her dream of being pervaded by ecstasy and passion, of taking leave of the world. Coming through the windows, still without curtains, the late afternoon sun settled on their bodies as they melted into each other in a single current of pleasure that passed rapidly back and forth between them. When Deb opened her eyes, she saw Steve's face illuminated by the colors of the evening.

Later Deb went into the bedroom and emerged wearing a raspberry silk dress. They sat on the balcony. Steve poured champagne from the bottle he had brought, and they sipped slowly, watching the rich shifting reds and oranges of the sunset. The silent river grew pale as it rolled into the twilight toward the sea, and soon the last rays of the sun disappeared, reflected on the red flank of Mt. Hood. Darkness set in.

Steve called for a reservation at a nearby restaurant, and, taking two roses, offered Deb his arm as they went out the door.

Steve could see the color of Deb's face through the flickering light from the candle on the table. She looked peaceful and loving. It wasn't easy to break the beauty of the moment and talk about Bev. He reached across the table to take Deb's hand.

"It you want to tell me about Bev and last night go ahead. But I can wait, too, if this isn't the right time for you."

"No time is right for that when I'm with you. Just remember how much I love you, always. If you do I'll be able to talk about it."

"Here, I'll help. You talked to Bev last night."

"Thanks. I don't know which is harder, talking to her last night or to you now. She cried and sobbed all the time."

"At least I won't do that. What did you tell her?"

"That you and I are in love and that I want to live with you."

"That sounds reasonable."

"It didn't to her, though. She's finding it difficult to understand that changes are occurring. At first she's incredulous, then she's furious, and then tenacious, declaring she'll never let me go, under any circumstances."

"Maybe she is going through stages, like denial, and will eventually come around to accept the inevitable."

"I hope so. But at he stage she is in now I am completely tied. There is no way I can even make a suggestion, much less make a move."

"Like moving to my place? Or some other place for us both?"

"It will be a couple of weeks at least before she can face the facts with any kind of calm. I haven't the slightest idea what mood she will be in when I go home tonight, for instance."

"That's a disappointment, Steve, since I was so hoping we could be together right away. Then again, I don't want to put you through additional stress by insisting on anything. I can wait, Steve, until you think the ice is thick enough for us to venture out on it, safely."

He poured himself more wine and drank.

"How did you broach the subject?"

"I didn't. It broached itself. Here's how. You remember, don't you, that our beach house was vandalized? It was while you and I were up in Washington State. Bev went over to check it out two days ago. Nothing was stolen; it was destruction for destruction's sake, so to speak. But the really scary thing is that—you won't believe this—prominently displayed on a pile of broken glass and torn sheets in the bedroom were a couple of photographs of you and me coming out of the hot tub, naked of course. This is what Bev found in the midst of all the destruction, and last night she threw them in my face. Without those pictures, she wouldn't have suspected a thing."

"None of this makes any sense How could that have happened?"

"I haven't the faintest idea. Somebody took those pictures of us, and there is no clue who could have done it. The police and the investigators don't know anything about the photographs. They still suspect teenage marauders with nothing better to do.

But it looks to me as though the destruction was done for the sole purpose of exposing our relationship. I expect someone will be after me with a demand for blackmail soon. You can see why we have to be careful just now."

Deb looked at Steve. He seemed lost in some kind of labyrinth, unable to think his way out of an impossible situation.

"Steve, this may sound awful, but maybe it is the best thing that could have happened. Bev knows, and that means we can start our life together sooner. I want to so badly!"

"We will, Deb, we will," he said as he caressed her hand. "In a week or two, a month at the most, I promise. I'll figure something out."

He gazed into her eyes. It must have been a long, profound gaze, the kind meant to communicate feelings and hopes which, put into words, might have sounded confused and empty.

"I love you, Deb," are the words he managed to say.

"I love you, Steve," she whispered back.

The waiter came to remove the empty plates and brought dessert. They left the restaurant and walked slowly back to Deb's apartment. Steve went briefly inside and kissed her goodnight. He then drove home to Lake Oswego.

Steve parked his Jaguar next to the house. The windows were dark, except for Scott's room. There was time enough for a walk around the lake before going in and facing reality, which was bound to be difficult. He thought he heard the sound of animals moving in the bushes. Two ducks were still swimming in the water, and Steve observed their rippled wakes spreading behind them in ever larger intercepting triangles as the ducks gently progressed in the quietness of the night.

He started along a path that followed the shore. He knew the way well and was able to walk while his mind wandered through corridors of the past and empty yet obscure passageways to come. The pervading quietness, intensified by the steady sound of frogs hiding around the lake's edge, and the clarity of the moonlight reflecting on the surface of the water helped him delve deeper into himself and discover there something like honesty which, like a shy nocturnal animal, ventures forth from the shade when no predator is watching.

How could he have promised Deb just now that they would be free to live together in a week or two, that he would "figure something out"? Had he the slightest idea, really, where to start? It was like trying to figure out how to travel due north and south at the same time. If only he were two people! On the one hand Steve the First, the dutiful husband and father, who can't bear to hurt anyone let alone the two people for whom he has so long striven to make life tolerable, the skillful attorney who sticks with a meaningless job and colleagues. Then in a clash of thunder, Steve the Second would break free, the one walking down a midnight path, still inhaling the scent of Deb's skin, who would chuck everything—wife, invalid child, home, profession, routine—to satisfy his heart and senses in an open future. I might just as well strip off my clothes, dive into this lake, and seek my new life on the other side, wet and naked!

What do I want? To be with Deb, of course! He stumbled on a root sticking out of the path and nearly fell into the water. But if I end up staying to take care of my family, then I suppose that is what I really want. He brushed a spiderweb mixed with sweat from his face. He remembered how Deb had told him, talking about her adventures in Brazil, that you can't live "without taking risks." Either way, I'm risking something. I'll feel guilty if I go off with her, and if I don't I'll feel even more guilty. Bev and Scott are taken care of, so I'm only risking myself and my cherished sense of decency—do the right thing by others, live up to my commitment, and so on. Which one will be sacrificed, Steve the First or the Second? Which is more essential? A dog barked at him from somewhere in the woods.

Steve continued walking in the night, groping through the obscure ravines where the moonlight did not penetrate, trying to reason in a straight line while following a twisting and circular path. Twice he stopped to catch the breath he had held during a particularly tortuous dialectic. As he drew near his home, having circled the lake, he noticed that a full moon was shining down on him, and he discovered, to his honest surprise, that he had already decided earlier that day, without knowing it, to leave, to live with Deb, and that he had just been exhausting himself finding reasons for doing so. He felt refreshed.

He also felt jittery. As he approached the house he could have sworn he saw the shadow of a person disappear into the trees toward the road.

Located halfway between the county dump and a slough filled with rotting algae there is a private rifle range, where the next afternoon Ralph and Darryl have been practicing sharpshooting. They have been there in the sun for three hours, and they are cleaning their guns before going to a gravel pit to take a swim in one of the ponds

"Hey, come on, Darryl, what's it with you and the gal by the hot tub? You say she's your woman, but there in the picture she's with the old guy, coming out of the hot water and making for bed. I don't get it. Is he her dad or something? What's going on?"

"I'll tell you, but keep it to yourself. Cause it ain't funny. She's a friend of my mom's, believe it or not. Not that they have anything in common. She's a ritzy dame, and you know my mom! But they're friends anyways. They work together, talk, and tell each other things, you know, woman's crap. The thing is, the woman's beautiful, I mean, beautiful! Small boobs, you hardly know they're there, but you can see they're there without really seeing them, and they are sort of like . . . I don't know, like if you talk too loud they'll break into a thousand pieces. And she's got these eyes, you know what I mean, sweet eyes that never seen anything nasty like we seen all the time; and they look like it's too bad we are such slime balls. They sort of say she's never hated nobody, like she never even thought nothing nasty."

"Christ! You're really screwed up. I wouldn't have thought you'd go for a babe like that. You should take a cold shower or something. Go see a shrink. Or just jack off a couple of times, that'll get your mind off that broad!"

"It ain't what you think. You'll get it some day too, maybe, or maybe not. Depends. No way I can shake it, so I'm not trying. I'm just making arrangements that I lay her some day; that's all I care about. But it ain't going to be easy. Mom knows I'm panting for her, and Deb knows, too. She won't come to our place no more to see Mom unless I'm not home. You know! I musta said something the last time she was there, because she took off like a bat outta hell and Mom's been pissed ever since, saying if I ever touch Deb she'll have the whole goddamn army and marines after me. What the fuck? All I told her was she had a cute ass and we should get together and screw. Now that's a nice compliment, ain't it? Guess she didn't think so. And tonight Deb's coming to work with Mom and I have to stay away until midnight, for Christ sake! And it's my last chance, because Mom says she's not coming back because of me and my bad manners. What a pile of crap!"

"And you're gonna actually stay away like your mom says?"

"What can I do? If I'm there Deb won't come in. If I show up Mom calls the police and I'm locked up again."

"That's the trouble with messing around with women. Whatever you do is wrong, whether you slap 'em or treat 'em nice, and it's always your fault. But you have to think different. Remember what I'm telling you; it ain't never your fault, it's always theirs. They dig that too, if you show you don't give a shit about them. If they don't want what you got, tough balls! You go give it to another babe."

"Trouble with you, Ralph, is you don't know what the fuck you're talking about. Try usin' your head for once. But you sorta give me an idea. Tell me some more. What can I do to lay Deb tonight? I can't wait no longer."

"Well you got a problem I don't. When I want someone, I just sit there in front of her where she can see me and I don't even look at her. Soon she starts asking what I want. With you it's different. Look in a mirror some day. You ain't all that handsome. You'd make a dame shrivel up just from looking at you. So you gotta use another way, by getting them when they aren't looking, if you know what I mean."

"I don't, so you better explain quick. I ain't got all afternoon."

"Here's what I'd do. They're in there at night doing their work or whatever. You show up, kick your mom's ass until she leaves and then grab the dame, strip her, and lay her then and there. She'll never leave after that hero stuff."

"You're outta your friggin' mind. Mom will go to her boyfriend's downstairs and call the police, for sure!"

"Tie her up or lock her somewhere, put a gag on her if she yells."

"Got it! The bathroom! Lend me a hammer, and I'll nail the sliding bathroom door shut for good; she can scream the paint off the walls and no one will hear. In the meantime Deb's cowering in the corner, scared shitless of what I'm gonna do. First I'll try to talk her into doing it my way, real nice and easy. Or do I just grab her an' rape her, screaming and bawling herself sick? I never done that before. It's always been they wanted it, or we're all stoned, and then it's easy. The place is going to be noisy with them both screaming."

"Stuff toilet paper in your ears. I think you got it figured out. Let's get a burger and a couple of beers to put you in the mood. You can call me in the morning."

Deb arrived a few minutes before seven. She felt a bit nervous, going back to Glenda's after what Darryl had done the last time. But Glenda's place had everything they needed to finish their project, which they intended to do that night, and Glenda had promised that Darryl would be gone. Even Liz wouldn't be there to interrupt their work. They started right away, Deb holding the material while Glenda worked the sewing machine.

"I don't really know what got into Darryl. But don't worry, he won't be around, I can promise you that."

"He really frightened me. After all I've been through, I don't need him to go after me again. And I was starting to like him. He seemed quite sincere and almost gentle, despite his looks."

"He wouldn't do anything to you anyway, because I can't help thinking that deep down he's a good boy and wouldn't hurt a fly. He just looks fierce. I've seen lots who are like that. They make a big racket, but they're like sheep when you tell them to knock it off. Darryl's like that."

"I hope you are right. But I'm not going to take chances. Life in the city is dangerous enough without looking for more trouble. At least it is quiet tonight, Glenda. We can concentrate and maybe finish before it is too late."

When it was dark Darryl crept up the concrete stairs outside, holding his boots and a hammer in his hands. He could feel the three inch nails scratching his thigh through his pocket. It sounded as though Glenda and Deb had forgotten him, absorbed in their work, hardly exchanging more than a few words. He waited at the door and listened to the whirring of the sewing machine and the occasional noises indicating human presence within. Having rehearsed in his mind the motions he would perform, he knew that he would have to act fast to pull this one off.

Without uttering a word, he threw the door open, slammed it shut with his foot, glared at Deb and picking up his protesting mother, carried her to the bathroom. He slid the door shut and nailed it to the floor. Deb sat terrified, unable to move. Glenda pounded at the door, screaming for help.

"Get your ass over on that couch. Quick. Don't waste no time. You'll like it, Deb! Really!"

"Darryl! Come to your senses!" Deb shouted. "You can't do this to your mother or to me, it's criminal, and you'll only get into trouble. You're a fine guy, Darryl, big, strong. Show me that you are human. Let your mother out, now!"

"You heard what I said. Old Darryl gets what he wants. No broad is going to tell me what to do. Git over there and strip!"

As she doesn't move, he pushes a chair out of his way to reach her, picks her up, carries her kicking and scratching over to the couch, throws her down, holds her still, and starts to cover her face and neck with kisses. Glenda is still screaming, and the sound of running water is heard from the bathroom. Deb tries to scream, but Darryl places one large hand over her mouth as he begins to tear her blouse with the other. He reaches down to open the fly of her jeans. She is wearing a belt, which takes two hands to open, especially since she is kicking and pushing. He puts his knee on her chest to hold her still while he labors to pull her jeans down. They are tight and don't budge. Glenda is still screaming, and water is coming under the bathroom door. Darryl shifts his tactics. He tries the loving approach, slobbering over her arms and neck with mouth and tongue, murmuring: "Deb, come to me. I love you. I gotta have you. Take off them fucking pants!" He comes down with all his weight—legs, arms, head, torso, everything—on top of her. With that, the front foot at the head of the couch breaks, toppling Darryl on to the floor, while Deb barely avoids falling after him. He changes strategy once again. He stands up, watching her as she stares at him wide-eyed with fear, and with deliberation unbuttons his overalls at the shoulders and lets them fall to his waist, then pushes them and his shorts down to his ankles, in preparation for the last plunge onto Deb.

"What in tarnation is going on here?" It is the voice of Mr. Harding, the downstairs neighbor and new friend of Glenda's. He has forced the front door open with his shoulders and heads for the bathroom. "Your mom is flooding the frigging place. We are soaked down below. Here I am sitting on the can enjoying the comics and suddenly the Niagara Falls is coming down over my head through the crack that stupid landlord never fixed.

Second time that happened, Glenda knows . . . Well ain't you pretty there!" he adds, catching sight of Darryl pulling his overalls up to cover his butt. "I'll be damned. The bathroom door is nailed shut! Who done that?"

"Get out of here, asshole!" Darryl yells, going toward the intruder with the hammer. "None of your fucking business. I'll call the police."

Mr. Harding kicks the nails out from the bathroom door, and Glenda rushes out.

"Grab him, Harding. He's dangerous. Where's Deb?"

Deb has already ducked out the door and is running down the street. Darryl is still trying to button his overalls with one hand while menacing Harding with the hammer in the other. The neighbor, who weighs even more than Darryl, wrenches away the hammer, sets his adversary down on the broken couch, and turns to Glenda.

"You know as well as I do that the floor leaks. What were you doing in there, Glenda? Taking swimming lessons? Did you nail the door for privacy?"

"No. Darryl did. Can't explain now. Watch him while I call the police. Don't let him get away!"

In the meantime Darryl has escaped into the same bathroom and locked the door.

"Leave him there. There's no window he can escape through. Just don't let him out of the apartment."

"He can't get no water. I turned off your meter before coming up here."

The apartment is suddenly quiet. Glenda starts mopping up the water that has escaped from the bathroom, and Harding looks at the couch leg to see if it can be repaired.

"That'll be easy; be right back. I'm going to get some glue."

"No, please don't leave now. I'm afraid something might happen with Darryl. I have the feeling I'm going to need you."

"At your service, neighbor. But you look like you just seen a ghost. You better drink some water instead of mopping it."

There is no sound from the bathroom.

"I wonder what he's doing in there. As soon as Deb has time to get home, I'll call her and find out what happened."

The phone rang. It is Deb.

"Oh, okay I guess. That was a real mess wasn't it. What did he do to you? Are you okay?"

". . ."

"Oh, my God! Really?"

". . ."

"Thank heavens! So he tried to rape you! He must have learned that in prison; never did anything like that before."

". . ."

"You must be all in. Take a tranquilizer. Did he ruin your clothes? I can fix them, of course."

". . ."

"Okay, Deb. Take it easy. I can understand. I'll try to do something with him now. Harding's here to help, so you don't have to worry. Call me tomorrow. Bye."

"You got your share of problems, don't you, Glenda? What with Liz and then your nieces who bug you for help and then cuss you out."

A long moan comes through the closed bathroom door. Glenda goes to it and knocks.

"Darryl! Do you hear me? Unlock the door! Deb's gone and you're all right, so come out and tell me your side of the story."

She is answered by another moan.

"I'll get 'im out," Harding says as he kicks the door with his boot. The sliding door does not respond to his blow.

"Got any tools?"

"Under the sink."

He takes out a crowbar and forces the door open. Darryl is sitting fully dressed on the toilet; his arms hang to his sides dripping with blood. His face is pale, without expression.

"Oh, my God! Darryl, what did you do?"

"This is what he done," says Harding as he picks up a large fishhook from the floor and shows it to Glenda.

She slaps Darryl's cheeks to bring him to, rolls back a shirt sleeve and sees a crooked slit extending on the inside of his arm from his shoulder almost down to his wrist.

"Don't worry," Darryl says in a weaker than usual voice. I'm okay; I just wanna be left alone. Where's Deb?"

"Forget her. It's you we have to take care of, right now. Stand up!"

She tears off the sleeve, turns on the faucet for water to bathe the wound. A gurgling sound comes up from the depths of the building. No water.

"I'll go and turn it on," Harding says. "He's not going nowhere in his condition."

Glenda goes to the living room and phones 911, giving her name and address.

"Please send an officer right away. My son has gone off his rocker and is menacing people with a hammer. He has just cut his arms and I'm afraid for him and for us. See if you can send Officer Bill Jones. He knows us, yea, and he can handle big guys."

The water returns. Glenda bathes the wounds with the help of Liz, who has just come home, and lays a light bandage on Darryl's arms. They help him to his bed. Liz, nearly uncontrollable from grief and fear, begins to sob and ask questions at the same time. No one can understand what she is saying. When she sees a cop come in the door, her hysteria knows no bounds. Glenda has to take care of everybody at once.

When Liz finally calms down, Glenda turns to the new arrival.

"I'm glad it's you, Bill. You're used to this kind of thing."

"If it's not this it's something else. What's up?"

"It's Darryl. He's been sorta strange since he got home. So tonight he locks me in the bathroom and tries to rape a friend of mine; then he shuts himself in there and slits his arms with a fishhook. That enough for you?"

"They called me off a big accident on 405, three cars and a

semi. I don't know if the sirens or Liz's howling is worse. What do you want me to do?"

"Take Darryl to the hospital. He'll need stitches, and I want him to cool off there and get evaluated by a shrink, like they did for Mike Klauser last month."

"Where is he?"

"Here!" Darryl says, coming out of his room, dressed in a black suit coat, a shirt and red tie, and a clean pair of slacks. His hair is combed and he shows no sign of blood. "What's all the fuss about? Don't pay no attention to her," motioning to his mother. "She makes even less sense than her," pointing to Liz, still sobbing, quietly now. "You don't need to stick around. Better get back to that accident. It sounds real bad. I'll go with you." His speech is measured, controlled.

"Since Glenda called, I gotta look at you. Where did you say it was?"

"Both arms."

"I tell you there's nothing wrong. I ain't done nothing to nobody!"

"Darryl, take off your goddamn jacket and show 'im. If you didn't do nothin', he can't see nothin' either, so what'ya fraid of?" Harding breaks in.

"That's right. Roll up your sleeve and let us peek . . . Farther, please!"

Blood starts to drip down his wrist.

"Okay, Glenda, we need to call an ambulance. He's bleeding like a stuck pig, and he'll mess up my squad car."

"How about I take him in my car and you lead with a siren and flashing lights. Better have another squad follow, like when we took Liz in when she was raped."

"That would be okay. I'll call in. Have your friend in the back seat to control him if he needs it."

Soon the caravan leaves with Glenda's tiny car sandwiched between two police cars with lights flashing in the night. The other traffic waits respectfully as they speed through the stop lights on their way to the hospital.

It took a good two hours at the emergency department for Darryl to receive stitches up and down his arms. Glenda had to fill out countless forms and questionnaires. When she could finally ask the receptionist about having her son spend the night in the psychiatric ward and take tests to see if he should stay locked up for a while, she was told that there was no room in the ward. She should take him home and give him "a sedative, here's a prescription; he will be fine in a day or two."

As he walked out to the car behind Harding and Glenda, Darryl tossed the prescription and the invoice into a trash bin.

DARRYL REMAINED IN his room for a couple of days. His mother heard him rolling over in his bed and occasionally moan.

"Going to look for another job; donno when I'll be back," he told her when he finally came out of his room and headed for the door.

"How's your arm? You feel okay?"

"I'm great! Never felt better in my life. Just leave me alone, for crap's sake."

He walked up 18th Avenue and entered a coffee and doughnut shop with tables next to the window.

"What'll it be, Darryl? Ain't seen you for a while."

"Make that a coffee and one of them sweet rolls, maybe two. Been busy, I'll tell ya."

"Yea, I figured. Here you go. That'll be one dollar even."

Darryl carried the steaming mug and the rolls to the farthest table, picking up a newspaper on his way. He held the newspaper in front of his eyes without reading while he poured and stirred three spoonfuls of sugar into the mug.

"Fucking life! Gotta do something with it. Ain't getting nowheres this way."

The establishment's only waitress came up to ask him what it was he wanted.

"Nothing, babe. Just talking to myself."

"Don't pay no attention to him. He's just weird; aint ya,

Darryl?" the man behind the counter said, pointing an index finger to his temple.

They all think I'm crazy now, Darryl said to himself. Just as well. If I flip an' screw things up I can plead insanity. All I gotta do is forget that Deb dame. She's nothing but trouble, that's what. No problem. I'll find somebody who likes to screw and don't make no big deal out of it and hasn't got a lawyer she's panting after. And she ain't going to be no friend of Mom's, neither; they won't be making any goddamn curtains together, messing up my life. That's what loused it up with Deb, for sure: Mom putting her big foot in it all the time, trying to be nice to everybody. If it hadn't a been for her, me and Deb would be on our way to Reno or something right now instead of me feeling like my arms are on fire and muttering like a madman in this stupid joint.

Better shove. Like: get my life in order. Here goes!

With that project in mind Darryl walked out, jaywalked across the street, and entered one of the large public parking buildings made of concrete columns and slabs, where pigeons fly in and out through the open spaces and you can hear horns and sirens from the street below. The third floor should be already full, and it's too early for people to return from shopping. Darryl walks slowly along a row of parked cars looking for a partly open window or a lock button that isn't depressed. He has a clothes hanger in his pocket, but it will be easier if he doesn't have to pry open a window. Just for kicks he tries a few door handles. Nothing. He climbs the stairs to the fourth floor. The only movement comes from a car cruising back and forth to find an open space. Darryl walks more slowly now, sensing that he is close to a vulnerable Japanese compact or German import. There! An 86 Chev with a back window rolled two inches down. He can barely fit his hand into the opening without rubbing his stitches against the top of the glass. Suddenly an angry barking and snarling makes him leap back; a German shepherd is clawing at the opening to get at him.

I didn't want that one anyways. Since I'm not paying for it I can afford something more classy. It's old enough I'd probably have to jump it to get it started. And I don't need the dog, neither. He probably smells fresh blood and is ready for chow, something like my raw arms to gnaw on.

He continues walking, now going up the other aisle.

A 92 Mazda lies concealed between a VW van and a F250 pickup, obviously unlocked and waiting for him. He glances around; no one is nearby, no dog sleeping in the back seat. The door responds easily to his grasp and opens, allowing him to enter the intimacy of the dark vinyl seats, dials, wheel, and controls. He sits down, keeping the door ajar while he manipulates the wires behind the ignition. Pulling two wires loose, he ties the ends together, and soon the engine obeys his command to start. It idles quietly while he glances a final time to see that no one is approaching. He backs out; the car jerks a few times as if unused to being hurried, and then accepts its new driver. Darryl pays $3.50 at the exit.

"It's a bargain, when you think of it."

He drives over a bridge and heads south to Ralph's place in Milwaukie. That's his place, one of those cabins behind the filling station. Must have been an old motel; some day it'll get cleared out and they'll build a bowling alley. He rings at the door for a long time. Someone's gotta be here because a Pinto's parked in front. Finally Linda comes to the door, looking half asleep under her curlers and real pissed.

"What d'ya want? Oh! Hi, Darryl! It's you, ain't it? Ralph's not around. He's flying today and then he's going to see his kids. Won't be back for a couple of days. Ya got a cigarette? C'mon in." Her voice sounded like layers of gravel rubbing together.

"Here! Take these," he said handing her a half-empty pack. "Just tell me where he is and how I get there."

"It's somewhere on the highway between Sandy and Oregon City. Just drive around those farms down there; you'll see his plane easy. Sure you don't want some coffee?"

Half an hour later Darryl could see from the road a small plane passing back and forth above a field, just missing the power lines at each end, spewing out a yellow, foul-smelling mist over the vegetation. After another half hour, the plane landed to reload. Darryl walked slowly toward the refueling area and called over to Ralph.

"Wanna go up for a ride? Plenty of room. Keep a hand free to hold your nose. You don't wanna inhale this stuff!"

"The car's hot. I gotta get rid of it. Just tell me where I can get some crank."

"Go to my place. Tell Linda I said to give you a couple of rocks. Enough to keep you going for a while. If she acts dumb tell her they're stashed behind the toilet tank, in the wall. There's enough if she hasn't used it after I left this morning."

"How long will she be there? It'll take me a while."

"Aw, she's not going nowheres before the soaps are over. Wanna do me a favor, Darryl? Just keep this somewhere for when I get back."

He walked to his Mustang, unlocked the trunk, and took out a paper bag. Darryl knew right away that it was a pistol from the weight and the cool metallic feel.

"Tonight I'm off to Klamath Falls to visit the girls, that's where they are now. I don't want this around when I'm there. It wouldn't take them ten minutes to snoop through my stuff and find it; then they'd tell their mom what they found in daddy's suitcase and I'd be fried."

"You know I'm not supposed to have none of them things around. It would be just my luck to get caught with yours on me; then I'd be fried worse than you ever was. I'll take it to Linda and leave it there."

"The parole board won't search you out if they haven't yet. They got too much to do keeping sex offenders from hanging around schools. The reason you gotta take it is because Linda shouldn't have it in the house in case she gets a depression when I'm gone. You can bet your life's savings that's what she'll have.

Just put it under the seat or something. Don't show it to Asco; he could blab."

"Can I use it for target practice at the range? It would give me something to do."

"You'll need ammo. Go to Jake's, off I-205 on 82nd St. Talk to Jake himself; tell him you know me and it's for my gun. He don't ask questions."

Darryl drove back to Milwaukie, bought a six-pack and a carton of cigarettes for Linda, and, after receiving what he wanted from her, left her in front of the television with a can of beer in her hand. Back in Portland he ditched the Mazda behind a factory on 81st Street, walked into a record store, and while the owner looked for a used CD he had requested he quietly emptied the cash register into his pocket and left. He walked toward the corner; Jake's was only a block away.

"Two second-hand ones like that just came in," Jake told him. "This one is a little worn on the handle, so I can make you a good deal. See, it's clean inside; hardly been used. Belonged to an old lady for protection."

"How do old ladies manage to wear out the handle when they keep it in their underwear drawer all the time?"

"Beats me. I didn't ask the guy that brought it in."

"He probably shot his old grandmother and took her cash to buy dope. How much you want for it?"

"Where did I put the tag? Here!" he said, handing Darryl a greasy piece of torn cardboard. "You can deduct 25% for being Ralph's friend."

Darryl knew he had at least that amount loose in his pocket. "Go for it."

"Got your license here? Otherwise let me see your ODL, and I'll issue you one."

Darryl had neither.

"It's for Ralph I'm buying this. Make the bill of sale to him. You have his registration number on his last receipt."

"How will I know he gets the gun?"

"He'll call you in a couple of days, when he gets home from Klamath Falls from seeing his kids. Poor guy thinks about them all the time, sends them dolls and toys and his ex won't hardly ever let him see them. When he's through with his children, him and I are going target shooting in California. He'll phone you when he's back. Take my word for it."

Darryl paid for the pistol and left, with a weapon in each one of his pants pockets. Carrying these around will cool off anybody's balls. Good way to forget about women. By the end of the afternoon, Deb's a thing of the past. He walked across town to Asco's place.

"Hey, buddy. Let's go shoot. I got everything we need, excepting your Plymouth."

After two hours of target practice in the sun they went to a nearby bar for a few beers. Darryl told his friend how he had spent the morning and described his decision to get Deb out of his hair.

"Never could figure what you saw in her anyhouse! No boobs, no fun. At that cabin, when we was trying to take their picture for you, they just sat and talked all the time, and half the time they didn't say nothing. That aint my idea of sex. What got into ya? They torture you or something in prison? Give you electrical shock on your cock so you forget about fucking?"

Darryl wanted to order another couple of beers, but Asco had to go to work.

"Let me borrow the Plymouth while you're at work, will ya? I'll pick you up when you're done. What time you finished?"

"In three hours. Must be crappy not having wheels. Watch it, though; the tires are real thin."

After letting Asco off at the back entrance of a small factory, where he cleaned floors and took out the garbage, Darryl drove home.

Glenda was having a glass of juice and looking out into the street when Darryl burst in the door.

"Find a job?"

"Sure did."

"When do you start?"

"Right away. No more questions, you hear?"

"At least tell me where you'll be. I got a right to know, since I'm your mom."

"I'll tell you when I'm ready to."

He went into his room, slamming the door.

"What is the package you're carrying?"

"Never mind. Just leave me alone."

"What's the matter with you? What's the secret about?"

"Ain't no secret. You're just too damn curious."

"Then tell me what the package is."

"The secret is you can tell that friend of yours that she can go whoring around all she wants with that lawyer. I don't give a shit."

"What are you talking about? What friend?"

"Deb, you stupid . . . And tell her to stay clear away from here. If I catch you or Liz around with that bitch again I'll whip you both. Understand? And when I see that fucking lawyer he'll wish he'd never laid eyes on her, if he survives long enough. I'll get even with that son of a bitch."

"Darryl! Come back to your senses! You have never talked like this. I'm not about to take any more of that crap of yours. You come here and sit down!"

"Can't," he said, coming out of his room and heading for the door. "Going to work now; gotta earn our bread and butter. You sure as hell aren't going to support us three making whorehouse curtains."

He went down the stairs three steps at a time, laughing loudly.

"She believed every word I said, the stupid bitch! Just living in her vicinity makes me feel like a moron. Now what the fuck am I going to do with these guns?" he said out loud as he drove off in Asco's green car.

I've got it! I'm going to ask for a job at that lawyer's place. If Asco can sweep a floor, I'd be a genius at it! Sweep it so clean them lawyers can lick it any time day or night and say it tastes like ice cream or champagne. Here goes! I can get revenge in little ways, like putting a dead rat in his desk drawer or pissing in his drinking water!

As he drove into the parking lot behind the building, he caught sight of Steve hurrying out of the back entrance. He watched him go to his Jaguar, unlock it, and drive out.

Fun! Darryl thought as he followed. This will be the best drag race ever, me and the lawyer on I-5. I'll get there first, and he'll be so pissed. If he don't scrape into another car trying to avoid me, I'll be waiting for him in that driveway of his, and I'll tell him what a turd he is.

After Darryl left, Glenda sat speechless, not noticing the carrot juice dripping from the table where she had tipped the glass over.

The way he talked to me! I should turn him in for that, for swearing at his own mom! Wonder where he's working. Probably just a story. But then what's he up to? I don't like doing this, but I'm going to. She opened the door to Darryl's room. There under a pile of dirty clothes beneath the bed she found a receipt in Ralph's name for a pistol and a dozen cartons of ammunition.

In a daze, Glenda picked up the phone and dialed Deb's number.

"What is it, Glenda?"

"It's Darryl; he just left. I think he has a gun. He said something about Steve."

"Oh, my God! I'll call and warn him."

"Call him right now. Does he know what Darryl looks like?"

"He's never seen him, and I have never described him. Shall I come over? I can make it in ten minutes. What should we do?"

"Describe him to Steve over the phone and wait for me at your place. I'll pick you up as quick as I can. Then we'll decide what to do."

Having run up the stairs to Deb's place, Glenda had to catch her breath before she was able to talk.

"Tell me again what happened, so we know what to do. I can't make sense out of it."

"Darryl showed up a half hour ago. He's been strange ever since he went after you and then cut his arms. Remember? He was out looking for work all day, or says he was, and when he came home he acted real crazy. Said he'd found a job but wouldn't say where or doing what. Just told me to shut up. He was carrying a package and started cursing me out, saying awful things about you. Then he warned if he ever saw Steve something bad would happen, that he would get even with him. That's all. He just took off."

"What do you think he's up to?"

"It's for sure he's been drinking; I could smell it. And he's driving, too. I heard a car roar off, just after he went out. The worst part is he's got a pistol on him. He's after someone, I'm afraid it's Steve. Did you call him?"

"Steve had just left the office. I tried to talk to his secretary, but she wasn't there. The new receptionist doesn't know me from Adam and wouldn't tell me anything about where Steve was going. Let's go check things out, Glenda."

"I'm ready. Just need to fill up on gas. The tank's almost empty."

As they waited in the car while a young man washed the windshields, Deb explained to Glenda that it was Scott's twenty-first birthday and that Steve's household was to be the scene of festivities that night. In fact the guests were already due to arrive.

"Are you going?"

"Of course not! I'm the last person his wife would invite to an affair for important friends and lawyers."

"How did you know about the party?"

"Steve's been telling me about all the preparations, the presents, the people who are expected to come. Let me pay for the gas, Glenda. We may use a lot."

"Here you are. Thank you," Glenda said to the young man who waved them off. "Where to, Deb? If you want my opinion, we should go to Steve's place. If Darryl isn't there, then it's no problem, at least for now."

"Okay. Go to I-5 and turn south. I'll show you where to turn off."

"Here goes; hold on tight! Hope the traffic doesn't get in the way, because I don't want to bend any fenders."

Once on the freeway, Glenda weaves in and out of lines of traffic, switching lanes whenever an open space between two cars beckons. In no time she turns off on the Lake Oswego exit and tears down the two-lane blacktop road; Deb gives her instructions well in advance so that she can cut each corner without slowing down. Glenda can feel her own heart beating fast as she hears Deb tell her to turn right into the next driveway. They enter a thickly wooded area, proceeding more slowly now. They come to a fork in the road.

"Which way?"

"Right, I think. I've only been here once. Watch for a sharp curve."

On the far side of a sudden bend in the road, Glenda sees two cars ahead of them. One is Asco's Plymouth; the rear tire looks flat. Behind it is a Jaguar; someone in a suit has come out and is walking toward the Plymouth.

"Oh, God!" Deb murmurs as she fumbles to open her window. Then she shouts: "Steve! He has a gun! Let me get out, Glenda!"

Glenda watches Deb run stumbling toward the two cars where the man is already approaching the Plymouth. Suddenly he staggers, falls. Glenda is paralyzed, unable to move or scream. She hears the sharp sound of more shots. Deb rushes up to the man who is now lying on the asphalt, kneels down to him. Darryl comes out of the Plymouth, looks at Deb and shoots her twice. He then takes aim and fires again at the man on the ground, who is bleeding profusely. Glenda, helpless, watches her son walk over to the Jaguar, which is still running. He throws the pistol on the seat, gets in behind the wheel, and takes off toward the road with tires screeching against the pavement, almost striking Glenda as she pulls herself out of her car.

A few minutes later Glenda found herself driving back to Portland. Her mind was blank; the windshield wipers scraped against the dry glass. She wanted to say "Oh, God!" but couldn't. The image of her friend lying across Steve's body, her blank eyes turned toward the sky, with two bleeding holes, one in her forehead, the other in her abdomen, was still before her eyes. Finally Glenda was able to push through her mind a confused thought about her friend being united in death with the man she loved, but there all thought came to an end.

Unaware of the heavy traffic to every side on the freeway, she drove as if in trance. The sunset sent golden flames against flimsy quilted clouds. Must be that bad weather is coming, she thought as she drove into the parking lot of a branch police office in Portland. At the reception desk where she leaned for support, Glenda looked at the face of a tired officer and forced out the words "I want to report . . ." Then she broke down and sobbed.

Not far from Asco's place of work, Darryl drove straight into a telephone pole. Bummer! That jag drove real nice. Have to get me one some day. He had to work to extricate himself from the wreck. He put the polished wooden steering wheel, which had come off its mount, under his arm and took it with him. My trophy after a hard day, he thought.

Asco was waiting on the sidewalk.

"Where's my car? You smash it?"

"Naw. It got a flat. You were right about them tires. Left it out at that lawyer's place. We'll have to figure out how to get it back, 'cause I don't want to go there right now. There a tavern around? I could use a drink."

Seated at the bar, Darryl told Asco in minute detail what had happened since late that afternoon.

"You mean you killed 'em? Dead?"

"You don't never seem to understand when I tell you

something, Che Asco. Or maybe you're just plain dumb. No one ever seen anybody deader than those two, old buddy. How bout another round? I'm still thirsty."

An hour later, the police came to arrest Darryl. Asco was released after questioning.

IV

Portland, Oregon:
Scott

AT SIX IN the evening of my twenty-first birthday, my father was murdered. His body was found next to that of his mistress at the bend in the road leading up to the house. The record indicates how many times each had been shot. How or why it happened is still far from clear, and I am writing my recollections in order to shed whatever light I can on the event and perhaps restore some semblance of order to my thinking.

That Friday was particularly hectic. Mom, or Bev as everyone else calls her, spent hours preparing a big birthday celebration, having the house cleaned from top to bottom, talking about the menu to the cook, setting and resetting the table, phoning her husband to consult with him about this or that detail. None of this really concerned me. The dinner party was for friends and colleagues of my parents; my own friends weren't expected to arrive until sometime afterward, and a band had been engaged for dancing. In addition, there was much hush-hush about an important gift, the nature of which I was to discover only when it arrived. I spent the day reading and listening to music. Diane was so involved with Bev making preparations that I hardly saw her, and we skipped most of our therapy routine.

In the middle of the afternoon, Bev descended to the storage area in our basement to bring up the silver place settings she still needed for the table, some brass and silver serving platters, and the champagne and table wine that would be served before and during the meal. She took Diane along to help her carry these items up to the dining area.

Now this storage area is usually kept locked, for fear that robbers might break in and steal the expensive ware, much of it imported, that had been collected over the past ten years. The locking device to the area has always been a problem, which is that if it is difficult to enter without a key, it is nearly impossible to get out of unless you have taken the key with you inside, either hanging it around your neck or safely attached with other keys to your belt. Apparently Bev had opened the door and left the key in the lock while she groped to find the string that hangs from a ceiling light in the center of the room. Of course the metal door slammed shut, leaving Bev and Diane in total darkness and Bev in a state of panic. When they were finally able to turn on the light they began shouting and banging on old pots and pans to make enough racket to rouse the rest of the household, if not the dead. At the moment I was listening to a Mahler symphony with the volume turned all the way up to test my speakers and consequently did not hear anything from down below. It was only when Melissa came into my room with a concerned look on her face, holding her ears and gesturing at the same time, that I realized something was amiss and turned off the music. When it became clear what had happened, I must confess that for a moment I was tempted to leave them down there and thus make it impossible for the birthday celebration to take place at all, for I was already dreading the whole business.

Two factors made it doubtful that we would be able to extricate Bev and Diane from the bowels of the building. First was Melissa's profound superstition, her sense of foreboding—it is not for nothing that she hails from Malheur County—which was intensified by an attack of claustrophobia when she approached the steep, dark and narrow stairs that lead down to the storage room. She quite simply refused, with terror showing in her eyes, to go down one step. That left me, Scott, as the person appointed to save the day, which was the second factor. I have never learned to navigate a set of stairs alone in my wheelchair. So, with Melissa's help, I was able to slip down and sit on the top step. From there, using one hand to hold on to the banister and the other to lift up and swing my rear down to the next step, I maneuvered my way downward, all the time letting my useless legs dangle in front of me and get caught on the carpet. When finally I reached the last step and turned the key in the lock, Bev was just about to have a nervous breakdown. I don't remember exactly what she said as she jumped over my legs to reascend to the upper world. Getting me up the stairs was not easy, either. We tried several strategies, but nothing worked until we discovered that a rope could be tied to the railing at the top and that I could pull my way upward while Diane prevented my feet from dragging on the steps.

For the last few days, furthermore, Bev had been quite peevish with Steve, although she never let on what was bothering her. Of course, I knew perfectly well why she was in a bad mood, but the matter had never surfaced in a family discussion at the dinner table or during a walk, so we all had to endure episodes of sullen silences and irritated looks. Therefore when Steve did not arrive home from the office at five-thirty as he had promised, the mood around the house deteriorated noticeably. There were so many things he still had to do: set the fire, prepare the drinks, review with her the seating arrangements. He would never have time for a shower! "Where could he be? I'll bet he . . ." Bev went up to her room to dress. Diane, having to take more and more responsibility, was giving instructions to the temporary help called in to serve the tables. Meanwhile I posted myself in front of a window so as to be able to signal Steve's arrival or give a warning if a guest should arrive early. I kept thinking how much I regretted that Deb, the person we were all thinking about, hadn't been invited.

Bev looked ravishing when she reappeared. Dressed in a long black gown with ruffled sleeves and bare shoulders, she appeared fully in control, her expression confident and composed. After I had bathed and shaved, Diane helped me into a new suit.

Then she showered and dressed, for she was to take part in the festivity.

The first guests to arrive were Mike and Flo Hoffman. Wasn't it a beautiful day? What, Steve not home yet? Big day for you, isn't it, Scott? What are your plans? Are you getting enough exercise? Flo Hoffman chatted with Diane about something; Mike agreed to make some drinks.

Benny Brooks, his wife Hilda, and one of their daughters arrived, all dressed elegantly and full of smiles. "The other two girls are away for the summer, and we miss them so! Fiona is visiting her college roommate in Atlanta, and Mona is learning about psychology and Spanish verbs on a cruise ship in the Mediterranean. But our dear Bette stayed at home to keep us company. Without her we would simply be lost!" Bette Brooks is standing, holding a soft drink, in a straight dress that matches her red hair and freckles, her mouth partly open. How plain she looks next to Diane!

"Well, haven't I seen you somewhere before?" Mike asks Benny, having been with him the whole day.

"You do look somewhat familiar, now that I think of it. Flo looks great. She must keep busy. By the way, Mike," Benny whispers, "did you see the homeless couple sleeping on the driveway, right where it curves? Way out here in Lake Oswego! It might make sense downtown, but not here! I wonder if Bev knows about them."

"I didn't see anything, and I've been here all of twenty minutes."

The doorbell rings again; Bev receives the new guests, in this instance, Mary and Milton.

"Bev, dear. There's a homeless couple asleep in your driveway, did you know? Steve should go out and chase them away before more guests arrive." Then in a whisper: "They are in a very compromising position, too. It would make a perfect sculpture for our foyer in Seattle."

"There's an old wreck of a car with a flat tire there, too. It's probably what they came in. Oh! how do you do? I'm pleased to meet you," Milton said, nodding and smiling.

"Oh, dear! Steve hasn't come home yet. But when he does, he will certainly deal with them. Do come in and have a drink."

More people came, and the room filled with talk and laughter. I was stationed in a corner where most of the guests came soon after their arrival to shake my hand and offer me their best wishes. Inevitably each one asked what I planned to do with myself, and I stumbled on my answer each time, trying to make light of not having the slightest idea.

"Steve must be held up by a freeway accident, or maybe he stopped off somewhere to buy flowers or the cognac he said we needed. I can never depend on him to be home on time. Diane, my dear, please go and ask Melissa if we can hold off serving for another half hour."

The final guests to arrive mentioned to Bev that the "homeless" couple in the driveway didn't look asleep but rather as if something was wrong with them. "With all those psychos being released from the mental institutions, it's no wonder the streets aren't safe any more. They drink themselves into a stupor, and then freeze to death, at least in winter. Maybe they were hit by a car and crawled off the road to die, like stray dogs."

Bev phoned the local police and asked for someone to come to investigate.

"Imagine that! A recording said: '. . . all our operators are busy; please leave a message at the beep!' With our tiny police and fire department, that can only mean they are having coffee at the counter across the street."

"Aren't you in Lake Oswego?" someone asked.

"We're in the one of the last unincorporated areas around, so my call had to be taken by the county."

I was a little uneasy. I was sure Dad was with Deb and just couldn't tear himself away. But at the same time it was unlike him to take a risk on a night like this. I looked for Diane across the room. She was listening to Mike Hoffman describe one of his exploits. She smiled at me and shrugged, as if to say: "I'm helpless."

It was becoming dark outside when the doorbell rang with insistence. Two police officers were at the door, and sets of blue, red, and yellow lights flashed maddeningly from the roofs of two squad cars outside.

"We're very sorry to bother you, ma'am, but there's been some violence on your driveway. I'm Sergeant Butler from the Township of . . . I need to ask your permission to remove evidence from your propertry. This is Officer . . . "

"Sergeant Percy of the Homicide Division of the OHP, ma'am. I need to ask your guests some questions about what they saw when they . . . Please tell no one to leave, I mean everyone not to leave, I mean . . . "

"Yes, Officer. They all saw those homeless people sleeping out there, and I hope you can do something to get rid of them. It is so disturbing to know that strange people are around, especially when you have a party planned.

"They aren't sleeping, ma'am. They are dead. You see . . ."

"What he is trying to say is: under the deplorable circusstances we all have duties to preform. But there is a conflict of juristriction between the Township, the Highway Patrol, and the Lake Oswego P.D., which is still out at the scene of the crime . . ."

I didn't wait to hear the rest. In an instant I was out of the door racing down the driveway as fast as my new wheelchair could manage. I heard steps following me, but I was so intent on the dozens of flashing lights out at the driveway curve that I didn't look behind. Fire engines, ambulances, and police cars were everywhere with diesel engines running and spewing forth the most sickening smell. The men at the scene appeared to be talking on or listening to walkie-talkies as they paced back and forth. A van from a local TV station was just pulling up to the scene, and a man with a camcorder on his shoulder was running up, accompanied by a woman in high heals talking nervously to a microphone.

Then I saw them. Dad was on his back, lying on a stretcher. They were just covering his body with a plastic blanket. His face was unmistakable, yet without expression and grotesquely disfigured. Next to him was Deb, who had the same peaceful look I had seen when I met her. Then I couldn't see any more. From behind me a pair of soft hands covered my eyes and wheeled me back to the house. Diane took me into my room through a side door, and, after having told Mom and a few guests where I was, sat next to me in the dark and began quietly to sing songs she had learned in her childhood.

I don't know how long this lasted. Time didn't seem to matter, nor did life. My mind tuned into the voice and the sweet, monotonous melodies enough to exclude everything else, especially the scene I had just caught sight of. Slowly, numbness so completely enveloped me that only the thin line of song was able to relate me to the world. I felt the insensitivity of my legs spreading throughout my body and brain. I knew that a raging sea of suffering was out there ready to destroy what little desire I had to continue living, waiting for me to venture forth from the shelter of the voice and the dark.

I would have been content to remain like that forever, but a knock at my door told us that I was needed. In the brightly lighted living room there were a number of guests still standing and whispering. Policemen with their bulky jackets, belts, and guns and some plainclothes cops had moved the furniture around to create an office where they were talking on phones, typing on portable computers, and doing interviews. Some were smoking, others just sitting, waiting. A tall fellow had even helped himself to one of Mike Hoffman's manhattans. Most of the guests had already been interviewed; the questioning Bev had been subjected to was long and probably grueling. Melissa had been spared, I learned later. The combination of the tragedy and the burning of the roast she had left in the oven during the confusion had apparently unhinged her, and she proved unable to answer even the simplest question without sobbing and exclaiming that it was all her fault because she hadn't told anyone of her premonition of disaster. The smell of burnt meat was still strong, mingling in the room with cigarette smoke and diesel exhaust. They took Diane's deposition, which was short and simple. Mine was longer, because apparently I was the only person present who knew who Deb was and what her relationship to my father could be. As soon as the questions pertaining to Deb began, Bev went upstairs, accompanied by Flo Hoffman and her friend Mary. I have little memory of the interview or the person who questioned me.

Soon my friends started to drift in with startled looks on their faces. Somebody cued them in, and most left quietly. Suddenly from the patio came the noise of a band setting up and connecting loudspeakers. The clarinet ran up and down an arpeggio, an electronic piano experimented with different pop rhythms, and a sax wailed out a blues air while the drum and the electric guitar began to drive the characteristic rock beat, which rattled the sliding glass windows. Benny went out to convince the band to leave or at least quiet down, but the players refused to pack up before the lead singer came and could decide what to do about the musicians' contract. Meanwhile a clown came rolling head over heels out of nowhere, gesturing, and making announcements no one could hear. With him three or four girls in miniskirts jumped into the room, cheered, and released red, white, and blue balloons. Another clown followed pounding on a bass drum which had Styler's Volvos printed in large letters on the drumhead. All of this created so much noise and confusion that no one was able to warn the first clown before he came up to congratulate me and hand me a set of keys hanging from an automobile-shaped balloon and invited me and the guests (including a handful of police) out to view the marvelous apparition, the miraculous birthday present that had just driven up to the front door and parked between a squad car and the dark gray hulk of a funeral limousine.

It was at this point that I turned my wheelchair around and

headed as fast as I could for my quarters. For good reason, too,
for right away I threw up and passed out in my bathroom. When
I came to, Diane was wiping off my face and jacket.

"Did you lock the door, Diane?"

"I will. There is a doctor out there now, seeing to your mother.
He wants to know if he could give you a pill or a shot to help you
sleep. It might not be a bad idea."

"I don't want to see anybody, except you. Let's barricade the
doors and windows. When will all the people be gone?"

"Your mother has retired, and Mary is trying to shoo
everybody away. She is so brusque about it she may even
convince the police to leave. Her husband is sound asleep on
the couch. We don't have to let anybody in here. What about the
pill?"

"If you sing some more, I think I'll be able to sleep."

"Maybe a swim would relax you, and a massage."

About an hour later all was quiet except for Diane's voice
singing close to me as I floated again and again into sleep only to
awaken to the memory of flashing lights. At one point I must
have drifted deeper, for when I came to everything was dark and
silent. I remember staring into the darkness and wondering if
light would ever return, feeling blind as well as paralyzed. I
remember also making some kind of noise, perhaps it was a long
sigh or dry sob. Then I felt Diane's hand on my forehead, and
that touch suddenly released an unending stream of tears. It was
as if she had opened dikes to let out all the sorrow that had
collected over the years and all the solitude that I knew awaited
me. My entire body, even my legs, shook as if I were abandoned
in a freezing snow. I must have sobbed for a long time. I remember
being comforted only when Diane crawled next to me under the
cover, resting her arm and hand on my chest.

Soon after I was driving my wheelchair over one of the bridges
high above the Willamette River. Large semitrucks and buses
with flashing lights and wailing sirens were to my left, causing
the bridge to sway as they thundered by. The sidewalk on which

I was driving caused my wheelchair to shake as it moved over the rough grillwork. Through it one could see the gray rippled surface of the river below. Not wanting to take my eyes off the roadway or stop, I avoided looking at the bolts and nuts that secured my right wheel, which I feared was coming loose, and I continued as fast as I could toward the middle of the bridge. When the wheel began to wobble seriously, I signaled and pulled over to the railing to stop. Fortunately my tools were under the seat, and I began to tighten the bolts with a wrench. It was hard to know which way to turn them, since some bolts had to be tightened clockwise and others in the opposite direction. To be on the safe side, it seemed best to alternate, with the result that half of the bolts fell through the grill into the water. When I tried to catch them as they fell, I lost hold of the wrench, which also slipped through an opening. To make things worse, the wheelchair, now running smoothly, began to roll down the bridge toward the streets on the other side. With time it went faster and faster, and all I could do was watch it speed toward the busy traffic at the corner.

I awoke with a jolt, hearing Diane's voice telling me to wake up, that it was only a dream. That didn't make particular sense to me at the moment, but I was thankful to find myself in a warm bed where an immediate crash seemed less likely. Postponing a decision as to whether the nightmare or the events of the day was the more terrifying, I sank back into semiconsciousness. I could feel Diane's hand move gently on my chest and her voice say soothing words. Something in the air smelled different, more fragrant than what I was used to breathing. Then the dim awareness that Diane's hand had come across something unexpected woke me again.

"*Oh! pardon*," she murmured, moving it away.

It was well known to her that my legs did not move on their own accord. That what is situated between them should enjoy a life of its own and a certain independence of movement had perhaps not occurred to her. I must have emitted a grunt or a sigh of contentment which had the effect of bringing her hand back and of letting it remain. It moved ever so gently and filled me with a sensation I had given up the dream of ever experiencing. I don't have a clear memory of what ensued, but certainly a remarkable shift of roles took place when I began to unbutton her pajama top and let my hand explore inside. Suddenly I appreciated what Chuck had always described to me of the joys of alpinism, in particular that sensation of coming, after great toil, to the summit and finding oneself alone, victorious, and surrounded by the most wondrous landscape and topology that nature has to offer our senses. Here truly, he said, reality never fails to go beyond our expectations. Diane must also have had an instinct for mountain climbing, for after our pajamas somehow mysteriously fell away she scrambled deftly up to what one might call my *spitze* or *pic* and, settling down upon it, brought about the most violent volcanic action I can remember ever having experienced. This went on for some time before both of us fell asleep, exhausted.

When I woke up to the warm light of the morning, Diane was still next to me, smiling. Remembering a phrase I had learned a month ago but had not dared pronounce to her, I said, as well as I could:

"*Je t'aime.*" We kissed.

"Scott, love! Today will be rough for us both. I don't know what you will have to endure. Just remember that I am here with you."

10617-LIND

THE DAY WAS anything but restful. Melissa had to be taken to the hospital in the early hours of the morning, and was said to be under observation. After spending the night in Bev's room, Mary got up early and treated the household to a large batch of burnt French toast. I didn't see Bev until after lunch, and then it was because she wanted to enlist Diane's help that she came downstairs.

An endless line of officials, friends, and visitors started to arrive in midmorning, and the phone rang continuously. Since I turned out to be the only person available to deal with it all, I set up a kind of office in the dining room, not unlike what the police had done the night before. There I sat and officiated at the big mahogany table, yelling at new arrivals to make themselves at home in the living room, answering the phone, and trying to listen to whoever happened to be seated at the table with me. For peace and quiet, the doorbell was silenced and the door simply left open so that people could enter and exit at will.

My first guest was Officer Minsky from a homicide squad; he had been assigned this particular case and desired to present himself to the family. He spoke at length of his experience in this kind of work and then went on to explain how his job was complicated because of the lack of solid information about the people involved, including my father, and, of course, the woman who perished by his side. I took note of everything he said, which makes it unnecessary to remember and repeat here all the details.

He did say toward the end, and I think that this was to be the climax of his presentation, that a suspect had been apprehended and that this person had readily admitted guilt, although he subsequently withdrew his confession after seeing a lawyer appointed by the court for his defense. The police were in possession of the weapons used. It was reported also that what is left of the jaguar has been recovered and was being towed to a wrecking yard, where it will be "thoroughly examined for fingerprints and other evidence" and then disposed of. Beyond that, nothing made sense, even to Officer Minsky. There were no evident motives or other indications of why this crime had taken place at all.

"But we'll find out; we always do. I'll keep in touch," were his final words.

Among the phone callers was the minister of Bev's church, the Rev. Smythe, who wished to confer with us and would it be convenient for him to stop by this afternoon at one-thirty? Various newspapers called to confirm the information they had on file for the obituaries that would appear in the next day's issues. When there was a moment's pause, I phoned Steve's sisters to inform them. Benny Brooks called to make an appointment and soon thereafter came carrying three legal suitcases full of papers. Just as he entered the dining area I caught sight of a tiny woman dressed in black waiting on a couch in the living room. When I asked what I could do for her, she said she needed to talk to me but preferred to wait until I was through with everyone else.

Benny was visibly shaken. After all, as he told me, Steve was his best friend, and losing him was a terrible blow to the partnership and to him personally. "It isn't often," he went on, "that one comes across a person like your father, and I have little hope of ever forming a close friendship again." After pausing he went on to say that he needed a number of signatures, which I gladly gave him, eager as I was to put the day behind me. He also left two tall piles of papers to read, as soon as I felt able to concentrate, in order to become acquainted with Steve's will and the financial situation.

"I don't know if you are aware of this, Scott, but your father appointed you executor of his will and manager of his estate as of your twenty-first birthday, which, if I am not mistaken, was yesterday. That puts a heavy burden on your young shoulders, but I applaud his choice, nevertheless. What complicates matters is that Steve had accepted to manage the affairs of his former client, Deb Myers, in case of her death. She in turn had the care of her ward and husband, Hank Myers, who is incapacitated and needs to be looked after. This second collection of documents pertains to Deb and her husband, and you will want to peruse them rather soon in order to determine what action to take in regard to his care. Your father has probably kept a number of personal documents here at home—I have seen his study upstairs and suppose that is where he would have been likely to store them. You may want to go through the papers on his desk and in his files for further insight into what his intentions were." Benny paused. He looked tired.

"You have inherited a great deal of responsibility, my boy, and it is important to realize that before you decide to take a long vacation in Hawaii to get away from it all. Let me know soon if you want our firm to do your legal legwork. I will appoint the best one of our young partners to help you out."

"Why not yourself, Benny? It would seem to me that . . ."

"No, Scott. Your father was too close to me. It would almost be a conflict of interest. By the way: I took it upon myself to inform Deb Myers's family about what happened yesterday. Also, I phoned the care center where her husband is staying; they have agreed to continue his care until they receive further word from you. Let's arrange to meet at my office when you have recovered from your shock. It will be easier than you think to . . . I wonder if I may pay my respects to your mother. Is she upstairs?"

As Benny went upstairs, the Rev. Smythe was coming down; I could hear their polite but almost frigid greeting from where I was sitting. Benny is a Unitarian, and the Reverend is rector at Portland's highest Episcopalian church. I asked if the little lady in black could wait until I was finished talking with the clergyman.

"I was just conversing with your mother about the funeral arrangements. We have tentatively scheduled it for Tuesday morning at eleven. That gives us three days to prepare. Your father's body is at Goode's Funeral Home, where he will lie in state. Visitations can be Monday morning or afternoon. The burial will take place Tuesday, immediately after the ceremony. Your mother is going to see about buying a family plot at Sunset Lawn, where there is still available space, although not much, I dare say. She is right in assuming that if you order a stone now with her name next to his the saving will be considerable. Then when she passes on, the mason only has to carve the date, and if you pay for that now, you will save even more. Jay Goode is due to be here soon to finalize the arrangements. I must say, Scott, that I'm impressed with your mother. With all the pressure she is under at this time, she has a clear head and is able to make the best decisions for her husband, for herself, and for you. Steven would be proud of her, yes, very proud, if he were able to behold her at this moment."

I thanked him for his kind words about my mother and asked what the funeral service would be like.

"They are all basically the same, although some are more elaborate than others. Your mother has chosen Number Four, and I applaud her for her choice, since the next step would be the type usually reserved for eminent public servants, politicians, bishops, the kind of people half the city would want to come pay their respects to. Although I didn't know your late father very well, he seemed to be a fairly modest man in his outlook and ambitions, and the basic expanded service would be the most appropriate in his case. Of course, extras and add-ons are available if your mother or you wish to include them. My list of the different services and available options is in your mother's room if you want to see it."

"You must have to perform a number of memorial services during the course of a week. I am wondering how the service for Dad will be different from anyone else's."

"In many ways! You and your mother will be given an opportunity to offer suggested solos for the singer and interludes for the organist; we will consult you as well regarding the choice of hymns, Old and New Testament lessons, prayers, the Benediction, and so forth. But the most personalized section will be the Celebration for the Life of Steven Thornton, which will be like a sermon consisting mostly of a paean of praise for the good works he accomplished during his lifetime, which was cut so tragically short. There will also be four prepared statements, or thanksgivings, by appropriate persons and members of the Church that bear witness to his life. Your mother has already said she is willing to speak to the congregation, which she has done on other occasions and can be depended on to do very well. I am sure Mr. Alexander, the head of your father's law firm and a respected elder of our Church, will be more than willing to give a short presentation. One of Steven's sisters might be able to tell about his early life, which would enlighten and amuse us all."

"Who will give the fourth presentation?"

"Why you, of course, are certainly the designated person. I had taken it for granted that you would make the most important contribution, and I hadn't even thought of asking you! Isn't that silly of me!"

"In that case I plan io describe the way he died. That seems to me a useful sort of thing to tell people who might otherwise be unaware of the violence that may be waiting for them in their own driveways. And it is very much on my mind."

"Well, in those matters caution is always in order. After all, we don't want a memorial service to take on the tone of a television crime drama. Our purpose is to uplift spirits and give thanks for the privilege of having known the deceased. Perhaps a subtle allusion to the events of last night might be admissible, one that stresses tragedy, not gore, and the mystery of the Lord's wisdom in taking the innocent. If that is what you had in mind . . ."

"Then I suppose cute memories of little foibles and meaningful virtues would be appropriate, along with what a loving father he was, what an inspiration he was to me, and how I will always cherish his memory."

"Yes, exactly so. That is what we want people to hear. We will have a ramp so that your wheelchair can make it to the raised platform without noise or extra fuss."

"And I would also like to say during the service that my father's mistress died at his side while she was defending him from an armed gunman, as an illustration of the great courage human love is capable of."

"Now, Scott! We should talk about this again, since I really have to leave now. Oh! My goodness! I'm very late for my next appointment . . . I sincerely believe you should reconsider what you just proposed, if you did so seriously, and I suspect hopefully that you did not. It is essential to consider your father's honor and your mother's peace of mind. Need I say more? Just let me know if you decide to speak on behalf of your father. If not, we can always ask one of his friends."

Dr. Smythe left somewhat in a hurry, and I was glad because I needed to collect my thoughts and feelings. Diane came in briefly, which revived my spirits, and then returned to help Bev.

Finally the lady in black came in, smiling meekly and speaking softly.

"Hi," she said. "My name is Glenda. Deb Myers was my best friend, outside of family of course. You should know that my son Darryl is the person who shot them last night. I saw it; I was there. Darryl is now . . ." She broke down and was unable to say another word through her tears sobs for several minutes. I went out to get her a glass of water and some tissues and then waited, with my hand on her wrist, until she was able to speak again. "I couldn't help overhearing what you said to the minister about Deb's courage. You are right. If we had gotten there just a few minutes earlier she could have saved him, and herself." She started to cry again. When she was able to speak, she told me the whole story of Deb and Steve, as she knew it, and the story of her son's childhood, his violent nature and life on the streets, his insane jealousy. The whole story came out in an easy flow of words, without embellishment or detours into her feelings or her guilt. By the time we had finished talking, I felt enlightened and glad to have made a new friend.

Others came, but I was too exhausted to listen attentively. Thus when Jay Goode, with his serene face and curly hair, his voice dripping with compassion, spoke to me on behalf of his funeral business—referring to himself as "counselor to the bereaved"—my mind went dead inside and amnesia regarding his speech set in.

There was some turmoil when Melissa rushed in after returning in a cab, muttering "my place is here, helping my people in a time of sorrow, not simmering in bed and answering silly questions about my childhood." She went straight into the kitchen, signaling to the cabby that I would pay the tab.

"I didn't know what to think, Sir. Was she a loony escapin' from the bin? Am I in for some trouble for fallicitatin' her flight? She told me they were keepin' her there against her will, she said. Was I correct in bellievin' her, Sir? I hope you will protect me if there are any repercussions, Sir. I certainly don't want any repercussions for what I did!"

At that point an ambulance screeched to a stop at the door; two paramedics, dressed in white, one of them carrying a package large enough to conceal a parachute or a straight jacket, announced that they were here to take their patient back to the hospital. Fortunately, Glenda, who for some reason was still waiting at the entrance, recognized one of the men and, when she heard me refuse to permit them to recapture Melissa, told them to retreat peacefully and tell their boss that they had lost her trail.

"They haven't enough beds at the hospital anyways, you know that, Marcus! They'll be glad you lost her so they don't have to turn out some guy tonight to die on the street. Anyhow she's not here; the cab was empty, just ask the driver."

After everybody left all was quiet for the first time that day. Diane finally came downstairs and cheered me by announcing: "I really admire your mother! She is strong and knows what she wants." I told Diane what I had learned from Glenda. As if by silent consent, when it was time for my usual exercise, swim, and massage, neither Diane nor I wore anything.

Bev came down for dinner, looking tired but otherwise healthy. We talked quietly about the funeral and burial arrangements, and for the moment I felt it unnecessary to mention my misunderstanding with Dr. Smythe.

"Thank you for letting me have Diane today," she went on to say. "And thank you, dear, for being such a good secretary! We accomplished an enormous amount of work. First there was the gallery to put in order. I won't be able to go to Seattle for at least another week, and Mary will have to bear the responsibilities and make the decisions. Maybe you should go up there, Diane, and help poor Mary out! But of course not! You need her, don't you, Scott? Well anyway, we went through all my clothes to see if the black dresses and suits fit. Well none of them do! I've gained at least ten pounds since Aunt Barbara's funeral, and that is extremely depressing for me. How are you feeling, Scott?"

I described the day's activities to her, ending with an account of Melissa's return.

"How fortunate! Remind me to congratulate her after we have finished dinner; she used good sense not letting herself be pushed. And the dinner is really excellent, isn't it? I wonder how she managed to prepare it so fast. Of course we had so much food left over from last night. Your Diane took notes on everything, Scott, and she's a wonder on the telephone! When we realized I couldn't fit any of my black outfits, I had her call Nordstrom's and ask for Maurice in Women's Clothing. She got him away from a client, described the situation to him, and arranged a private viewing Monday in one of their special rooms. No one but he will be there, only a seamstress or two. Maurice is such a dear! So smooth and understanding. He was really overcome by our tragedy; he just couldn't believe it."

We talked on until a phone call interrupted us. It was for me.

"Hey, Scott!"

"Hey, Chuck! What's up?"

"I know this a rotten time to call. You know how bad I feel about all that, really the whole thing makes me want to . . . to rebel, that's what."

"Actually I'm glad to talk now, it may be what I need."

"Well, here's what's up. I've got this girlfriend here; she's Polish. Her name is Anitka, and she is the most wondrous pianist you will ever hear for a long time. Thing is, she's leaving for Krakow in a couple of days, and if you want to find out what her fingers can do, it's now or never." Then, in a lower voice: "I've been trying to make her stick around Portland to play more chamber music, but no luck. I even invited her to climb Mount Hood with me—you'd think at least that would convince her! Is your piano in tune?"

Here I have to add a parenthetical note. I haven't mentioned, because it really wasn't relevant to anything, that I had a baby grand installed in my room about four years ago and have used it regularly for hand and finger therapy and for the pleasure of thumping out melodies that I forget five minutes after inventing them.

"It was tuned in anticipation of last night's party."

"Then can we come over Sunday? I'll bring my cello. We're doing some pieces together that you will enjoy, and Diane, too, if she's there. Do you have any beer?"

"Enough for an army."

"Who was that, dear?" Bev asked as I made my way back to the table.

"Chuck. He's coming over tomorrow with a friend. We'll be quiet and try not to disturb you."

"Don't worry about that, please. With the pills Dr. Merced

gave me I sleep the whole night through. I'm about to take one now. But before I forget, Scott: will you be sure to take care of all the legal red tape that Benny told me about this morning after he saw you? I just haven't the mind for that sort of thing at this moment, and I know you want to take more responsibility. And also, please write it down that you must call the insurance agent, what's his name? . . . first thing in the morning. He has to turn in claims so that we get Dad's insurance money without waiting forever. I don't know how much it will be, but it will certainly be a handsome sum. Part of it goes directly to you, isn't that nice? Good night, all. Give me a kiss, Scott! Diane, would you check out Melissa, please? See how she is and tell her how good dinner was!"

We transported the dishes from the table to the kitchen and found Melissa busy washing pots and pans.

"Will you be needing me tonight? I might take in a movie. My friend, Charley, is coming to fetch me in a half hour."

Chuck drove up on Sunday afternoon in his little pickup with a passenger next to him and his cello and a new dog riding in the bed.

"Aren't you afraid it might bounce out at one of those sudden stops you take? An instrument like that can't be easy to come by."

"My cello doesn't chase cats, but this puppy here does, so I have to keep her on leash. Meet Umma, part collie, part husky, part shepherd, other parts unknown. Scott, Diane."

It was typical of Chuck to introduce his dog to us formally and ignore his friend, Anitka, who was standing there, somewhat chubby with a round smiling face and large light blue eyes staring candidly at us. Chuck had his usual old woodsman look with unkempt hair and curly brown beard (he is all of twenty years old), dressed in army surplus shorts, climbing boots, and a navy blue T-shirt.

When Anitka joined the conversation, she spoke in a soft,

lilting voice, choosing her words with care, all the time smiling. She wore a long peasant dress with lace on the sleeves and across the bodice.

"Let's make music before it's too late!" Chuck intoned. "What did you bring to play for them? Is it okay for Umma to look around for a place to sleep? Once the music starts, she'll conk out and start snoring."

"I brought some Chopin. I'm working on the nocturnes for a competition back in Poland. Would you like to hear some?"

Diane and I sat on the couch, Chuck was on the floor next to his dog, while Anitka sat at the piano and meditated a few moments. She then paged through a volume of music, which was barely held together by a few strings still attached at the spine. Closing the book she began to play slowly, quietly, one of those longing pieces with a constant movement in the left hand while the right spells out a plaintive melody, often with flourishes and thick nests of rapid interspersed notes. The effect was that of a boat song, and it navigated on through different moods and modulations but remaining always in the same moonlit landscape.

She played another nocturne, this one a slow waltz with an agitated middle section in which a turbulent left hand deftly thunders forth; then the melodic line returns to the quiet motion of the beginning. As far as I could tell, she made no mistakes, and her rhythm was infinitely fluid. Turning to Diane to share my enjoyment, I saw the tears streaming down from her closed eyes, and I realized how much she, too, needed this release of feeling.

Diane brought some beer and sandwiches to the patio, where Anitka found her tongue and told us how much she had benefited from studying in this country and how various teachers had helped her find her way as a pianist. "Now I have to go back to Poland, yet I would rather continue here." She went on to talk about the friends she had made and that she feared she might never see again. "When I come back maybe in ten years, I hope you will still have your beautiful forests."

"You will be returning sooner than that, even if I have to go to Poland to get you!" Chuck exploded. "There is still the whole piano and cello repertoire for us to explore. You don't expect me to wait that long, do you?"

We moved back into the house for more music.

"This is Beethoven's Opus 69," Chuck went on, "we've only read through it together once, and it may have pretty rough edges. I've played it a lot, but it's new to Anitka. Here goes."

He set up a music stand, tuned his instrument, and found a nick in the floor for his end pin. Anitka paged through her part at the piano, as to remind herself of what was coming.

"May I turn pages for you?" Diane asked. "Two hands can hardly be enough for all those notes."

I watched the three of them as they started. Chuck began alone, slowly and sonorously in his middle range, moving upward then downward, ending on a long low note that palpitated as the piano came in higher, liquid, insisting, then disappearing down a slide to the same low note, only to pick up the same melody where the cello had left off. I couldn't help reacting with something akin to joy to the openness of the key and the way the notes seemed to separate and come together. The music went on, sometimes loud and furious, then lyrical, then running in all directions. At one point Chuck broke in with:

"Let's do the repeat, so I can fix the mess I made of the second theme!"

The piece went on. Another section came, in a different mood. Then another, slower and searching, which ended before I could fathom what it was searching for. The finale was good-natured, fast and at times downright comic; I had to hold my breath every time the two hands of the piano rose furiously and the cello caught up with them, all ending triumphantly on the same note at the same time.

When they had finished and Chuck was packing up his instrument, we didn't say much.

"It's a shame Anitka's leaving. We really need to work on that piece. It went okay, but now it needs to be made more connected. We need to start breathing together, and that takes time and practice."

Diane asked if Beethoven was deaf when he wrote that piece.

"I'm not sure if he was stone deaf yet, but if not he certainly knew that it was just around the corner. Amazing, isn't it?"

As they left, we all hugged. Later, in bed next to me, Diane talked on for a while about how she felt listening to that music.

"For me it was like going into another world," she said, "a world where things are in harmony and people are courteous with each other, and the whole blends into a kind of beauty that is new to me, except that I think I felt it once or twice in the woods around Québec, when the first snow was beginning to fall and some of the leaves were still on the trees, moving ever so slightly . . ."

She talked on for some time while I dozed, half-listening. A short time afterward I could tell by her breathing that she had fallen asleep, and I was able myself to finish her thought. I went over the opening theme of the sonata we had just heard, and then the realization came to me that Beethoven was deaf, that later on he died, along with all his friends and acquaintances, and everybody else living around then, and yet the joy expressed in that A major melody is so perfect that neither all the sorrow nor all the tears shed on this earth can blemish it. I listened to Diane's breathing for a while, then fell asleep myself.

AFTER A NIGHT of deep sleep and dreams, I awoke to the touch of Diane's hand on my body. We made love. It was like the first time, yet entirely different. Gone was the element of surprise. Instead there were anticipations and realizations, waiting for a particular caress, and when it came, letting the sensation of it flow to all the corners of my being where I could savor it. I learned new tricks, like rolling over at just the right moment, or lifting myself on my elbows while using a hip as fulcrum, which freed my hands for more important matters. Out of respect for Diane, I won't mention all she did to make me deliriously happy.

Afterward I was relaxed and full of energy. Diane went to the kitchen to help Melissa, and I wheeled over to a table and wrote a neoclassical ode "To My Knees." I won't reproduce it here, in deference to my hurried reader who undoubtedly has an overloaded schedule, but the sense of what I had to say was that, lacking operative knees, I was deprived of an important and powerful sexual tool. My ode starts with an invocation to Pan, who was blessed with hairy goat's knees, which are by far the most desirable kind, as we have learned in countless poems. From there the focus shifts to my own knees in their current condition: wilted, yielding, incapable of holding my weight. I'm not sure I will keep the last section, which ends with: "Oh Knee, it's at your altar that I kneel!"

When Diane came to call me for breakfast, she was carrying

a five-foot long package gift-wrapped in elaborately spotted and striped paper.

"This was to be your birthday present, Scott; you might as well start using them."

Opening the package revealed a pair of aluminum crutches; the bottom of each divided into three points that formed a triangular contact with the ground, which made it possible for me to use them without immediately falling flat on my face or on my ass, depending on which direction I was leaning, as had always happened whenever I felt brave and risked navigation without my wheelchair. They worked! In just minutes I had crossed the living room and made it to the dining table, where Bev was already seated, looking relaxed and rested.

"Good morning, Scott, dear! Isn't that a nice way for you to get around? You really look quite agile! We have to plan our days very carefully. I'm going downtown after breakfast. The funeral is tomorrow at eleven, you know that, don't you? Are you sure you don't want to address the congregation? I really think you should, to make it a memorable occasion for everyone. Oh yes! Where should we put Steve's relatives up? They say they want to sleep at a motel or hotel, but wouldn't that be a little chintzy if we don't have them stay here? But I don't know why it is that in this big house there's really no room for anybody else. At least we should hold the reception here, since we have the food anyway, and everything is still pretty much picked up, unless of course you messed things up with your friends yesterday."

"I'm going to try out the Volvo, Mom. That means getting a driver's license, and then I'll do some errands. Weren't you going to take Mary with you to buy new outfits?"

"Yes. And Flo is coming, and someone else, too, but for the life of me I've forgotten who. They will certainly be more help than you, Scott. What do you know about women's clothes? But I would like to have Diane there, for I value her judgment."

"I'll try to come, Mrs. Thornton. Just tell me where and at what time."

"Please! Diane, call me Bev. We have all been through so much together that we can be friends. I'll be at Nordstrom's at two. Just ask for Maurice. I do so hope you will be there. Then I could buy something for you, Diane, which would be nice."

My Volvo was, as Chuck and his friends might say, a dream. The hard part was learning how to drive the wheelchair up a ramp, through the door, turn, and secure the wheels in special grooves, all of which puts me in front of the steering wheel and numerous handles and buttons, many of which are surrogate pedals. I had learned to drive before the accident, so a few trips up and down the driveway were sufficient to remind me how to start, steer, stop, park, cruise, and the like. Before long I was driving Diane to the Motor Vehicle Department, where we arrived without incident and where I was issued a learner's license with my picture on it and a handicapped driver's sticker permitting me to park almost anywhere except in the middle of a freeway.

We drove to the Friendly Lawn Home, where we sat with Hank for a couple of hours. Diane took his hand in hers and stared into his expressionless eyes.

"He is beautiful, you know," she told me on our way downtown. "I have seen many blue eyes, especially among my relatives, but none as deep or transparent as his. The more I looked into them, the more I saw only peace. I wonder what he was like before whatever it is happened to him."

"I've seen papers and documents about him from Dad's office; they can tell us something."

"I can understand how Deb could have loved him."

"Can you understand as well how she could love my father?"

"That's not as easy. They seemed so different. But the real mystery now is Hank, and I hope we can visit him often."

We stopped for lunch. Diane continued her thought:

"What did you decide with the director of Friendly Lawn, while I was still with Hank?"

"Nothing definitive. I asked her to continue taking care of him as they have been doing until I can figure out what to do next. The only difference is that the bill will go to me from now on?"

"I think you should check out other facilities for him. Which one would he be the most happy in? He can't tell us, but there are ways we might know."

"Makes sense. But beyond those reasonable ideas what do you suggest?"

"Bringing him home and taking care of him there. We could get some professional help, and you already have lots of equipment that could be used for him."

"Well, why not?" I said, after recovering from the shock of hearing her idea. "Hank isn't the kind of responsibility I had in mind when I was thinking about what to do next with my life, as they say. Let's consider it for a while. Could we actually care for him better than those people are doing right now?"

"Where he is now he will never improve. With us, at least the doors in his future can stay ajar."

Later I parked at Steve's office building, just a short walk for Diane to Nordstrom's, and I spent the rest of the afternoon listening to condolences from lawyers and secretaries. I was able to page through mountains of papers and files. It was decided that Minnie would help me for the next few months, either at the office or at home, with the paperwork that would be inflicted on me. She would also be in charge of feeding the tropical fish in the tank in Steve's office. I met Tim Jonas, a young lawyer who would do the legal legwork for Dad's estate. It turned out that this Tim was currently sleeping with a friend of Deb's. I invited them both to dinner the following week.

Before leaving the office, I called Glenda and asked her to meet us at a cafeteria close to her appartment.

"I thought you'd be interested to know that Darryl is in the County Jail. I don't know how long he will be there since they may move him somewhere before his trial, whenever that is. He has confessed twice and recanted both times. They say he is obstreperous, is that the right word? He bangs things around and won't talk to anybody, not even his sister or me. We've gone there to see him, but he refuses to come to the visiting area."

"Maybe if I went there he could be convinced to talk to me."

"If you dressed like a priest, you know, or a minister, maybe. He's already got himself converted to a religious cult some felon talked him into joining. He says the only one he'll talk to is Shah Allah, but nobody knows who that is. What would you want to see him for?"

"I'm not sure. I find it hard to believe that anybody would want to kill my father, so if I saw Darryl in the flesh I might start to understand what has happened."

"There is something else I want to tell you, Scott. In the last few weeks, Darryl had these two friends. There's Ralph and there's Asco. Maybe you could talk to them to find out why things happened the way they did. Here are their phone numbers. I'm not sure how to spell Ralph's last name."

Later I phoned the jail and found that Darryl would most certainly not talk to me—I could hear him cursing in a hallway when someone informed him of my request. I phoned Ralph. His girlfriend answered and said she had no idea where he could be. The most she would say is that he had kidnapped his two children during a visitation and that the police of several states had warrants for his arrest.

Asco Derm, according to the owner of the warehouse where he worked, was currently undergoing treatment for alcohol and drug abuse, and was not expected to return to his job. But the boss did have the name of the treatment center where he could be reached. I left a message for Asco to phone me.

My father's funeral was midway between a disaster and a fiasco, and I am largely to blame. It took place at the local Episcopal Church, where the Rev. Smythe presided. Mr. Goode's assistants whispered guests to their pews, and Ms. Andrea Walker-Hugh, the organist, and Ms. Bonnie Blankenship, the soprano soloist, filled the vaulted ceilings with sound and echoes. Friends, acquaintances, and the curious tiptoed to their places as the organ modulated from one key to another, waiting to begin the opening anthem with a blast. Relatives and close friends of the deceased were sequestered in a special parlour. There I saw Dad's two sisters, their husbands and children huddled in hushed silence, Mom seated in a corner surrounded by Mary and her husband, some of Dad's partners with their families, including two of Benny's daughters. No one was speaking; a few sniffles were heard. Many eyes were moist and red. The organ started a vaguely familiar hymn, which faded out into another melody without beat, as if Ms. Walker-Hugh's fingers were wandering aimlessly over the keys. Then without warning, the pedals and the keyboard issued forth a blaring announcement that a marching hymn was about to begin; Mr. Goode took Bev by the arm and led the sequestered guests through the Tudor hall and down the main aisle to the front rows, which were protected by a black ribbon hanging from the end of one pew to the next. I brought up the end of the procession since my wheelchair would need to be parked in the aisle. I was followed by Mr. Smythe and two other men dressed in black, who, after making a slight detour to skirt around me, took their places on a raised platform and waited for the organ to come to the end of the musical statement it was attempting to make.

Mr. Smythe stood up, gave and asked for blessings, and called all to worship. He then led an invocation, which was a kind of dialog between pastor and flock, printed in full on the program. What Mr. Smthye's voice lacked in volume was amply supplied by Ms. Blankenship's, which then sang the Lord's Prayer, beginning quietly, as if holding back unlimited resources, but becoming louder and higher as she moved through "temptations" and "evil" to land on "for-EEEV-er," seeming to hold that note in constant, wobbling vibrato while the audience wondered how long forever was likely to last.

The program listed the names of the people scheduled to give testimonials to the achievements and character of Steven

Thornton. I was happy to see that my desire to remain silent had been honored. Mom gave a four-minute speech about the loving and thoughtful husband. Then the senior partner of the law firm, Mr. Alexander, spoke of the lawyer's sterling qualities of thoroughness and perseverance and of the deep religious convictions he had always so modestly concealed. Aunt Paula narrated some anecdotes about life in Massachusetts as the youngest sister of an earnest, hard-working boy; she went on to say that my grandmother, already deep into Alzheimer's, could not know of Steve's passing, and that was a blessing. Finally, Benny described the friend he had lost. Throughout all this, Diane, who was sitting at the end of the pew beside me, held my hand tightly, which, to judge from the expression on their faces, was noticed by the people seated nearby.

Mr. Smythe asked if any other person would like to say a word. A few people I had never seen before stood up and spoke from their pews, among them one of Dad's old clients who admired his skill and generosity. Then I signaled my desire to say something, wondering if I had suddenly gone berserk.

One of the minister's helpers placed a ramp for my wheelchair. As I drove toward it I realized my head was empty, that I hadn't the slightest idea what I was going to say. Then halfway up the ramp my wheelchair motor killed, causing me to roll backward. I started it up again, backed up ten feet so that I could gain enough momentum for the climb, barreled toward it at top speed and roared on to the platform, causing the audience to laugh quietly at the comic interlude. I turned around to face the people, recognized Chuck and a few other friends, Glenda with her daughter. I'm not sure if my words made any sense. But I do remember starting like this:

"Let us speak plainly and with honesty. Everything that has been said so far today about my father has been kind, thoughtful, and partly true." I continued along these lines for a few minutes wondering what point I was going to make. Looking at the expression on the faces in front of me I saw that the people were undoubtedly wondering as well. "Ask yourselves," I went on, "how often you told Steve the beautiful things you have said about him here in this noble edifice. When did you express to him the appreciative thoughts you just had while listening to this ceremony? Did he ever directly feel the love, the respect, the admiration, and the thanks you express so publicly now? Or did he have to guess? Steve, you will say, was such a private person you just couldn't tell him those things. But why? He was private because he was loyal to the truth, and to him anything less was a lie." I was about to give up at this point, but the smile I saw on Diane's face encouraged me to go on. "Unfortunately, funerals propagate myths which suppress the truth. And the truth nobody has dared mention today, although it is foremost on all minds present, is that Steve was murdered, brutally, for no apparent reason. The next truth is that he was murdered along with the woman he loved, the only person who ever told him everything we have been saying today. Steve Thornton died happy, in a state of happiness few of us will attain. For that let us give thanks." No one came up to gag me or to usher me back to the parlour where I couldn't do any more harm. The people simply stared at me in silence. I continued: "Steve enjoyed a spiritual affinity with nature, and he did enjoy reading the Bible. His favorite verse to quote was, forgive me if I get it wrong: 'And the meek shall inherit the earth.' But then he always added: 'What's left of it, that is.'"

My wheelchair responded immediately to my bidding and carried me quickly down the ramp and up the aisle toward the back of the auditorium where Mr. Jay Goode and his two stuffy helpers looked at me in dismay. As I turned to the right and made my way into the lobby I could hear Mr. Smythe ask the congregation, as if nothing had happened, to begin Hymn number so and so, after which the organ struck up introductory chords. The lobby was empty as I crossed it toward the exit with the wheelchair access. To leave that place as soon as possible was the sole thought my mind was capable of. As I drove down the ramp toward a line of long black limousines waiting to lead a procession of cars to the burial ground, I could hear Diane trying to catch up with me.

"Wait," she cried. "It's impossible to run in these heels. I tripped and almost fell halfway up the main aisle while everybody was watching. My ankle hurts like mad; I hope it is all right. Can we sit for a moment?"

"I'm glad you are still talking to me. No one else will for quite a while."

"You said what you had to say, and that's better than remaining quiet. Sometime you can tell me what else you had in mind to add. You would make a terrific minister, by the way."

"You are making fun of me!"

"No. I'm admiring you. What do you want to do now? It's almost time for lunch, we haven't any transportation, and I can hardly walk. You don't intend to wait here for the end of the service, do you?"

"Let me rub your ankle a little, there . . ."

"Ouch! It must be sprained, or broken. *Aïe!*"

"I'll rub more gently. We need ice and a tight bandage. Do you remember which one of those vehicles brought us here? That one can manage the chair. Slip over on my lap, Diane, and we will check them out."

The third limo waiting in line was the one; we could tell by the mustache of the driver who was dozing in the driver's seat with his visor cap covering his eyes. Knocking at the tinted window we woke him from his dream.

"Help us in, please, and load the chair. Let's get going."

"Uh! Can't. Gotta follow the hearse to Sunset Lawn. No side trips if they aren't prearranged."

"You will be back in time. Can't you see the lady is in agony? You don't want to be accused of obstructing medical assistance, do you?"

"Huh?"

"Take us quickly to the closest drugstore. This is an emergency."

"Do you think . . .?"

"And there is a bonus for you if you get back in time for the procession, so better get started now!"

"If you think . . ."

At that point Diane started to moan, winking at me.

"Hear that? She's either going to die or have a baby, take your choice. In the meantime let's shove!"

By that time the other drivers had approached and were helping us aboard. Our driver seemed pleased now to be of service. The boredom of his work had been interrupted by the unusual, and he seemed to enjoy, through his rearview mirror, the sight of Diane removing her panty hose. When we got to the pharmacy, he even volunteered to go in and buy the orthopedic stretch bandage we needed and a bag of chipped ice. When he reappeared he brought the pharmacist with him, who carefully tightened the bandage around Diane's ankle and showed her how to apply the bag of ice. Telling us we needed a pair of crutches to "prevent the young lady from doing further damage to herself," the portly pharmacist disappeared for a moment and returned carrying wooden crutches and a rental agreement.

We asked the driver to drop us off at a good restaurant. Once we had disembarked, wheelchair and all, our driver thanked us several times for the fifty-dollar bill I handed him and drove back to the church hoping that the caravan of limousines would still be there. I headed into the restaurant with Diane seated on my lap, holding in her arms the crutches, her shoes, and a crunched-up pair of panty hose. It was too early for lunch, so we enjoyed a drink at the table with the best view and then spent the next two hours over the most expensive seafood item and dessert on the menu. After enjoying the rest of the afternoon in a nearby park, we found a cab that could take us home and arrived in time for dinner with Melissa in the kitchen. Bev had called, saying that she would dine with friends.

When I awoke in the morning, I found that Bev had returned home in the night only to pack her car and set off for Seattle. Chuck called to congratulate me on my "sermon." He was heading for the wilderness, the best way he knew of to cope with Anitka's departure. There was also a call from Asco Derm. He said that when he was "clean," after finishing the drug treatment program, he wanted to make "restiputation" for what he and his buddies had done to our beach house.

I HAVE BEEN spending several weeks going through the papers on Steve's desk. Trying to put order in other peoples' lives isn't easy, especially when one is still picking up the pieces of one's own. So far what I find most interesting is a folder of yellow legal-size pages in Steve's handwriting: notes he took during his first interviews with Deb and his own annotations in the margins. Obviously he was attempting to reconstruct her disjointed story into a coherent narrative, and this must not have been a simple matter. "Here she broke down in tears," he observed. "It seems that the memory of waiting for Hank, whom she hadn't heard from for a couple of months, has a new and vicious ability to make her suffer, since he did come back to her only to be torn away again. I need to verify the dates." Then, further on: "Deb is very sweet and trusting; that alone makes me want to do my best for her. She is also realistic about her situation, about the power and ruthlessness of her opponents, which depresses her, and I wonder whether she will be an effective witness for her cause." One day, without telling Deb, Steve went to visit Hank at the Friendly Lawn Home. He reported that just by appearing in court Hank would win the hearts of the jurors. "I myself found him appealing," he went on. "He's the kind of guy anyone would want as a friend." In another folder are the pages Deb wrote detailing her life in Rio while she was waiting to hear from her husband. She even kept an agenda, where she listed, week by week, the appointments she had with different people and the times she expected to be gone with her mobile health unit.

Deb's mother wrote me a few days ago inviting me to a "resurrection service" for Deb, which she says will be celebrated in October in a little Swedenborgian chapel on the west side of the Puget Sound across from Seattle. She asks me to bring Deb's ashes along (the cremation was done here in Portland) and, if it isn't too much trouble, to make arrangements for Hank to come, too. I plan to take a copy of the pages about Deb that I have been reading and give them to her mother.

Last night Diane and I entertained Deb's friend Jenn, along with Tim, her young lawyer boyfriend, for dinner. Melissa had prepared us a wonderful roast duck with orange sauce, and during much of the meal Jenn spoke almost without interruption about the Deb she had known for so short a time and yet with such intensity. Jenn and Tim are also planning to drive up to Deb's funeral. Perhaps we can all travel together.

After they had left, Diane and I sat in the dark on the patio. I told her how strange it seemed to be entertaining just like some middle-aged couple, as if we had suddenly broken loose from the straps of time to enter another era where I felt a little ill at ease and somehow misplaced.

"That reminds me of something I need to tell you," she said. "I'm almost positive that your first child is on the way. She has been speaking to me almost incessantly for the last week or so. I haven't quite been able to define her voice yet, because it seems to sing in different registers, but it is very melodious and beautiful. In a few days I will be able to hear it more clearly."

I was astounded and for a while speechless, until I was able to come up with something to the effect that it was wonderful news, that I was happy as could be, when would she know for sure, and so forth. Finally I asked a sensible question.

"Shall we get married?"

She turned toward me and, as far as I could see in the dark, smiled.

"Scott, love," she answered. "I hope you will understand this. When I was a child there was a moment when I learned that there was suffering in the world with each breath I took. That's when I made a solemn vow to the Virgin. I'm not even sure of the occasion, but I promised Her that I would never marry a rich man."

"That disqualifies me, then."

"It looks as though you will inherit all this," she said, gesturing toward the house and the grounds. "And I've already forgotten how much insurance your mother told me you will receive. I hate to sound brutal, but you are out of the question."

"Do you still believe in the Virgin?"

"My vow was sincere, and I intend to keep it."

"So I have no choice but to divest myself of all these riches. How poor do I have to be? I'm serious!"

"I'm not sure. Until tonight the thought hadn't really occurred to me that I would marry anyone."

We sat in silence for a few minutes. I took her hand in mine.

"Our child needs a father," she said. "And we will have other children as well, and they will also need you. The more we are together, Scott, the more I feel I need you, too."

We sat watching the stars. Diane went inside to get a sweater. I wheeled in to get a bottle of brandy and two glasses.

"Let's celebrate," I said when she returned and sat down next to me. "To a beautiful child, and to our love."

"You are still worried, Scott, I can sense it. I know this much: I don't have any desire for independence now, and I can't see myself leaving and letting you wheel around on your own for the rest of your life."

The next morning when Asco Derm came to visit, Diane and I talked with him at length over coffee. We accepted his offer to fix the damage he and his friends had inflicted on the beach house.

"Since them guys ain't around to help, I gotta fix what we all messed up. It's only fair."

I drove the three of us to Seaside in the Volvo. The house was a dreary sight: from the outside it looked abandoned with its windows and doors covered by plywood and the flower beds full of dead plants and struggling weeds. Inside we discovered that a raccoon family had set up housekeeping, adding to the disorder that had so distressed Bev earlier.

"You want it exactly like it was?"

"No. We would like it to be more simple. All you have to worry about is cleaning up and repairing structural damage."

"Well, I can do it, I think. It'll take time, and I'll need some tools. Maybe if I take a class in carpentry I'll do a better job. Trouble is, I'm broke. Have to borrow a pickup to take all this stuff to the dump before I can start fixing."

We agreed that Asco would start work on the outside while learning the basics of house repair. In the meantime he could work around our home in Lake Oswego to earn some spending money and satisfy what appeared to be a growing need to be useful.

Later that day, when we had returned to Lake Oswego, he started his chores by removing the lock to the storage room in the basement where Bev and Diane had once been imprisoned. Then he mowed the lawn and split some firewood.

Since everyone expected to return from Deb's funeral in Washington at a different time, it seemed sensible to use separate vehicles to drive there. We formed a convoy: Jenn and Tim, who had experience driving in Seattle, led the way. Glenda and Liz followed, neither one with the slightest idea where they were going or how to get there. Pulling up the rear was the white van, which for years Bev had used to drive me around Portland. It had barely enough room to fit my wheelchair, Hank's wheelchair, the equipment he needed, and a stout male nurse. Since the van wasn't set up for a handicapped driver, Diane drove. Hoping to arrive before dark and knowing that our progress might be slow, we left early, loaded Hank and his nurse at the Friendly Lawn Home, and headed north to Olympia.

Hank's nurse, a regular employee of Friendly Lawn, was cleanly shaven and sported a blunt black goatee. The smell of after-shave lotion and of a potent breath freshener seemed to float everywhere he went. He looked jovial enough: well-groomed black hair in the shape of a horseshoe surrounded a polished bald area, and a magnificent row of teeth glistened whenever he opened his mouth, which was not often. Ron Nolte did not smile, and he spoke little. I must admit that, try as I might to like this person, I ended by loathing him even before we stopped for lunch in a park near Shelton. All we could extract from him was that he was from Nebraska, that he did not dislike his work, and that Hank was "just like the rest of the blobs" he had to take care of. He refused to partake of the enormous picnic lunch Melissa had sent with us, saying that he was accustomed to eating at a restaurant when "on assignment." So while the rest of us ate at a picnic table overlooking the Sound, he sat impatiently at a table nearby drumming his fingers on the surface.

Glenda did her best to save the day by telling humorous stories about her family and friends. Jenn knew many of the people she referred to and was able to add further anecdotes. It was the first time I had been able to observe Liz from up close. She looked old for her age and related mainly to her mother and Jenn.

"She will accept you in her own time," Glenda told us. "Ever since she was raped and fixed, she doesn't trust people like she used to. She doesn't sleep good any more, waking up and crying in the night. But give her time; ignore her until she comes to you, then she'll love you to pieces."

It was already evident to everyone that the one she loved to pieces was Hank. While we ate, she took her sandwich and a soft drink over to where he was sitting in the shade and sat next to him, looking at his face. Then she turned to her mother and shouted something funny that I couldn't understand.

"He don't know how to eat any more," Glenda shouted back. "So don't give him nothing."

We arrived at a kind of hostel just beyond Poulsbo late in the afternoon. It consisted of a single-story rustic building that included a large meeting room with a fireplace, a kitchen, and several bunks behind curtains. Five small cabins and a tiny chapel lay nearby under the cover of tall fir trees. When it was not needed for church functions, the buildings were rented out for Zen Buddhist meetings or group therapy sessions. For three days they had been reserved for our group, and Norma, Deb's mother, had been inspired to set aside one of the cabins for Diane and me.

Norma was there to meet us when we arrived. She is a born optimist and planned the whole ceremony to be a celebration of life. A Swedenborgian for many years, she is the image of a calm peace, and her low speaking voice has the musicality of acceptance.

"Deb never belonged to the New Church, so we won't have a religious ceremony. I want it to be in harmony with her belief that life and death are so intimately connected neither is ever far away. I know she will be with us in everything we do, living invisibly among us, loving us all. I am so happy you were able to bring Hank. Do you think I could have him with me in my cabin?"

Ron Nolte objected vociferously, saying that he could not entrust Hank's care to anybody, that he intended to take Hank to a modern motel equipped with the necessary conveniences. Whereupon Diane offered Ron the keys to the van so that he could find an appropriate motel and suggested that he take plenty of time to have dinner along the way.

We sat at a large table in front of the main building where we were served a simple vegetarian dinner. Hank was behind Norma's chair with his new friend, Liz, next to him. Deb's two sisters were at Norma's side, and the three of them spoke to everyone at the table about life in and around Seattle when Deb was a child. Other people drifted in: friends from high school days now married and with children. Everyone conversed easily without asking questions; a sense of equality descended like a fog in waves from the branches of the fir trees to cover us all in a single blanket of intimacy. A high school teacher, now retired, spoke up about the adolescent Deb's joys and tribulations, to which fellow students added details and anecdotes. A tall man in his sixties spoke about his friendship with Deb and Hank when they were in Rio de Janeiro; it was Erik Nielsen, who had come up with his wife Maria for the occasion and with whom I was to talk at length the next day.

The minister also spoke, saying that although Deb had not been a church member, in her own life she had affirmed a belief in the connectedness of all created forms. "Tomorrow," he said, "we will celebrate her entrance into the spiritual world. Her life was useful among us. It will be even more so in the world to come."

Jenn and Glenda also spoke up, and then I joined in, describing the Deb I knew and giving the eulogy of my father I had been unable to finish at his funeral. The children were sent out to gather pieces of wood and bark, and before dark had settled in a roaring fire was burning near the table, each person approaching it just close enough to keep warm. Then we sang some of Deb's favorite songs.

By the time Ron Nolte returned we had forgotten him. He announced he was ready to take Hank to a motel thirty miles away. Diane walked some distance from the fire to explain to him that Hank would remain with Norma for the night and all Ron had to do was empty his pouches and make sure the intravenous connections were properly inserted and installed. Hearing some kind of altercation in the distance, I wheeled over to where I saw him holding Diane's wrist and spitting venomous words in her face. I fired him on the spot. Refusing to leave, he sat sulking on a chair near the entrance to Norma's cabin. Liz came up and told him the most insulting things she could find in her vocabulary. Fortunately few of the guests could understand her garbled pronunciation, and the children weren't paying attention. Diane and I ducked into the chapel and phoned Asco long-distance.

"How soon can you get here? We need help with Hank."

"In about five hours, give or take depending on how fast I go and if the Plymouth makes it in one piece. If I get a ticket, you'll bail me out, okay?"

"Sure thing!" And I explained the situation briefly, including the necessity of ridding ourselves of Mr. Nolte.

Everyone went to bed, ignoring the nurse who sat on a chair giving dire warnings: "If he dies, it's not my fault, but yours! You can explain that in court!" Norma and Diane, with the help of one of Deb's old friends from nursing school, prepared Hank for bed in Norma's cabin, while Liz watched attentively. About an hour later, when we heard Ron snoring loudly, we could fall asleep ourselves.

In the morning, it was Asco we found sound asleep in the same chair with a small dog tied with a rope next to his feet. When he awoke I asked him what had happened to the nurse.

"When I seen him there snoring, I figured that's the dude you didn't want around no more. So I took the tire wrench I had an started tightening his nose. He spills out swear words on me, so I'm like: 'This here is a tooth extractor machine. I'm gonna count how many new teeth Liz needs for her mouth. One! That shiny one in front. Two . . .' He split before I got to three," Asco said, pointing down the road toward Poulsbo. "Went that way. If he shows up again, tell him my count is up to thirty."

We partook in a communal breakfast. Later some of the guests took walks along the paths leading to and from the chapel grounds, others sat in the morning sun talking or reading. Norma sat down next to me, and I had an opportunity to show her the notes Deb had written for Steve to use in preparation for her trial. I went on to explain to her that I was interested in learning more about Deb as a way of feeling closer to my father.

"His love for Deb was the last important event in his life," I told her, "I was able to catch only a glimpse of that part of him, which was so different from the Steve I thought I knew well. Some day, Norma, maybe you will tell me about Deb, about her time in Brazil, and her feelings for Dad as well."

"You might be interested in seeing the letters she sent me from Rio; they read almost like a diary. She would write at least once a week. I have the letters at home and will send them to you if you like. There are also many she sent from Portland. I could tell she loved your father even before she admitted it to herself. You will take care of them, I'm sure. I am especially fond of the letter that describes a trip she took with Steve up the western coast of Washington."

After lunch the entire party drove north to a town called Suquamish, where we clambered aboard an old fishing boat that had been rented for the occasion along with its weather-beaten captain. We headed east, skirting an Indian reservation, and then north along the Sound for about an hour until we arrived at a particular location that Norma indicated. There the minister said a few words and read some poems. Norma opened the urn containing Deb's ashes, rubbed some on Hank's face and hands, which looked ruddy and healthy from exposure to the air and sun, and then she gave each of us a sprinkling of ashes to toss into the wind and sea.

Back at the chapel many of the guests began to pack their cars and leave after having hugged each other as if to confirm the memory of a treasured moment of closeness. When Jenn was just about to leave, she came over to us:

"By the way: Tim and I are moving into Deb's old apartment. Come and see us soon."

"Really? The one on the fifth floor?" Glenda was overjoyed. "Then I can give you the curtains Deb and I made to keep her place warm. You can have them; they're tailor-made for your windows."

When it was time for Glenda to leave, Liz shouted and sobbed that she wanted to stay with Hank, that she would never see him again when he went back to that Ron jerk, who was sure to abuse him, et cetera.

"Look, Liz," I tried to explain to her. "Asco is here to take care of him. Hank's not going back to that place any more, he's coming to my place. In two days you can come over and see him again. Okay?"

"When did you decide that?" Diane asked me after the sound of Liz's sobs had grown faint in the distance down the road.

"Watching him on the boat where he almost came to life. Is that all right with you?"

"You know it is."

That evening Erik and Maria visited us in our cabin.

"Deb's funeral was important enough for us to return to this country, even for so short a time. Now that we are here we're going to travel slowly across the states to show Maria the places I knew as a boy. If you ever visit Rio, Scott, please be sure to set aside plenty of time to stay with us."

"And let us know what happens with Deb's trial," Maria said. "Will it take place at all, now?"

"There's something else, Scott," Erik added. "Norma told us how you want to know more about Deb and Hank. Here is something that will help. This," he said holding a package wrapped in heavy brown paper, "is the diary Hank kept while he was out in the wilderness. Maria hid it in the kitchen when it looked as though Hank was in some kind of danger. We brought it for Norma, but it is written in a code that she can't read any better than we can. Maybe you will be able to break the code. I also have the letters Deb wrote to Hank while he was in the interior; she had no address for him and simply put them in a drawer. And here is a letter sent to me from somewhere in Europe by one of Deb's friends, Roger Bonot, when he learned of her death. Please write to Maria and me and tell us what you make of it all."

The next morning Diane and I left, with Hank securely locked in place in the van. Asco followed in the green Plymouth. After a ferry ride to Seattle, we left Hank basking in the sun in a park, with Asco and his dog.

Diane and I set out to find Bev's gallery. The galleries were closed in the morning, so we had to wait. Finally, after wandering through downtown streets looking at the crowds and storefronts, we saw a museum just opening its doors; there we received directions to the new Capricorn Gallery. It was closed until early afternoon, but after we pounded on the door for about twenty minutes, Mary came looking disheveled and washed out from what must have been a late night out. She recognized us right away and let us in. While she went to the rear of the gallery to wake Bev, we looked around.

"It's impressive, really," Diane told me. "Look at all those wild paintings and skinny sculptures. Far out, as your friends would say."

Bev came in, well dressed and groomed as usual, smiling, happy to see us. She took us to lunch; Mary came along.

"We are doing marvelously, much better than I would ever have dreamed we would. People here have taste, they want art, and they are willing to pay for it. Soon we will have paid our initial investment; then I'll send you some money, Scott. How are you doing, by the way?"

She went on to describe her life in Seattle, how busy she was, and how many new friends she had made. "Just last night, for instance, Mary and I were invited to the most elegant dinner at the home of a rich Hong Kong investor who is trying to fill his new home with paintings. And he is buying most of them from us!"

"You surely remember," Bev continued, "how I always said that the art market is so advanced in Seattle. People here are more attuned to the basic function of art in their life, which is to depict life, to imitate it."

Mary's face took on a roguish look. "Most of them also know that kitsch imitates art, so they spend less money on trash."

"Then life imitates kitsch," I couldn't help saying. "And not only in Seattle."

It was time for Mary to return and open the gallery. Bev asked what was new in Portland. Diane told her she was pregnant.

"Oh! dear. I do hope you can stay long enough for Scott to find a replacement. May I ask who the father is?"

Diane nodded toward me; I pointed to myself.

Bev changed the subject. "By the way, in November Mary and I are going on a tour of museums and private galleries in Europe. It is called, let's see, what was it? Oh yes, 'From the Hermitage to the Prado.' Sounds exciting, doesn't it. We will be back around the first of December, and I'll bring you something from Europe for Christmas."

BACK HOME IN Lake Oswego, life was becoming more complicated. I did not attend Darryl's trial, feeling that the sight of me in a wheelchair would sway the jury. I also let Tim do most of the work on the probate of Steve's estate. The space and equipment designed for me turned out to be not appropriate for Hank. We hired a contractor to make basic changes as well as install an elevator to give me access to the upstairs. Liz came over every day to be near him, even though it took her two and a half hours to ride the bus each way. After a few days, Diane suggested that if Liz was to spend so much time with us it would be more convenient if she could sleep here as well. Our contractor was able to add a guest room and bath to his construction plans.

Diane went to see a doctor. When she came back she looked concerned.

"Everything's fine. It's just that there are three of them. We'll have to adjust our thinking a little. No wonder I couldn't hear her voice very clearly! There were two others speaking to me as well. One has a boy's voice, I think. We'll see."

That night when we were in bed I went through all sorts of contortions to place my ear in a position where I might hear those voices from Diane's abdomen. To no avail. Perhaps they were asleep or being quiet. What I did hear, however, aside from the reassuring sounds of Diane's digestion, was something like the wind blowing through an orchard in bloom or water trickling from icicles in the morning sun. I fell asleep with my head on her stomach, letting those images evolve and become dreams.

Inevitably, changes took place in our daily life. To make matters easier, we started to eat our meals at a big round table in the kitchen. There were quite a few regulars: Melissa, her friend Charley, who often ate with us after doing chores outside, Liz, who was beginning to talk all the time (although few understood what she was trying to say), Asco with his dog under the table, Diane and I, and Hank next to us, as if watching and listening to everything. Now and then Chuck would drop in just in time for dinner and some music or talk. Jenn or Glenda might be expected on some evenings. Even Benny and his wife had to learn to bear with this extraordinary group whenever they drove up.

"You ugh, Scough," Liz said to everyone, "Ngee wally've to druve dunta Manesties." (I translate: "You know, Scott, we really have to drive down to Manesties.") She went on to say something to the effect that it's not that far away, either, that we could all get into the van and the Plymouth, and we'd be there in two days. "Come un, Scough! Promise ngee druve dunta Manesties!" Hank would just love it at Manesties, she added, and as a final argument told us that her friend Izzy had gone there with her dad, and "boy'd they ever've fun!"

"Can you tell us where Manesties is, Liz?"

She sure could, but her explanation was too garbled for us to understand. Finally one night Glenda came over and rescued us from confusion.

"She's trying to say 'Walt Disney's.' That means Disneyland. She has been bugging me for years to take her there."

I went through the papers I had brought home from the funeral and Deb's letters that Norma mailed me a few days afterward. They were full of enthusiasm or sorrow, depending on her situation when she wrote. There were also photographs Deb took in Rio. They are remarkably clear and detailed. Diane and I thoroughly enjoyed the three shots Deb had taken of Hank after his return from the interior. He was naked, and we could see the fantastic designs painted on his face and body. He looked very thin but obviously happy.

Reading Hank's journal was an arduous, if fascinating, task. The last part was fairly easy to decipher since it was in English. Scribbled on crumbling paper with dull pencil or ball-point pen just running dry, it was an account of his experiences in the Amazonian rain forest. But the first part was an enigma. What language was it written in? The letters of the alphabet Hank had used looked vaguely familiar, only backward sometimes, or upside-down. I made no further progress until one night when Benny brought his oldest daughter, Mona, just home from a language study cruise in the Mediterranean. When I showed her the mysterious text, she said right away:

"Oh, that's written in the phonetic alphabet. Only the symbols are facing the wrong way. I wonder why."

Then I remembered that in Bev's room there is a dressing table with three mirrors, the one in the middle stationary and the others attached to it like a triptych. We went upstairs and looked at the manuscript in various positions, reflected once, twice, three times.

"Stop there!" Mona said. "Now I can make out the symbols. That word says *entonces*. It's Spanish! I can understand it if I read it out loud."

She read and hesitatingly translated a whole page. Then she stopped.

"The words don't make sense any longer. If it's Portuguese I can't read it."

A few pages farther Mona thought it might be French. We called Diane; Mona pronounced sentences from the manuscript without understanding them, and Diane easily translated them into English.

The next day I had Asco move the dressing table to my work area. With a textbook in phonetics at my side and the help of Mona, Diane, Chuck for sections in German, and various other people to help out with Portuguese, and Latin, I was able eventually to enter into my computer more or less everything Hank had scribbled in his devilish code. It seemed appropriate to have him sitting next to me as the work proceeded. Occasionally I would ask him if a particular expression was the right one, and he seemed always to agree that it was.

"Hank," I asked him once. "Did you tell everything? Or did you omit some events, for Deb's sake? You are the only person who knows. Just tell me. I'll understand." Once I even said to him: "Now I know what that blissful look means, the one you always have when we look at you; you are thinking about your young bride, Meelú, seeing her walk ahead of you down a path in the forest." And Hank went on smiling. Finally, for some reason, when I had the whole diary written out, I read it to him. Did I think it might trick the neurons of his somnolent mind into coming back to life? Or did I need his silent approval?

The whole story is beginning to make some kind of sense, although many of the events and missing parts still baffle me. Asco loves to talk about his friends and adventures. Erik and Maria supply me regularly with information and interpretation. Roger Bonot helped me, by e-mail, fill in a few gaps. Diane is my greatest help, suggesting what Deb or Hank or Steve may have been thinking at certain times. She even corrects my English when I get sloppy!

As soon as I realized there was a book here, I called Bev to inform her that I was writing it, and I also told her that there were triplets on the way.

"The book doesn't interest me." She paused. "But I'll read it if you insist, once it is published." Then she added, more gently: "I am happy that I will have grandchildren. Will you invite me to see them?"

The other night, at dinner, Liz started talking about going to Manesties again.

"Look, Liz," I said. "We're not going to Manesties." Then I went on, without knowing exactly why. "Instead, we're going to

Amazonia. There we'll search for Hank's shaman, and if we're lucky enough to find him, he'll give you a brain, Liz. To Hank he will return his soul. Asco needs a conscience. And I will ask for two good legs."

"What will he give me?" Diane asked.

"He'll give you an extra breast to feed the third child, and the strength to help us all find our way."

Acknowledgments

THE STORY AND characters of *Searching for the Jaguar* are fictional. Nevertheless, they are situated in a real historical context. In order to become acquainted with the Brazil of the period described, the reader may wish to consult some of the books I found useful. *The Brazilians* by Joseph A. Page gives a complete portrait of Brazil, its people, history, culture, and resources. An excellent general history of Brazil is E. Bradford Burns, *A History of Brazil, 3rd. ed.* For a history of military rule, see Thomas E. Skidmore, *The Politics of Military Rule in Brazil, 1964-1985.* Gilberto Freyre's classical volume, *The Masters and the Slaves,* is a profound overall study of the formation of the Brazilian culture. Ronald Segal's *The Black Diaspora* is an account of the Atlantic slave trade and describes how it contributed to the formation of modern Brazil and other countries. An anthropological description of the peoples of the Amazon basin can be found in *The Amazonian Chronicles* by Jacques Meunier and A. M. Savarin. A thorough sociological inquiry into the African religions in Brazil is presented in the book by Roger Bastide, *The African Religions of Brazil.* An excellent introduction to the particular religious mixture of Northern Brazil is the novel, *The War of the Saints,* by Jorge Amado, which is also lots of fun to read. To keep abreast with current events in Brazil and the drug trade in South, Central, and North America, one can read articles appearing daily in *The New York Times,* as well as in local newspapers.

For the American Northwest, readers are encouraged to travel there and find out for themselves about the area, its people, and the beauty of its landscape.

BVG